In Praise of Deborah Kinnard

"It's about time! Deborah Kinnard's *Seasons in the Mist* embraces the classic time travel romance with medieval flair, intrigue, humor and bold, fresh faith. History grad student Bethany Lindstrom's strategy to make her academic imprint is sabotaged when she gets stuck in real medieval Cornwall . . . with a real knight in shining armor. Whoops! Kinnard is a natural teller of time travel tales. Once you read *Seasons in the Mist* you'll want to journey back and read this novel for the first time—again. I certainly did!"

—Linda Wichman, author of *Legend of the Emerald Rose,* 2006 Christy finalist

"From the favored quill of yon Lady Deborah comes this skilful tale of a brave maiden snatched from her own time. Verily, history doth come alive through her passionate eyes, with nary a word out of place. Amidst a high and noble romance and cunning courtly intrigue, a savvy twenty-first century wench discovers what is of true substance in life. Would that all time travelers had such a hand to tell their stories, for my lady is indeed subtle and fervent both—such words to carry the reader's mind to that other time in fullest hues."

–Grace Bridges, author of *Faith Awakened*

"Along with the heroine, prepare to have Deborah Kinnard draw you from the world you know to a past that still lives within these pages, thanks to Kinnard's skill with weaving history into a delightful story."

–Laurie Alice Eakes, author of *The Heiress*

"Rich with historical detail and lyrical prose, *Seasons in the Mist* takes historical fiction lovers on an emotional ride they won't soon forget. Is time travel a new trend in Christian fiction? This novel may very well start one because it grabs the reader and pulls them through a portal that is so realistic and convincing readers will be hooked and want more from this author."

–Michelle Sutton, author of *It's Not About Him*

"Castles plus danger plus romance all add up to one satisfying adventure in *Seasons in the Mist.* Author Deb Kinnard is a master at weaving history with fiction, so much so that it's sometimes hard to tell fact from fable. From the first page to the last, you'll enjoy a rollicking visit to the chivalrous realm of the past."

–Michelle Griep, author of *Gallimore*

Seasons in the Mist

Other books by Deborah Kinnard

Angel with a Ray Gun, Desert Breeze Publishing

Angel with a Backhoe, Desert Breeze Publishing

Damages, Desert Breeze Publishing

Acknowledgements

I'd like to thank the Katherine Swynford Society, particularly Graham Coult and Roger Joy, who have been a tireless source of information so obscure I doubted its existence. For the niceties of how a lord, lady, baron, baroness, and all their exaltednesses are addressed, plentiful thanks go to Laurie Alice Eakes and the HISWriters group. To my savvy editors at Sheaf House, much appreciation for helping make this book the best it could be. Any remaining errors, historical speed bumps, and plain old speculation are mine alone.

Thanks go to my agent, Tamela Hancock Murray, for her patience, kindness, and smarts—she deserves all the accolades I can find. Last and certainly not least to my critique partner and fellow Chicago Bears fan, Janet Butler, who saw the manuscript in its early stages and encouraged me more times than I can count.

Last and foremost, to Christ our Lord and His soon return. Amen.

Seasons in the Mist

Deborah Kinnard

Charlotte, Tennessee 37036 USA

Published by Sheaf House®. Requests for information should be addressed to:

Editorial Director
Sheaf House Publishers, LLC
3641 Hwy 47 N
Charlotte, TN 37036
jmshoup@sheafhouse.com
www.sheafhouse.com

Library of Congress Control Number: 2010921105

ISBN: 978-0-9824832-1-3 (softcover)

Published in association with Hartline Literary Agency, Pittsburgh, Pennsylvania 15235.

Interior design by Marisa Jackson.

Map by Jim Brown of Jim Brown Ilustrations.

10 11 12 13 14 15 16 17 18 19 — 10 9 8 7 6 5 4 3 2 1

MANUFACTURED IN THE UNITED STATES OF AMERICA

To Russ, Christina, and Sarah. I love you forever.
Thank you for liking and eating carryout pizza.
To Sandy, who saw this story very early
and encouraged me to keep at it.
To Barb, a lady of the first rank.

Jesus replied, "What is impossible with men is possible with God."
Luke 18:27

Author's Note

Bethany Lindstrom lands in the mid fourteenth century, a time of social and linguistic transition in England. After the Norman conquest in 1066, the Anglo-Saxon underclass held to their native English, while their "betters" spoke French. For 300 years English society had two tiers: the French-preferring aristocracy and the English-speaking peasantry. Many factors operated to change a French-speaking nobility to an English speaking one, including the Pestilence in 1348-1349, incessant warfare in France, and the loss of English possessions on the Continent. These factors made speaking English feel patriotic.

From the date of the Magna Carta (1215), French replaced Latin as the language of public documents and also the language of private correspondence. English speakers were not expected to be literate. French also took Latin's place as the language of poetry, the vehicle of satire, or the voice of faith. In an educated person such as Lord Michael, one would expect familiarity with three languages: the English his inferiors spoke; the Latin of the church; and French. Michael, of course, also speaks Cornish.

Until English was established by royal decree as the language of Parliament (1362), French was the tongue of the court and the upper classes, English the speech of the people. It's hard to say exactly when and how the upper class completed the conversion to English and how soon the commons stopped trying to speak French. By the time of Beth's journey, English had spread pretty thoroughly among the upper classes. In 1337 Edward III first addressed Parliament in English, and in 1362 English became the official language of both the judicial system and of Parliament.

Resources

England in the Reign of Edward III, Scott L. Waugh, Cambridge University Press, 1991.

The Mother Tongue: English and How It Got That Way, Bill Bryson, Harper-Collins, 1990.

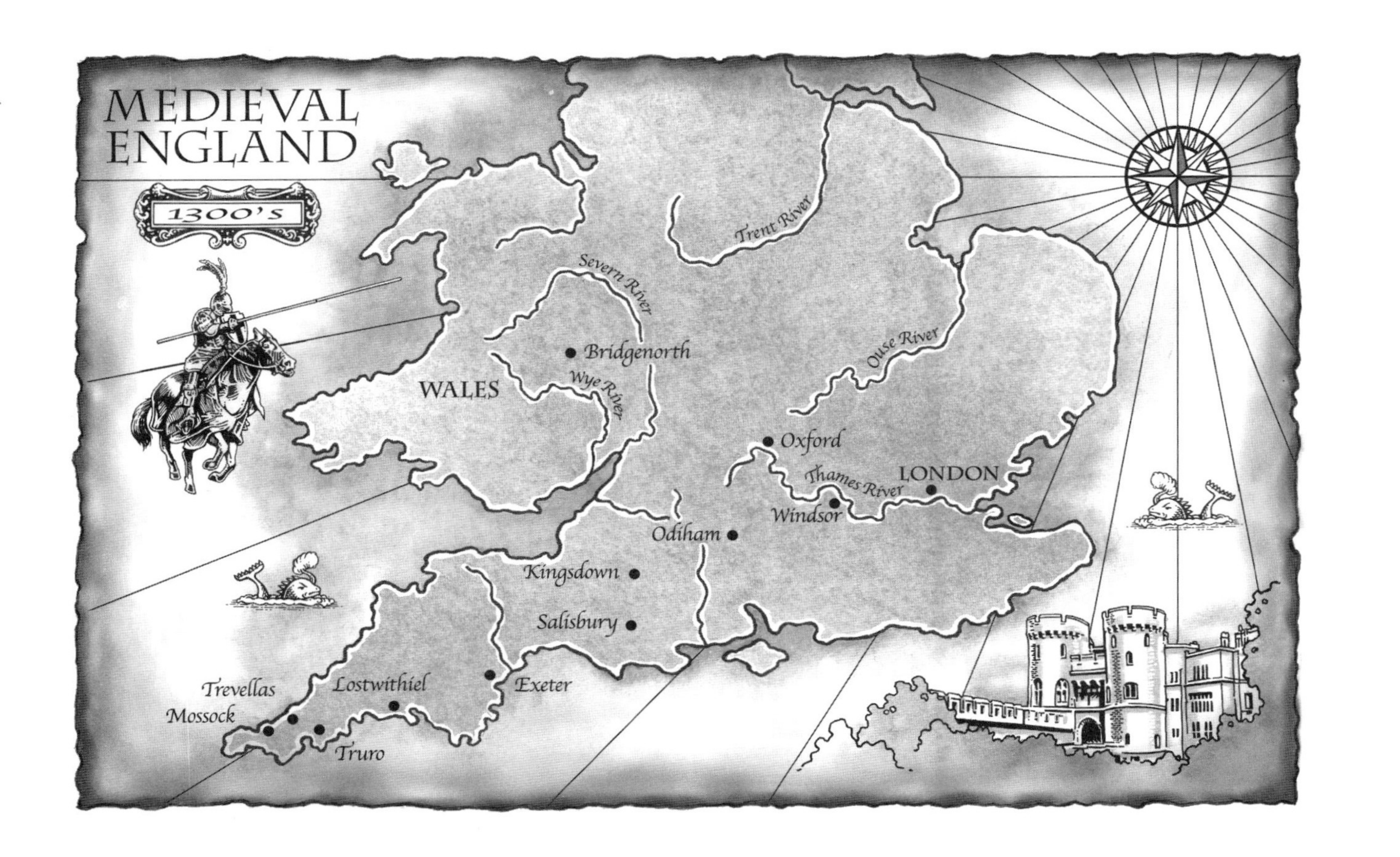
MEDIEVAL
ENGLAND
1300's
WALES
Trent River
Severn River
Ouse River
Bridgenorth
Wye River
Oxford
LONDON
Thames River
Windsor
Odiham
Kingsdown
Salisbury
Exeter
Lostwithiel
Trevellas
Mossock
Truro

One

I wish these clouds would break.

Bethany Lindstrom did an involuntary bounce in her seat and felt herself flush in embarrassment. Casting a covert glance around, she figured nobody had seen. Good thing, too. PhD candidate overachievers should not bounce.

Not long now. In a moment, in only a moment, this plane will break through this infernal cloud cover. It can't be long, we're descending so fast. Seconds now—my first glimpse of England. England, Avalon, Narnia. Land of my forever dreams.

She'd planned, fantasized, speculated, and schemed this trip all her life. As a child she'd read every book in the school library about medieval British history. She'd studied until eye drops no longer eased the strain. She'd outlined studies, written theses, defended her dissertation, labored over ecclesiastical Latin and legal terms, learned Anglo-Saxon and vernacular Middle English until she could converse with a contemporary, should one materialize. At last, she'd taken the prize. Through the efforts of her faculty advisor, the good Dr. Richards, the university had offered a summer semester at Oxford and finally—finally—she'd dug up enough grant money to make the flight and to support herself during three fantastic months in England.

England. The very word beckoned like a siren song. Beth leaned forward to see past the woman in 17-A as clouds scudded past the tiny window, obstinately refusing to clear on final approach to Heathrow.

"It's your first visit to the U.K., isn't it?" asked her seatmate with a smile.

"Yes," Beth answered. "I can't wait to see it."

"Oh, you'll see plenty in a moment, love."

She'd enjoyed chatting with her seatmate. Sheila Tyrrell lived in Cornwall and had visited Chicago on business. Violating every stereotype about the taciturn English, Sheila had talked volubly of her family, her small town on the coast, and the local amenities.

"You really must find time to visit," she urged as Beth strained to see through the clouds. "No holiday is complete without seeing Cornwall."

"Is it far from Oxford?" How would she afford bus fare, so tightly had she budgeted every last pound sterling?

"Oh, not so far. You take the Inter-City to Exeter, and from there you're just a short hop to Truro . . . "

Beth listened, fascinated. Learning she was a historian, Sheila mentioned many ancient sites in her native county. "Of course, most folks want to see the places associated with King Arthur." She snorted delicately.

"Not an Arthurian fan?"

"Well, he belongs to the English, doesn't he? Not the Cornish."

"There's a difference?"

That gaffe earned Beth a ten-minute discourse on differentiating the present-day English and the Cornish—a Celtic race, and therefore superior. Sheila's lecture fell apart in quiet laughter.

"My, I guess I do get rather passionate about not being called English. We're British, and visitors don't know it matters." Sheila dabbed her eyes with an airline napkin and gave Beth a helpless grin.

Then she said something Beth wondered about while watching the clouds part for her long-awaited first glimpse. "Passion isn't always easy, though, is it? You'll need all of yours, and more of strength, to finish your journey well."

"Journey?"

Sheila waved her hand. "Never mind. My husband always jeers at my 'seeings', as he calls them. Just middle-aged rubbish."

Seeings. Beth believed in facts, dates, translations, authorities, source documents. And her own intelligence. Not arcane glimpses into the future, or for that matter, into the past. So why, as the tidy rooftops of suburban London came into view, did Sheila's statement ring in her mind like the tolling of Big Ben?

She put it down to excitement, nerves, and jet lag. Not that she felt tired. Quite the opposite. She had arranged to be met at the airport by a transportation service, so she'd see Oxford within a few hours. She would ignore fatigue if it hit later, for the April day was still fresh, and an entire "sceptre'd isle" awaited inspection.

Finally. This is England. I'd pinch myself, but I'm awake and here at last.

At the customs queue, they parted with a civilized handshake. Sheila pressed a business card into Beth's hand. "Do ring," she said, "whether you're able to squeeze in a Cornish holiday or not. I'll be that glad to hear how you're doing."

Beth tucked Sheila's card away in her blazer pocket and nudged her carry-on an inch closer to clearing customs. An hour elapsed. She claimed her baggage, a single duffel. Her one good outfit sagged, travel wrinkled. She always traveled light, and for this trip, Mom had helped her ruthlessly prune her packing.

Beth disliked being overburdened. Her accommodations would be collegiate small and Spartan, like her tiny place at grad school at Midwestern. For a city-bred girl, she enjoyed a minimalist lifestyle, and she was more than ready to settle in. Now if only she could spot the driver from the transportation service. They said he'd be holding a placard bearing her name.

She wove in and out of bustling travelers until the offload from the 747 thinned out. No driver. Plenty of people holding signs searching for other arrivals, even entire tour groups. She hunted for a sign that read Bethany Lindstrom, Bethany, Ms. Lindstrom, even Beth. No sign. No transportation.

The last uniformed chauffeur gathered his group around him like a hen with a brood of jet-lagged chicks. She dug the transportation firm's business card out of her passport case and dialed. The cell phone seemed reluctant, but finally put the call through. "That number," intoned a British-accented voice, "is not in service."

She figured she'd misdialed, so she tried again. Same result. Her heart sank, speeding up with a healthy additive of fear. How was she supposed to get to Oxford? Should she seek out an airline representative? Was there a booth for stressed-out, abandoned international travelers?

"My ivers! You're still here?"

Beth whirled around to see Sheila Tyrrell bustling toward her, tugging a rolling suitcase and wearing a concerned expression. "Someone was supposed to come for me, but I think the plans got fouled up."

Sheila clucked. "Do you have a phone number? I have my mobile." She pulled the phone out of her jacket pocket.

Beth's heart warmed just to see someone slightly familiar. She'd been feeling six, not twenty-six, lost in a strange land with nobody to help—or care.

"I tried to call. More than once. They're not answering." Beth gnawed on her lower lip, a habit Mom hated. "For that matter, why are you still here?"

"Graeme was to pick me up. He's late, as always." Sheila gave a shrug. "Sons don't always listen carefully enough, do they?" Her expression lightened. "But I gave him a ring—he says the traffic on the M-4 is horribly snarled. I said, what do you expect, on a weekday noontime?" She chuckled, then raised her brows, apparently on a new thought. "Say—must you get to Oxford today, particularly?"

"Not today, but soon. I need to find another way to get there. My schedule's open enough, but I only have three months and I don't want to waste any of it."

"If you've nothing pressing today, then why not come to Cornwall? We've plenty of room, and we'll get you to Oxford on the morning train from Truro." She held up a hand. "Truly, Bethany, this will be no inconvenience. Blame it on my foolish 'seeings,' and I never accost strangers. Bertie chides me for being impulsive, but I've never had an instinct go bad, and well he knows it. You mustn't think me forward or brash—"

Touched, Beth chuckled. "Like Americans can sometimes be?"

Sheila smiled. "Do come to Mossock. Graeme won't be much longer, and we can chat more on the way."

"Mossock! You live at Mossock House? In Cornwall?"

"You've heard of it?"

"Of course."

Beth mulled her options for a quick moment. Her alternatives all looked bleak: Stay tonight at an airport hotel, wasting money she'd rather hoard for Oxford. Seek help from the airport staff, who might have the best intentions but couldn't offer temptation to equal a medieval manor house. Brave the bus to central London and figure out which train might get her to Oxford, then from the train station to the college. Keep trying to get hold of the transportation company.

Or spend a wonderful day or two making notes and sketches in one of the older listed homes of England. No—Britain. She spent no more time deciding.

"You're very kind. And I'd love to see your house. Thanks—I think I will."

Graeme Tyrrell pulled up almost immediately. Sheila's son turned out to be a long, thin man of about twenty, with a low-key manner and virtually no conversation. Beth yielded to Graeme's insistence that he load her duffel into the "boot" of a sleek black Land Rover. She froze for a moment when Graeme got into what she considered the passenger's side of the car—until she noticed the steering wheel was there too.

Duhh. Knowing they drive on the left side sure isn't the same as seeing it!

Sheila offered Beth the front seat, for the better view, and chatted comfortably from the back, pointing out various items of interest as Graeme wove skillfully through traffic and onto the M4.

"The West," said the large blue motorway sign. Beth rubbernecked without shame as the superhighway wound through tidy communities, industrial parks, farm country of a lovely, luminous green. Hedgerows, another first, bordered the country roads they passed. Occasionally Sheila pointed out a landmark visible from the motorway.

The *driving* part of the experience Beth tried hard to ignore. Graeme drove too fast for her taste. Knowing the British drove on the left hadn't prepared her for the visual effect. To Beth's eyes it looked as though driverless cars shot toward them at terrific rates of speed from the wrong direction. She gritted her teeth.

Calm. Blasé. Experienced traveler.

"Now over there—" Sheila pointed. "Up that road a ways is Stonehenge. I do hope you'll get a chance to take a day trip. Really, no visitor to the U.K. should miss it."

Beth nodded and smiled. Sheila continued, "Of course, you're not on holiday but on business. I keep forgetting you haven't sufficient time. A pity it is you can't sightsee."

Graeme glanced in the rear view mirror and chuckled, the first sound he'd produced in sixty miles. "She might get the chance, Mum."

Beth felt obligated to explain. "More than anything I'd love to, but my project won't let me. Given the short time, I'll have my hands full getting the work done."

Sheila and Graeme exchanged a glance. "Wait and see," said Graeme's mother. "Just wait and see."

Small towns along the way spaced out further. When she turned to ask a question, Beth found Sheila dozing tidily without sound, her dark head canted back on the headrest.

"Catch a nap yourself if you've the mind to," Graeme said softly. "We're still an hour from home."

"Thanks. It won't bother you?"

He made a dismissive gesture. "I drive this route often enough to do it in my sleep."

Beth shuddered. "Feel free not to."

Graeme chuckled and lapsed into silence. Taking Sheila's example, Beth rested her head and let her imagination take flight.

England. England everywhere. This earth knew the footstep of people I've only read about. They lived here—William Marshal, John of Gaunt, Julian of Norwich.

And I'm headed toward Cornwall, an invited guest at a house written up in all the architectural guidebooks. How lucky can one stranded academic get?

She drifted on a tide of jet-lagged fatigue, dreaming in spurts of Mossock House and of her project. For two months she would join the dig team at New College, Oxford, where a fourteenth-century plague pit had just been discovered. Then she'd have a frenetic month to analyze and write up her findings.

Though many academics were interested in the pestilence, her conclusions would not echo theirs. With her paper she would break new ground. With the excavation of the pit in New College's quadrangle, a veritable gold mine of facts would emerge. No longer would those facts lie buried with the bones of the plague victims, waiting for undergrads' eager shovels and historians' discerning eyes. Through providence and a timely research grant, Bethany Lindstrom, grad student, would join the ranks of the scholarly elite.

She knew the source documentation as well as any seasoned scholar. In old manuscripts she'd studied contemporary accounts, comparing the eyewitness version with that of modern scholars. Though the pestilence, as the contemps had called it, had depopulated all Eurasia, the decline had started in climate deterioration and famine three decades earlier. Had the pandemic never struck, the boom times were over anyway for unfortunate Europe. And the English had suffered worse than most.

Beth had written a bare-bones outline of her paper, needing only field study to prove her theory. On the pre-plague famine years, and how they had primed the demographic disaster that followed, she pinned her hopes for a distinguished academic career.

"We're home." Graeme's voice cut through the dreams, and she startled awake.

In the back seat Sheila was stretching; apparently both women had succumbed to jet lag. Beth stared into the hazy blue-gold of her first English afternoon and gasped. An imposing pile of gray stone and slate loomed before her, ready and willing to rob her of breath. Mossock's photos didn't do it justice.

Sheila laughed while unfastening her seat belt. "Go ahead and look, Beth. It's a bit run-down about the edges, but it's home."

"My word." Beth had trouble finding her breath as she got out of the car. "It's incredible."

"Mossock," Graeme said simply. "Welcome."

Again he insisted on carrying her duffel. Beth gaped some more as Sheila, quite wide awake, led her in through great iron-bound double oak doors.

"Bertie! Hullo, house. I'm home."

Two huge dogs with wiry gray hair bounded out to be rubbed and greeted. On their heels a tall man of about fifty, clear eyed and dark bearded, emerged from a side door.

He caught Sheila in a massive hug. "So you are, sweet." He kissed her soundly and set her back onto her feet on the stone floor. "And who's this you bring with you?"

Beth hastily put down her carry-on and took the man's outstretched hand. His paw enveloped hers twice over, warm and firm.

Sheila made the introductions. "Albert—we all call him Bertie—my husband. This is Bethany Lindstrom."

"Welcome," Bertie said with a smile. Puffs of graying dark hair stuck out over his ears like explosions, and his half glasses dangled askew on his brow. He reminded Beth of one of her lit professors, only warmer.

"Thank you for having me in your home." Beth gave a futile gesture around the hall and the grand room into which it opened. "Amazing. The photos don't capture its beauty."

"But you're not to tour it yet," Sheila declared. "That's for after tea. For now, let me settle you in a room. You'll want to clean up—I'm certain I do."

"You're right. I feel as though we've been traveling forever."

"Then come right this way, love. I have just the thing."

After showering and changing, Beth crept—she could find no other pace—down the great staircase. Her bedroom had blown her away. More a suite than a room, it was decorated in yellow and navy, with ivory accents, the patterns harmonizing with the eighteenth century elegance of Chippendale furniture. Ivory curtains gracefully draped a massive four-poster bed almost too tall to climb into.

Large, deep-set windows faced the ocean, which muttered and hissed against the rocks fifty feet below a stone garden wall. The private bath seemed minimalist by contrast, but proved more than adequate. She'd indulged in plenty of soap and hot water to make her feel more like a human than a piece of abused airline baggage.

The staircase was straight out of *Masterpiece Theatre,* its banister a solid foot thick, the wood so polished she checked for her reflection. Her footfalls made no sound on thick moss-green carpet as she entered the downstairs hallway. The air smelled of furniture polish, with an overtone of something sweet wafting from an oven.

On the right, two sets of closed pocket doors, also varnished to a formidable luster. On the left, an open set. Toward these she ventured.

Spotting her, Sheila waved her in. With a grin, Beth joined her hostess in a cheery parlor, where tea had been set up near French doors open to the summer evening.

"You'll have to excuse Bertie and Graeme for now. They went into Newquay to look at a grass mower or some such male concern." Without asking, Sheila dropped a half-spoonful of honey into a fragile cup of floral china and added a tiny drizzle of cream. "They might be back by dinner-time. Feeling more the thing, are you?"

Beth accepted the cup and sipped. *Hold on. How does she know how I take my tea?*

"I certainly do feel better. You didn't mention you live in a famous house. It's wonderful."

Sheila smiled as if pleased. "Mossock has been in my husband's family since the Civil War," she said with a hint of pride. "It's much older than that, of course. Parts of it—not the parts we live in, unfortunately—date from before Henry V. We're greatly blessed to have our home. So many Cornish families lost their family estates to bad political judgments, poor management, hard times. This is not easy country in which to prosper." She sipped from her china cup, and then handed Beth a plate on which many tiny sandwiches clustered as if fighting for the attention they deserved.

"Tell me about the house." Beth took a sandwich.

Sheila gave another smile, almost conspiratorial. "Eat hearty, love, and I'll do much better than that."

Beth obeyed and finished without delay. A girl in a black turtleneck and blue jeans came with a friendly smile to clear away. One of the hounds lying in front of the fireplace sighed and lumbered to its feet. With the dog for escort, Beth followed her hostess down a bewildering maze of passages. Sheila knew not only her ancestral home's structure but also its history, down to the fascinating personal stories and little details historians craved.

"You'll want to see the oldest wings, won't you?" she guessed with scary accuracy.

Beth could only nod and rubberneck. Sheila turned to regard her, and after a long moment, returned her nod. The glint in her eye gave her a sudden sly look, and a shiver traced its way up Beth's spine.

"This way, then. Mind your step. These stairs are old and not in the best repair."

From a pocket of her slacks, Sheila removed a huge cast-iron key and tried the lock. Beth expected the heavy iron-hinged door to creak in protest, but it swung open silently as if kept well oiled.

Sheila flipped a wall switch. "It's not very well lit, either. We've neglected this part of the house. A pity, but family fortunes don't grow on trees, do they?"

Beth followed her into a narrow passage that opened onto a large, high-ceilinged space. Walls of the local gray stone formed bays along each side, with rounded arches framing doorways into other parts of the wing. A fireplace that could have cooked an entire ox took up one end of the room, its mantelpiece a narrow, angular funnel with carved corbels as trim. The roof beams, dim in the late afternoon light, appeared be hewn from entire tree trunks.

The room smelled of dust and sunshine. Vagrant beams slanted, dancing with dust motes, through narrow leaded glass windows.

"Wonderful," she breathed. "It's the great hall, isn't it?" She whipped her tiny notebook out of her pocket and began sketching the fireplace and its glowering corbels.

"Yes. The oldest remaining part. We think this range might have been a fortified manor house, but the rest is long gone." Sheila worked her fingernails into the dog's coat just behind the ears. "There's an undercroft, of course. One of the rooms has a manacle set into the wall. We can't prove it, of course, but it might be where they stuck people they found—inconvenient."

Beth laughed. *A dungeon, eh?* "Those high windows look defensive." She pointed and did a quick thumbnail sketch. "Before they were glazed. And those squarish holes, up high on the wall? See the ones I mean? They could have held beams for a second story. That would be the solar, if this dates back as far as I suspect it does."

"My word," Sheila said on a chuckle, "you are the genuine article, aren't you? And a fair rendering of the window, so fast! You're good with a pencil."

"My uncles were all in commercial art. The youngest taught me to draw. And as far as the historical details, I've lived and breathed the Middle Ages since I learned to read."

Beth turned three-sixty, taking it all in, breathing, dashing off quick thumbnail sketches, drawing the feel of the old hall deep into her bones. And yet the experience wasn't entirely pleasant. Like a roller coaster—scary and exhilarating, and vaguely unnerving because it must end all too soon.

"How can you bear to leave it unlived in? Not to use it?"

"Well, there's a reason." Sheila's expression changed, took on a sorrowful air. "It looks long abandoned because it was. Bertie's ancestors had the money to restore it. They didn't want to."

Beth looked a question at her hostess.

"They feared the places in this wing where one can sense something." The dog gave a fretful whine and Sheila reached to scratch her huge bristly head. "There now, Wenna. That's the girl."

The dog's unease triggered Beth's. "Something unpleasant?"

"Worse, I'm afraid. All these old piles have their ghost, their cold room—call it what you like. I almost think we English would be disappointed if they didn't. As for Mossock's, it's no Victorian ghost. Ours goes back many generations. The tales Bertie's grandmother threatened him with! That old harridan. She put fear into that boy, let me tell you. She warned him if he were rude, she'd let him spend some time in the old hall with the 'Gray Lady.' " Sheila scratched the dog's ears, making it sidle closer.

"What? Who was she?"

"Nobody now knows. But she's called gray for good reason. Nobody's ever actually seen an apparition, mind you. It's more sensed than visualized. Those who report her presence call it an overwhelming feeling of displacement. As though she's lost somehow, and grieves for someone. Yes, grief. Soul deep and almost too much to bear." Sheila's eyes clouded. Beth wondered why, but in a second, the look vanished. "According to legend, the Lady first appeared in the Trevorgas' time. They held the manor in the sixteenth century. The Lady wouldn't make herself known to just anyone. Only those of the family—and sensitives—could feel her."

"Sensitives?"

"People like me, love. And like you."

"I'm not." Beth took a step back. "There are no such people."

"No, of course not. You're a modern woman. Practical. Such stories are no more than rubbish, aren't they? Feelings, impressions, they have no root in fact." Sheila spoke without emotion, but watched Beth's face for reaction.

Something prompted Beth to whisper, "And yet—I've always had the strongest possible desire to come here. To visit England. To do my work. To learn the stories forgotten long ago, and tell them to others."

"Yes." Sheila sounded unsurprised. "You were called, maybe by the Lady herself. Maybe, in time, she will tell you why."

A link clicked shut. "You spoke of passion, and how it's not always easy."

"I spoke on impulse, but it's true. Even before you got stranded at Heathrow, I felt our paths would cross again." She gave a grin almost impish. "My foolishness doesn't always make sense, even to me. What your journey entails, I can't say. But I do feel that, in time, you'll know."

"God brought me here," Beth said quietly.

"You're a believer?"

Beth mulled her answer for a moment. "Not active. I don't attend church, if that's what you mean. I did, once."

"Well, then you already know He has many mysterious ways," Sheila replied. "Past finding out." The dog gave a higher, more insistent whine. "But that's a conversation for another day. Come, the stables are out this way. Wenna wants to show you her new litter of puppies."

Two

Despite the "Gray Lady" and Sheila's enigmatic words, Beth slept well that night. The disturbance of her inner clock meant that she snapped full awake at four a.m. Combing her fingers through her hair, she went to the deep window seat and opened the casement. The air smelled of dawn and kelp, seawater and anticipation, with a faint and unfamiliar floral tang. Below the window, birds heralded the morning, foreign English—Cornish?—birdcalls, gentle and insistent.

The ocean muttered accompaniment below the cliffs. It waited to be explored, and she felt it beckoning. She pulled on jeans and a T-shirt. After a quick call home to let Mom know she'd arrived safely and of her unexpected change of plans, she went to make her own discovery of a Cornish morning.

Aimless, basking in her surroundings, she strolled down the garden toward the ancient hall. All around her wildflowers, colorful annuals, and other plants she didn't recognize bloomed in a lush profusion of color and scent. Behind her a premature sun crept over the horizon. This puzzled her until she remembered England lay at a higher latitude than Chicago, making for shorter nights at this season. The damp-spangled richness of early dawn added its special luster to a trip that already seemed surreal.

Dew wet her sneakers from the thick grass near the old hall. She wished she'd brought her notebook to make sketches as she strolled its perimeter. The architecture strongly reminded her of photos she'd seen of other manors of similar date. Mid to late twelfth century, she calculated, and no later. The long-and-short corner detail, the shape of the arched doorways, the narrow semi-defensive window apertures—all these features shouted of an early date.

She stepped across a ruined stone wall to approach the hall more closely. Beyond one corner, a worn dirt path led to an area she hadn't explored. Funny how this path alone looked ungroomed, lacking the fastidious upkeep of Mossock's other areas. Beth shook the dew off her sneakers and followed the dirt trail around the corner of the building.

Set exactly at the wall's midpoint, an ironbound oak door beckoned. Smaller than the others, it almost looked out of place. She tried the handle and it swung smoothly inward. After a brief hesitation, she tiptoed in, afraid it might lead to an ancient privy or something equally uninviting.

She looked around a cool stone corridor, as yet untouched by the warmth of morning. Faint, dust-laden dawn beams served as its only illumination. Though the passage obviously wasn't often visited, it had once been tidy and maintained. She took a step away from the door.

Between one heartbeat and the next, the narrow hallway went cold. Mind-numbingly cold. Beth gasped and reached for support, her hand landing on the wall stones. She found them almost icy. No help here. The sensation lingered and deepened, and another overlay it.

Grief. A woman's whisper, soft with sorrow too deep for tears.

She almost cried out, so overwhelming was the sensation. Around her, something shifted and went dark. At the same moment, her surroundings tore loose from their moorings and swirled crazily around her. She felt consciousness ebb. Though she'd never felt faint in her life, she couldn't mistake the sensation. Her clammy hands slipped on the dank stones, and her knees buckled. Beth collapsed to the floor, crying out as her head struck the wall a glancing blow.

By degrees, the blackness ebbed. Her head quit whirling and the wall stopped quivering. The dizziness diminished and her surroundings resumed their proper places. Her world righted itself into a normal Cornish early morning.

Outside the open door she heard the birds' random twittering. The sense of sorrow had fled, and the passageway's temperature was only the expected chill of a shaded stone building.

She took a shaky breath. Wiping stinging hands on her jeans, she struggled to her feet. At the sensation of warmth trickling past her eye onto her cheek, she lifted her hand to her throbbing head. Her fingers came away sticky with blood, the palms scraped and dirtied from the attempt to prevent the fall.

Oh, great! How am I going to explain this without looking totally ridiculous?

She hesitated, but she couldn't figure out anything else to do. The cut on her forehead hurt and wanted attention. With luck, no one would be awake yet, and she could escape to her room to tend to herself in decent privacy. The last thing she wanted was more Sheila-fussing. Taking a deep breath, she edged back down the passage and out the door.

The man in the garden hadn't been there a moment before.

He saw her at the same moment she saw him. She stared and the man stared back, his jaw hanging open.

He looked a mess—tangled dark hair hanging onto the shoulders of a dirty, loose shirt, baggy shorts ending just below the knee, and bare, grimy feet. On his head sat a shapeless cap, looking like a chair cushion emptied of its stuffing. In his big, gnarled hands, he pushed a crudely constructed wooden wheelbarrow with no sides. It overflowed with small wood and bare branches.

His appearance jarred her, so badly did he stick out in Mossock's tidy world, but it cost nothing to be courteous. "Good morning," Beth said, her voice sounding hoarse in her ears.

The man jumped as if she'd thrown a rock at him. He gabbled something in a tongue she didn't recognize, made a hasty sign of the cross at his chest, dropped the barrow, which dumped its contents, and ran.

She gaped after him. He ran as though he wouldn't slow down till London.

"Well!" she muttered, taken aback. She'd known nothing but kindness in England so far, but apparently the U.K. had its rude people just like America.

Shaking her head, she rounded the building's corner. And stopped dead in her tracks. Her heart sped up alarmingly, and she felt cold again, a new chill.

Mossock—the Mossock she'd slept in—wasn't there.

In its place she saw several moldering stone buildings attached to the great hall. Two-story ranges in the same architectural style straggled to the right, including a high, round tower with arrow-slits in place of windows. A single-story range off to the left backed onto wooden outbuildings with roofs of slate or thatch. The ruined stone wall over which she'd stepped had morphed into a wall higher than her head, enclosing a garden fragrant with herbs and undersized, richly aromatic roses. Further away, a horse stamped and blew through its nose in a wooden stable. The aroma of the stalls almost overwhelmed that of the garden.

She took another step forward, her heart hammering. Smoke rose lazily from the chimney of a wooden outbuilding, carrying a scent of cooking food. Hens scratched, loose in the rutted yard. A rooster greeted both Beth and the morning in the usual way.

But this was not the morning that should be.

"Where is it?" she whispered. She grabbed a fold of skin at the back of her hand and pinched hard. Nothing changed. She was awake and not dreaming. *Where is Mossock?*

A woman—not Sheila—emerged from a doorway adjacent to the hall, and Beth gaped some more. She wore a long tunic-over-tunic garment in a grayish blue color, and its fit showed the lines of early pregnancy. Her hair was hidden, wrapped in a dun-colored cloth. Unlike the oaf with the barrow, Beth noted, she wore leather shoes that appeared to be of fine quality, though badly scuffed.

Her eyes widening, the woman took Beth in, a puzzled expression coming over her face. Lifting her skirts, she approached, picking her way between the hens and across the ruts.

"No. Help. This can't be *happening*," Beth whimpered under her breath. She hated whimperers.

The woman stopped several feet short of her, inclined her head with lifted brows, and said something quick and questioning in an unfamiliar language. Beth made a two-handed gesture she hoped communicated, *I don't understand you.*

The woman frowned more deeply and repeated her question.

In Middle English. English heavily influenced by Norman French.

Beth gulped a breath that didn't have enough air in it. Her brain would not produce words, so she blurted the first thing that came.

"Je suis perdu." I'm lost. Would she communicate? She could not think or remember, or feel anything but terror.

The woman clucked her tongue. "You poor thing. And such clothing! I've never seen the like. How came you to be lost?"

Though Beth understood the archaic accent, she couldn't produce an answer. The woman scanned her up and down and appeared to reach a decision.

"Come inside," she said in a tone of command. "You look fair beset. Mossock has ever offered its welcome to those in need. You must take wine, refresh yourself, and say what has befallen you."

Apparently thinking her tongue-tied, shocked, or stupid, she led Beth by the wrist as if reluctant to touch "such clothing." Beth followed, mute, fighting panic.

This isn't Mossock. Well, it must be—the great hall looks the same. But so different. This is not the house I saw last night.

Indeed, the hall had changed. Where last night it had stood empty, populated only by dust motes and legends, today the expanse bustled with people. In the enormous corbelled hearth, a merry fire snapped and sent flames high up the chimney. Along one wall, plainly dressed men set up a long trestle table. With impatient gestures, a middle-aged woman urged them to haste. Across the end of the room before the fireplace, a second, shorter table had already been set up and covered with white cloths. To this table her protector tugged her.

"Maude! Bring sweet wine."

The middle-aged woman left off harrying the men and hurried to obey. Beth sank down upon a long bench.

This can't be. These people wear medieval clothing. They're setting up a great hall for a morning meal, and they're going to bring me wine, not coffee. This lady who greeted me isn't Sheila. She isn't anyone I know. She belongs here, and this is her time, not mine.

What am I going to do?

She closed her eyes. The darkness brought an unpleasant distancing feeling, so she opened them again. No good—the strange hall hadn't morphed back into the place she knew.

Muttering under her breath in sharp disapproval, the woman called Maude brought a goblet of white metal with an engraved bowl. Beth tried to ignore the servant's narrow-eyed scrutiny as she sipped its contents more to gain time than for any refreshment it might offer. The wine, however, tasted light and sweet, and it restored her. The younger woman, sitting at her side and watchfully waiting, apparently saw she was doing better.

After sending Maude to bring a cloth and a basin of water, her hostess gently washed the swollen scrape on Beth's forehead and sponged away the drying blood on the palms of her hands. She dabbed a soothing ointment on the wounds, then sat back and regarded Beth with kindly interest.

"First, your name, *s'il vous plait*."

"Bethany." Her voice was toneless, so she tried again. "Bethany Lindstrom."

The woman repeated it. With soft, French-influenced vowels, Beth's name sounded both foreign and somehow comforting.

"Unusual. How did you become lost?"

"I wish I knew."

That caused another frown. Beth said quickly, "You're very kind. I thank you for the wine, but I should go and try to find my—" She choked. *What? My people? That magic hallway? My century? How am I supposed to find that, when I can't guess how I got here?* "Lord help me, I remember nothing . . . nothing!"

The woman seemed to soften at her distress. With a kind pat on the hand, she said in the low, soothing tones one uses to a frightened child, "You must not worry. You shall bide here in safety. When Geoffrey returns, he will send to ask after your husband and family."

"Geoffrey?"

"My husband," the woman explained with a smile. "Geoffrey de Tallac. Surely, you have heard of him—but forgive me! I did not give you my name. I am Alys de Tallac. We hold Mossock and many other honors. My husband is vassal to Lord Michael Veryan, a baron highly respected at court."

Beth grabbed for her goblet and drank, more deeply this time. The wine buzz penetrated the shock flooding her mind.

At court. Whose court? Not Elizabeth the Second's, that's for sure. Elizabeth the First? Earlier? Later? Good grief, what's happened to me?

"Are you the Gray Lady?" She bit her lip in consternation. What bit of terror had that come from?

Alys let out a chirp of laughter. "Not unless my hair turned color in the night." From under her workaday headdress, she pulled a thick dark braid and held it out for inspection, then tucked it back away. "Not yet, it would seem."

"Forgive me. I misspoke. Perhaps a memory . . . "

Alys's eyes widened in what could only be disbelief. "This night, then, we will pray the rest of your memories soon follow."

Beth gulped. "May God grant it, lady."

"Lisstreau? Linstrow? Your name is not Cornish. There are no such names here, but in the ancient Danelaw. You are from the

North Country? Perhaps that accounts for your strange dress as well." Alys looked at her expectantly, and Beth lifted both hands in helpless distress.

By now they had attracted an audience. To all appearances overcome with such curiosity at Beth's highly unusual ensemble that these normally reserved English folk had forgotten their habitual respect for others' privacy, a cluster of servants edged closer for a better look. Seeing that her Reeboks attracted special interest, Beth quickly tucked her feet under the bench and shrank away from them, tears welling to the surface.

Casting a quick glance around her, Alys waved the servants peremptorily away. "Enough for now. We must get you properly dressed, and then you will feel much better."

Upstairs in a busy solar, Beth endured the open-mouthed stares of Alys's maids while plotting how she could return to the back passageway of her entry into this world. Alys reprimanded her maids in stern tones, telling them to serve her guest, Lady Bethany, as they would their mistress.

When Alys pulled shift, gown, surcote, and soft leather shoes out of her own wardrobe trunk, Beth insisted on a private chamber to replace her own "strange clothing" away from prying eyes. The last thing she wanted were questions about her zipper, Reeboks, and bra.

I have to seem normal . . . though heaven knows I'm not! In these superstitious times, it might be one short step from stranger to witch.

Alone in the small bedchamber off the solar where Alys led her, Beth donned the clothing she had been given, her fingers fumbling with haste. But where to hide her jeans? The curious stares and disapproving expressions of the serving maids had left her feeling queasy. It was clear they did not accept her presence or story with the unquestioning sympathy of their mistress.

She glanced around her in desperation, heart hammering. All it would take was for one of them to get a close look at her outlandish clothing and she would be undone. If not Alys, then surely the lord of the manor on his arrival would put questions to her for which there could be no answer that did not lead directly to a stake surrounded with firewood.

Hurriedly she rolled her jeans and T-shirt into a ball around her underwear and sneakers and pried open a commodious, iron-bound coffer that stood in a shadowed corner. Thrusting the ball beneath what appeared to be clothing, she smoothed the concealing fabric, then cautiously eased the lid closed, wincing at the slight creak of the hinge. She strained to catch any sound from outside that might betray someone listening at the chamber door, but heard nothing. Straightening her overdress, she strode to the door.

"Your hair," Alys said once she emerged. "Have you no veil?"

Beth poked at her curling dark brown hair. Her stylish layered cut, falling just below her shoulders, now seemed garishly out of place. "I must have lost it."

Forgive me, Father . . . if You can still hear me who's ignored You so long. I'm out of my depth here. I'm a historian, but I have no clue what to say or do, and I'm scared. Just help me fit in as best I can, till I can get back to that passage, and get home. Her eyes filled.

Seeing, Alys offered a quick and bracing hug. "Do not weep. You are frightened, naturally. You miss your people, but for sure your husband will soon come for you." With one finger she lifted Beth's chin until Beth met her gaze. "Such odd coloring, and yet so fair. I am sure he misses you sore and will make all haste to find you."

Should she confess to being single, at her age? Girls married young in the Middle Ages, and Beth didn't want to seem abnormal, but she had no choice. "I think I have no husband."

Alys winced in consternation. "Ah, this you remember then. The mortality. Perhaps it is grief that has robbed you of memory. I understand, and I will speak of it no more."

The mortality? She means the pestilence. I came to a year sometime after 1349? Whoa, I hope not. That's not my period of study.

Beth cast her eyes down, hoping silence would let her hostess draw her own conclusions. Alys chattered of domestic issues, praising the rich curling mass of Beth's hair, as she sat her down and began to braid. Beth's hair, never obedient, was no match for a determined medieval matron, however, and Alys soon had it tamed and hidden under a starched white wimple.

"There. You must feel much better."

If I must, I must. "Thank you."

Beth scanned Alys's solar for a mirror, and found none. The off-white gown itched and fit too big in the chest and too long in the hem, as did the tunic over it, which showed at neck, sleeves and sides. The shorter surcote, cut away at the sides to show the tunic, was a dark mossy green in color. Its lack of ornamentation suggested an everyday garment, twin to the one Alys wore.

The lack of panties, bra, and slip felt very strange and yet light and well ventilated. That would take some getting used to.

If Alys was pleased, however, she must look normal. Whatever a twenty-first century historian was to make of that . . .

Unbidden, anticipation bubbled under stark fear. *However this happened, I'm here. I need to get back to that hallway ASAP, but until then . . . I didn't ask for this, despite Sheila's "seeings." I'm scared spitless, but if I'm supposed to be in this century for some strange reason known only on high, let me accomplish it fast as I can.*

The newly dubbed Lady Bethany slept that night, when she slept at all, in the same wall chamber off Lady Alys's solar where she had changed her clothing—now secured in the coffer with the key she'd found on the mantelpiece. Though Alys's serving maids slept wherever they could squeeze their pallets on the solar floor, Alys had not allowed Beth to do so. A "highborn" visitor must occupy a guesting chamber. Thus it was that Beth found herself stuffed naked into a cupboard bed built into the chamber wall.

The room itself felt dank with moisture from the thick stone walls of the manor house. A well-banked fire in the small hearth provided welcome warmth and its own aroma to add to many others. Her tick smelled of straw and past occupants. Though the linen sheets seemed clean, they abraded her skin. She turned and turned on the goosefeather pillow, covered in the same scratchy linen as the sheets. Sleep would not come, not that she expected any. At odd times, she fought hysterical laughter, remembering feeling jet lagged twenty-four hours ago, and now staring at a rising fourteenth-century sliver moon through the gaps in a wooden shutter.

The atmosphere in her bedchamber warmed slowly, gradually stopping her shivering. Though at times she shuddered from purest trepidation, Beth decided to make the best of her situation. And carefully too. She must watch every word and never, no matter how dire her need, tell any of these fanciful, credulous people the truth.

The truth would smack of sorcery. She'd have to walk the thinnest possible tightrope. Surely, surely this experiment—whatever had caused it—wouldn't last long. After a few days she'd find a way to escape the women and find her way back through whatever portal lurked in the back passage, back to the Mossock she knew, or even home. She wanted only to return to her own time and figure out how to incorporate this bizarre experience into her research. She nearly moaned in anticipation of the possibilities, but until she got home, she couldn't risk running afoul of medieval sensibilities.

Why me? David Graber or the Millards know this era better than I do, and they'd have been delighted to slip back in time. Any of them would've been a better choice than me. This isn't even my time period. Not that I know what year this is. I'll have to find some way to ask without asking.

She turned over and tried to punch the pillow into a different shape. It wouldn't punch, but gave off a faintly dry smell as air puffed out. Panic surged up again. She beat it down with as little effect as she had on the pillow. If only finding out what year she'd landed in were her only problem . . .

If only. She could foresee a dozen, a score, a hundred different pits into which she might fall, a stranger in this strangest of lands. Her hair was too short. Her attempts to speak the language were off base, if Alys's occasional puzzled expressions were any indication.

Her teeth were too straight, thanks to Dr. Banks and expert orthodonture. Heaven forbid anybody should glimpse her lone filling. What would they make of her appendicitis scar?

"That's nothing," she could see herself blurting out. "Just modern surgery."

They'd tie her to the stake and hurry off for kindling.

She rolled again onto her back. Like any avid historian, at times she'd speculated about time travel. Was it possible? Would it be, someday, with future technology? What would it be like to live in the Middle Ages?

The reality, at least the first twenty-four hours, was nothing like her romanticized images. She'd never conceived of the hardships, the dust, the lack of conveniences, the everyday odors they all apparently took for granted. Even Lady Alys, higher born and cleaner than the rest, smelled of skin and sweat.

For Lady Bethany de Lindstrom, one hundred percent liar and fraud, the smell of fear.

Sounds. Beth awakened to the manor beginning to bustle. Grainy-eyed, she stretched and yawned. Then found herself without sleep shorts or T-shirt and remembered.

A sick feeling socked her like a fist in the gut. Yesterday she'd stepped off a jumbo jet in modern-day England, excited and rubbernecking. Today she'd been cast back in time through what mechanism she couldn't guess. Groping for new ways to cope. Trying to fit in where she most assuredly did not belong.

I'd give my eyeteeth for a shower. And what about brushing the teeth? My teeth feel like . . . good grief. Why stress about hygiene when I'm not even going to be around very long? I'm a tourist, and I have to mimic their ways as much as possible. Above all, try to fit in.

Gathering her courage, she rolled out of bed. Thankfully, her scrapes had already scabbed over, and a brief inspection assured her that they would heal quickly.

Remembering the key to the coffer, she removed it from under her straw tick. An intensive hunt yielded a chink between the stones of the outer wall below the window ledge just large enough to conceal it from all but the most determined investigation. Praying that no one would need the contents of the chest and question why it was locked and what had happened to the key, she hurried to dress.

Donning her single outfit took no time, but night's leftover taste in her mouth was more than she could bear. With an impatient cluck, she scrubbed her teeth with a finger and the hem of her chemise. Pulling the tangles out of her hair with her fingers defeated her, so she went downstairs to the hall as she was.

Alys, already up, greeted her warmly. "Maude, bring my second-best comb."

When Maude returned, Alys did Beth's hair quickly and efficiently, chatting about the day's plans. Mass first, of course, and then sewing. Alys had some stuff they would make up into a gown just Beth's size. After fastening yesterday's linen coif over her braids, Alys handed over the comb.

"It is made of sandalwood," she said. "It will impart its aroma."

"Lady, no, I can't take your comb."

Gently, firmly, Alys closed her hand around it. "Do not say me nay. It is my gift to you."

To refuse the gift would be to insult her hostess. Beth gave in and managed a smile.

In the distance, a bell rang out for mass. The manor folk trooped behind Beth and Alys out the big main gate and down the road to the village church. She kept trying not to stare at the villagers bowing or tugging their bangs—no, forelocks, she reminded herself. A sign of respect for the gentry to whom she didn't belong. The village lay just beyond the round-towered church, crowded with homes little better than hovels, each one low to the ground and thatch roofed. From the nearest house window, an incurious ox peered out, chewing his cud.

Beth felt challenged not to openly sightsee the interior of the church. Older than Mossock, its architecture called the eleventh century to mind, rather than the thirteenth. Round-headed arches formed the doors and tiny, high-set windows. Two great candles smoked with a vaguely sour smell, competing with wisps from a censer the priest jerked around like a pup on a leash. Whitewashed walls instructed the faithful with brightly colored paintings of the Virgin, Christ Triumphant, several anonymous and uncomfortable-looking saints, and the harrowing of hell.

The priest looked to be in a bad temper. His robe showed many mended spots, and the short brown curls that bordered his tonsure jiggled every time he moved.

"Father Stephen," Alys whispered. "He would rather putter in his garden than say mass. He is new to us, so I do not know him well, but other than his inattention to his priestly duties, he does well enough."

The gardener priest ran through the liturgy quickly, enunciating without inflection. Beth decided Father Stephen was one of those post-pestilence clerics who lacked education and had to memorize the Latin liturgy by rote. His stomach made irreverent hungry rumbles, just like Beth's.

Out of courtesy, she followed Lady Alys, who tried to present her to Father Stephen. He gave both women the slightest nod of greeting and disappeared into the tiny sacristy.

"Welladay," said Alys on a sigh. "He is ever busy about his vegetables. Come, let us break our fast. I will bid him come to supper. That will give time enough to get his counsel on what you should do."

Beth said a fervent prayer that his vegetables would sprout six different kinds of root rot. Anything to keep the good priest far from her.

Back at the manor, Maude served breakfast, consisting of another jug of wine, some stewed fruit, and a large meat pie. Too hungry to worry about cholesterol or the strangeness of pie for breakfast, Beth consciously aped Alys's table manners and dug in.

Before they'd finished, Maude returned with the aggrieved expression Beth had already noticed. She didn't seem to approve of Mossock's houseguest. Or should Beth blame her own paranoia, since she was truly not what she seemed?

Maude and Alys had a quick exchange in the tongue Beth didn't understand. *Cornish? English, but a dialect they didn't teach us?*

Maude finished up, gave a stiff little bow, and turned to leave. As her eyes drifted to Beth, her gaze became calculating.

"If Lady Bethany will tell me where she has put the clothing she wore when she came to us, I will take it to be washed. It appeared to be dirtied, but I did not find it in her chamber. Perhaps it will tell us where she came from," she concluded with a thin smile.

Panic rose in Beth's throat. When Alys turned to her, brows lifted, she shook her head vehemently.

"Please . . . it is all I have left," she managed, her mind racing to find a plausible explanation when there was none. "Do not take it from me—" To her dismay, she broke down into sobs.

Alys placed her arm around Beth's waist, clucking soothingly. "Do not trouble yourself. Of course, the servants will not touch your things." She directed a reproving glance at Maude. "This clothing is, no doubt, all that binds you to your family, and it is understandable that you do not wish anyone to take it away."

"Thank you," Beth whispered, dabbing away her tears.

Maude gave her a sharp glance, but then shrugged and left them.

Coaxing a smile from Beth, Alys said, "Maude has brought good news. Kei—my husband's master-at-arms—has returned this morn. My husband is but a day's ride away. By vesper time tomorrow—or, please Mary, sooner—he will be home."

Beth nodded approval, though she felt only trepidation. What would Sir Geoffrey de Tallac make of her? Would he offer her the simple, open-hearted hospitality Lady Alys gave? Or would he demand a better story, a more plausible explanation of how a woman came to be battered, lost and alone? Would he look skeptically on her half-baked untruths?

She lifted another bite of pie on her borrowed eating knife and hoped heartily that Sir Geoff's horse would throw a shoe.

"Let us see." Upstairs in the solar, Alys opened a large wooden chest. A moth escaped into the sunshine, and a faint aroma of lavender wafted out. "Berta, take Lady Bethany's measurements. Then can Ela cut the linen for shifts. Three, I think; certes no less."

From a woven wicker basket, Berta unearthed a cord tied with many knots equally spaced. The maid held it up to see how many knots would measure from Beth's crown to her ankle. Beth felt led to object.

"Lady, I hope this is not for me."

Alys turned on her a round-eyed expression of surprise. "*Mais oui*. You cannot live forever in my old work shift and gown. They must be washed. And if Geoffrey wishes to take you to Lord Michael, as I think he will—"

Beth's spirit quailed. "To Lord Michael?"

Alys held up a length of bleached linen. "To find your family. Truro is quite a big city. And Veryan has wide connections, both at home in Cornwall and in England." She clucked her tongue. "Where else will Geoffrey seek them, if not in bigger towns? They will not think to hunt for you in a place as small as Mossock."

Alys unearthed several lengths of fabric, considered them, laid aside a length of teal blue, then a deep red, and put the rest back in the chest. "This, I think, for a best surcote. Ela can handle the seams, and of course, it will require embroidery. You do embroider?"

"I am . . . unskilled."

To Beth's surprise, Alys nodded with admiration. "You have the running of your dower properties, of course, and no time for trivial arts. You can sew the straight seams?"

"I can manage those."

Over the plain fabrics she'd chosen for gowns, Alys spread the length of warm blue-green cloth, then the second of maroon.

"These colors suit you. Such light eyes. If we are industrious, with God's grace we can have you ready for Veryan by the time Geoffrey sees fit to take you."

No choice. Beth swallowed. Sometime today then, she must sneak back to the portal—if there was a portal—and to these people, she would vanish. She'd been foolish to assume she could linger here at Mossock, free to investigate this current era to her heart's content. No, unless she found a way back to her own place and time, events would move, and she with them.

But what if she couldn't find the portal? The thought chilled her. Being a competent woman in her own time gave her no feeling of power here. Far from it. In this age, women worked their will through subtlety and by bringing some man around to their way of thinking.

Very well. Wasn't she a daughter of Eve? She had her own feminine wiles, though she'd have to tailor them to the current century's ways. She'd fly by the seat of her pants . . .

She almost laughed aloud over so modern a simile in this very medieval world. If it became necessary, she would work on Sir Geoffrey's liege lord. By the time she was done, Lord Michael would want nothing to do with her.

She waited until all the women were comfortably set up in the solar. Berta had satisfied herself that Lady Bethany was both shorter and thinner-built than Lady Alys. A third maidservant, introduced as Ela, dipped a shy curtsey of greeting and asked Beth to raise her skirts. Ela knelt and outlined Beth's foot on parchment with a lump of charcoal.

"Shoes," explained Alys. "Young Wat at the village inherited his father's lasts."

Ela giggled. "That is how he came by his name—Wat Cobbler."

Alys nodded. "Tell him to cut Lady Bethany a purse as well. She will need to carry her belongings when she goes to Truro."

Ela vanished on her errand. Maude, Berta, and a maid named Hawise got busy cutting and piecing Beth's new shifts. Alys insisted on doing the cutting of the more precious fabric for the tunics. Fascinated, Beth tried to watch without watching.

The process showed every sign of being a masterly operation, done with the speed of familiarity. Pins, it seemed, were not greatly used, since Alys owned but six. She accounted for each pin with a swift, calculating glance after each maid finished. Beth was ensconced in a tall-backed chair near the open casement window with a silver needle, fine white linen thread, and pieces of an undergarment.

"Do you know Lord Michael?" Beth asked once the maids had begun to chat amongst themselves. "What sort of a person is he?"

One of the maids giggled, to be quelled by Alys's swift glance. Alys put her thread into her mouth to point it for the needle. Beth smiled. Apparently, some human habits never changed.

"Hmm, how to describe him? He is a hard man. He speaks little, save to those vassals and retainers he has known the longest. Geoffrey is among those closest in his councils."

"Not given to conversation. I understand."

"Oh, he was not always thus. When first I met him—he honored us by guesting at my father's manor for our wedding celebrations—my lord was as merry a man as you could hope to meet. Always with a laugh, a jest, a charming new step to add to the country dances."

Alys plied her needle with frightening speed, setting tiny, almost invisible stitches into the fabric. Though she'd never heard of multi-tasking, apparently medieval women were as good at it as their modern counterparts. Beth wasn't sure she could talk and sew at the same time. Alys had seamed two inches of fabric before Beth set the knot in her thread.

"Perhaps your own lord was known to him," said Alys, "before the pestilence."

Beth tensed. She had not yet come up with a plausible story to explain her shocking lack of interest in finding her relations.

"I doubt it." In that instant, it dawned on her. "Lady, I must make full disclosure to you. I do not recall where I come from nor who is my family."

That was enough to stop Alys's needle in its tracks. "You do not remember?"

"No. When I told you I was lost, I meant it full sure. If I belong anywhere, I cannot say where that might be."

Lies. More lies, but what else can I do? I don't dare tell the truth. She'd never believe me. And in a way, I did get lost—didn't I? I just don't know how. . .

"*Ma pauvre*. You are frightened, and understandably so. No wonder you have been so silent. No doubt you were traveling, for you are not Cornish—it is clear from your fairness that you are not—and your party was set upon by brigands."

One of the maids made a distressed mouth noise.

"*Sans doute* your escort was roughly handled," Alys said, shaking her head.

"And those clothes." Maude gave a snicker. "I thought me, when Bruse ran in gabbling about an apparition, he'd gone daft. Your proper clothing was stolen, lady?"

"I suppose so." Beth stifled a sigh. Why couldn't Maude give up her fixation on the strange clothing?

"Your memory must have gone a-wandering for the time being because of the bump to your head," said Lady Alys.

"For the time being. Yes." Beth put a self-conscious hand to the scrape on her forehead. "It aches since I came to be here."

That much is a hundred percent true.

"You see. It is just as I say. Such times! Brigands, runaway serfs—there has been no peace. First the cattle-murrain, then the cursed pestilence." Several of the maids made a fervent sign of the cross. "And the Welsh, who live and breathe rebellion. Not here in Cornwall, *grâce a Dieu*, but elsewhere. Sufficient men cannot be found to till the soil or take in the harvest, but plenty to take up outlaws' ways." Alys shook her head and finished off the side seam.

Beth found herself staring at her thread, knotted in a fair imitation of an interlaced Celtic serpent. Compared to Lady Alys's, her stitches looked like a backward child's.

Carefully she unthreaded her needle and set the mess to rights. *Smaller stitches and much faster or I won't be taken for a gentlewoman, that's for sure. It would be nice if I could fake it a bit better.*

She ventured a comment. "Labor has been scarce here since the sickness?"

Alys nodded. "Mossock is small, but we do well enough. With Christ's grace, the murrains are behind us, and the rains come as they should. Geoffrey keeps our serfs' obligations light. Lord William—my father-by-marriage—followed the old ways. By the rood, to hear him speak, villeins should eat grass like the cattle."

Beth intercepted an eloquent glance between Ela and Maude.

Alys continued, "My husband sees things differently. He believes the manor is best served by leaving them time for their own crops. They should not be burdened with overmuch boon work. He follows Lord Michael's example and has even freed many of our serfs."

Beth made a sound she hoped indicated approval. "Did you lose—" She stopped as Alys's pleasant face set in a stoic expression.

"Many," Alys said quietly. "Maude's husband and both sons. Ela's sister and brothers. My mother-by-marriage and my young son."

"I am sorry," Beth murmured. "I'll follow your advice and discuss it no more."

"We gave them to God," said Maude, "four years ago August month. We grieve still, but it does no good to rail against Him."

"No," Beth agreed. "His ways are not our ways."

At least, not that I remember. I walked away from God a long time ago. But now, at least I know when "now" is: 1353. Unless the dates we've always used are off by a twelvemonth. Or more.

Alys nodded, while Maude and the maids stared somewhat uncomfortably at her. "You speak like a priest, lady," said Maude.

Ela clucked her tongue. "No use at all, they were. Why, didn't dear Father Launce die the first, right here at home, and the friar the bishop sent for replacement soon after?"

"You must have been—" Beth bit back *shocked out of your gourd,* "—sore beset."

Alys's voice softened. "We served each other. What comfort was to be had we shared between us."

Beth remembered that the Bishop of Bath and Wells had advised his flock on the relaxation of strict church procedure during the crisis of 1349—though how he had dared send a messenger while the plague raged, she couldn't guess. He'd instructed his frantic parishioners to give each other spiritual support to the best of their ability. Even women. The bishop had no idea he'd anticipated the ways of some modern churches by so many hundreds of years.

For a time she mulled over their words, sewing in silence. The maids, too, seemed pensive. Beth had no doubt each thought of her losses. How had they gotten through such a shock?

If she was permitted to stay here for a while—who knew how long?—she could learn how they'd managed. And so many other things. She must make hyper-efficient use of whatever time here she had. When at last she got home, somehow she would find ways to validate what she'd learned. She would astound every English history expert on the planet. Her dissertation would not only be excellent, but brilliant. She'd be preeminent in her field. She all but licked her lips at the prospect.

To do that, I have to get back.

A glance upward showed the sun descending. If she was to seek the portal, now was the time. She murmured a vague excuse about the privy and set her needlework aside.

Gathering up her skirts, she trotted back to the sun-gilded great hall and through the door of the buttery, where great casks of wine and ale were stored. This led into the hallway she sought, which now in the light appeared disused except for storage. Several half-empty barrels and a broken bucket littered its walls, looking forgotten in the bustle of a busy manor.

Beth slid along the wall, heart pounding, seeking with her fingertips on the rough stones.

Here. Just here. Wasn't it? That cold feeling, and then I got dizzy and slipped back in time. Funny—it still sounds incredible, yet here I am. Please, let this work. Let this be my way home.

She clenched her eyes shut, leaning against the wall, willing its unknown magic to whisk her back where she belonged. From a distance came the voice of a serving man calling to one of his mates in that oddly musical and unfamiliar language. Though out of practice, she prayed violently, her hands clutching at the surface, hoping through sheer will-power she could force her way through . . .

No cold sensation. No vertigo. The serving man laughed at a comment from his mate and replied in kind—in that unknown tongue.

Beth opened her eyes. Nothing. She still heard all the sounds, smelled all the rich and foreign aromas of the old Mossock, and none of the new. If the portal existed, she couldn't make it work.

She let go of the wall. So . . . analyze. Perhaps the portal wasn't a matter of a specific place. Obviously, she couldn't simply lay her hands on the wall and invoke time travel at will. Since that was true, time travel was a random event. But what sort of random event? What generated her journey in the first place? How could she reproduce a random happening to get home?

She let out a deep and unsteady sigh. She'd already lingered here longer than a trip to the privy required. Gathering her borrowed surcote in her fists, she muttered a resentful prayer for resignation.

The solar welcomed her back. The sun had settled lower, sending peach-pink rays through the casement in the western wall. The fire burned low, setting its warmth at odds with the cool of early evening. The maids murmured soft commentary one to another, desultory talk that did not disturb Alys from her thoughts or Beth from hers.

Maude had already finished hemming the first shift, and Ela was rapidly completing the seams of a tunic. Under Alys's skilful hands, Beth's "best" tunic took shape. Ela tied off her thread, sketched a curtsey to Alys and vanished down the solar stairs.

Beth's stomach rumbled. She hoped Ela went to hurry supper. This night, perhaps, she would sleep more soundly than last. Minding her tongue and aping the ways of the others put stress-knots into her neck muscles. And no ibuprofen to ease the ache.

"Let us finish, *mesdames*," Maude said at last. "The light fails."

Beth slept better that night. Though worry over Sir Geoffrey's reaction to an amnesic stranger kept her tossing for a while, eventually she closed her eyes. On the rare occasions when she woke, moonbeams filtered through the wooden shutters on the single narrow window. The dim light seemed comforting somehow, telling her that some things remained unchanged. Though she had walked away from God, He seemed still available—for emergency use.

Dawn came too early around here. Up with the sun, Beth did her best to contribute to the heightened activity of the manor. Sir Geoffrey's impending arrival threw the household into excited disarray. Lady Alys clucked and tsked and harried the servants until Maude felt led to intervene.

"Lady," she suggested, "the embroidery for Lady Bethany's bettermost tunic is yet unfinished. The sun shines on the plesaunce garden, and the wind off the sea will cool you."

"We are *de trop*," murmured Alys with a chuckle. "Let it not be said that a lady rules her home. In truth, uppity maidservants have their way in all things."

Beth picked up her sewing. Alone with Lady Alys, she might get a chance to ask discreet questions about both Sir Geoffrey and Sir-Michael-to-be-Managed. Shooed out of the great hall by Maude and her sweating minions, Alys indicated a wood-and-iron bench with the sunlight at their backs.

"That sleeve with the flowered border goes ill, does it not?" She pointed to an error in the embroidery Beth had hoped nobody would notice. "What say you give that garment to me, and you finish the seam on this tunic?"

"Yes, please." Beth handed the messed-up piece to her hostess. "I did warn you, in all truth—I am poor at this. Thanks, lady, for saving my pride before the maids."

Alys laughed. "Let them think we are less than perfect, and before you can say an Ave, they will feel free to banish you from your own solar."

Beth giggled, then broke forth into a hearty laugh. They bent their heads over their sewing.

The peace of the morning's embroidery broke with the noontime arrival of Sir Geoffrey de Tallac and troop. Lady Alys ran forth out of the gates with a little squeal to greet her dirty, tired husband in the dust of the road.

Beth held back, uncertain. Sir Geoffrey's steel helm hung by its leather laces. He pushed his chain mail hood back to reveal copper-dark hair plastered to his skull with sweat. Without wasting time for words, he dismounted, tossed his reins to the nearest retainer, stripped off his gloves, and caught Lady Alys's face between his bare hands. The kiss he offered and Alys's response left no doubt in Beth's mind—some small percentage of medieval marriages were contracted not for property, but true love.

Her discomfort deepened, along with a pang of deep sorrow. No man of this time would take her cheeks in his hands and cover her face with kisses. *Not that I have anybody in my own world either. I've been so busy getting my PhD and making a name for myself . . .*

The pang took on a name: Loneliness.

Lady Alys straightened her headdress, knocked completely awry by her husband's greeting. "*Warlinenn,* my dear lord," she said breathlessly, "and let me make known to you our houseguest."

With a crisp gesture, she motioned to Beth. She came forward reluctantly, casting around in her mind for whatever form was appropriate. All she could think of was to curtsey low, in the dusty road between the gateposts.

"My lord." Anxiety froze Beth's tongue to the roof of her mouth. Though she wanted to search for his reaction in his face, she kept her gaze on her soft-leather shoes.

"My lady." His voice sounded cultured and smooth, but under simple courtesy she heard an undercurrent of caution. She could hardly blame him for being wary. His wife had welcomed her, swallowing her lame story while manifesting no sense of self-protection. Men of parts would not be so trusting. Beth couldn't expect a seasoned warrior to accept her, or any stranger with a weak excuse for being here, at face value. She swallowed through a dry throat.

Father, please stick around, though I don't hang with You much. Lately I've been whining to You every chance I get. Just . . . let me know what to say without telling too many lies. Oh, and it would be nice if Sir Geoff here doesn't consign me to the local dungeon.

Didn't Sheila say Mossock has a dungeon?

"*Warlinenn.* Be welcome," de Tallac continued. His gaze lingered on the scabbed scrape on her forehead. "Over dinner, tell me your story and how I can assist you."

So I can get out of your hair as soon as possible, Beth interpreted.

"You are very kind," she said. "I owe all to your lady."

Sir Geoffrey slanted a glance at his wife. His mouth softened in what must be amusement, for his eyes lost their cautious expression at the same time.

"Aye. Lady Alys is much given to the protection and succor of the lost and hungered."

Beth found no answer.

"Hungry!" Alys squealed. "Dinner. The meats have been held back half done, my dear lord. I must away so there may be a fitting dinner for your return."

"Let me," Beth begged. "How about—" She caught Alys's frown that said, *I'm not reading you.* "Do you welcome Sir Geoffrey, and with your permission, I will see to the meal."

I can, right? Any idiot can bid them turn up the heat under the roast goose—or whatever she's got planned for the feast.

Lady Alys shot her a grateful look. "If you please, Lady Bethany. And you, piggy—" She wrinkled her nose at her husband, "—you smell like six weeks of horse and road dirt. *Deus a ji,* now, inside with you, and get you to the bath you so sorely need."

Beth fled to the kitchen outbuildings to announce that the lord had come. The cook and staff tolerated her interference with silence, if not grace, so once she'd set them to their work she relieved them of her presence. In the plesaunce garden, she located her dropped sewing and set back to work. Her heart hammered loudly enough to hear over the *siss-whomp* of a heavy swell smashing on the cliffs beneath the garden wall.

Sir Geoff doesn't trust me. Of course he doesn't. Why should he? Why would he believe my story as easily as Alys did? Will he maybe hustle me off to Truro for his overlord to deal with?

She rose and opened the garden gate to peer down at the noisy surf. The current ran at angles to the sharp rocks, and graying clouds scudded on a breeze that lifted her borrowed veil. Somewhere out in the Irish Sea, a tempest built. Would it hit Cornwall? A good squall might delay departure for Lord Michael's, but not forever. Hot tears rose in her eyes, as insistent as the storm-borne swell at sea.

Ah, Bethany, eager to prove herself, as always. What if all I discover here is how it feels to die in a dungeon?

Lady Alys made sure supper was served in a manner worthy of her lord and his welcome return. Many candles glowed from the iron-pronged holders ranged on the tables, and every torch bracket shed additional light. The high table and even the lesser tables bore linen cloths of the most immaculate white. Despite the spring evening's warmth, a large fire had been laid in the hall's massive hearth, its fragrant wood smoke enhanced by the addition of sweet herbs.

At first Beth held back from the revelry, reminding herself she was but a tourist here. She had trouble doing so. Sir Geoffrey abandoned his initial reserve and regaled his people with stories of his travels, both current and in the past. His retainers shouted, striving to outdo one another, telling many tales of bravery in service to the baron de Veryan, at one remove to King Edward himself. As home-brewed ale and imported wine flowed freely, they vied for the floor, relating tales of their lord's exploits—and their own. Beth had to laugh at some of the stories, for no knight could take down a hundred armed men alone—could he?

She drank with the others. The wine soon stole her resolve to remain aloof. To the high table at which she, Alys, Geoffrey, and Father Stephen sat, the servitors brought a rich pottage redolent of leeks, removed with lamb patties and meat pasties glazed yellow with saffron and egg white. There followed venison, a small roast goose, dishes of boiled and sauced vegetables, a whitish cheese baked *en croûte,* and artfully braided loaves of finest white bread.

She sampled everything, even the highly flavored sauces. With a qualm she remembered her studies, which claimed that such sauces were devised to hide the taste of meat about to spoil. She couldn't taste any off flavors, so she put it down to yet another scholarly theory that didn't hold water.

The welcome feast held but one disquieting note. Later, as she removed her shoes in her chamber, she thought back to Father Stephen and the low-toned discussion he'd held with Sir Geoffrey. What had he said in such urgent tones? Of course, she'd understood no word of the priest's insistent Cornish, but the tension in his body language needed no translation. Something about her, the newcomer with a suspicious past, bothered Father Stephen. What had he urged Sir Geoffrey to do about it?

She crawled naked into her bed. In the morning, she'd try again to get to the hallway. The passage held the key—the portal, whatever it was. However it worked. The sooner she left here for her own time, the safer. Father Stephen's reservations about her would soon be academic, his only concern to explain how she'd vanished from this place forever.

She wondered, though. Would the disappearing Lady Bethany make her way into legend, larger than life, as Sir Geoffrey's men made him out to be? She'd come into an age that loved—and believed—marvels. What tales would local history tell about a disappearing stranger? *I don't care what they think or how I leave them.*

She turned over, upset, but not too upset to wonder whether to ask God for help. Somehow it seemed more natural to pray in this age of faith than it had in her cozy apartment in Chicago. *Lord, I can't care. Just let me get back to my own century, as rapidly as possible.*

With the rest of the household, Sir Geoffrey broke his fast early. At the high table he courteously informed Lady Alys that he must see to his accounts, then ride to the nearby manors, which owed him Eastertide rents.

"Before I ride out, I would speak with you, Lady Bethany."

Uh-oh. Here it comes.

She allowed Ela to pour her more home-brewed ale, for which she'd already developed a taste, and hoped her answering nod looked calm.

Sir Geoffrey apparently believed in the direct offense. "I would hear your story from your own lips."

"My lord, please excuse me. Would that I knew it to tell you. I came here with no memory of my own people or my life before I walked onto Mossock land."

Lord God, if You can still hear me, forgive me for lying.

"So says my lady."

"It is the truth." And now she was lying about the lies she told. Where would it stop?

"You were some hurt when my lady found you. Were you then attacked by outlaws? If so, I must hunt them down and drive them off my lands."

"I am sorry. I know not."

He studied her a moment in silence. "Father Stephen claims you are telling less than the truth."

"I cannot claim otherwise. For all I know, he may well be right," she said, keeping calm with an effort.

That git. He's never so much as spoken to me.

"I would not willingly deceive." That much, at least, was plain truth. "For your kindness alone I owe you all honesty. I cannot give it, for I do not know exactly what happened. But Father Stephen has never asked for my ideas on what befell. He bases his suspicions on rumor, an uncertain source of information."

"I did suggest he ask you himself," Lady Alys put in. Her expression seemed serene, at odds with Beth's emotional turmoil. She rested her folded hands atop her baby bump, a gesture Beth found poignant and lovely. "He said he would come to you, but has not."

Geoffrey snorted and gestured to Ela for more ale. "He is not as dutiful as our old priest."

Alys laid a hand over her husband's. "He is yet getting acquainted with the parish. He has had scant time to do the necessary work on his glebe lands, much less learn all Father Launce and Father Tom knew."

"But this is nothing to the point." Geoffrey offered his wife a tender smile and turned his scrutiny back onto Beth. She much preferred his attention where it belonged, on Alys. "Priests should hold themselves apart from gossip, though Mossock village is fonder of gossip than work . . . enough. Father Stephen fears you might be possessed of demons. He seemed much disturbed by reports that you lacked proper clothing and that you have no Cornish. I disagree. Many nowadays dress above their—ah, that is to say, differently than their stations might indicate. And how many speak proper Cornish, particularly among the Sawsnachs? Neither of these lacks are any sign you serve the Evil One."

Alys crossed herself with an impatient gesture. "Of course she does not. And her clothes were in no wise improper. Was she not covered, neck to ankle? I have seen worse at court. Not immodest, merely . . . odd. And I need no priest to tell me what is what. I can judge character for myself. I should have seen by now were Lady Bethany evil. She is anything but."

Geoffrey gave Alys another fond glance. "My lady wife suggests we seek your people in Truro. I am inclined to agree."

Beth swallowed. How was she to find her way back through the portal—the portal she couldn't make work—if she left Mossock?

"My lord?"

Sir Geoffrey must have seen her shock, for he held up a hand in a *work with me here* gesture. "Hear me. Father Stephen seems indolent for a priest, and certes he is no deep student of the faith. Nonetheless, he is well connected at court and in the bishop's palace. One hears worldly rumors that he is the bishop's nephew, though he has never said so. It would be well to separate you from his area of influence. If he take an offense against you to his superiors, the consequences could be—" He cleared his throat. "—most unpleasant."

Beth suppressed a qualm of fear. Images of fifteenth-century illuminations crowded her memory, the worst showing Jeanne d'Arc, hands folded in prayer, small and alone at the stake. Time to play the submissive medieval female and give lip service to acquiescence. She drained her mazer, hoping the brew might lend false courage to an uncertain spirit.

"If you wish it, Sir Geoffrey, I will go to Truro." And then, somehow, she would have to find her way back here.

She knew nothing of how time portals worked. Were there other doors in this misty realm of legend and fairy tale? Perhaps King Arthur had left for Avalon using just such a portal. She had no way to prove he hadn't and no way to investigate.

Did the Cornish slip easily back and forth through time? She couldn't imagine them doing so.

Mossock itself must be the key. She would not lightly let go of it.

Three

The party left for Truro after mass the following Sunday, after a delay caused by intemperate rain and a shrieking wind that felt as if it blew straight off Greenland. Once it cleared, Beth made ready, donning a hand-me-down riding habit, hastily cut down from garments Alys pulled from a coffer belonging to her late mother-by-marriage.

The gray wool habit, freshened with some cinnamon filched from Cook, was not Beth's best color. Alys clucked her tongue over this, but Beth didn't care—her only concern was the skirt. To her relief she found it full enough to allow her to bestride her borrowed palfrey. She'd dreaded encountering anything resembling a sidesaddle.

On parting Alys had expressed the hope that they would soon meet again. In addition, she'd been more generous than Beth could imagine, pressing on her three gowns and two fine veils. In addition to the newly made soft-leather shoes, the cobbler had provided a capacious traveling pouch, into which she surreptitiously tucked her "strange clothes." She also possessed a secondhand eating knife, the sandalwood comb, a tiny vial of lavender water, and six silver pennies.

So, the road. It stretched before the gates of Mossock, a muddy challenge. Beth returned Lady Alys's tearful wave. Had a lost traveler ever happened upon a kinder soul? She and her benefactress had bonded, and Beth felt sorrow at the parting.

At the same time, a thread of excitement built at the idea of experiencing travel during the Middle Ages. Would they meet outlaws, pilgrims, a merchant band conveying their goods to a summer fair? No matter what they might encounter, Beth didn't fear for her own safety. Far from it, for Mossock in the last days had felt uneasy. Father Stephen's parting blessing had sounded sinister and most insincere, his small opaque eyes revealing only suspicion.

Sir Geoffrey's instincts were sound. Despite the reason—the search for her nonexistent family—she did well to leave Mossock.

That in de Tallac's train rode no fewer than thirty keen-eyed, seasoned men at arms was reassuring. Their leather helmets and ring-sewn jerkins had seen hard wear, and their leader's face bore an old scar from eyebrow to chin. In what battle had he taken so fearsome a wound? And how, with medieval medicine's coarse knowledge, had he survived it? The scar made Kei look foreign and barbarically threatening, and Beth couldn't help shuddering at the sight.

Their road led downhill into the village of Redruth. The sun pierced early through the leftover mists of morning. Beth felt a bead of sweat trickle from under her wimple and trace its path down her back. She couldn't swipe at it without upsetting her mount, for the palfrey called Caillin had bad habits. Though gentle enough, she gave an unannounced two-inch bounce at anything that discomposed her, and she found plenty to upset her on the road. A laugh from one of the men, a seagull passing too close, a startled hare—almost any interruption set her off. Despite the leather-covered wooden saddle with its comfortably high pommel and cantle, Beth didn't dare let her guard down for fear of winding up flat on her bottom in a mud puddle.

No thanks, Caillin.

The men already thought her strange, with her unplaceable foreign accent and her borrowed finery. The last thing she needed was to give them a laugh by failing to keep her seat.

The road treated them kindly enough, offering neither brigands nor pilgrims as distraction. A mile outside Redruth, a pair of mendicant friars kept pace with the troop for safety's sake. Beth nodded greeting, which the good brothers ignored, marching stolidly, chanting under their breath, their hands buried deep in brown woolen sleeves.

The sun was just finishing its descent at her back when the party rode at last into Truro. Beth roused from a muscle-sore, fatigued doze to gawk around her. Outside the city walls, shacks of wattle plastered with clay leaned against each other for support. Beyond them, the tide had gone out of the estuary, exposing wide gray flats of sea-smelling mud, where a few ragged children scavenged for any treasures the sea might have left behind.

Kei, Sir Geoffrey's battle leader, spurred his tired mount toward the gates of the town. With a bellow that made irritable Caillin bounce her bridle tassels, he demanded entry—and got it. Beth patted her mount and assured her she'd soon be tucked up in a warm stall, for the looming battlements of a tall keep told her the journey was ended.

Kei gained access to the keep in the same way he'd shouted at the town gates. The guards raised the portcullis, and they rode inside. Sir Geoffrey told Beth to wait with the troop in the bailey until he found Lord Michael to welcome them.

Welcome. Yeah, I'll bet. Any delay will just give him more time to erect the witch-burning stake.

The days waiting out the storm at Mossock had revealed much Beth hadn't understood. Sir Geoffrey had never voiced disbelief of her story but left her to read skepticism in his body language. Only this morning, as they'd ridden out in the dawn, had he summoned her to spur Caillin forward in order to explain his forbearance.

"I am much indebted to you," he'd said formally. "Of late, my lady has suffered sore unease of spirit."

Beth knew better than to ask questions. Sir Geoffrey didn't like women who spoke up—unless they were Alys.

"She miscarried of our last child," he continued. "You know, do you not, that she is *enceinte* again? She frets much over the babe. Save once, she has not carried to term."

Beth bent her head. *And then your son died in the pestilence. I understand.*

"The manor folk say she has been much lightened in her mind since your coming."

Beth felt bold enough to venture, "If I helped at all, I am glad of it, my lord."

Sir Geoffrey's frown lacked punch. "If it is my lord Veryan's will to bring you, I would welcome you back to Mossock for her confinement or at any time."

"No one could have been kinder to—" She was about to say *a liar,* but bit the words back. "—to a stranded wayfarer such as me."

He'd cast her another speculative glance and said no more, so Beth figured the conversation had run its course. She let Caillin fall back a few paces.

Clear as dawn, Sir Geoffrey's expression said, *Veryan has no lady to cozen him, and you will not find him as forbearing as I have been.*

He returned now to the bailey with a plainly dressed man in his wake and beckoned her inside the walls. She relinquished Caillin's reins to a skinny stable boy and retrieved her leather pouch from the cantle. Without shame, she took in everything.

My first castle!

The main tower of the keep loomed, sternly granite, some four stories overhead. From a mast, a red and gold pennon fluttered in the breeze off the estuary. The bases of three outlying towers were smothered in the same sort of clustered outbuildings as at Mossock—wooden structures, roofed in thatch or gray granite slates—around which people scurried, busy about eventide tasks.

Sir Geoffrey led the way to a forebuilding of the main keep. While studying the place, Beth trotted to keep up, trying to commit every detail to memory.

Just within the doorway into the great hall he stopped. "Wait here," he commanded, and left her edging toward a huge granite hearth to warm her stiff fingers.

A maid approached, dressed somewhat similarly to her own and Alys's "work clothes" at Mossock. "God's greeting, lady."

She pressed a silver goblet into Beth's hands, sketched a curtsey, and hurried off. Presumably, she had many other duties besides welcoming strangers. Beth sipped sweet wine—a better quality than Mossock's—and studied her surroundings. Oh, for paper and a pencil!

As at Mossock, men set up long tables along both sides of the hall, with a shorter table on a dais near another large hearth. As soon as the men had propped each tabletop on its trestles, maids scurried to spread them with white cloths, folded back upon themselves at the edge nearest the diners. On the high table the maids spread more than one layer, creating the folds with precision. These cloths gleamed snowier white than those for the long tables. In the center of the high table, a man set a replica dragon ship, complete with silver sail and colorful enameled shields at the gunwales.

The saltcellar, she guessed. The arbiter of who's highborn and who's not. It graces the high table, splendidly dressed for the use of the lord and those noble guests he sees fit to honor.

Where will Veryan put me? Below the salt, with the retainers? When Geoff tells him about me, will he send me outside to sup with the stable boys?

"Ah, there she is." Sir Geoffrey approached with a taller man. "My lord, allow me to make known to you Lady Betaine de Linstreau. Lady, Lord Michael, baron de Veryan."

Again, her name hashed into Frenchified nonsense. She dipped to a hesitant curtsey, afraid her wine would spill. The gesture made the strap of her leather pouch slide down her shoulder, and she rose with greater speed than courtesy demanded, hooking a finger around the strap.

"My lord."

"So, de Tallac."

Their host's voice sounded light and pleasant, not the deep bass she'd expected from a man so big. He had ebony hair in dire need of a haircut, for it feathered around the embroidered neck of his russet tunic. Its wool, she noted, was finer than any she had yet seen. His eyes were the color of the last autumn leaf, and right now they narrowed as they scanned her up and down—somewhat insolently, she thought.

"What is this you bring me?"

She felt her cheeks grow warm. In few words, Sir Geoffrey detailed Beth's encounter with brigands and the blow on the head—creations of Lady Alys's imagination—that had robbed her of memory. Lord Michael gave a nod, and Geoffrey bowed and left them. Another peremptory gesture brought a manservant scurrying with a large carved chair for him and a stool for her.

What? I'm no lapdog to sit on a hassock at my lord's feet!

A smile teased mobile lips, but a hard one, without warmth. "Lady, rest," he said. "It is a long and weary journey from the coast."

She lifted her chin. "If it please you, my lord," she said in a manner she hoped was haughty, "I shall stand."

He gave a negligent wave. An observant manservant rushed up. "Tamkin, a chair for the lady."

Her cheeks heated, and she studied the hall, ostentatiously ignoring him until the chair arrived, then nodded thanks at the servant.

Lord Michael studied her. "You are comfortable?"

Hardly. Comfortable means not afraid of every word and glance.

"Very much. My thanks."

From the hearthside, a huge hound rose, sniffed the air, and ambled over. Her host reached out a hand, but the gray monster passed him by in favor of Beth. Gravely she offered the dog a hand to sniff, which he did most thoroughly before licking her fingers.

Then she felt free to scratch his enormous, rough-coated gray head.

"Bran, what ails you?" The baron snapped his fingers. "Your pardon, lady. He is usually most standoffish, certes not accustomed to be so forward with strangers."

"He but welcomes me."

She scratched some more and Bran responded with a low rumble, not a growl but a moan of pleasure. He resembled Sheila Tyrrell's wolfhound, Wenna, enough to be her litter mate. Could he be a distant ancestor of Sheila's pet? She remembered the way Wenna had followed her around the later Mossock as if aware of some impending distress. Bran seemed to share the bond with her that Wenna had shown.

"I am glad he does not unnerve you. From what de Tallac says, you have been unnerved enough and sore beset these weeks past."

The servant approached with a small table, on which a maidservant set a goblet, a flagon, and a bowl of nuts holding an iron nutcracker in the shape of a stylized horse. Lord Michael, ignoring the servitor, took his time selecting a walnut. Beth all but jumped when the crack echoed in the hall.

"Your party was set upon by miscreants."

"I beg your pardon. I do not remember."

"You stumbled into Mossock wearing strange clothing."

"I wore what I wore—that is all I know." She licked her lips, and finding them dry, sipped more of the light red wine. It emboldened her to add a comment. "Lady Alys was most kind."

"That is Lady Alys." He popped the walnut into his mouth and chewed reflectively with strong white teeth. "Kindness itself."

"I owe her much."

"Indeed." He chose another nut. His fingers, though scarred in places, were long and artistic, not the blunt hands of a soldier. "You should repay her kindness—and de Tallac's, for indeed all Lady Alys gave you comes from his bounty—with the truth."

Her anxiety cranked up another notch. "I have told the truth as far as I can tell it."

"What of the part you cannot tell? I would hear that."

"You yourself have said it. I cannot."

He offered her a freshly cracked nutmeat. She shook her head.

"And would not if you could, I think."

Beth rose. "I will not play at words. You are Sir Geoffrey's liege lord and, from what I hear, a hard man but not a wicked one. Ask your questions, but I cannot give you answers I do not possess."

"Be seated, lady. You need not eye me like a doe eyes a hunter. If you mean no harm, you are in no danger here."

She complied, but warily, watching him like that hunted doe. She did well to stay alert, for Lord Michael seemed nowhere near as trusting as the de Tallacs.

Which of her facial expressions gave her away? Worse—if he suspected her story as the fabrication it was, what did he assume the truth might be?

"I mean no man harm," she murmured. "Not you or yours, nor those at Mossock."

Lord Michael-to-be-Managed, who was supposed to tamely accept her story and let her hurry back to Mossock, proved not easy at all. Beth sent up a swift prayer for guidance, for his every sentence sent fresh fear down her spine.

If he meant what he said, she was in no danger. But what if he hid suspicion and threat behind considering glances and calming words?

He studied her. "You are very fair."

She decided to take his meaning in the modern way. "No doubt my ancestors had light coloring. Lady Alys thinks I am not Cornish."

"Certes you are not. You sit glaring at me like a Norse reaver of old."

Her pulse sped up, and she could have stamped her foot against the floor rushes in pique. How did he do it? She was no blushing teenager, but every time he scored a point, she felt her cheeks get hot. And he scored like Jordan with a basketball.

"I am no invader, of any race."

To her surprise, he gave a rusty laugh. "I shall believe you, my fair new guest—at least for tonight."

He put the nutcracker down and rose from his chair. With the bow of adversary to worthy opponent, Lord Michael offered her his hand. Beth placed two fingers on his wrist to rise, hoping she did it the way she'd seen in manuscript illuminations.

"Come. A maid will show you to your quarters. You will wish to refresh yourself before the evening meal. I offer you my protection and the comforts of my home. Let us sup together, and you shall tell me more of what you are—and are not."

Lord Michael Veryan, knight and baron of Truro, of Mossock, St. Anne, Kingsdown, Trevellas, Odiham, Ivel, and Trevorgas, tenant-in-chief of King Edward III for these properties and others of dubious loyalty in Wales and the Marches, ordered Beth seated above the saltcellar. As his master of ceremonies gestured her into place on a bench to the right of the single chair at the high table, she felt tense enough to break out either into silly laughter or panicky tears.

She glanced down at her finery, so lovingly and hastily sewn by Alys, Maude, Ela, and the others. A pang of homesickness shook her for Mossock and those she'd grown to respect. But at least she'd come clean to the meal. Before supper she'd had a chance to wash off the road dirt, surprisingly in a private chamber.

As they'd adjourned from their sparring, Veryan had, with a negligent gesture, summoned an apple-cheeked brunette maid. "This is Teagen, who will serve you. Show Lady Bethany to the south tower wall chamber."

"My lord?" Teagen hid her reaction behind her hand. Sir Geoffrey simply gaped.

"The south chamber, wench. Have you porridge in your ears?" He did not raise his voice, but Teagen gave a hasty nod and bow.

Beth had tried to follow her, but the maid would have none of it. "Please precede me, lady, as is seemly. The chamber is through that door, then up the stairs."

The maid seemed willing, though obviously she had hang-ups about precedence and order. Beth had given up and let Teagen help her to dress in the best blue gown and surcote. Like Alys, Teagen had muttered imprecations under her breath while doing Beth's hair, but for now it behaved, decently pinned and hidden under Alys's third-best silk veil.

She smoothed both sweaty hands down her skirts. If a twenty-first century woman could look acceptable in fourteenth-century gear, Beth figured she'd do. Now to rein in her up-and-down emotions for supper. For sure she felt as flighty as Caillin.

Now, in the great hall, a servant drew out the bench where she sat for an older man. Beth bent her head in greeting, and the man followed suit. Old enough to be Veryan's dad he was, and owing to the quality of his worn blue velvet tunic, she guessed his status was at least that of knight. Mumbling into his mustache, he introduced himself as Sir Andre de Giscard of Odiham. Beth offered her own name, to which he responded with an inarticulate grunt and thereafter made no further conversation.

For table manners she covertly watched Sir Andre and the few ladies present. She noted gestures and etiquette she could copy. Water vessels called *écuelles* were brought to table, so she dabbled her fingers in the warm, scented water as Sir Andre did, wiping her hands on the linen napkin folded next to her trencher.

Panic drowned in a surge of wonder so acute she had to blink back moisture. *I'm here. A medieval banquet like I've read about, and I'm really here.*

The high-raftered room roiled with conversation, spiced here and there with laughter. A stray zephyr teased smoke from the huge hearths, setting the perch-hung tapestries on the walls gently astir.

Along the columns supporting the wooden roof, many iron torches gave out a pine-scented, inconstant light.

Pages and lesser servitors darted here and there with pitchers almost too big for them, replenishing wine or ale at the diners' demand. "Anon, madame," they puffed, struggling from low table to high and back again. "You shall be filled, sir—anon!"

The pitch of the conversation ebbed when the baron strode into the hall, announced by a flurry of attention near the lesser tables. He did not enter as much as make an entrance. Several men and two boys kept pace with him. In the dim torchlight, Beth made out Sir Geoffrey's face, like hers cleansed of travel stains. Veryan, clad now in dark green velvet tunic and somber brown hose, took his seat without ceremony at Beth's left.

She swallowed. Since the grand chair beside her bench boasted cushions and carving, she hadn't had to wonder whose it was. But she'd hoped to get through the supper by chatting with Sir Andre, not her clever, observant host.

"God's greeting, lady."

He did not wait for her murmured reply but made an impatient gesture to a priest hovering behind the high table. The priest stepped up, cleared his throat noisily, and made an attention-grabbing sign of the cross. Sound stilled in the huge room, save only for the scuffling of tall, hungry hounds amongst the rushes. The priest intoned a short Latin blessing over the meal, and Beth murmured her amen with the others.

Immediately the chatter swelled back to full volume. From a balcony at the far end of the hall, pipes, lute, tabor, and harp crashed into a lively, if raucous, measure.

Baron de Veryan cleansed his fingers and accepted wine from a sweating page. There was no goblet for Beth, but after my lord drank deeply, he wiped the rim with his napkin and proffered the vessel. She touched the wine to her tongue the first time, but the tasty flavor warmed her through. The second time he offered, she drank in earnest.

"You are fond of music?"

"Yes, indeed."

"Are your minstrels skilled?"

Beth kept her temper with an effort and bought time by removing her eating knife from its scabbard on her belt. "I have explained before. I do not know if we have minstrels."

"Ah, yes. The loss of memory. You did mention something."

She felt like stamping her foot. How was she supposed to get through an entire meal with an inquisitor as dinner companion?

Between the baron's place and her own, a servitor placed a fragrant tureen of pottage, set a single large bowl between them, and ladled a generous helping of the tureen's contents into the bowl. Another man set out similar bowls between each additional pair at the high table, placing silver spoons before them instead of the horn spoons provided at the lesser tables. No fork, of course—she recalled the fork hadn't come into use until much later.

Maybe I'll invent one. And buttonholes instead of these pesky cloth loops and laces, and drawstrings, and knitting and lace, and flush plumbing.

The ideas gave her a little lift, which deflated in the next second. She couldn't do any of that. She must mess with this foreign time period as little as possible, nor interfere in the natural order of their era.

In any case, she doubted the opportunity would ever arise. With God's blessings, she'd get back to her own time and write up any of her findings she could defend without telling the truth.

Veryan indicated she should sup first from the pottage. But a new realization made the delicious soup taste of ashes on her tongue.

My word. I come from the future, and I can't tell them that here. When I get home, I can't tell anyone I've visited the past or they'll write me off as insane. Whether I stay here or go back to my time, I'm doomed to spend my life in lies.

She recollected herself with an effort. "I shall be grateful if you recall my loss of memory and not ruin so pleasant an evening in pointless questions."

He let out another rusty laugh. "How can I deny so fair and unexpected a guest? Come, let us cease sparring and enjoy the meal. My cooks' skill is known throughout Cornwall and eke into England."

Reprieve? Let it be, if only long enough for me to get some chow here. My stomach thinks I'm on a no-food diet.

For some minutes, both gave their attention to the pottage. When they finished, my lord motioned a perspiring page to serve the fish. As the boy filled their trencher, Beth watched hungrily, considering the possibility of a life of lies while her stomach responded to the delicious aroma.

But the baron was not finished after all. Feeling his gaze upon her, she raised her eyes to his.

"Tomorrow, lady, we will discuss the truth."

Four

Beth snapped awake in darkness. She had dreamed she failed a final exam. All her classmates and even Dr. Richards, dressed in medieval linen and wool, had lined up along the walls of the great hall to jeer and chuck used trenchers—and worse—at her.

"Brr." Her tiny chamber had gone cold overnight, so she wriggled further under the thick feather-filled coverlet in search of warmth.

A strange evening, her first at Truro. Baron de Veryan had seen to that. At the high table, he'd caused Sir Geoffrey's mouth to fall open, not once but several times. He'd perpetrated the worst outrage at the end of the evening's entertainments when he'd seen Beth hide a yawn.

"Forgive me," she'd said. "I'm travel-tired."

Veryan rose, appropriated her hand, and raised it to his lips. Had he held it there a second longer than necessary? She couldn't tell, but she'd felt the warmth of his courteous kiss down to her toenails. And equally, the embarrassment of Geoffrey's stare. Apparently this was not a courtesy offered to every female stranger.

His eyes glinted at her obvious discomfiture, but he said only, "Give you good night, lady. Rest well."

"And you also, my lord."

Seeking warmth at the bottom of the coverlet with her toes, she studied the images dawn light made as it trickled through the shuttered casement of her room. Another puzzle, this private chamber. Far from uncomfortable, it was crowded with a bed curtained in embroidered maroon velvet, an ironbound chest, and a small hearth. For the duration of her stay in Truro, she would enjoy unwonted privacy.

Shouldn't she be lodged in the women's quarters? Or did my lord mean to keep her sequestered until he pried the truth out?

In the interest of peace with her host, she'd accepted his assignment of a room without question. She felt gratitude for his kindness—a space all her own made it possible to think more clearly—but to be marked out by unusual courtesy made her uneasy. What game did he play?

She'd heard Teagen muttering as she followed her back to her room. Yet the maid hadn't looked reluctant when she'd held out her hand for Beth's veil.

"The lord bids me serve you."

Slowly Beth pulled out the two silver pins anchoring the veil into her curls and handed the items over. "Does my lord's order displease you?"

Teagen shook her head. "His pleasure must be mine."

"That is too much compliance. That turns you into—" She was about to say, *an automaton,* but the girl wouldn't understand. "—a cipher, without thought or feeling. I see you are more than that. How say you?"

A more natural smile had curved Teagen's generous mouth. Beth noticed the cleanliness of her simple tunic and gown and the tidy braids beneath a plain linen wimple. Intelligence gleamed in the girl's brown eyes.

An ally? Perhaps, given time and opportunity to build trust.

"I' truth, it is my liking to serve you, lady."

"And mine, also. As long as you are content. Come, help me undo this tunic. I am clumsy with the laces."

A strange affair. Beth turned over now, seeking any warm spot. What did Veryan make of her? How would she protect herself under the cross-examination he'd promised for today? Worse, how did she fight this bone-deep awareness of him?

Dawn turned to full morning. Teagen greeted her with a jug of wine and an ewer holding water for washing. Beth spared a moment to regret her shower, a good shampoo and conditioner. Maybe later she'd find a way to get a proper bath, for she felt grubby.

"What gown, lady?" After the wash-up, Teagen held up a plain gown and the dark red surcote in tactful suggestion, and Beth slipped into the garments. Hopefully looking good might give her confidence to deal with the baron. She'd made a fair beginning, but she could see a thousand conversational pits into which she might tumble. My lord was no dummy, and he'd already heard Geoffrey's spin on Alys's embroidered version of Beth's half-baked story.

Lord, if You're still paying attention to a sinner like me, stick close today.

Teagen patiently did up the laces that fastened the surcote up each side under Beth's arms.

Let me not say anything foolish. Keep me from getting into a snit when he provokes me.

"No braids today," Beth decided on the spot. "Just the veil. Hand me that comb, please, and I'll get the tangles out."

Teagen shook her head. "Lady, nay. It is not fitting. Only harlots prance about with loose hair."

"My hair is not fond of braids."

Teagen was too much the good servant to disagree. "It is not. Where had you so ragged a cutting? But, lady, you must. An it please you, I can borrow a net and coil it up therein. I trow you will not be displeased, and it will look most proper."

Beth gave up. Although it would have helped her confidence to wear her own hairstyle, she didn't want to introduce either *harlot* or *witch* into anyone's vocabulary concerning her.

"Very well. But Teagen—"

"Lady?"

"This incessant borrowing. All I wear, all I own is Lady Alys's gift. If I do not get something of my own soon, I shall weep."

Or go nuts, but that's a concept we shouldn't suggest, either.

The maid didn't bother mincing words. "Have you money?"

Beth rose and opened her big leather purse, careful Teagen should not glimpse the modern clothing tucked inside, and extracted six small pieces of silver, Alys's gift. "Just these pennies."

"Sixpence! Marry, we are rich! I will go arrange our escort."

"Escort?"

Teagen fairly bounced. "To the fair! Do you not know? Did you not see? St. Piran's fair is this very week."

"St. Piran?" Beth had thought herself acquainted with most major medieval English celebrities, but this one escaped her.

"Our very own Cornish saint, though some say it is St. Petroc. It's the second fair—after St. Augustine's, of course." Teagen's brown eyes sparkled with enthusiasm.

"Of course. And you have not yet had opportunity to visit it."

The maid blushed. "I had no need."

Beth chuckled. "And now that's changed, for I have great need."

Teagen hid her laugh with her hand as she'd done the night before. "The morning flies. By your leave, I shall go to Bifan and ask for a man to escort us."

Beth thought she saw an added spark of enthusiasm. "Any man in particular?"

Teagen colored more deeply. "Well, of all the men at arms, Ennis is the most dependable."

"And the most handsome?"

She giggled. "Some say so."

Beth made a shooing motion. Strange, how easily she'd adapted to having a servant of her own. Certainly her middle-class upbringing had never taught her how to deal with one.

"*Vite*, then. Go and arrange escort as pleases you."

A thought hit her. Hadn't she arranged to talk turkey with Baron All-Seeing? A naughty thought, for he couldn't prise the truth out of her if she wasn't here, could he?

"Teagen?"

"Aye?" The maid turned in the doorway.

"Let us go early. Right after mass. And tell nobody."

Dimples appeared alongside Teagen's smile, unhidden this time behind a modest hand. "As you wish, lady."

How far could she make sixpence stretch? With the dependable Ennis as escort, Beth explored St. Piran's fair like a wide-eyed child in a toy store. Spread out in a grassy field she hadn't seen on the road into Truro, vendors had set up both stalls and wains to display their varied wares.

Beth wandered, charmed and amazed, through sellers of fabric and thread. Goldsmiths, Teagen explained, did not risk their expensive goods at the fairgrounds, preferring to remain safe behind the town walls. But silversmiths had come, and workers of less precious metals. Other vendors sold foodstuffs, spices, earthenware, and the wooden kitchen implements called treen.

Beth drifted from booth to wain to table, generally failing to understand the vendors' urging to buy since most spoke Cornish. Occasionally she fingered an item or admired its craftsmanship, then set it back down with a regretful smile for the hopeful seller.

Teagen chatted with Ennis as both trailed a discreet two paces behind Lady Bethany. Mid-morning, one of Beth's precious pennies bought them three rabbit pasties and tankards of cool barley beer. An entire lunch for three people—one cent! She marveled as they lingered to nibble and drink under a bright canvas canopy that fluttered in the brisk April breeze.

At length Beth saw the sun cast almost no shadow. She remembered Veryan's ominous last words.

"Teagen, Ennis—I fear we've stayed overlong. I must return."

"As you wish," said Ennis with a smile.

Despite the gap between his two front teeth, Beth quite understood Teagen's fancy for the lad. She warmed to her earnest young escort. He seemed a merry sort, though over solemn with the weight of his responsibilities.

Teagen apparently felt the same way. "By our Lady, Ennis, you spread duty too thick. Must you so easily cut short our mirth? Look you, if we needs must leave, let us go past the mercers'. Master Jonas had the exact blue shade I need for my best tunic."

Ennis made Beth flush with pride when he looked her way for permission. "Lady?"

"We might return that way."

At the mercer's booth, Teagen pored over the rich colors of embroidery threads offered. Beth drifted, fingering fabrics, threads, ribands, a snood of netted cording to hold the braids, all the while humming under her breath.

For the moment she wanted for nothing, content just to be here. Fear and exhilaration alike had eased. The colors, the smells of pasties and geese and trampled young grass, the flutter of canvas and insistent cries of the peddlers, all served as balm to her stressed-out soul. She would remember her fair day long after she returned to her own time.

Then it hit: There *was* something she wanted, and wanted badly.

"Ennis," she called, keeping her tone casual as though remembering a minor need. "Do you know of a seller of parchment, ink, and quills?"

Ennis gaped but nodded. "Near to—behind the mercer's, lady."

"Then let us linger a moment longer. I would see his wares."

Ennis led them in that direction, fortuitously along the way that led back to the keep. At the stall, Beth fingered parchment, asking the price of several sheets, plus a small inkhorn and a single quill.

"What would you of these?" Teagen made bold to ask.

"I would—" She bit back *write a journal of my travels in time.* "—draw. I would make a pleasing picture to thank Lady Alys. If my lord will allow me to send a messenger, I would gift her with a drawing of the Holy Mother and Child."

Both puzzled faces relaxed. Beth reminded herself to keep her writings secret, perhaps storing the parchment under her jeans and

T-shirt for safety's sake. It would never do to confess abilities—such as literacy—she shouldn't have.

The shopkeeper quoted a price. Teagen made a rude mouth noise but held her tongue.

By now Beth had gotten used to the local price structure, and she pretended umbrage, giving him her coldest *my lady* stare. "I will give you fourpence."

The merchant cast his eyes toward heaven and countered her offer with a price of ten pennies. Beth gathered up her skirts as though to move on. He whined some more but gave in, and Ennis stepped forward to accept the cloth-wrapped bundle.

"Permit me," he said with a smile. "Not seemly to bear your own parcel, lady, whilst I am here to carry it for you."

Yet another custom she hadn't discerned. "My thanks, Ennis."

Teagen had wandered one stall ahead. "Look you here, lady," she called. "Saw you ever so delicate a silk?"

Beth fingered the fabric. "Fine, indeed." The fabric glided over her fingers, tender as a baby's cheek, glowing with ivory color. "But I cannot think seriously of it," she added to Teagen in an undertone. "Such a piece will cost far more than I have left."

"Ah." Teagen nodded, and put the bolt down. "I'll have this." She shook the blue thread in the mercer's face. "And I'm no gentry, to be daddled out of my money. A halfpenny for the length."

"Mistress, forbear. Fourpence is the least I can take. You see yourself the quality of the dye." Taking the thread from her, he held it up into the sunlight to show off its even coloring through the length of the strands.

"What! I could dye better myself on a bad day. A halfpenny and not a groat more."

"Tuppence. I and my children shall starve."

Beth watched, amazed. They haggled like contenders at an Arab bazaar. Teagen finally settled for a penny and came away chortling over her bargain.

"I'd have given three." The trio walked back through the gate into town. "But scratch a merchant, find a robber. All alike under the skin, are they not?"

"No peddler will get the best of you." Ennis's gaze lingered on Teagen.

Beth hid a smile. Teagen's admiration for the young soldier looked to be mutual, and she couldn't fault the taste of either of them.

They walked back through the narrow rutted dirt streets of Truro. Cats fought vagrant rats in the corners for scraps not worth tussling over. Down the gutter in the street's center ran a malodorous rivulet, to which housewives added from time to time.

"Gardy-loo!" would come the cry. Most pedestrians would look up, dodge a chamber pot's contents flung from an upper story of the houses on either side, and remain dry. But not everyone.

Beth wanted to sneak into the keep without Veryan noticing. Better if he hadn't even realized they'd been gone. His remonstrations would blacken her memory of a beautiful and peaceful morning, but she felt a sneaking guilt for seizing on Teagen's fair trip as an excuse to put off the hour of her interrogation.

Ennis shepherded them in through the main entrance, gave a single bow, and escaped with his parcels. Several of Teagen's friends accosted her, accusing her of shirking embroidery time in the lesser hall. "My lady would see the fair" was all she gave as answer, but Beth saw the mischief dancing in her eyes.

"It pleased me much," she added to support Teagen, in as gentle and civilized a tone as she could produce. "Look you here, the quality of the thread Teagen bought."

Then Teagen had to show her purchase to all who would see it. The moment the chattering maids' attention focused on Teagen, Beth slipped out of the great hall with her prizes to run up the curved stairwell leading to her chamber. In the doorway she stopped short.

On the oaken coffer next to her bed lay an assortment of items that hadn't been there before. She crept near to examine them.

A length of fabric slipped through her fingers. Ivory silk, soft as an infant's cheek. Nearby lay a scrap of parchment carrying four figured silver hairpins, a needle, and a half-dozen sewing pins. A paternoster—at home she'd have called it a rosary—of smooth greenish stones, whose beauty she'd admired at the carvers' booth. The netted snood from the mercer's. She fingered that, then set it down.

She'd thought herself clever to have eluded the baron for the morning, but he'd bested her after all.

In the lesser hall, Teagen taught Beth how to set embroidery into a glove cuff.

"Nay, do it thus," she said, demonstrating the correct method.

Beth copied the maid's quick, competent stitches on the scrap of velvet she'd been given on which to experiment. Teagen liked to talk while she sewed, and her explanations of quick tricks and techniques helped Beth understand why she'd made such a mess of her embroidery at Mossock.

Around them the other women chatted or hummed while they worked on their sewing. In a corner one worked a great loom whose heddles clacked an accompaniment to the melody of conversation. Under the window, a trio of ten-year-old girls in training produced neater embroidery than Beth's.

Another maidservant entered and spoke quietly to Teagen, who passed the information on in an undertone. "Lady, my lord requests your presence."

Beth's heart hammered. She set her scrap in Teagen's wicker workbasket and smoothed both hands down her dark red surcote. She had no time for more. The maid led her downstairs from the lesser hall of women and across the great hall where hounds snoozed before a merrily popping fire.

From the tangle of wiry-furred limbs, Bran disentangled himself and trotted over to nose his way under her hand. She gave him a perfunctory scratch on the cranium, which seemed sufficient. The dog's claws made soft click sounds on the plank floors as he followed her and the maid up a staircase Beth hadn't seen before. At a door the maid rapped once, curtsied, and left Beth alone to face her accuser.

"*Entrez.*"

Beth took a single deep breath but decided to make him wait before she obeyed. Let him see she was free—within limits—to order her own ways in this strange place. She would jump to obey no man, no matter how grand his title.

After a deliberate moment she stepped boldly through the door, Bran at her side. She tangled her fingers into his wiry gray fur, and the dog didn't seem to mind.

"My lord," she said, keeping her tone neutral.

The small room reminded her of an office cubicle, except with stone walls and a small, smoking hearth with a chimney painted in a rose and vine design. Candles thick as her wrist provided light, augmented by sunshine dancing through an open wooden casement.

Veryan rose from his carved wooden chair behind a matching table. The sheer power of his size reminded her he could break her in two if he took the notion. Yet she didn't sense any overt threat in his body language. She bent her head in a gesture she hoped was sufficiently courteous, then lifted her chin.

He motioned her into a smaller chair. "We had a pact, did we not? And I see your protector remains with you still." With a gesture, he indicated the hound, who flopped onto the floor and scratched with a paw the size of Beth's hand.

"My lord." Without seeming to hurry, she took a seat. "It is unseemly to ask questions to which you already know the answer."

"Yet you chose the fair over my company, and the conversation of servants to mine."

His spy network serves him well. "It seemed the better choice."

"The safer choice."

"Have I reason for concern over safety?"

"You would do better to speak plain words to me, and at once. Advise me if you concern yourself over your safety."

He fingered an ivory paperknife. Did everything he owned have to be so lovely?

"My concern is over my memory. I pray God it soon returns."

He slammed the paperknife onto the table top and leaned on both fists. "Your memory is unimpaired."

"Not so. Why would I lie?"

"Because you are not what you would seem."

"Which of us is all he seems?" She gave a dismissive toss of her head, hoping her headgear wouldn't fly off and cause further scandal. "You have treated me with respect, for the most part, as befits one of your own station. Why? I might be the meanest peasant, and unworthy."

He shook his head. "Not so."

She met his gaze, hoping she seemed unafraid. How clear his eyes were. Not brown as such, but the warm hazel color of an oak leaf in autumn. With a glint of humor in them, they could be beautiful eyes.

Oh, no. Don't go there.

"Why no?"

Swift as a lion pouncing, he reached over the table and grasped her hand, turned it over to inspect the short, clean nails and unblemished palm. Nor did he seem eager to release it. His capture imparted no sense of constraint, so Beth did not pull away.

"A lady keeps her hands like these. Yours are not a peasant's hands."

I never thought of that. "That tells no story of who I am or where I come from."

"No. But Lady Betaine—"

"Bethany." She corrected him without thinking.

He gave a quirk of the mouth and tried to wrap his French-accustomed tongue around so foreign a name. "Bettany. If lady you are, and I believe that is so—it is time to stop dissembling. Open your mouth now and speak truth. By my father's bones, I will hear your story in silence, and in full, before I comment or question you further."

Temptation hit like a freight train. She weakened ever so slightly. Was secrecy as necessary as she feared? So far nobody had screamed "Witch!" or hauled her before the local justiciar. Why should she not tell him what had happened? Was there any chance he wouldn't laugh in her face or have her sent off to face charges?

Her safety was at risk, not his. Her honesty would cost him nothing, but might cost her dear. Then why did she even consider coming clean?

In the warmth of his austere hazel gaze, she saw a keen intelligence devoid of malice. If he disbelieved, she couldn't imagine him using her tale against her or making her suffer for circumstances not of her making.

God, please. You're all I have. I just need some guidance here. Shall I obey Your law not to bear false witness and trust him?

Almost before she'd phrased the petition, she found herself speaking. "My name is Bethany Lindstrom, that is truth. But the rest of my story—I do not know it to tell you."

"Tell me the part you do know."

"Only that I wandered onto Mossock lands. Lady Alys there did take me in and give me shelter, food—" She lifted a corner of her surcote. "All I have comes from de Tallac's bounty."

"You must have tried to guess whence you came and where are your people?"

"Aye. And I have arrived at nothing I can use to find them or they me." She began to relax ever so slightly, for he didn't seem to be attacking. Yet. "When Sir Geoffrey suggested I come to you here, I was much taken with the idea. If any folk are missing such a woman as me, they will belike seek here, not at remote Mossock."

"You speak aright. Yet you seem quite calm for one lost in this failure of memory. You do not seem prone to a disordered brain."

"I have no choice but to remain as calm as I may. My faith is tested. To wail aloud will not help me or those who would give me aid. I have tried to upset no one."

She found her fingers twisting a pinch of fabric, and forced herself to let it go, smoothing it out of its wrinkles on her knee. "I told Lady Alys the truth—that I am lost. Perhaps," she added, her voice catching, "no woman has ever been as lost as I."

He sat back in his chair as if trying to assimilate her words. "Certes. Yet you are a most singular woman. You get separated from your people and lose all memory of how to find them. You must be sore afeared, and yet you weep not."

Beth tried to glare but had to fight a smile. "I weep not where other eyes can see, my lord."

"The fear you do not deny."

"No. I cannot deny."

She sat back in her chair, shaken by stress. He apparently swallowed her story of amnesia, a circumstance that must seem like the wildest fiction. Where did he find this ease of belief, or was he an actor worthy of an Oscar? Yet she was glad she hadn't yielded to the temptation to spill her whole tale. God wouldn't blame her for lying by omission, would He?

After all, think of what would happen if the tables were turned. If Veryan had arrived on campus in twenty-first century Chicago and announced he was from 1353, she'd have thumbed 911 on her cell phone for the authorities to cart him off to psychiatric intensive care. Yet his expression remained merely thoughtful, as if he tried to fit her disingenuous story into his reality.

"I have told Alys and Geoffrey, but no other," she added. "I do not wish to answer questions from all and sundry, so I ask that you keep my plight to yourself."

"Indeed." He nodded. "When I asked you to tell me your story, you seemed hesitant. Do I have so fearsome a reputation?" In his palm, he toyed with the ivory knife as if it helped him think. "I may not know your family or discover how to get you back to them. Yet you trust me, as if I had this power. Perhaps my good lord the king will know of your family. But you do not ask to be taken to court. Why?"

The Plantagenet court? Going anywhere near it had not occurred to her. Cornwall's straightforward ways she could handle, was handling. Sort of. She could not imagine the much greater challenge of trying to fit into a bunch of eagle-eyed courtiers, every last man and woman out for personal advantage.

Nor could she tell him she'd taken interest in his heaviness of spirit, the incipient light in his eyes that seemed quenched. She knew she should object to staying here in Truro, much less traveling further afield. She must return to Mossock, must she not?

And yet for a split second, she strained to remember why.

The portal. I need to get back to my own place, not to wonder about this gentleman, no matter how interesting he seems.

Nor should she put too much confidence in a stranger's expressed desire to listen and to help. A poor basis for trust, wanting to see a man's expression ease in laughter. Irrational, but it was what she wanted.

"I trust you," she said simply.

"You should not offer trust so easily. I must think on what you have said."

She rose, relieved enough to throw her arms to the sky and laugh aloud, though she resisted the urge. The burden of her lies, embellished by the de Tallacs, seemed somewhat lighter. Ease in her spirit told her she'd made the right decision not to tell him the whole truth.

She could always 'fess up later. Right?

Veryan rose also. "I must get me to my affairs. But tomorrow, before Teagen entices you away to some womanly nonsense, come seek me. I would ride out. Due to needful travel, my lands hereabouts have gone weeks without my eye. I would see how the planting goes, make sure the farmer folk put good effort into a healthy crop this season. Will you accompany me?"

"As you wish." She sketched a curtsey.

He let out another rusty laugh. "You curtsey ill. At social graces, *ma petite*, you seem most unskilled."

"I learn apace, my lord."

"Perhaps they use not this custom from whence you came?" He angled a skeptical eye at her, lifting one dark eyebrow.

"Perhaps. If they do, I am out of practice."

He gave a naughty chuckle low in his throat. "On that we are *d'accord*."

Five

A Traveler's Tale. Beth dipped her feathered quill back into the ink and continued to write with care in modern English.

I came to this place unwilling. I can't tell exactly how. The portal thrust me back in time, and I'm still at a loss to explain it. But this place! It is a time of fair folk and foul smells, of barbarian ideas and exquisite courtesy, of massive inconvenience and the cleanest wind this side of heaven.

She cast a glance toward Teagen, already asleep on her pallet, and tried to quiet the scratching of fresh quill on scraped parchment. She kept reminding herself to dip the quill in the small inkhorn, not too deeply, and let the excess ink drip back in before starting a new word.

Ink was supposed to flow from a plastic tube, ceaseless until she lifted it, and a ballpoint that obeyed. The hand-sharpened nib had an annoying tendency to create marks she didn't want.

Nonetheless, she took simple pleasure in writing. The blunt nib made her plain-print characters look more elegant than any she could produce with a ballpoint pen on notebook paper.

She wrote of the terror of the portal and, briefly, of Mossock and Lady Alys's kindness. She described the freshness of a sunny morning; the bone-seeping chill of Cornish mists; the taste of home-brewed ale, smoked fish, and fresh-snared rabbit; the raucous music of Truro's minstrels, the peddlers' brash cries at St. Piran's fair. And she wrote of her hopes and fears.

When she finished, she wiped her pen on a scrap of old linen Teagen had found for her. She blew on the page to dry the ink since she must hide it in her coffer before sleeping, and she didn't want it to smear.

While waiting, she began her sketch for Lady Alys, necessary to lend truth to Beth's need for parchment as well as for Alys's enjoyment. The bare outline of the mother emerged under her pen, for she had to relearn how to draw with a quill instead of a fine-point Sharpie.

Blowing gently on the sketch to dry its first few lines, she reread the last part of the journal entry. Why, it almost read as though she longed to stay! Foolish and untrue. She must go home, and soon.

She'd either carry this journal back with her or find some place at Mossock to hide it. If she had to conceal it and she got very, very lucky, the hiding place would endure a six-century wait until she could retrieve it in her own time.

And with a quadruple helping of luck, prove her story.

After stowing the parchment, she sought her bed and slept without dreaming, waking as dawn sent tentative light fingers through her casement. Teagen on her pallet stretched and groaned.

"Rest," Beth urged. "I do but seek the privy. I will return."

Teagen gave what might have been a nod and rolled over. Apparently, she'd spent a late and fun-soaked evening after her trip to St. Piran's fair. Amused, Beth wondered if Ennis or a surfeit of ale were more to blame for her maid's drowsy state.

Returning to her room, Beth assessed the day from one of Truro castle's small, deep windows. Fair, it appeared, and with a fitful early sun peeping amongst shreds of last night's clouds. A fine day for riding out with the baron.

Teagen, yawning and moving slowly, brought washing water and a small earthen jug of wine. Beth bade her take some also.

"Unless," she suggested, "you took overmuch last evening."

"It was ale, lady."

She winced as she spoke, so Beth desisted. Teagen, however, did pour out a sip or two of the sweet red vintage and seemed better for it afterward.

"What will you wear?" she asked.

"My riding habit. Gray. Yes, that." Beth pointed into the oak coffer that had become hers. "Lord Michael bade me ride out, and so I will after mass."

"Where do you go?"

Beth wriggled into the clean shift Teagen had laid out, then stood still as her maid laced it at the neck. "Around his lands. More he did not say."

Teagen scowled. "Do you go alone?"

"No," said Beth, startled. "Lord Michael will be . . . oh."

"Aye. Unmarried ladies must tread cautiously. Is it not so?"

"I am no blushing girl," Beth remonstrated.

Teagen tittered. Apparently, wine woke her easy laughter. "Except when my lord be present."

Beth gaped. Teagen sobered and patted her on the arm, then turned her round to face the comb.

"None has remarked it," she said as she coaxed the night's tangles from Beth's curls. "Do not trouble yourself. My own doltish fancy sees what is not there. Indeed, my mind is much taken with Ennis, so mayhap I see St. Venus's light in every pair of eyes."

"Do not talk foolishly." *What does she see in his eyes? Or in mine?*

"I will do so no more, lady." The maid gave her a wink.

After mass in the keep's drafty chapel, Lord Michael nodded to Beth and she made her way to him. At the hearth, the hound Bran stretched, rose, and trotted toward them with a whine, reminding her to scratch just behind his ears.

"Good morrow, my lord."

"And to you."

Crossing the great hall with Bran at his heels, he snatched hunks of steaming bread and cheese from the platter a young servitor held. He didn't even break stride while handing her half the food and tossing a big chunk to the dog, who caught it in mid flight. Beth broke off a piece of each and ate hungrily.

"Cicely, fetch a skin of the Gascon wine."

Through the hall he strode toward the stables, Beth following dubiously in his wake. Panting, Cicely caught up with his long strides, lugging the wineskin.

Michael issued orders in Cornish to the stable boys. In no time they led out Caillin and a tall gelding, frisky and full-accoutered for the ride.

"Lady Bethany, meet Broc."

She noticed he had no further trouble pronouncing her name correctly. Had he practiced?

From a leather pouch at his belt, he dislodged two apples, offering one to each animal. The gelding tried to snatch both, but Michael withheld one so Caillin could lip it delicately.

"Wicked lad! He likes to be scratched, just here."

Beth obeyed, and the gelding nosed her purse as if telling her to offer him fruit also—as was only right.

"Broc, you are a glutton, I fear."

"Aye, he would eat all day if I let him."

She startled as he put his hands around her waist and lifted her competently into Caillin's saddle.

He lifts me like a feather. How strong he must be.

She determinedly ignored the flush of awareness his touch had caused. Lord Michael mounted and touched Broc gently with his gold spur, and Caillin obediently followed the gelding. Bran trotted in their wake, sniffing at the grass, checking out an interesting hole near the stable wall.

"Herd animals," Beth chided her mount. "You are on your best behavior for my lord, aren't you? Why would you not behave so on our journey here? It is false service you give me, my girl." She patted the mare's neck in case she'd given offense.

One of the stable boys made a hushed comment to another. Lord Michael turned in his high leather saddle to cast them a single glance. One touched his forehead, and both hefted their wooden pitchforks with fresh energy.

Side by side, the horses trotted out the bailey. As they passed under the portcullis, Beth glanced up, hoping the chain would not pick this moment to snap and cut them in half.

Just outside the castle wall, a huddle of ragged people held up dirty hands with importuning pleas in Cornish. The baron reined Broc in and dug in his waist purse, scattering coins into the huddle. Incomprehensible shouts of joy greeted his action, along with a lot of scrabbling in the muddy road.

"Hold a moment."

Beth curbed Caillin, who seemed more interested in the tall grass by the verge than in her rider's commands.

"You, there. Aye, you—in the jerkin. You seem ill-suited to begging. What are your skills?"

A ragged man at the edge of the pack moved a foot closer, casting the huge hound an anxious look. What Beth understood of his mangled Cornish Middle English reply sounded like "miner and blacksmith, lord."

"You wish work?"

A fervent nod from the man in the torn and shabby jerkin.

"Get you to my steward. Ask for Peter atte-Well. If anyone resists, tell them Veryan sent you with his gage." He stripped off his worn leather riding glove, and the man grasped at it like a drowning man at a plank. "They will know it within. Peter will see to the rest."

The man yanked violently on his forelock and gabbled something full of Cornish and gratitude. Broc sidestepped away from the fuss, and Caillin, ever-obedient when it didn't matter, followed suit.

Beth watched the byplay with interest, admiration, and a smidge of fear. What instinct had led the baron to single out that particular man? Her heart warmed that a landowner with so much else on his mind should stoop to better the life of a single laborer. What manner of man was this, whose protection and attention she enjoyed?

He urged Broc forward, and she kicked Caillin into motion. "Where do we go, my lord?"

"I bethought me that you might like to see the lands along the river. It was near dark when you arrived, and you had scant time to view its beauty at so late an hour."

She smiled in pleasure. Had he known she longed to see more of the English—no, Cornish—countryside?

"I would like to see the river."

The sun picked that moment to emerge from sly flirtation with high, drifting cloud. It sent a single beam to strike lights off Lord Michael's hair. Dark, soft-looking strands glistened, holding her attention to his face. The light found his autumn-leaf eyes and made its home there.

In stasis, they sat their restive horses, locked in a moment. For a heartbeat she reflected she'd never seen more comely a man.

Careful, girl. I'm a tourist here, and very temporary. For all I know I could land back in my century five minutes from now. No business noticing what he looks like . . . or how considerate he's been . . . or how he trusts me as honest, when all I can do is tell lies.

Apparently, the moment struck him with a similar impact, for he kicked Broc into an easy canter. They rode in silence for a pace, followed at varying distances by the hound. The road, little more than a cattle trail, climbed gently.

Beth glanced back to see Truro resting in a shallow bowl between three lines of low hills. On the horizon, she glimpsed the squat tower of St. Mary's Church and the taller donjon she knew as Truro keep. Toward the south, morning sunlight glinted on blue water. Lord Michael shaded his eyes against the reflection, reined Broc in, and pointed.

"The river," he said. "At Falmouth it forms a deep harbor, the best berth for large ships in all the West Country. Yet it is a river.

Rightly, three rivers, the Kenwyn, the Allen, and the Fal. Here at Truro they form an estuary leading to the sea."

"It's very beautiful."

"Yes," he said in a low tone. "*Très belle*."

His gaze didn't rest on the river, and she felt her cheeks flush. "The sea, then, is always with you," she said hastily.

"Yes." He curbed Broc who danced impatiently, wishing to be off once more. "You wear naught of the finery you bought at the fair."

"I purchased only chicken pasties and some parchment." She felt relaxed enough with Caillin's improved manners to take the reins in one hand and rest the other on the high pommel. "You mean it kindly, no doubt, but why did you do it?"

"Cannot a man gift a fair woman? Cannot a woman accept offerings made in simple kindness?" he parried. "You were quick enough to accept Lady Alys's."

"I would repay Lady Alys, if I could. As for your gifts—maybe other women can. Not me."

"You question my intent? Welladay, read my motives as you choose, but I pray you, keep them. They are but trifles, and you have few of the gewgaws women love."

"I do not incur debts I cannot repay. I beg you to reclaim them."

"You jest." His expression remained serious, though she caught a glimmer in his eyes. "The snood would ill become me, and you must see I would look a proper fool in hairpins."

She chuckled and was instantly annoyed. If she couldn't take her predicament seriously, how could she expect him to?

"My lord," she said on a choked-off laugh, "such gifts may start tongues wagging. I must look to your reputation and my own."

He turned Broc onto a narrow path, scarcely visible between scraggly hedges of prickly bushes to which he pointed. "Furze. Practically our native plant," he said absently. "Aye, you have the right of it. Tongues are already busy, I'm told, and people are sometimes too hasty to put their own meanings to what they see."

She sat up straighter with alarm. Caillin, preferring that Beth stay motionless in the saddle, gave one of her ill-tempered hops.

"Tongues?" What are people saying?

"Castle folk. None outside. Of course, there is reason, not that my people know of it. I have dealt with you duplicitously." He cast her a glance she guessed was meant to rile her.

You incredible . . . man! How dare you tease me?

"How have you treated me dishonestly?" She kept her tone as lofty as she could manage.

"Ennis told me you were for the fair. I bade Teagen keep watch for what you fancied. I gave him coin to purchase anything you admired." His expression remained straight-mouthed and forbidding, but she glimpsed mischief in his eyes. "Anything and everything."

She frowned. "Again—why?"

"It pleased me." He lifted a shoulder in a shrug. "By God's grace I am so placed in life that I can indulge my whims, within reason. And you needed those trifles. When you arrived I saw in your eyes . . ." He left off, finishing his thought with another shrug. "You came here scandalously ill outfitted for guesting at Truro. De Tallac did mention how Lady Alys furnished all she found needful for your journey here. For which," he added hastily, "I have repaid him amply. But she found you shockingly lacking in fripperies."

"I had little when I came here," she admitted. "Only the clothing I wore."

"And I'm told your clothing is out of the modern fashion."

He guided Broc up a little hill, then steeply downward through a small copse of beech and overgrown fruit trees. Into this copse, horses and hound made their separate ways, accompanied by snorts of disapproval from Broc and a lot of chuffing from Caillin. Beth found reason again to pray the mare would not tip her out of the saddle. That furze bore evil prickles.

Abruptly the path widened into a leafy clearing. Vagrant shafts of sunlight shot through the branches overhead, creating a green and private space. She breathed deeply of its scents, redolent with damp life and springtime. It whispered welcome as she touched Caillin with one heel, turning her three-sixty to take in the lush and tangled greenery, the wildness and the mossy trees.

Lord Michael dismounted and led Broc over to a chipped granite trough from which the horse drank. Bran slurped up water noisily, and Caillin moved to follow suit. Michael looped both sets of reins around a dry branch, then lifted Beth from the saddle and set her on her feet.

"How beautiful! What is that building?"

At the end of the glade stood a tiny roofless chapel. Built of the ubiquitous gray Cornish stone, its windows gaped like vacant Norman eyes, round-arched and contemplative.

He answered without glancing at the structure. "St. Aldhem's. Before that, who knows?"

He caught her fingers, causing that sneaky tingle in her skin, and tugged her over to a fallen log. On this he sat, urging her silently to sit at his side.

"Before the church, certes another building stood here. I daresay this place has been in use continually since the first sons of Adam came to this island. It is due to the water, you see. The horses know. Sweet water comes from that spring and fills their trough. Always clear, even in dry years it runs cold and fresh, never brackish, though we are so near the sea. It is an important place. The old ones built here because of the spring. First their places of worship, whatever they were, later the church."

"Why does it then lie in ruins?"

"None knows. I have made inquiries, but the story of St. Aldhem's has been lost. Only the older tales remain of what this place was before Christ-lore came to Cornwall."

Oh, for a spiral notebook and a stub of pencil! All she had was her memory. She'd have to rely on it to recall the tale he would tell. Somehow, this day would linger in her mind once she returned home . . .

His voice called her back from her reverie. "The place has always been holy. The church in her wisdom assigned the spring to St. Aldhem, but we Cornish know better. St. Aldhem is but a *nouveau arrivé*. This well was sacred long before we Christians changed its name."

"Sacred to whom?" *He loves this place. And its legends.*

He shrugged answer. "Who can say? The Cornish are good sons of the church in these modern times, of course, but we are an insular race. Too long separated from the rest of the realm, mayhap. We cling to our old beliefs, our ancient ways. Perhaps a water sprite made this her home. Perhaps not. The grannies claim piskies still dwell amongst us, causing mischief."

He picked a long blade of grass and chewed reflectively. The gesture reminded her of neighborhood boys back home—boys in blue jeans and sneakers, not woolen hose and gold spurs. Despite his attire, somehow he had a familiar look.

"If the best milch cow fails or the cream turns or the barley beer goes sour, why that is the piskies' work. The villeins leave small offerings at night—a crust of barley bread or a ripe apple—in hopes of placating them. Most unwise to allow the local piskie to feel neglected."

Beth chuckled. Bran sidled over and collapsed into the long grass next to the log. Scratching the rough gray coat, she watched Lord Michael gnaw on his grass blade, lost obviously in childhood tales.

"Piskies? I had thought an educated man would not believe in them."

"Here we believe. They live near such springs as these. Piskies and others."

She leaned forward, fascinated. "What others?"

He threw the grass blade into the spring, watched as it spun on the unquiet surface. "Water sprites, of course. Spriggans, giants, and all manner of unholy creatures."

She felt affronted. "You play with words."

"What else are words good for?" He yanked at the edge of her wimple, making her giggle.

This was so wrong. Twenty-six year old doctoral candidate time travelers should not giggle.

His eyes sobered. "Your words—they call up many questions and few answers."

"Ask, then. I may not be able to give you the answer you desire."

He stretched out his long, booted legs. His first question surprised her.

"Since that is so, I would ask—what are your thoughts? Why did this calamity befall you? Lady Alys says you seemed uninjured but for scrapes. When you washed, she saw no other hurts. What befell those in your traveling party?"

Beth frowned. More lies?

"I pray they came to no harm at all, and I merely became separated from them."

She picked her own grass stem to play with. Aye, more lies, and yet she could not envision any other path. Increasingly, it bothered her.

"I must put them from me for now and let God care for them," she added, her voice muffled.

He digested this for a moment. "I tend to ask overmuch why a thing happens. Yours is the better approach. All my life I have been a soldier, not a student of holy writ. Things of the spirit are not my work. Of the ways of the Blessed Lord and His saints, I know only what the priest tells me, and that faith in God leads to life. But when why is asked, I consult Father Gedren."

"If he has any insight into my problem, I would take his counsel gladly."

"Depend upon it, he will have none."

He plucked a stem holding a fragile blue flower that looked something like lavender and tucked it under her wimple. She drew a long breath of delight, for the bloom smelled wonderful, and his touch felt even better.

"There is too much in this life that is closed to human understanding."

Beth nodded. "Plenty."

"The sickness, to start. Why were some spared and some taken? Why did the strong ofttimes die while the frail survived? This, as you say, we must leave in God's hands, for none can explain to satisfy."

"You do well to commit it to God. Your faith must have been a great comfort to you in so fearful a time."

"The church gave little comfort. Each man came to his own answer," he said grimly. "Certes the priests were no help. Of those who did not flee, none could do more than commend the sickness to God. Yet was God so wroth with us that He took so many—saint and sinner alike?"

This hurts him, and he turns to me for answers. Why?

"I do not believe the pestilence was God's judgment for sin, but a natural event. And some may have had more efficacious prayer."

"Many prayed. Few recovered. The sickness came to all lands—certes many were also lost in your homeland. Yet you believe in the power of prayer?"

She scanned his expression for a clue as to whether he still believed but found only curiosity. Discarding her grass stem, she said, "It is all we have. I struggle sometimes to believe. But you say each of you found your own way to faith after the sickness. It seems to me, though I remember little, that I too have found my way . . . and I like it not."

He gave Bran's ears a rough caress. "That lies in your power to change. God does not desert us, though ofttimes we leave Him. Faith lies always within reach."

"Perhaps," she said. "I must depend on Him and on you. I would go back to my own folk, of course." *And yet . . . and yet.*

"Perhaps *le bon Dieu* placed you here, away from your own people, for a reason." He regarded her, his expression more open than on her first night in Truro. "Perhaps you have work to do here that requires your parting from those you love."

She considered that. Could God have work for her to do that she alone might accomplish? Did the people here have attitudes, mores, mindsets that made the task impossible for them?

"Perhaps. When I discover what that work is, it might become easier to sojourn here for a time."

He shifted on the log, studying her face. With a swift gesture, he reclaimed the sprig of lavender from under her wimple and cast it into the spring.

"There."

"What?"

"An old custom, and hardly Christian. Legend says if you offer the well a belonging, it creates a binding. We Cornish are a fanciful people."

"Binding?"

"I have bound you to the well." His eyes glinted mischief, then sobered. "And to Cornwall. And in a very small manner, only as much as you yourself permit, to me. But lady, you should take care."

"My lord?"

"Tell no one your tale. I will keep it secret. Others may be less easy of belief than I." He shook his head, his expression making Beth wonder if he thought he'd lost his mind. "I cannot say why I believe, for I never have known such a thing to fall out as you say it has. Yet I would counsel you to mention your history as little as possible. I accept it, but there are those who will disbelieve for reasons of their own. Others may use your . . . "

"My strangeness."

"Aye. They may use it for their own ends, and not for your well doing. Enough. You shall bide at Truro until I must wait upon the king. When I am summoned, will you travel with me to court?"

Court. He invites me to go with him to King Edward's court. The Black Prince will be there, and Queen Philippa of Hainault. How many of them might I see?

Her spirits rose at the very thought. "I had not thought on it. Yet if you wish it, I will go."

"We will take the greatest care for your safety."

She decided to tease him out of his worry. "What ill can befall me while under your protection?"

He ran a single finger from her temple to her chin, his expression lightening for a moment, then sobering once more. "I am only a man, not a saint, and a soldier at that. A man so long under arms sees danger behind every gorse bush. I cannot help fearing for you. So lovely, and no history. No father or brother to protect you. Other men may—nay, will—covet the beauty I now look upon freely. Strangeness attracts in its own manner. Some may try to use your extraordinary position for their own ends. Yet I will do my best to protect you, my lady. I swear it by whatever spirit still inhabits this well."

She stared into his eyes, moved beyond words. "Whatever you can do, it will be enough."

"My lord." Peter atte-Wood scurried up as they reentered the hall. "Guests are come from Bristol."

"Hmm?"

Michael—this afternoon she'd jettisoned the honorific, at least in her mind—handed his short cloak to his steward. Beth gave hers and her gloves to Cicely the maid.

"Who comes?"

"Sir Cadwr of Bridgnorth and a small troop."

"You have quartered the men?"

"Aye, my lord. He awaits you in the hall."

Michael nodded, and the steward moved purposefully away to his next duty. Michael offered Beth his arm.

"Let us go, lady, and welcome my guest."

"You know this Sir Cadwr?"

"Of course," he said, "for regardless of what mischief's in it, he is my brother."

"Mischief?"

"My half-brother, *ma petite*. I will tell all where no curious ears can hear."

She chuckled and put her fingertips on his wrist.

They found Sir Cadwr rolling between his hands a chased silver goblet, turning it this way and that in the light to display the richness of its decoration. He rose from a cushioned chair Peter had placed before the hall's great fireplace.

"God's greeting." Sir Cadwr approached with a wide smile for Veryan. "Michael, it has been too long."

The men embraced in a hearty fashion, yet Beth read restraint in Michael's body language, and he was first to withdraw. What, she wondered, caused such reticence while greeting a brother?

"Renegade. You are well come," the baron responded. "Your only sin is not coming sooner. We dine anon. I see Peter brought you wine."

"I am well provided for."

In Cadwr's expression Beth saw he accepted Truro's hospitality as no more than his due. He either had some importance in local affairs or thought he did.

She sized him up as the baron questioned Sir Cadwr about his recent movements and what brought him to Truro. Cadwr was an inch or two south of six feet, making him a hair shorter than Michael, but he was more conventionally handsome in a light-haired, blue-eyed way. At home, she'd have called him a surfer boy. His attire screamed of riches; the quality of his velvet tunic far surpassed the homely wool of Michael's riding clothes. The sword at Sir Cadwr's belt boasted an ancient and lavish art, with an intertwined animal design on the hilt and a scabbard so heavily decorated with gold wire that the leather wasn't visible.

"Lady Bethany de Listrom," Michael was saying.

Inwardly she shook her head. His pronunciation improved, but still missed slightly. How many more variations would the locals find before she was done here? From the first time Lady Alys had tried to pronounce it, her surname had mutated into a word more

French than Scandinavian. They'd butchered Bethany just as badly. The way things were going, she'd become known by a mere approximation of her real name.

"Allow me to make known to you my bastard brother. Sir Cadwr ap Gwillem of Bridgnorth."

"My lord." Beth added a smile to her curtsey, stung by the casual way Veryan used the term *bastard*.

Cadwr didn't seem fazed by it. He bent over her hand but did not touch it with his lips as Michael had at first meeting. Had his brother perhaps taken umbrage at the derogatory term?

She'd noticed Michael had presented Cadwr to her—hinting that hers was the higher rank—not her to him. She cast a glance sideways at Michael. Plain as day, his stern expression said, *This man is my brother, or said to be, yet I do not trust him. No unmerited courtesy here for such as he.*

Peter called the party to dinner. Beth found herself famished by the morning's ride, and the noon meal smelled most welcome. With due ceremony Peter seated Cadwr at Michael's right hand as honored guest, with Beth at his left.

Cadwr dipped his fingertips in the *écuelle* and began to speak, praising the beauty of Truro's lands and the good order of its people. Then he turned his attention to Beth.

He told her that his lands lay in Wales and the Marches. He held the bulk of his lands as a vassal of the great abbey of Valle Crucis near Llangollen. Despite their location in the hinterlands, he had plans to expand his territory. Though by English law he'd been unable to inherit from his and Michael's father, Lord William, his father had secured his Welsh mother's lands to him, chiefly the great border keep at Bridgnorth, for which he owed knight's service to Henry of Grosmont, the saintly and much-admired duke of Lancaster.

Without undue modesty, he credited his mother's blood bond with the Mortimer family for his preferment. He would advance in the world, of course, for Bridgnorth, a strategically important keep, commanded one of the Roman roads into the half-tamed lands of the Cymry.

"Alas, the Cymry. Love us or hate us, the English must endure." Cadwr permitted the page Richard to refill his goblet with wine. "At war-craft there are none to match us. We plague them without ceasing. Foolish Saeson, they cannot bring us to set-piece battle in a chosen field, for we wage war at our own liking as we are poor folk. Always flashing down from the shelter of our hills. A few cattle taken, a guard shot, a wain stolen here and there. Some say we Welsh are mad, and of course it pleases the English to think so. But the Cornish are no different, being of Celtic blood themselves."

"I know nothing of the Cornish in battle, my lord."

He laughed and speared a chunk of spiced venison with his eating knife. Unlike Michael, he had trouble remembering to offer her the morsel first. "No, of course not. Where did you say your husband's lands lie?"

Beth studied him. Michael had not mentioned her family, and she knew nothing of this stranger, so she must watch her words with redoubled care.

"I did not say."

"No . . . you bide here at Truro." He chewed, regarding her speculatively. "With Veryan."

"He has offered his protection," she corrected, "until I find my family."

That stopped his contemplation of the next dishes the servitors set on the high table. "You were reft away from your own folk?"

"So it seems." She dipped a morsel of capon into the mustard and honey sauce, and took her time to savor it. The cooks had obviously improved on her suggestion. "Lady Alys de Tallac and her husband helped me much. Once I recovered from a blow to the head, they suggested I come here to seek my kin. And here I am."

"Indeed." He chewed, eying her. "Here you are."

Cadwr changed the subject, telling her an anecdote intended to amuse concerning the king's latest paramour. Beth ate and nodded, trying to look interested while guessing the mistress of the moment. She came up blank, since her readings in fourteenth-century history had focused not on King Edward III's time, but on his father's and the pre-plague famine years.

As dinner wound down, the men's talk turned to politics. Beth found her attention drifting, though she tried to follow. Cadwr criticized the king's debts and the constant push-pull of Edward's claim to the French throne. Michael's opinion was that if there must be war, better it be overseas than in England. As for the validity of the king's claim, he called that a tired old tale he did not care to hear again.

"But thank all the saints, this season my lands will bear well. Given continued fair weather, we need not fear to see our peasants starve. Have you forgotten the famines? Only two years ago we scarce had sufficient corn to grind for bread."

"I remember it right well," Cadwr growled, while motioning young Richard to refill his cup. "Famine, war, pestilence—ever something. France, now war, now peace. The king's lust to rule there leads to naught but clamors for yet more money. My shilling's on wool—do you not believe so? Since the sickness, there are scarce enough peasants to plow and harvest. Where are we to find men to raise more sheep? Taxes on wool, taxes in wool. All so my lord king can pay his bankers and prosecute his claim to the French throne."

Michael selected a pear from the bowl on the high table. "As if he had not enough trouble here. I trow, at times these Plantagenets seem like to run mad. A hunger gnaws at their bones to swallow everything. Even his sons, barely dry behind the ears, thirst for power."

Hungry to rule, eh? Beth considered the later career of the king's third son, John of Gaunt. He was only a boy now, but oh, they'd see, once he grew to manhood. She barely suppressed a giggle. Both men turned to stare at her.

"Your pardon, gentlemen. Richard, a little more wine, if you please?"

Michael continued to reason in conciliatory tones. The Plantagenets did none so ill, free now of the old king's unpopular favorites. Taxes on wool should not burden the country unduly, and none would suffer for a larger wool pack. He himself was doing everything possible to put sheep on his manors.

"The men are keen to raise them, and so far the clip pays well. Best in both quality and measure, of course, comes from my lands worked by freemen."

"A credit to your methods," Beth put in.

Cadwr turned a startled expression her way, as though the *écuelles* had spoken.

"My lord Veryan believes the manors are better worked by free tenants looking to their welfare as well as the lord's. Freedom is the best spur to diligence."

Cadwr returned his attention to Michael. "I had heard something of it. Is this true indeed—that you free your serfs?" When Michael nodded assent, Cadwr gave a guffaw and drained his hanap. "Ever you had *fou* ideas and, by my feet, now you put them into action." He nodded sagely, while giving Beth a considering glance. "Brother, where will your mad ways take you next?"

Six

Beth drew her cloak further around her shoulders. Up here on the battlements, the breeze rose from the river, bearing the sea-smell on a damp mist. The fair day had given way to a muffled evening, as if night itself held its breath. On the battlements she'd found a *soupçon* of privacy, but paid the price in a cool breeze determined to tease the curls out of her snood.

Supper, served with all the fanfare and rigmarole a medieval keep could manage, had dragged on interminably. Cadwr, well into his cups, had spoken in dark and uneasy tones of the rumors now rife at court. From what his overlord Abbot Boniface had heard, the king intended to put forward a most unnerving new law.

"An this madness goes through—and I doubt not the king shall press it—Englishmen will be forbidden to seek redress anywhere but the royal courts." Cadwr drained his wine and motioned to the page for another refill. "It tastes bad. I mislike it, brother. It will not irk Saint Henry of Lancaster one iota, but what will it do to the monks? In any dispute between them, they must be subject to the *king's* pleasure, rather than take the matter to canon law."

"In truth, is it of such great moment?"

"It changes everything." Cadwr's expression grew morose. "I hear it said that England pays still for the Church's attempt to curb King John, may his name ever be forgot. There are long and mournful faces at Valle Crucis, and I daresay every other abbey in the land."

Beth wasn't following this. Cadwr continued to predict bad times ahead, if the law he called *praemunire* were to pass. At length she put in a question. "My lord, how can this affect you? Of course you hold some of your honors from the church, but will you not do better if your holy overlords must wait on the king's justice, same as your worldly lord must do?"

Cadwr gave his head a mournful shake. "Alas, lady, you know naught of the church's ways. The fines that now go into the abbot's coffers will go into the royal till instead. *Peste!* If the abbot suffers, he passes it down, as it were. The abbey must pay its lawyers, must pay for the writs, must pay and pay and pay—where think you that money will come from? From squeezing us who hold of them, that's where."

Michael replied in soothing fashion. Likely this new law the king put forth would not beggar vassals of the church, nor was it in the king's interest to do so. In the past, English kings had exerted some control over whom Rome appointed to powerful sees, making sure the candidate knew and accepted English ways. "It is far better now than in the days of Edward II. Do you long to have our spiritual lives ruled by those who cannot even speak plain English?"

"Never that," Cadwr moaned. "But there must be some other road. By the rood, plenty of us there are who would help find it. In this latest lunacy lies ruin for the abbeys, and double ruin for anyone unlucky enough to call an abbot lord."

Michael continued to reason, occasionally defending a concept or a man unfamiliar to Beth. At those times, seated at his left hand with Cadwr on the honored right, she kicked Michael under the table.

Though he put away enough wine to float an aircraft carrier, she didn't believe that Cadwr was drunk. His eye held a determined gleam, not the unfocused stare of a boozer. Was he trying to draw Michael into talking recklessly? Into criticizing the king's pet project? Saying something Bridgnorth could repeat at court to Veryan's detriment?

Brother, ha. I never had a brother, but this one's got some odd ideas. I see now why Michael doesn't trust him.

Glad supper had at last ended, she pushed a strand of breeze-whipped hair back into her snood and politics out of her mind. Tonight she'd been aware of looking good in some of her finery, evidence of Michael's generosity. He'd noticed at once. He hadn't smiled or nodded, but his eyes had glowed approval.

Beth groped toward a grudging recognition of her status as dependent. A woman in her position existed only through the generosity of others, a state she didn't like. But she hadn't counted on the pleasure in his eyes on seeing her wear his presents.

A strong hand slid onto her shoulder. "What do you here, lady? The mist grows cold."

"I came seeking quiet. And I am warm enough."

"You cherish peace. Do you require quiet as well?"

"Often, yes." She turned to face him. "My lord, what of Sir Cadwr? Such strange comments after supper."

Michael grimaced and rubbed his leg. "I noticed your disapproval. My shins will ache for days." As though her concern for his welfare gave him certain rights, he put his arms around her waist, letting his full cloak shield them both from the wind-borne mist tendrils. "Tell me your thoughts. Though he is my brother, he is Welsh, and therefore half crazed. All know they are madmen. But he seems fair beset over this new law. What say you to his fears?"

She spent a moment mastering her emotions. His arms felt good around her, too good, and his larger body served as windbreak. She wasn't here to fall in love—therefore she wouldn't. Simple as that.

"His concern is real enough. And he took his wine well watered—I saw him motion several times to Richard for the water jug. Yet he wished to be seen as . . . "

"Wine sotted?"

"Yes. Why?"

He remained silent for a time, while the fog muttered its own reservations. Sheltered against him, Beth no longer felt cold.

"You take a keen interest in my welfare."

"Your well doing is mine also."

He stilled, then his arms tightened around her waist. "So. You feel it, too."

Beth attempted to demur, but he forestalled her. His lips brushed a tendril of hair where it blew free from the snood's confinement.

"*Tu es dans ma tête.*"

He used the familiar form—*tu* rather than *vous*—a term used only for family, friends, or loved ones. She frowned. "I should not be in your head. I do not belong here."

"And yet you sense it as strongly as I."

"How can it be so? We know little of each other, and not for long."

"What window does time make for such things? By all that is right and holy, lady, you should be with your family and not here at all." He tightened the embrace. "Much less in my arms."

"No, my lord. I should not be."

She drew breath to continue, to remind him that she belonged elsewhere, to point out how far his station lay above hers, to bring up every possible impediment, to tell him—

He put a single finger to her lips and the words died unborn. "You draw not away."

"Not yet," she whispered. She felt his finger trace from her lip over her jaw line, to the spot where the snood confined her hair. "In a moment, but . . . not yet."

"Bethany." Her name suddenly sounded like the tenderest endearment. "Attend. Do but give me some time to think. Your—situation—your coming here is difficult of management, but we must deal with what we have. You hold an unusual position in my home, but not impossible of solution if we are patient and discreet."

"What are you suggesting?" Her breath shortened. "That I become your paramour?"

"No." From the folds of her cloak he unearthed her fingers and lifted them to his lips. "I would not so dishonor you. But an unmarried lady, guest in my keep yet not of my household? In the strictest sense, unprotected. Cadwr is no man to keep a still tongue if he finds reason to let it flap. Your presence here will give rise to talk of sin, or worse. Many tongues wag freely at court, especially when they should keep silent in Christian charity."

"I can sure understand that," she muttered.

"Then can you keep patience?" His eyes glowed into hers. How did the light always find them? "You have confided your tale and put faith in me for your safety until your family comes for you. Can you trust a little longer?"

With my life, and maybe my heart as well.

"I trust you," she breathed.

Their faces were inches apart, and for a wild, reckless second she wished he would bend down and cover that last crucial space. She wanted his kiss. Oh, she wanted that.

Apparently, he did not. He drew away.

"Come, dear lady. You grow cold. Let us seek the warmth of the hall."

A Traveler's Tale. Today we visited a holy well. Not exactly a Chicago-style date. Michael could've turned barbarian on me at no notice at all, and yet his behavior was everything honorable. I don't think he's quite as suspicious as he used to be, though I don't know what changed that. He urged me to tell him all the truth, and I came that close, but at the last minute I wimped out. Funny, I almost felt I could spill it and he'd believe me, because of this strange connection between us. And I'm not just imagining it—he feels it too. At St. Aldhem's well he threw a flower of mine into the water. He claimed that bound me to Truro, and in a small way to himself. I need to be free. I should resent him trying to tie me anywhere. Wonder why I don't.

Later on I went up to the tower and he followed me. I needed to think, but how am I supposed to think when he's around? He held me and I felt safe, almost, for the first time.

He says I'm in his head.

She lifted her gaze from the parchment to gaze out at a gray and overcast dawn, then jarred into action and tucked the journal safely away as Teagen stirred and muttered in her normal wake-up mode.

The dull skies added to her feeling of letdown. Michael would not be present this morn, for he had mentioned his plan to take his brother hawking. Courtesy obligated him, and while out he intended to draw more information from Cadwr, both his reasons for a rare visit to Truro and for his dark speech of the night before.

"What's to do?" Teagen asked, yawning from her pallet on the floor.

"Needlework, I suppose." Beth closed her coffer, turning to make a face. Her maid laughed. "Do you bring wash water and some ale. I cannot look at wine so soon after last evening." She ran her tongue over her lips. "Do you know any substance that will clean the teeth? Mine need it badly."

"Mayhap I can find some salt and sage. Do you not use your finger, thus?" Teagen demonstrated.

"Yes, but I need more than that." Beth shrugged a helpless gesture.

"I shall ask the other maids." Her servant drew on clothing and left.

Now, during the minutes Teagen was gone, Beth could solve part of her problem. From the depths of the coffer she extracted the leather pouch that held her modern clothing. She handled the items thoughtfully. Zippers and buttonholes and elasticized cotton felt strange to her touch now. In these few weeks she'd grown used to loose-fitting, natural-fabric garments, more comfortable than she'd realized.

She turned her jeans inside out and ran her finger along the seam. From a frayed spot she drew a long, strong cotton thread. Hastily shoving the jeans back into her pouch and the pouch into the coffer, she ran the thread between her teeth.

Ah. Not totally effective as dental floss, but an improvement. Now to finish with whatever Teagen finds.

The maid rushed back into her room. Beth slammed the coffer and whirled around.

"Lady, hasten." Teagen flung a small clay pot of gray-green powder onto the small table that served as washstand. From the coffer, she dug everyday clothing. "You must dress and come below. The hawking party is back, and hungry as a sow wi' nine piglets! The kitchen wenches throw breakfast all higgledy-piggledy on the tables."

"Slow down!" Beth made haste in donning the plain linen shift, gown and surcote, all the while trying to slow Teagen with linen-swathed gestures. "And speak English only—you toss in so many Cornish words I cannot follow."

"Hasten, lady! The priest says he grows hungry too, and will not wait mass for laggards."

Beth laughed and thrust her feet into shoes. Together they hurried down the curved stone stairs with a hand on the wall to prevent a tumble.

In the curve of the hallway, however, a low hiss of conversation stopped her in her tracks. She grabbed Teagen's elbow and gave her a warning glare and a finger to the lips.

A short arched passage to one side of the stairway led into a lesser hall. From this hall came men's voices, barely raised above a hush. Teagen shrank back with Beth, and they held their breaths.

" . . . this pretty story of brigands, a knock on the head." Cadwr's voice. "I do not say she lies or intends you ill, brother, but I can smell a double-tongued woman quick as a rat in rushes."

"She means no ill," returned Michael's tenor voice, sounding irritated. "You do not know her."

"And you know her right well, just in these few short days of guesting," Cadwr scoffed. "Years are not enough to know some women."

"Certes that is so. Put your mind at rest. Lady Bethany—"

"That is the other question without answer," Cadwr interrupted. "How came you to think she is noble born? What is her family? Where lie her lands? She wormed herself into your vassal's good graces, and now into yours. De Tallac is a fool if he—"

"Geoffrey is a good man of hands and eyes both and no man's fool. Nor, despite an elder brother thinking the younger weak-witted, am I. If Lady Bethany intends harm to me or mine, she will soon come to regret it. In any event, the problem is mine to resolve and none of yours. Let this go for the nonce. Come and break fast in amity before my people catch us gossiping like fishwives."

Beth restrained Teagen more forcibly, preventing her from shooting out into the passageway to deny Cadwr's suspicions. She counted to thirty before releasing Teagen's arm, giving her head a warning shake. With due decorum and a seemly pace she entered the great hall, trailed dutifully by her fuming maid. Beth cast a glance back to find on Teagen's face an expression of total innocence, despite a stream of muttered Cornish curses. She had all she could do not to laugh aloud.

Cadwr stood at the fireplace, a pleasant expression like a mask on his surfer-dude face. He and Michael accepted silver hanaps of wine from Richard the page. Beth greeted the men, and Michael's expression cleared almost imperceptibly.

It was easy to see that Cadwr's suspicions had awakened his own.

"Good morrow, my lords—lady." Peter gestured toward the high table.

Beth deferred until the steward had seated the men, and then took her seat as last night, at Michael's left. She remained silent as the pages served them with cheese, bread, and an egg-and-herb dish called tansy. The men rehashed the morning's sport.

Cadwr waxed eloquent on the manifold delights of hawking. "The hounds flushed a covey of doves. My falcon rose smartly—and Michael's peregrine also, to be sure. We followed hard after and brought them down."

"Roast dove will add to our dinner." Michael gave Beth a smile that calmed her unrest a bit, for she saw nothing of suspicion or stress in his eyes. "We had no fitting meal for a guest yesterday, Cadwr, but now you will see Truro's cooks at their best."

I'd better go tell them not to boil the vegetables to mush, then.

Beth dipped her fingers in the *écuelle* and wiped them, then pulled her eating knife from its scabbard. While dining, she studied Cadwr whose motives Michael distrusted. What game did he play? Why criticize her, whom he'd never met before yesterday, and why suspect her of being less than honest? Not that he was wrong.

That thought murdered her appetite. She set her knife next to the trencher. Why not tell Michael all the truth? Until now, she hadn't realized how heavy a burden it was to hide behind a tapestry of lies. It weighed her down like a thick, dark shroud. If ever she discovered how to safely set it aside, how free she would feel!

"You do not eat, Lady Bethany?" From Michael's other side, Cadwr leaned forward to examine her trencher. "The tansy's excellent."

She forced a smile. "A momentary vapor, my lord. Women have them."

"Women," said Michael, "have many mysterious and vexatious ways."

"Why say so? I am the least vexatious of women," she said, her expression saucy.

"Truly, most ladies grow fretful when bored. Brother, you must devise some mirth for the Lady Bethany lest she grow tired of endless sewing in the women's quarters." Cadwr nudged Michael. "Do you enjoy hawking?"

Beth drained her ale, and the ever-watchful Richard refilled it. "I think I have had little opportunity to try such sport—to the best of my knowledge."

"We must do better than hawking," said Michael. "I have the idea ready to hand. In a few days comes the feast of St. Petroc. Some say he is our own Cornish patron, others claim him for Wales."

Cadwr nodded vigorously and opened his mouth to own the saint, but Michael was quicker. “Truro folk hold the day sacred for sport and feasting.” He regarded Beth, a sly and eager smile curving his lips. “What say you to a proper celebration? First we must go to the bottom land by the river. That is where the country folk have their dances and their bonfires. We will honor their festivities for a time. Once the villeins have drunk and eaten and danced themselves to distraction, what say we return here for gentler revels?”

Cadwr brightened. “It is just the thing.”

A medieval feast day.

Beth pretended to consider. “I do not know,” she said slowly, as if speculating. “Do you know the ways of gentle revels, my lord? I might decide to remain with your villeins.” She cast him a glance to show she was teasing.

“No, oh no, my lady.” Peter leaned over the table. “Veryan keeps most seemly holiday. I will make you a fine celebration, worthy of a master of many honors. There will be naught lacking that belongs to St. Petroc’s day.”

The other three chuckled. “I trust you, good Peter,” said Michael with a slap to the steward’s shoulder. “Let there be bonfires to delight Lady Bethany’s eyes. And dancing. There must be dancing. Scour the shire for jongleurs—scour Devon if you must! We will make right merry.”

The days until the vigil of St. Petroc passed quick as thought. Beth had to constantly remind herself she was but a tourist here. Temporary. Not someone who belonged.

The thought discomposed her. While sewing in the women’s quarters, she had too much time to think.

For the first time in an active life, she took the time to examine herself. What, in truth, did she want most? Who was Bethany Lindstrom if you discounted family, hobbies, a historian’s career?

She couldn't be so shallow that if you stripped off the twenty-first century woman, it left but a husk. Could she?

A thread knotted, and she struggled for a few moments to untie it, then made an exasperated huff and took up small iron shears to clip it off. She did want the respect of her peers—nobody liked to be thought incompetent. She desired quiet acclaim, not the clamors of a crowd. She wanted friends and her family around her.

She forced herself to examine a deeper layer. Yes, she wanted God back. But she did not know how to approach Him, though here people tossed His name around as though on the most intimate terms with the Almighty. Yet how did a self-recognized liar approach the holy and perfect Truth?

I don't need to figure that out now. But Lord, if You've got a moment to spare, it'd be nice if You'd make a way for me. I need You.

Besides renewed relationship that must remain on hold for now, what else lay at that depth?

She let the needle rest idle in the linen glove cuff and closed her eyes. Instantly an image came, not visual but bone deep: the sense of completion she'd felt when Michael had embraced her on the battlements.

I want to make a difference in someone's life. To love and be loved.

She sat up straight. Her life schedule had omitted that. She'd run on the academic treadmill nonstop since age five. She hadn't dated much in high school, and in college and grad school she'd taken brutal course loads, concentrating on her studies to the exclusion of a social life.

She had the grades, the sheepskins, and the *cum laudes* to prove it.

She must go home to all that, though the idea of home felt more sterile by the day. This was not her time, no matter how seductively familiar it became, and she must remember . . .

Lately she found herself repeating mentally: *You don't belong here.* Yet it felt increasingly as though she *did* belong.

Cadwr was uneasy about the king's proposed legislation. Michael's worry over what Cadwr might say or do in a fit of pique shadowed his eyes every time he and his brother spoke. His tension hurt her, and she found herself seeking ways to lighten his load.

Peter sought her out to ask advice over plans for the feast. Did she think ten large pasties sufficient for the high table? And though spring was not the correct season and the stars not auspicious, perhaps a pig should be slaughtered in order to make pork pies? Or would rabbit make a tempting change? He went so far as to press upon her the keys, the precious large iron and brass keys every chatelaine carried to unlock the spice coffers and the best plate.

The first time Peter offered them, she declined with a qualm. It felt odd, as though she usurped a privilege not rightfully hers. The next time he urged them on her, Beth bit her tongue, for it no longer seemed so strange.

"Naught unseemly, my lady," Peter assured her. "It is a woman's place and duty to bear the keys. My lord is right well aware of what I do and approves it."

She'd known that before he spoke. And Peter seemed almost tearfully grateful when at length she gave in. The keys felt heavy and strange, clanking a muted music as they swung from her belt. But Beth soon grew accustomed to the burden.

Loving carried its own weight.

She spent time, as Cadwr predicted, on improving her embroidery in the women's hall. One fair morning she visited the hut of one of the serving women accompanied by Teagen, who knew the woman from childhood. Inside the dim hut that huddled against the inner wall of the bailey, she found a marvel of artistry.

Agnes, Truro's best weaver, led them to a corner totally taken up by a huge floor loom on which grew a wonderful cloth in reds and deep brown and cream. Its design, a fanciful creation of birds and rabbits, seemed almost to breathe and hop and fly, so skillful was the execution.

"I would have this," she murmured to Teagen. "Tell her to name her price. I would gift it to my lord as thanks for his kindness."

A quick and intense discussion ensued in Cornish, while Beth admired the marvelous cloth. A wall hanging? A magnificent surcote?

"Lady, she will take no coin. Agnes was widowed in the pestilence and would wed."

"Tell her to make Peter aware of her wishes, and I will speak for the man to my lord."

When Teagen translated, Agnes beamed and bent in a deep and thankful curtsey.

"What is *thank you* in your tongue?"

Teagen told her, and Beth repeated it as best she could. "*Meur ras,* good Agnes. *Meur ras.*"

Agnes smiled wider, baring several brownish teeth, and added a last comment to Teagen, who laughed and nodded agreement.

"What was that last?" Beth asked as they quit the hut.

"Agnes said Truro has long needed such a lady."

Beth felt her face flush, then lifted her head to listen. "Noises. Do you hear? The hunting party is back."

They picked their way across the sun-washed courtyard. A hen fled at their approach, squawking alarm to her sisters.

"I hope they brought down enough game to satisfy Peter," Beth added. "His plans for the feast grow ever more elaborate."

Cadwr beckoned as he dismounted. "Lady Bethany, hasten. Lord Michael is sore hurt."

Her heart lurched. She ran past the storage buildings, sending more livestock scurrying out of her way.

"What befell him?"

"A low-hanging branch."

Cadwr helped Michael down from his mount, concern written large on his surfer-dude face. Michael lifted a confused gaze as she drew near. Instantly she saw the trouble—a large bruise rose on his temple, surrounded by scrapes smeared with dirt.

"My lords, come into the hall where there is comfort. You, lad—Kennet, is it? Run for Peter—*vite!* Quickly! Teagen, bring both warm water and cold. Rags for washing and the strongest lye soap you can get. None may touch him before they have washed."

Peter lumbered up, wringing his hands. "I sent for the leech, lady, but I hear he attends a brewer's 'prentice who fell from a wain."

"Then we must do without him."

Probably the best plan anyway. The leech isn't likely to be clean, and I don't trust medieval medicine as far as I can throw this keep.

She let Cadwr help Michael up the entry stairs and into the chair that stood always near the great hearth. "My lord, attend. Can you see me?"

Michael's looked dazed. "Aye. Any man with eyes would . . . "

He bent over, retching. Peter, hovering and attentive, held up a basin into which Michael emptied his stomach.

Beth stooped at his knee once he was finished. "Have you ringing in your ears? Pain in the other side of the head? Does it pain you anywhere else?"

He shook his head slightly and winced at the movement. "None worth speaking of, save for all you hens fluttering about me."

Cadwr spoke for the first time. "A most annoying accident. The hounds bayed as though they scented boar. We followed hard after, for roast boar is just the thing for St. Petroc's feast day. There were trees, of course. I cleared them, but Michael must not have ducked in time." He made an irritated clicking sound with his tongue. "Great looby. I have not seen you come off a horse since you were nine."

She studied the bruise, large and swelling. Michael kept blinking as if not quite sure where he was. Teagen arrived with two tiring maids on her heels, bearing ewers of water, rags and a clay pot Beth hoped held soap.

"He was unhorsed?"

"He jumped clear, praise Mary. That rouncey's hooves might have caved in the cage of his ribs, but he came well away."

Cadwr ordered Peter to bring ale or wine. Peter's mouth tightened, his expression saying he would rather take commands from his own lord. Beth confirmed the request with a tiny nod. Peter sketched a not quite subservient bow and vanished.

Teagen poured warm water over Beth's hands into a slop basin. A maid proffered the pot, which indeed contained soft grayish soap. Its lye content stung her skin, but Beth assured herself that meant it would kill germs. She cleansed her hands thoroughly before dipping a rag in the cooler water and pressing it to Michael's bruise.

He flinched away. "Ayiee! Do you probe for the bone? Have a care, lady."

"Be still, or I will hurt you further."

With care, changing linen rags frequently, she soaked the bruise clean, then used warm water and soap to wash the abrasions. From them she coaxed copious amounts of tree bark, lending credence to Cadwr's assertion that Michael had been hit by a branch.

The bruise seemed darker than it should, however. Beth cleansed and pondered. She didn't trust Cadwr, and he clearly did not trust her. Something about his political problems seemed to have a darker undercurrent that didn't ring true enough for her taste.

I'll make Michael go up to his chamber to sleep. In private he'll tell whatever else befell.

Finished, she dipped another clean rag in cool water and bade Michael hold it to the bruise to take down the swelling. "Now you shall rest. If your brain is—" She tried to think of a medieval term for *concussion.* "—addled from the blow, sleep is God's remedy."

Not that she intended to let him sleep long. She would wake him soon to hold a candle near his face and check the response of his pupils. Just as Mom had done for her when she'd ridden her bike into a jungle gym . . .

Strange how the memory didn't hurt, though the thought of her mother's gentle care warmed Beth. Would she ever see her again?

At moments like this, it would be nice to pick up the phone and seek sound advice.

Unsteadily Michael rose, Peter hovering to lend a hand if he wobbled. After offering his own strong arm to assist and being waved away, Cadwr retreated to the fireplace, sipping ale from a silver hanap as he watched them through hooded eyes. Beth thanked him nicely, relieved Michael had declined his assistance. She didn't want Cadwr anywhere near her lord until she'd heard his side of the story and could figure out what to do next.

Please God, let his memory not be damaged.

Some hours later—occasionally Beth found it irksome, never to know exactly what time it was—Michael stirred in his big curtained bed. She lay her sewing aside and rose to attend him.

"Turn your head this way."

She held up a carved walnut stick holding a thick, bright beeswax candle, and in its light, peered closely. His pupils contracted in response to sudden light, relieving her fears of concussion, or worse.

"Orders. Ever these terse orders. When did you leave off being a gentle, lost wench and turn into a harridan?"

"The moment you rode under a branch too low for you," she responded.

He frowned. "My mouth is that dry. Give me wine."

"Terse orders, my lord?"

He gave a rusty laugh.

She poured well-watered sweet wine into a chased silver goblet. He rose on one elbow and drank thirstily while she watched for signs of nausea.

"My head is much better."

"I am glad of it."

"I must resume my duties." He rolled onto his side as if to rise.

She put her hand on his shoulder. "You must rest. Peter will see to all, and I've bade him not disturb you unless some matter needs your urgent attention."

"You command him as well, *ma petite?*"

Without thinking she replied, "I would order the king himself, were it to your benefit."

His hazel gaze softened. She set the candlestick on the floor well away from the bed hangings and brushed back his dark hair. His bruise had deepened to an angry bluish purple but seemed less swollen due to the repeated change of cool compresses she'd applied as he slept.

"You do care for me, then."

She felt her cheeks heat. "I betray myself."

"Yet you do not trust me fully."

"Forgive me. A woman alone has but one defense—not to trust."

He mulled her words for a moment. "Aye. I can see that. You are a merlin flying amongst falcons and know not what might befall from one moment to the next."

"I know whom I do not trust at this moment."

"Sit here nigh me and speak." He patted the bed at his side.

Beth gave the spot a wary once-over. In matters of the body, he might not be as harmless as he looked. Deciding she might chance it, she took the seat he indicated.

"Sir Cadwr—forgive me, my lord. I know he is your brother, and he speaks fair enough, but what really befell? I saw not the truth in his eyes."

He gnawed at his lip. "Repeat this to no one."

"I will not breathe a word."

He sighed and took her wrist in his fingers. Her pulse quickened as he played with her hand.

"I lied. My memory is whole, not as I let you think in the hall. I saw quite clearly also. My brain is not addled, and I am not about to sweal away. Cadwr called me aside saying his dogs tracked a boar. While I sought for what he saw, the branch—" He made a disgusted snarl. "I swear by all the saints it was not there a moment before."

Beth drew a sharp breath. "Did Cadwr—"

He snorted and fingered the contusion. "I do not know—and that is the plain truth. No man saw him release the branch that sprang back to knock me from my horse—if he did so. My men rode up only after I lay flailing in the forest dirt like a green boy. Is he capable? Again, I do not know. If he meant mischief, he lacks skill. I have taken sharper blows on the tourney field and in pitched battle. My head is not so soft as to be broken by a tap.

"Certes he and I scrapped over any excuse as boys. My father brought him here for a time, you see, to learn English ways and manners, and for us to come to know each other. He and I often battled to a standstill, though I was the smaller. Age has but refined his sneaking ways, though not his cunning."

"What then?"

"Pah! Mine are good men who'll say nothing to my face or to anyone else. They will think their own thoughts. If they suspect aught amiss, they will come privily to tell me, but they may do no more than laugh behind their hands. I have not been unseated—aside from jousting practice, which does not count—for years." His mouth twisted as though in contempt for his own weakness.

"What could be Cadwr's motive?" Beth prodded.

Michael made a dismissive gesture. "When last we spoke at any length, we were half grown. From what I hear of his reputation since, it is checkered for good and ill. I can prove naught, but at court men do say he looks sharp to his own advantage. Sometimes, by accident, what is best for his liege lords and for him coincide, and then he plays the loyal vassal. Is he faithful at heart, or not so? I cannot see into his inward parts. Only God can do that."

He sighed. "He must know I travel soon to court, for he does also. Abbot Boniface will want his voice heard at court in this *praemunire* matter, and Cadwr must attend on both the abbot and Henry of Lancaster, for he owes fealty to each, just as I attend the king. Does he wish that I fail? A device to keep me from answering the summons so the king's grace can levy a heavy fine?"

He moved his head on the pillow. "But to what end? My attendance—or failure—cannot be of such great moment to his cause. It can harm only me. Cadwr cannot turn the king aside on any course he has chosen, and I will not use what influence I have to do so. Nor has my word such weight as Cadwr supposes. Mayhap my brains are indeed addled. Unless my brother has gone utterly mad, I cannot fathom this."

An idea hit Beth. "Then you will not leave Truro. You are sore hurt and will not depart for court no matter how urgently summoned."

He glared at her. "I will do naught of the kind. Women! King Edward is not one lightly to be disobeyed. Besides, I will not shirk my duty. All the barony must attend—willingly—when summoned for parliament."

"Oh," she said on a laugh, "if you needs must go, then go you shall. But your brother will not know of it. I will have it said that I forbade you to travel until you are well healed. We can make away in private, I with you. You asked me to go, and I have a great desire to see the court. But Sir Cadwr will hear none but the tale we wish him to hear."

"Dishonorable."

"Needful."

His brow creased, then eased as a smile played about his features. The smile captivated her mind and her heart both.

Holy cow, I'm in love with this man. I, who don't belong here, who must go back and write my scintillating doctoral dissertation on the pre-plague famine years in the early fourteenth century, am falling in love.

"I knew when first we met, you would do me good in some way."

"Your eyes are overeager to find good," she said, "before it is meet to see it."

"Wise as a serpent," he quoted, still grinning. "Gentle as a dove." He pulled gently on her wrist, easing her down to him. Ever so slowly, ever so deliberately, he captured her lips in a feather-light kiss.

She drew herself upright, her heart pounding. "That was from holy writ. You claimed you know naught of it."

"I know enough, lady. Just enough."

Seven

St. Petroc's eve signaled the welcome onset of summer. The blessing of warm weather softened the faces of the castle folk. In the expressions of the townspeople and peasants, Beth sensed a strengthening hope. She stood in the castle's chapel for vespers with those of the castle. The very air seemed dressed to honor the blessed saint. Thick candles of the best beeswax lit the chancel. Incense perfumed the soft evening air, wafting about in the sweet breeze from the open doorway.

Anticipation thrummed in excited chatter before Father Gedren called them to worship. "By my troth," Beth heard behind her, "this will be the best holy day ever. It's said the lord will roast three oxen in the bailey and provide ale for all who are thirsty!"

She smiled a secret smile. She'd been able to encourage Michael to expand good St. Petroc's obsequies into a general holiday of two days for castle and townsfolk alike. They would party hard—she'd seen to that. Peter had sidled in close this morning to ask about the extra hogshead of ale. Did she really intend the churls to drink so much? She assured him they'd indeed need to broach a third barrel, and he should keep a fourth in readiness against need.

Her scheme was that everyone, Cadwr's party included, should be well-soaked. During the day of recovery, she intended to find an opportunity for Michael's meinie to slip from Truro keep unbeknownst to his brother. Although he scorned the idea of "skulking away," he'd promised at least to consider doing so.

If it lay in her power, she would protect Lord Michael—and at one remove, herself—from any evil intentions his bastard brother might harbor. If it took the simple and available remedy of getting the castle folk sloshed, she had no problem with that.

"Ite, missa est," Father Gedren intoned.

Beth startled. Lost in plotting, she hadn't attended to the holy words as she ought, and had missed the bulk of the mass.

Michael stirred at her side and began to speak before the last word echoed in the great vault overhead. "Let us to the bailey" he said, offering her his hand. "They will expect me to open the feasting."

At his other side, Cadwr yawned and stretched his yellow-velvet clad arms. "I'm told, lady, you have ordered special dishes. I am eager to sample them."

"I hope you will be pleasantly surprised, my lord."

Cadwr eyed her in a way that irritated her—as though she herself was an added dish for his sampling. Michael moved slightly to one side, blocking Cadwr from further conversation. Beth let her eyes speak gratitude for his sensitivity.

He led the way out of chapel, for the castle folk were too well trained to rush toward the bailey and the heavy-laden tables set up there. Baron's and knight's rank must precede theirs—so said every custom they knew.

The feast started out calmly enough. Father Gedren called the multitude to order, thanking their good lord for his bounty and the Lord above for His great saint Petroc, honored in the memory of all Cornishmen forever. Michael stood after the priest had done.

"I am no man for long speeches." He spread his arms wide to encompass roasting pits, barrels of ale and mead and wine, tables groaning with meat pasties, fish pies, fried pilchards, vegetable and egg dishes, huge cheeses, marchpane, dried berries and nuts, seasonal fruit tarts and honey-cakes. In great baskets, many loaves of barley, oaten and manchet bread steamed gently in the morning. On its own table, apple in mouth and a-rest in a "hedge" of boiled greens and pastry, waited a whole roast pig. "Blessed be St. Petroc.

May he ever intercede for all Cornishmen good and true. Behold his feast. May it well become you!"

A roar of approval went up from the crowd. Peter made sure the high table, set up near the doorway to the great hall, got first crack at the finest treats, which included Beth's own suggestions. On her first taste, she decided the cooks had done themselves proud with her approximation of pizza.

"What manner of pie is this?" Cadwr demanded.

"A dish from my mind's eye, sir. Naught but a simple cheese and garlic pie."

"It is beyond words." He beckoned the flushed and weary head cook over to the table, and into the man's open palm, he pressed a coin. "My compliments."

Can he be truly evil? If Michael cannot fathom his intentions, how am I supposed to?

Her gaze sought her lord. He appeared to have come far from the sorrow-heavy, taciturn man Lady Alys had described. He roared with laughter, drank deeply, ate heartily. From all appearances, he partied as vigorously as any of his people.

Beth scolded herself to stop fretting and enjoy the feast. She'd told herself to affect nothing here, and indeed, it was sheer presumption to think that she might be responsible, in a small part, for Michael's improved demeanor. How could she affect him in any way? After all, she was only a tourist.

"Richard? A touch more ale?" she requested.

Further down the bailey, a table of weavers raised their voices in contention. Loud Cornish imprecations followed, quieted only when Bifan strode down toward them and brought his wooden ale-mazer down on the loudest weaver's head.

Party, Cornish style.

Two days later, headachy and feasted out, Truro's inhabitants made a final night of special merriment as farewell to Cadwr and his troop. Though Beth had watched him closely as a dove does a merlin, he had attempted no further harm to Michael. During the full two weeks he'd guested, he had created no more untoward moments.

She thanked God for his restraint. She only had to get through tonight, for Cadwr of Bridgnorth left at dawn. As this final night's feasting wound down, Beth excused herself to the men, pleading fatigue. At the entry to the curved tower staircase that led to her chamber, Cadwr loomed out of the dark.

Beth squeaked in alarm. "My lord!" Her candle flickered and almost went out, so she sheltered the fickle flame with her hand. "How can I serve you?"

She tried to stay polite, not willing to give him reason to raise his guard. Besides, if he wanted more wine or some ale, or a finer beeswax candle to light his chamber, she'd comply with all speed . . . the better to see the last of the man.

"You know the answer, *ma belle*." He crowded Beth into a window embrasure and tried to loosen the nice veil she'd worn to supper. "Sweet burde, you bewitch me, as you have done Michael. What harm in our sharing delight? Grant me the favor you show my brother."

She hissed between her teeth and tried to squirm away. "You speak from too much wine, my lord."

His laugh held an off-center, unpleasant sound. "I've eyes like any man, sweeting. As a son of the wrong side of the blanket, I am the more assiduous in looking after the family honor. A pretty story yours—a faulty memory." He turned his head and spat onto the floor.

How had he heard that? It hadn't come from her.

"You are no man's wife," he continued. "You belong to my brother, not as wife but leman."

"I belong to no man. Either way, I would grant you no special attention."

As though Beth wasn't worth answer, he pulled her veil off and yanked at her hair. Her temper boiled. She tried to pull her eating knife, but he pressed too closely against her for her to grab it.

Suddenly she lost it. She whipped her hand from his grasp and slapped him hard across the face.

"You're no true brother to my lord. You are a fool and a churl. Never again bespeak me in such a manner."

He jerked back and rubbed the mark on his cheek. For a moment, she thought she saw fear in his eyes. Fear made him dangerous. Through his teeth, he hissed something crude Beth didn't catch, and then slammed her back into the wall and strode back toward the hall.

She escaped to her chamber to cool off. Later, wakeful, she took out her journal and wrote of the encounter, hoping that might steady her enough for sleep. The night candle cast a wavery light on her parchment. Beth cast a glance at the worn-out, slumbering Teagen and dipped her quill into the ink.

A Traveler's Tale. She brushed the tail of the feather quill against her chin, frowning. *Tonight's incident still has me shaken. I didn't even tell Teagen, but I'd like to.* Her pen scratched slowly. *It hurt my hip when he threw me against the wall. I hope he rots and his nose runs and his teeth fall out.*

I rubbed my hip for a while and then came up to bed. I wish I could understand the expression in his eyes. In my nostrils I can still smell the faintly sour odor of his breath. Drunk? Worse? Maybe just drunk—though he didn't slur his words. Maybe he's one of those drunks who can talk all right when he's sloshed. By then we were all a little overcelebrated. Blame St. Petroc.

She stared into the fire. Cadwr had said he'd leave at first light, but he couldn't scram too soon for her taste. Writing the incident brought it back, fresh and unnerving.

She sat quietly, lost in thought, the quill idle in her hand. The fire's snapping, hissing song spoke peace to her. Did the flames not consume wood in exactly the same way at home? Teagen's soft snores added a lower note to the fire's melody. The fire had fallen to embers before she calmed enough to roll the parchment and stow it.

She slept uneasily. Before dawn, Teagen woke her, holding out an everyday dress. Beth saw she'd made ready the gray riding habit for later.

Though she woke up with Cadwr's affront still fresh in her memory, she resolved not to mention the incident to Michael. He'd only overreact. Or worse, catch up with his brother on the road and challenge him to some sort of medieval grudge match. She couldn't stand the idea of causing more disharmony between the brothers, and Cadwr had excited Michael's suspicion enough already.

After early mass and breakfast, she cleaned up as thoroughly as possible, giving extra attention to her teeth with the salt-and-green-sage mixture Teagen had provided. Ablutions would have to last a while; she couldn't foresee the road ahead offering much chance to wash. Teagen, who'd never before left Truro, chattered excitedly about the journey beginning this morn, for she would accompany the party, as befit Beth's status.

Teagen slammed Beth's hair with the comb until it wilted, then coiled it tightly for tidiness underneath the riding wimple. Washed, dressed, and ready, with new lambskin gloves, Beth descended the narrow staircase, while Teagen trailed behind carrying my lady's traveling basket and pouch.

They emerged from the big double doors to the bailey. Cadwr's troop had left more than an hour earlier, and now Michael strode around Truro keep's bustling courtyard, managing preparations for the journey. The broad expanse was aswarm with men at arms, half-packed wagons, whinnying horses, cursing servants, and Peter anxiously striving to bring order out of chaos. He'd had straw spread thickly over the muddy ground, for it had rained steadily all night.

"*Myttin da*—I mean, good morrow, my lady."

"Good day to you also, Peter." Beth surveyed the bustle in the courtyard. "Will we be ready to depart, think you, before midday?"

He chuckled, then touched his forelock respectfully. "Well ere midday. It looks like a grand muddle now, but you have never seen my lord's meinie make ready to travel." He scanned the confusion and yelled at a manservant to make that cart secure or, by the mass, he'd know the reason why!

Beth and Teagen waited on the stone steps, out of the mud and the men's way. Bifan bellowed orders to the men at arms, while Peter prodded the castle folk to greater efficiency.

Michael, Beth saw, was having a bit of difficulty with a great gray horse. It kept rearing and trying to bite the grooms. Finally, after he'd wound the reins several times around his gloved hand, he brought the animal's head down where it could no longer lash out. The huge gray snorted and stamped with hooves the size of dinner trenchers.

"There," she heard Michael soothe, "my great looby fellow. You are anxious to be off, are you not? And mislike that I am not yet mounted."

He spoke more words of encouragement to the horse, then glanced around the bailey. His gaze brightened on seeing her and clung in approval.

"God's greeting, lady!"

"And to you, my lord."

"Stay as you are. A pox take this rain—it left much slop to avoid. I'll have Caillin brought to you and Teagen's palfrey also."

She nodded agreement. When the grooms brought her horse, Michael handed his gray's reins to a stable lad and strode across the courtyard.

"I claim the privilege," he murmured.

Beth smiled into his eyes as with one easy motion he lifted her into the saddle, while a groom held both palfreys' leather bridles. Teagen followed suit, mounting from the stairs.

Order slowly devolved from chaos. Once Beth was mounted, curbing the fractious Caillin with a pat and a soft word, Michael returned to his gray. It took a cuff from his gauntlet, and more coaxing, before he also mounted.

"Great idiot," he said cheerfully. He accepted his peregrine from the falconer, settling her onto his gloved wrist. "War horses are not fit to use as hacks, but Giffard is none of those devil destri-ers. His conformation is as theirs, but bred down, of course, so his temperament is a shade nearer malleable. But he thinks he must act up so as not to shame his noble ancestors."

He pricked the gray with his gold spurs, and Giffard pranced into forward motion. Caillin the follower moved off as well. Beth reined her in so as not to come into range of those huge, gray-feathered hooves.

"Do you not take Broc? Will this horse act up the entire journey?" Beth asked with some trepidation.

"Broc is not the mount for a long journey," Michael responded. "Giffard will steady. A rouncey like Giffard can go without faltering for many miles. If not for his tireless nature, I would not use him. You see, high-bred animals mislike an empty saddle. It speaks to them of danger, then they attack anything in reach. The better bred are like to run mad with rage when deprived of a man's weight. Even a rouncey can be difficult of management. But for a long distance, I own no more dependable horseflesh."

Beth eyed the horse and thought back to her studies. *In my time, the destrier is an extinct breed.* War horses were bred to be vicious, the tanks of the Middle Ages. She recalled seeing their closest living relatives once at a country show near Rockford. The Percherons had been enormous enough to make her eyes roll, but Giffard made them look small in her memory.

She also remembered the telltale sign of God's touch—Jeanne d'Arc had been enabled from on high to ride and control a destrier. Certainly, no woman lacking God's anointing would try. She certainly would not dare approach the animal. Giffard was not Caillin.

Thoughts of medieval virgin martyrs always unnerved her. She suppressed a shudder so that Caillin would not prance in that irritated way.

Behind her, Teagen whimpered audibly. Michael turned a considering expression on her.

"Do you steady yourself, wench. We overnight in Lostwithiel, so we must arrive there safely. Can you ride that nag, think you?"

"I shall not fail, lord."

"If I thought otherwise, you would bide here." He gave Beth a conspiratorial wink. "No matter how much store my lady puts in you."

"I could not do without Teagen," Beth said. "She is clever and faithful both—rare qualities that should be rewarded. Do you not think so?"

"Aye so. Bifan! Get those wains to the rear! I would clear the portcullis by the sun's rising."

"As you wish, lord."

Obedient to Michael's spurs and a firm hand on the reins, Giffard trotted through the archway. In the fresh light of the new day, the party wound through the wide-flung gate and into the narrow way leading down into the awakening town.

Beth noted the protocol in riding out with a large party. Bifan led, followed by her and Michael. Next, their personal servants, then a party of men at arms before and behind the baggage wains.

Early-rising locals scurried aside. Some of them looked a bit the worse for the feast. She picked out a word or two of appreciation in Cornish. Michael nodded and waved, greeting one or another he knew. On his gauntlet, his peregrine bated, beating her wings wildly with a harsh cry of protest.

He feared none of Truro's people, he'd told her the previous evening, but he'd assigned a larger guard than usual due to the women's presence in the party.

"I inconvenience you," Beth had apologized.

"No, *ma petite*. I take but the usual precautions to protect ladies from highwaymen and miscreants, suchlike as attacked you and caused your loss of memory." He'd yanked on her veil, as he often did since she'd told him it irked her.

She'd tugged his hair in retaliation. She smiled now, remembering his yelp of pretended outrage.

As the party trotted through what Beth thought of as downtown Truro, many of the shopkeepers and burgesses greeted Michael or touched the brims of their hats, a few bowing to her as well. It moved her to see evidence of the regard they held for him. So why didn't Cadwr respect him?

Don't think of him again. He's already gone and can't hurt Michael. Think instead on the fact that it's a warm June morning in 1353, and I'm going wayfaring through the countryside with my favorite person in all of time.

Past the tall town gates of Truro, just opening for morning, their road took them east and north, bypassing the trampled, littered field of St. Piran's fair. Beth marveled at how rapidly Truro and its sparse suburbs gave way to open country. Fields hedged with blooming gorse and furze straggled in furlong strips over the gently rolling land. A crew cutting the season's first hay rested on their scythes to stare at the travelers.

One worker, bolder than his mates, waved his shapeless hat in the air and bellowed a greeting in Cornish. At his side a woman, knee-deep in cut hay, regarded Teagen and Beth with open mouth and wide eyes. Beth smiled with what she hoped was a gracious demeanor.

"Teagen."

"Aye?" The maid kicked her palfrey to catch up with Caillin.

"Why does that woman stare?"

Teagen turned to glance back at the hay field. "Oh, villeins. They do gape so. Likely she does not often see a lady. Your dress alone is enough to draw interest. Ignore them. That is the best way to deal with serfs—as befits your station."

Ah, yes, my station. By now you'd think I'd remember.

Beth straightened her spine like a real lady, and the party left the haymakers behind.

The road wound out of sight of the estuary. Michael rode now alongside his men at arms, now at Beth's side, ever busy about the troop's vigilance and efficiency.

"Tomorrow," he said to Beth, "we cross the River Tamar. Once we ford that, we are no longer in Cornwall."

"Aye," put in Teagen, "but in England, where the wicked Sawsnachs live."

"Hold your tongue, wench, or I'll nip it out."

Teagen subsided, but didn't seem at all cowed.

"Then over Dartmoor," Michael continued. "A bleak place that—different from our moors. We sleep tonight at Lostwithiel, still on the right side of the Tamar."

"At an inn, lord?" Teagen's eyes lit with excitement.

"No, maidservant of the saucy tongue. We overnight at the keep of a vassal, Henry de St. Just." Michael chuckled. "He is greatly skilled on the lute and cither. Likely, lady, he will want to show off his talents to you who are new come among us."

"He sounds a most pleasant fellow."

"Aye. He and his troop will accompany us, possibly to London itself."

Beth figured the stronger the party, the better, for in numbers lay safety. "Teagen," she said, "do you ride back and ask how the larger wain does. I would not have the furniture jostled overmuch."

Teagen kicked her palfrey into an awkward turn, raising a small swirl of dust.

"What do you now?" asked the baron.

"I would speak of her."

"Have your say."

"She is clever, my lord, and obedient. A ready tongue, aye, but a good nature. I would satisfy a desire of her heart." Watching Caillin's head bob with each step on the rutted road, Beth sought words that would make her case.

"What desire?"

"She and Ennis of Kenwyn are much attached. I believe they wish to wed."

He made a mouth-sound but didn't look disgusted that she'd mentioned it.

"It would be a good thing."

"Perhaps. I will think on't. Now, while we speak privately, there are matters of greater weight."

"I'm listening."

He allowed Giffard to pace a half mile beside a stream. The party forded before he spoke.

"You were much incensed that I purchased certain necessities for you." She opened her mouth to elaborate on unseemly high handedness, but he forestalled her. "Yet in time you came to see reason. I did none so ill. A woman's rightful place is under a man's protection."

"My lord—"

"Allow me to finish. You share this fault in common with Teagen Quick-Tongue. It must be why you two treat so well together. Enough. You mislike being dependent. Your own folk must have very odd ways, for what choice has woman but to live in a man's protection? But I have bethought me of a solution."

What? She frowned and decided to hear him out.

"I plan to enfeoff you—give you a modest estate that will supply your needs."

"Lord, I am grateful for the thought, but I cannot."

Lands here? Impossible. She wasn't staying here! She bit her lower lip, bitterly regretting that she hadn't leveled with him when she'd had the chance. Why had she let him believe an untruth? Why hadn't she told him by now that she must travel back to her own time?

Despite the uneasiness she'd felt while idly speculating on the desires of her heart, she could not lightly put her obligations aside. She must tell Mom her incredible story. That first. Then finish her studies, write her paper, forge her reputation, pursue her brilliant career.

And all the while, create lies—to cover knowledge that could have been gained only through time travel.

"You have little choice." His glance should have looked stern, but did not. "Either you accept my giftings and hold your tongue about my *indigne* behavior or accept lands of your own to provide for you."

"I scarce know what to say."

Thank God he doesn't suggest marriage. Of course, I can never do that—I have to go back.

As soon as I figure out how.

"*Merci* will suffice," he said dryly.

She thought on it. A temporary fix, for when she returned to her own time, the lands would automatically revert to him. While she remained here, though . . .

"If I were to agree—and I do not say I will—it would not harm you that I accept these lands?" He shook his head. "Where do they lie? Near Truro?" *Near you?*

"Trevellas is close enough. And you do not impoverish me. I have sufficient honors to maintain my rank. Your holding these lands in fief means I will take fealty of you. The king must approve, of course, but he will, for we will pay entry fee into his purse. Your vassalage will do him no harm, nor Veryan either."

He went on to describe the manor. Beth watched as enthusiasm lit his eyes. "Not heavily fortified, of course, since it be small, but a comfortable house and close. The demesne is profitable. Several goodish farms of some thirty virgates each. The land is in good heart and will give you an income of perhaps forty marks *per annum* after feudal dues. The house is poorly furnished as I recall, which you will want to set to rights when at last we visit. The chattels go with the land, *naturellement*, and the manor owes the service of one knight—normal military duties only."

She blinked. "Military?"

He let out a sharp bark of laughter. "Think you to don armor and lead your men? Nay, lady-dear, I do not suggest such delights for you. This is my duty as your liege lord. Of course, no woman can be vassal except in name, for she cannot lead men to war. If the king calls a levy, I will use troops from Truro, and Trevellas will pay scutage enough to cover the costs."

"I do not worry about the costs. *Grand merci* for your kindness. I know I seem ungrateful not to accept without question, but you see, I do not believe I am used to depending much on others." For the life of her, she couldn't figure out what to do. "May I think on the idea?"

"Until we reach London. There we approach my lord the king for his yea-say."

Beth mulled that over. "This manor, this gift—it will give me income of my own?" He nodded. "But still be yours."

"Aye, in a manner of speaking." He curbed Giffard from sneaking near enough to Caillin to nip her croup. "Trevellas was part of Joan's dower property."

His wife? Never before had he used his wife's name in her hearing. Her heart constricted in sorrow for him. And yet . . . if he gave her Joan's manor, didn't it speak of healing?

She let the clop-clop of hooves lull her into an introspective state, almost dreaming. While she remained here, she would hold lands. Trevellas, his free gift, would remain essentially his, no matter that the income would devolve on her. But her possession of the manor would turn out to be quite temporary, more so than he knew. It must! Weeks? Months? When she returned to her own time, Trevellas would revert to him. And she had to return soon, she had to—

Why must I?

She sat up straighter, making Caillin dance a resentful sidestep at the shift in weight. Of course, she had to go back. She was a historian, not a medieval landowner. It didn't matter that she knew not how to travel in time. In due course, after she'd accomplished whatever task she was supposed to do here . . .

What if it takes years?

A frisson of tension tracked up her spine. She forced it down to consider the possibility dispassionately. What if she *did* stay here longer? What would that entail but more of this new life as she knew it? Would current-day mores allow her to remain single,

Teagen at her side as servant, confidante, needlework instructor, and advisor on proper ladylike behavior? Would she stay friends with Michael, possessor by proxy of a small and productive manor?

She feared the answer to that question. She'd read of the beliefs and folkways of late medieval society and understood them as much as a modern reader could. A woman's place was under a man's authority. A single Bethany would be an anomaly, more so than most spinsters. An unmarried woman had but three paths: matrimony, a short widowhood between husbands, or lifelong chastity in the church.

She snorted silently. Yeah, right. Her, a nun! That was funnier than Bethany Lindstrom, feudal landlord. But current ways wouldn't allow her to drift forever in-between.

All right, then, what if things played out differently? What if Michael's healing led to other more interesting outcomes?

Down, girl. No matter how attracted I am, I'm not free to think about a relationship, much as I'd like to love somebody and be loved in return. Oh yes, I would, but I have to go back.

Once admonished against it, her mind insisted on contemplating an end to her solitude. In her own time she was accustomed to being alone much of the time, though some evenings she'd speculated on what it might be like to have someone special. Now she wondered: If she lived out life in this age, what if she and Michael decided to spend time together? What if she did remain here, "bound to him" as he claimed she was? What would the world lose, really, for the lack of one more scholarly dissertation on the tumultuous fourteenth century?

She trembled at her audacity at considering any other ambition.

The road wound on before them, climbing a little, then descending as the sun sank at their backs.

"Lostwithiel."

Michael pointed to a village nestled alongside a streamlet. On his gauntlet, his peregrine bated, fretting at the motion of her perch. In the soft, still air, smoke rose from several dozen rooftops.

"And a league past the town, the keep. Small, but it will serve your comfort, lady. By dusk we will rest."

"Glad of that I shall be," put in Teagen the Irrepressible.

So will I. So much change, so many new possibilities. So much that tempts me and yet frightens me at the same time. How can something so dicey feel so attractive?

"Lead on, my lord."

Eight

Beth woke scratching her first ever flea bite. Her own bites put Teagen in a foul humor before they broke fast at Lostwithiel's small keep.

"By St. Sebastian's wounds, could they find no fleabane for the guesting chambers?"

"Have you salve or something to stop this itching?"

"Naught with me, lady. But I am ready dressed. Do you finish washing while I go below stairs to find some." Teagen glared. "And give a gaggle of lazy serving maids the wrong side of my tongue."

From her fierce expression as she slammed the door, Teagen would do that job quite thoroughly. Beth chuckled at the image and dabbed cool water on the bites she could see. A lame remedy, but it would have to do for the present. Longing for an antihistamine to soothe her itches, she drew her journal out of her pouch.

A Traveler's Tale. I'm covered in bites. Fleas, Teagen says. Hope they don't carry a nasty little bug called Y. pestis. It shouldn't be lurking here so long after the initial outbreak—I hope! My textbooks never dealt with this.

These folks know remedies for any number of human ills. They haven't figured out germ theory or communicability or even basic sanitation, but their medical knowledge seems rooted in practical and observed effects. So far, nobody's spouted theories about the four humors. I brush my teeth with sage and salt. I've seen willow bark used for painkilling, yarrow for scrapes, and rosemary burned to inhale. To hear them talk, rosemary cures everything from minor skin infections to smallpox.

It's not all practical, though. Besides the herbal remedies, each woman has her favorite patron to pray to—St. Stephen for a pesky headache, St. Brice for upset stomach, St. Dominic to ease a villein woman's labor, even below-the-breath invocations to the piskies against leg cramp. I listen and don't say anything about why this isn't the best idea. Mostly I make mental notes, more to remember which herbs are used for which illness than the saints they invoke. Above all, I use my bogus authority to insist they all wash their hands thoroughly with strong soap before touching any patient. They grumble under their breath and think I don't notice, but so far they obey me.

Hearing Teagen return, she thrust the parchment back into the pouch. The maid bore a small clay pot of salve, smelling strongly of lavender and rue. This she smeared over the bites, first Beth's, then, grousing, her own. Beth admitted that they both smelled pretty good as they descended from the women's quarters to the great hall for the meal.

Michael, she soon discovered, was in no hurry to leave. Over wine, bread, and cheese he dawdled in serious conversation with Sir Henry, who hadn't offered any lute serenades as yet, apparently preferring to talk urgently to his guest. Beth caught anxiety in both men's voices and eavesdropped as unobtrusively as possible while they discussed the king's latest tax.

"If we plead our case on this accursed tax," Sir Henry said as his squire presented a large meat pasty, "the king must see reason. Certes the clip will show better this year, but not to the point of thrupence on the virgate! We have not sufficient men or beasts to pay such a sum— not this year. Maybe not next. If the king will not support a base price for wool, I fear it will beggar us."

"Some speak of persuading the king to accept some portion of the tax in kind." Michael accepted a second slice of pasty and speared a hunk of meat on his eating knife. "A tax in wool, rather than on land, would be better for us all and give his grace more coin withal. But think you, had you rather squeeze a few pence more out of the land now or answer the king's next levy of troops in your own person? For he will soon find reason to go again to war."

"I'd answer the levy, my lord." Sir Henry's voice rang with passion. "With my sons in my tail."

Michael's voice dropped. "As would I, had I sons to follow me."

Her heart ached for the leaden quality in his tone. *I could give him sons.*

The thought shocked her into forgetting to eavesdrop. She chewed and swallowed mechanically while giving herself a mental shake. She hadn't the right to think in such terms. Better concentrate on figuring out how to get home, not envision Michael's face alight with the joy she could give him.

Joan bore him no heir, but I could. Barring disaster, like the next plague pandemic that's coming in 1361, my kids would live. I'd create a much better environment. No midwife would touch a newborn of mine till her hands were cleaner than its little soul. I'd make sure . . .

Her thoughts scampered lightly over possibilities, then stopped capering and sank to desolation. "I can't," she muttered under her breath.

The men, deep in their own conversation, did not attend. *Lord, help me . . . I start to want this, and I cannot.*

"I dare not."

"Lady?" Sir Henry stared at her, a bite of pasty frozen on his eating knife, halfway to his mustached mouth.

Beth could feel her cheeks heating. As nonchalantly as possible, she said, "Forgive me, my lords. I but spoke a thought aloud."

Sir Henry nodded and returned his attention to Michael, who seemed not to notice her flush. She stared down at the eating knife in her clenched hand and called herself time's own idiot.

There were no possibilities. A leaden weight pressed down on her chest.

The journey, exciting and new at first, began to fall into a pattern. Wake, hear mass, break fast, mount, ride. Beth chuckled at the way she and Teagen exclaimed at every new sight. She noticed the way her maid signed the cross when they forded the Tamar.

"Bear up," she urged. "You will come to no harm here. England is Christ's, same as Cornwall. Both belong to our Lord."

"And His blessed mother. You are right, lady, and I am foolish to be afeared." Teagen gave an audible swallow.

"But you have never been far from home," Beth guessed. "Journeying is a hard thing, but exciting, *n'est-ce pas*?"

Teagen nodded and looked thoughtful. Beth left her in peace as the horses splashed their way across the shallow river.

One of the wains managed to get a wheel caught between two rocks on the river bottom. Michael urged the women up the opposite bank out of the range of mischief, well guarded by Ennis and several other men at arms. There they watched the tedious, wet operation of freeing the wagon wheel, several men pushing, several pulling and urging the struggling, neighing horses. At last the wain popped free with a muddy, sucking lurch, as though the river suddenly relented and set it loose against its better judgment.

On the bank, Caillin nickered approval, and Teagen gave a last shiver. "The wain did not want to leave Cornwall."

"It must," Beth reminded her, "if it wishes at last to see great London."

Teagen brightened and afterward showed keen interest in every new sight. On the third day, riding the bleak stretches of Dartmoor, Beth worried not about her maid's misgivings, but her own conflict. Round and round it went, like dough kneaded for the sweet rolls they sometimes ate at breakfast.

In a bare and windy silence that muted the horses' hoofbeats, Beth mulled all the changes she'd assimilated. She'd had no idea that she could adjust so rapidly. Meat pasties for breakfast, ale in lieu of coffee, natural fabrics instead of synthetic, snatching baths whenever possible and missing her daily shower. The taste of sage instead of mint when she cleaned her teeth. Speaking medieval English instead of American slang. She still received blank looks, but not so often anymore.

And her studies, the dig, her doctoral thesis, the things that couldn't wait? Somehow they could. The idea of returning home no longer seemed desperately urgent. Necessary, of course. Most of all, she missed her mother, though she kept that thought at bay as much as possible. How was she supposed to cope with never seeing Mom again?

Without a means of returning, however, all points were moot. Did time portals lurk in forgotten passages elsewhere, or was Mossock's the only one? She must find some way to access that portal, she knew, and soon.

It gave her a weird light feeling to realize that every mile they traveled toward London was a mile further from the necessity of seeking passage through the portal. She could not, of course, while my lord wished to make all haste to court. She need not seek a way home for a while longer.

A half-forgotten dream, to travel into the shaded past. But as the weeks had passed, 1353 had gradually lost some of its strangeness. And she need do nothing to pursue the vision, only go on as she had done—as she would continue to do—at the side of a man she admired and respected. All might yet be well.

"Lady, look you there." Teagen trotted up beside her, reined in her mare, and pointed. On the crest of a nearby hillside, a rocky outcrop sprouted as if planted ages ago by a Titan farmer. On the grass-covered slope below, shreds of morning mist hid a herd of small ponies. One tossed his head at Caillin and the other mares and gave a shrill whinny. The echo off the outcrop lent an otherworldly afternote to the stallion's call.

Beth shivered and drew her cloak tighter to close out both mist and unease. Behind them, Giffard snorted as if such mini horses were beneath his notice. Caillin, in her usual fretful mood, pranced and blew through her nostrils.

"Moor ponies." Michael's voice at Beth's elbow startled her; for once, she hadn't sensed his approach. "We call ours goonhillies. Good for use in the mines since they do not grow large. That stallion you see challenging Giffard—that is as big as he will grow."

"His head would not reach Giffard's withers. For sure, so bleak a land must keep them small, for even the grass grows stunted."

"I saw you shiver. The moors do not invite you?"

Involuntarily she tightened her hold on the reins, to which Caillin objected. "They have beauty, but of a wild and haunting nature. All these rocks lie as though scattered here by some giant."

He nodded. "Folk say the giant Cormoran himself left these rocks behind, scattering them as trash while he dug the Tamar with his great fists."

Teagen listened big-eyed as he told the legend. Beth found herself distracted from the shiver Michael had so easily seen. Did his gaze seek her as she found herself constantly noticing him?

The moor seemed endless, though by afternoon the land changed. The stark, windswept rocks gave way to a lightly wooded, shallow valley, dry at first, then yielding to a broad river. At Michael's order, they did not seek a crossing at once, but tracked the watercourse a few miles inland, then forded and turned back southward. A downhill ride through mixed farm and woodland led to a first sparkle of the sea. The late sun picked out glints of silver and gold on a wide expanse of water.

Michael held Giffard back. Beth, grown familiar with this wordless signal, cantered up to join him.

"Yonder lies Plymouth."

"I am glad to see it."

"You are weary, lady?"

She smiled at the concern in his voice. As she caught his gaze, her heart melted.

"None too weary. The road is toughening me, dear-my-lord."

He growled in his throat, amusement in his eyes that did not reach his straight-lipped mouth. "See that it not toughen you overmuch. Maidens should not taste like an old rooster in the stewpot, but remain ever tender." He removed his leather gauntlet, yanked her glove off, and in front of God and his retinue, lifted her bare fingers to his lips.

Her heart stammered a half-hearted protest. "You would stew me and dine on me, then?"

He gave a low chuckle, her fingers still entwined in his tender grasp. "We must come home to Truro by sea, not over Dartmoor. I like this mood of yours better than the silence you kept whilst crossing moorland. Silence does not become you."

"Whether I am silent or talkative, you must not think to predict me." She freed her hand with a flounce of her head, smiling to show she was kidding, hoping he would not see the havoc his simple hand kiss wrought with her emotions.

"Indeed."

He spurred Giffard to an easy canter, with Caillin keeping pace. The road broadened toward Plymouth town, following the estuary past docks and a solitary mill whose great wheel creaked and turned with the force of the water. Around the mill clustered wattle-and-daub huts, like a brood of goslings about their mother.

"Predict you? I would not presume so far."

"Presume! You have done naught else since first we met."

In comfortable banter they led the way, lord and lady, through the open gates of the port. Beth refused to dwell on the fragility of the present mood between them.

Let me have this a while, her heart pleaded. *You who are master of time, let time not slip by. If we could but stay locked here now, riding these narrow streets, with him at my side humming that catchy tune . . .*

Nine

They overnighted at Plymouth and the following night at Exeter, another estuary town. Exeter, the biggest city Beth had seen so far, lay more steeply packed into its hills than either Plymouth or Truro. From there they went to Ilminster, the small and wealthy abbey town of Shaftesbury, then Salisbury.

Though Lord Michael denied her casual request they visit Stonehenge—saying it was naught but heathen rocks strewn there by the devil—he indulged Beth in her desire to hear early mass at Salisbury's great cathedral. The pristine beauty of the church almost stopped her breath. The chants and singing of the mass echoed off the high, brightly decorated carvings of the roof. Mist-dimmed sunlight threw subtle shades of ruby, emerald, and citrine light on the worshippers, elusive as fog and seductive in its ever-changing radiance.

Their stop the following night at Odiham castle, near Basingstoke, found the entire party saddlesore and irritable. Sir Andre welcomed them heartily, but Beth begged off the formal supper. Michael scowled and opened his mouth as if to demand her company. But then his eyes cleared, and he gave her leave to seek the women's quarters.

Sir Andre's kindly wife Amicia, over fifty and prone to mother, ordered a light supper of soup and roast fowl for her and Teagen. While they sat drinking soup by the fire in their shifts and close-wrapped cloaks, she insisted her serving women must clean and freshen their stained riding clothes.

That evening the strangeness of the journey mixed with fatigue and got them slap-happy. Or was it the Gascon wine Lady Amicia served? Beth emptied her brain of every translatable joke she knew, and Teagen managed a few saucy tales of her own.

The night candle burned low before Teagen groaned and suggested they seek their beds. "My word," Beth muttered, "was there ever a pair as out of hand as we two?"

"By my troth, the nobleman who takes you to wife will get a termagant."

Beth gave one last hiccuppy laugh. "Wench, for you I could say the same."

The morrow brought tidings both good and ill. Michael had sent Bifan on ahead of the troop to question at various keeps regarding the court's whereabouts two days hence. King Edward was not one to abide at his favorite hearth fires for long, but journeyed constantly from this keep to that manor. The court followed wherever the king's whim took him, and parliament met wherever the king was.

A tired and travel-stained Bifan returned that morning as they broke the fast. "Lord, the king bides at Windsor, as you guessed."

"Aye and good. St. George and his dragon grant the king's grace stays put. What sense have you of the barons' mood?"

"All well on the surface. I heard not much grumbling. The men at arms are watchful and say little, proper enough. But the soldiers will know naught of high doings."

Michael nodded and bade him refresh himself. Bifan would rest here at Odiham this night and rejoin the troop two days hence at Windsor, Michael told him. From there they would travel together, following the court, and stay at Veryan's house in London.

"My lord, I would rest me as you command, but I cannot." Bifan accepted a wooden mazer from a maidservant and took a long and thirsty quaff. Michael motioned him to take bread, cheese, and stewed fruit, forbidding him to speak again until he'd eaten.

Beth watched with approval. *A trusted servant, and Michael treats him well, looking to his welfare before he demands news.*

Bifan wiped crumbs onto his sleeve. "My other news is not so well to speak. As you commanded, I did question about Cadwr ap Gwillem. He is by now at Windsor. Reports are that he rode in great haste thence, as if the devil himself nipped at his heels."

Teagen crossed herself. Beth stared, wondering which name concerned her maid—Cadwr's or the father of lies.

Maybe she feels the same toward both. I'm not sure she's wrong.

Michael waved Bifan's words away. "Pah! No matter what mischief he plans—and surely he can do no more than vent his spleen against the new law—he can do naught against me. Should he try some foolery as at Truro, I'll bring complaint against him to the king."

Bifan's somber brown eyes met his lord's. "Lord, I like it not. Why such haste? Unless he mean some treachery."

Michael threw his bread crust down on the table. "A pox take him. What treachery can my brother do me or mine? He forgets I have both the king's favor and his own liege lord's. Very well. I see you readying your mouth to spew more words of caution. I shall take extra care. As will you. Pass the word to the men to keep sharp watch and double the night guard."

"My lord." Beth put two fingers on his wrist and saw his high color diminish somewhat. "Since you know Sir Cadwr's whereabouts, keeping watch will be no burden, will it? When watched for, a trap is easily avoided."

He kissed her fingers in a caress that turned her whole metabolism awry. "You speak wisdom. But while you are in my care, I will keep doubly watchful, lady-dear." His eyes glinted mischief at hers, though his face remained straight as ever. "Who, I wonder, do I summon to protect you from me?"

"I need no such protection," she murmured, "for I trust your better nature."

He frowned a fake scowl at her. "Sadder-But-Wiser oft becomes the nickname for those who trust."

"That is not my name." She winked. "At least, not yet."

His scowl grew real. "And shall not be, whilst I have soul and body together."

As too often of late, her heart again melted. Did he have such great regard for her then? Never had any man stated his attachment to her welfare with so much passion. She wanted to kiss the scowl from his brow, but contented herself with a caressing gaze.

My lord decided the troop should rest their horses that day. Windsor lay only a half day's ride away and, once there, London's walls were no great distance. He even hinted the core of their party might travel from Windsor to London by boat, for the Thames gave a wide and easy road, and it would be a novelty for Lady Bethany.

Beth gratefully joined Teagen for a morning of embroidery and gossip. The women's quarters at Odiham keep lay in a very old section, and to this they returned. Beth missed the private chamber she'd enjoyed in Truro, but she and Teagen had managed well enough.

"More sewing." Teagen grumbled, following up the outdoor stairs into the shadowed old keep.

"Of course—always more sewing," Beth said with a laugh.

Today the task appealed to her. She was eager to start on the ivory silk from St. Piran's fair. From the moment she'd handled the cloth, she'd known exactly what use she must make of it. An under shift, they'd call it here, but she envisioned a wedding negligee. Did she dare dream of a night to wear it?

While she and Teagen worked, Beth pondered her future. She'd tried to push the worry down, and simply enjoy the novelty of a medieval journey, but she kept returning to it as a tongue does to an aching tooth. The knowledge that sooner or later she must go home made a constant minor counterpoint to the joy of her sojourn here.

She could dismiss her career ambitions. She'd started to harbor a secret and inarticulate contempt for history. For indeed, what was history but these people's stories? What better way to learn their tales but to live in them? The need to theorize about demographic decline, climactic conditions—these she had already left behind. She recognized that now. Below this certainty was the nagging longing to see her mother, to tell her of all she had seen and experienced in this vanished world. And Beth found herself increasingly haunted by the image of Mom's eyes filled with grief. What if she never knew what had happened to her only daughter? Was that kindness, to seek her own happiness here to the detriment of one she loved so dearly?

That this era was dangerous also concerned her. Not, of course, that the twenty-first century was safe, she reminded herself. Its street gangs, criminals, wild-eyed terrorists made a minor bully like Cadwr look like a paragon of virtue. In Chicago, a car might jump the curb, or some new and virulent germ might lay her in a modern grave.

No—her own century held as many ways to come to grief as this one. In either era, the only certainty was the love of Christ.

A new thought struck and her needle stilled. Hadn't she promised the Lord she would stay here if it were His sovereign will? Her spirits rose at the thought.

Should she not simply trust her future to God and let Him decide the matter? What choice did she have, after all? No amount of prayer or wishing would create a fresh door here at Odiham, through which she might return to her own time.

Smiling down at the smooth ivory silk, Beth focused on her stitches with a lighter heart.

Ten

At supper Michael announced they would leave Odiham early on the morrow to reach Windsor by midday. Lady Amicia gave a worried frown.

"But my lord, Lady Bethany has not court dress. And I fear our sizes differ too greatly to . . . "

Michael set his hand atop Beth's. "No matter. I set Teagen to the task days past. I fear, Lady Amicia, we have made free with your sewing women. This night they set the last stitches in the required embroidery." He gave a one-shouldered shrug. "I trust Teagen speaks true. I know naught of stitchcraft."

Beth let her glance scold him. *You devil.* He winked back.

"I suppose I may see what she and the maids have wrought?" If he'd ordered orange trimmed in red, she'd take his ears to garnish her porridge.

"Certes. Since the women will be well engaged, Sir Andre, what say you to a ride out? I would see your new saker hawk."

The men went down to the mews for their birds, Beth and Lady Amicia to the women's quarters.

"Quick," Teagen hissed when they entered. "My lady comes, hide it!"

"Too late. In any event, you need hide no longer," said Beth.

Morning sun streamed in through the open casements of the solar. Near the windows sat the women most skilled at embroidery, setting a deep border onto a summer-weight fabric of a lovely pine-green. Seated nearby, other women stitched skillfully on lighter cloth, the green of early spring leaves. The sunlight caught an occasional glimmer from something yellow and shiny.

"Concealment is useless, Teagen, for my lord told me all."

The maid beamed. "Come then, and see what we have made."

She grasped Beth by the elbow and hustled her to the corner nearest the hooded fireplace. With swift, rough skill and plenty of chatter, the maids stripped the bemused Beth down to her knee-gartered stockings and efficiently bedecked her, skin out, in new-sewn finery.

From the lighter colored green fabric, they'd fashioned the gown. It showed at neck, armholes and sleeves, bordered at neck and cuffs with intricate embroidery. Dark blue, white, and deep green silk, accented with gold wire, created fantastic images of leaves, flowers, and an occasional winking beast.

They'd echoed those motifs in the sleeveless surcote of pine-green. Cut away from the shoulders to just below the waist, its armholes showed the sides of the gown and its neckline dipped low in front. For the head, they provided a heavy net of woven gold cord, anchored at the crown with Michael's disputed hair pins. Completing the headgear, a fragile white silk veil.

Lady Amicia possessed but a small hand mirror, but Beth caught her reflection: a medieval lady of sophistication. She almost believed it, for they'd forgotten nothing. Her entire demeanor reflected everything of the women she'd seen pictured in manuscript illuminations, textbook illustrations, and medieval fine art.

Plain harried doctoral candidate Bethany Lindstrom from Chicago.

"My thanks," she managed to say. "All of you—such beautiful work, it stops my breath. Many, many thanks."

The maidservants, Teagen, and Lady Amicia all beamed.

"Come down to the hall," Amicia urged. "My lord will wish to see." One of the maids tittered.

"The men will be long gone a-hawking by now," Beth pointed out.

"I think not yet, my lady." Amicia gave a comfortable chuckle. "Not the way Lord Michael devours you with his gaze. You will ravish his eyes."

That'd be nice. Beth gave what she hoped was a modest smile, and went for the stairs with Amicia and a covey of giggling maids in her wake.

Father, let him appreciate. Just once in my life, I'd like to knock a man's socks off.

As she swept down the outside staircase, she felt her heart pound under the embroidery. Sure enough, as Lady Amicia claimed, Michael, Sir Andre, their squires and hunting hounds clustered by the hearth. On Michael's gauntlet, his peregrine stretched her wings and let out a soft cry of complaint.

In mid-comment to Sir Andre, Michael froze when Beth entered the hall. She tried for a brave smile, for so much depended on his approval. Without looking aside, he handed the peregrine off to a squire and approached her. At the last step, he stopped and lifted her hand to his lips in that caress that made her knees go weak.

"Lady," he said softly, "I shall put you under lock and key. You are far too beautiful to present to a sinful and licentious court."

"You may thank Lady Amicia and her maids. Their work surpasses anything I thought possible." She smiled at the besotted expression in his eyes.

So, after all, I can dazzle the one man who matters.

"Indeed."

He held out his hand, and eagerly she grasped it. His expression changed to amusement as he disentangled their fingers and replaced her hand atop his closed fist.

"Have you still no highborn graces? This handclasp is proper in noble company."

She chuckled back. "I shall learn, my lord."

In the correct manner, he led her to the hearth at the top of the hall. She accepted wine from one of the pages. Lady Amicia beamed at the lord's unspoken praise, but Michael wasn't finished.

"For you, gracious lady." From under his tunic, he unearthed a finely worked gold chain, drew it off over his head and spilled it into Lady Amicia's hand. "My heartfelt thanks."

"It is pleasure to serve you." Amicia's smile grew broader. "And now, by your leave, I must see my lady changed from court finery into her everyday things."

Beth thought it a shame to lay the beautiful garments aside in favor of a plain gown and surcote, but she couldn't parade around in fine feathers all day. While the men went hawking, she would ask Amicia and the maids to teach her more intricate embroidery patterns. She'd love to sew and embellish a fine surcote for him. Perhaps she'd use that marvelous fabric she'd bargained with Agnes for, at Truro.

As Michael's wedding gift? She barely dared hope so, but over her stitches she sent up a whispered prayer.

Eleven

A sulky sunshine, filtering through high clouds, blessed Beth's arrival at Windsor Castle. Side by side, she and Michael rode through the great gate in the lower bailey.

The enclosure buzzed with activity, so crowded that Bifan could scarce make their group's way through. Beth could not help gawking at the splendid display of courtiers, servants, clerics, supplicants milling to and fro, almost from wall to wall. And color! It seemed as though the courtiers vied with each other as to who could dress in a more outlandish combination of hues. Even the high-nosed prelates flaunted rich furs and boldest scarlet.

Noise also, almost enough to make her cover her ears. Horses that took exception to another nag too close on their heels screamed challenge. Dogs ran through the bailey barking warnings at each other. Hawks on nobleman's or falconer's gauntlet gave their distinctive harsh cries. And human voices, dozens—no, hundreds—vied with the animals' to make an unholy racket.

Dappled by sun and cloud, the stately yellow stone keep rose on its motte, looking down from a disdainful height at both bustle and everyday matters. Though parts of the Round Tower were encrusted with scaffolding and the signs of recent work, the building shone gaudy with banners flying from every tower.

Surmounting them all, a banner she easily recognized—the blue and red of England ancient, France quarterly—the king's own device.

Somewhere in this complex was Edward Plantagenet, king of England, of that name the third. Under her habit, her heart beat faster at the very idea.

Bifan gave a gesture as they reached a grand gate just to the north of the Round Tower. Michael dismounted Giffard and helped her down from Caillin.

"Welcome to Windsor, lady." His brow quirked in exasperation at the boiling of people around them amidst the chaos of a building under construction. "Such as it is!" he added with a glance around.

"The king looks to remake every structure here," she said.

"Even so. Building has been going on apace for years. An I get the chance, I will introduce you to the bishop. All here goes forward under Wykeham's keen eye, and well he knows how to please the king's grace."

"It will be wondrous fair when it is completed," Beth said.

Michael's hand felt warm and sure under hers as they ascended the wooden stairs into the Round Tower. From there, he explained, they would join the party in the great hall.

"This leads to the upper ward. There the royal family lives when in residence."

"Then Queen Philippa will be here. And Joan of Kent, mayhap? Edward of Woodstock, the younger ones, the Lady Royal?"

"Possibly. The prince returns from Aquitaine any day now." He gave her a quizzical frown. "But my young lord is a warrior. He'll have no patience at court for stubborn, outspoken, ill-governed *demoiselles.*"

She opened her mouth to deny she was stubborn. He prevented that.

"Enough, sweeting. I would talk of weightier matters than which ladies are present to have their gowns ogled."

"Always," she grumbled as he guided her across the hall in the tower, where around a merrily snapping hearth nobles drank wine, talked politics, and eyed the newcomers from toe to crown. "Always a more important matter than meeting the queen, or seeing the ladies and how they go on. I would study their ways, if ever I hope to meet your high standards in how demoiselles should comport themselves." She smiled to show she was joking.

"Why, that is easy." His turned to an innocent expression with raised brows. "Simply do exactly as I say and your deportment will certes be perfect."

"Ha!" she laughed, making sure her volume was soft enough not to attract undue attention. "How much study have you given to being the perfect maiden, my lord? I would learn from you who have learned the subject in such depth."

He laughed. "Depend on it, you will have your share of mirth. But we come primarily to do business—I to see that my brother does not alarm the great lords by talk of catastrophe. The rest of us, to attend the king's business. After that is finished, and not before, I intend to ask the king to confirm the grant of Trevellas to your keeping." He gave her hand a light squeeze. "Your meeting the ladies will be but a side benefit."

They walked back out into sunlight and across the broad lawn that comprised the upper ward. More buildings of the same warm yellowish stone, some being worked on by so many masons they looked like swarming ants, others complete and shining, their traceried windows reflecting an occasional sparkle of daylight.

Near the door of the great hall, Michael murmured excuse and waved a hand in the air. Cadwr, whom she saw a split second after he did, lifted his hand in response.

"We must greet him," Michael said. "To seem to snub him now . . ."

"Of course. I understand. And I was but jesting. I will take my manner from yours, nor embarrass you willingly. Having never been at court before, I grow . . . anxious to see and hear and learn."

His stern visage softened into a smile. He lifted her fingertips again to his lips.

"Since that is true . . ."

Beth groaned elaborately.

"Before we go to dinner, there is another matter I would settle, one that is not for discussion at court."

"What matter?"

He guided her around a muddy area, careful of her red leather boots. "Teagen. You did mention her as we set out from Truro—you thought I had forgot, but you see I did not."

She flushed. In fact, he attended to her words, as she listened carefully to his, and she shouldn't act waspish.

"Again I ask forgiveness."

"Granted." He winked. "Do you but remain complaisant, and you will give yourself—and me—less trouble. This way. We are to lodge in the Curfew Tower yonder." He pointed at an older building with battlements similar to those she'd sought to find privacy at Truro.

"What of Teagen, dear-my-lord?"

"The wench serves you well? Does she give you all due respect?"

He opened the door for her and they stepped into another hall, this one smaller and not as grandly appointed as that in the Round Tower. Michael greeted several men known to him who played chess near a window glazed with many tiny, diamond shaped pieces of greenish glass.

"She is clever and faithful, and does me true service."

"I have a mind to grant your request for her marriage. Ennis of Kenwyn has also proven himself. He is full twenty and no green boy, though not much tried. He is attached to her and says he would take her to wife."

"It would please them much, an you permit it."

His eyes narrowed as if he calculated a long and troubling math problem. Beth frowned. Then his expression cleared.

"It will serve in all ways. Summon her after dinner. As her liege lady, her marriage must be in your gift, not mine."

A plump maid barred their way with a bright smile and a curtsey. "My lord, may I show you your quarters?"

"Aye, for my lady is journey tired. I will lodge with the men. Give my lady my usual chamber since we are not man and wife."

"As you wish," said the maid. "This way, please."

She guided them up a curving stone staircase, sheltering her candle in its brass holder from the draft. At the top, she opened a stout wooden door.

"My lady."

Beth dug in her pouch for a penny. The maid's eyes widened.

"Thank you!"

"I have one further duty for you," Beth said. "Will you see for my maid Teagen? She entered the lower ward with the baggage wain and knows not the way."

"At once, my lady." The maid beamed and fairly scampered down the stairs.

Michael laughed, quietly but long. "And you say you do need training in command. You lack nothing."

"Wait until dinner, my lord. I am a-tremble at the thought of facing so many, so highborn, and . . . will they be unkind to a stranger, think you?"

He did not shut the door, but drew her over behind it and put both hands on her waist, the way he did to help her from horse. "If any are unkind," he murmured, "it will be the ladies, in jealousy of your beauty."

His face was inches from hers. This time, he offered the kiss. Readily she accepted.

The main hall, to which they made their way for dinner, lay in a separate building near the Round Tower. One end of the hall was under renovation, but as Michael led her in, she saw that the nobility of England thought nothing of the inconvenience of meeting in a place under construction.

And here they all were: the highborn, confident of their status; hangers-on looking to find any dropped crumb of gain; courtiers eagle-eyed for preferment; clergy anxious for this benefice or that inheritance. Her heart pounded at the sight and her stomach felt queasy.

Further up the hall, all eyes were drawn to the grandest table in the room, elevated on the dais above lesser men. There they sat, chatting comfortably—the Plantagenets. Through the candle and fireplace haze in Windsor Great Hall, like a distant sun they outshone their glittering court. Beth's hand, lying formally on the back of Michael's in the manner he'd gleefully taught her, tightened.

"You are afeared, sweeting?"

"Only dazzled, dear-my-lord." She gave her head a rueful shake, careful not to dislodge her gossamer veil, pinned carefully over the cord net. "Look at them—just look!"

He cast her an indulgent glance, his expression amused at her tourist-at-court manner. "Of course you would know which is which."

She studied the royalty arrayed before her, chatting so casually. Did they know they formed the stuff of dreams? Movies would be made about them, but they'd get it wrong. No Hollywood imagination could do them justice.

Snowy linen draped the high table, on which sat a huge silver and gilt saltcellar worth the ransom of an earl. Behind the table they stood or sat in intricately carved chairs, the king's chair bulkier and more ornately accoutered than the smaller chair to its right. Everywhere she glimpsed brocades, rich velvet in scarlet and emerald and sapphire, silk veils as ethereal as the drift of smoke haze that obscured the hall's great hammer-beam roof. Real gems winked from embroidery around cuff, headdress, and collar. Royalty.

"In the high seat—that must be the king."

"Aye. And the young man on his left is Edward of Woodstock."

"The Black Prince," she breathed. When Michael looked a question at her, she whispered, "Naught. I dream aloud."

She flushed. She must make no more mistakes of that nature.

"But tell me, who is the lady on the king's right? She looks overyoung to be the queen."

"Indeed she is not. That is Princess Isabelle, the Lady Royal. No doubt, the queen is indisposed. Mayhap some breeding complaint, poor lady."

Mentally Beth reviewed history she knew well. Somehow, historical fact became blurred in the push and pull of real life. Ten children before finishing, or had it been twelve? Several would predecease Philippa of Hainault, and at least one had died in the pestilence. Instead of dry historical fact, it tasted of brutal tragedy. Poor lady.

"And who is the fidgety boy beside the Lady Royal?"

Michael squinted, but seeing Cadwr approach, held his silence. After greeting his brother, Cadwr looked Beth up and down.

"You look well, my lady."

"As do you, my lord." She inclined her head and let her tone say what she really thought of him.

"Do excuse us. I must speak to Lord Michael."

"Lady Bethany stays. There is naught to hear that she does not hear also."

Cadwr looked irritated. "She has naught to lose. It will be on our heads the ill will fall if our plan goes not forward."

"*Our* plan?" Under Beth's fingers, Michael's hand tensed. "Do not presume so far. I am none of yours. And you cannot openly flout the king in this matter."

"Not openly, no." Cadwr glanced aside to a group half in shadow, variably dressed in cassocks or habits of snowy white, gray, and black. "But what I said in Truro has borne much early fruit. All feel great unease about the new edict barring our access to the church's law. My lord abbot has come also to take counsel of the others."

"Pah." Michael looked ready to spit, but he kept his voice low. He lifted his head and gazed openly at the clerical group who observed their trio so watchfully. "I recall a bevy of black crows moaning about the statute of Provisors, some years back. It came not to such moment as they feared. Like as not this *praemunire* will prove just such a storm in a mazer."

It will, she wanted to assure him, but dared not. More than ever, she wished she'd had the courage to tell Michael the truth. That way, once it was safe, she could tell him the historical outcome—the Statute of Praemunire proved confusing, unwieldy, but hadn't dealt the death blow to justice Cadwr claimed it would. Nor had it affected the church's pocketbook as badly as was desperately feared.

She could tell Michael none of this. *And even if I did,* she thought with a wave of despair, *he'd never believe me. He likes me, sure, but if I mentioned a word of this, he'd have nothing further to do with me.*

And Cadwr, she was sure, would be among the first to lug kindling to the witch-burning stake.

"We dare not take the chance," Cadwr told Michael. "Listen, brother—I said you had *fou* ideas, and so you do. But you are also highly regarded here. Can you not use your sway with my lord Henry or with the king's grace? Make them see reason? This statute will do nobody aught but ill."

The statute makes perfect sense to me. In the light of the anticlerical sentiment that's going to boil over in a few years, maybe the greedy ones among these churchmen have it coming.

"Least of all you," Michael countered.

Beth removed her hand from his, hoping it would give the impression that he spoke freely and not under any undue influence from a stranger. Cadwr scowled, but she read desperation in his body language.

Michael continued, "I am in no wise impressed by your Abbot Boniface. He cares not about the law's effect on the realm or the church either. He looks only to its impact on his own coffers. Were it to Valle Crucis' advantage, he would sell the very relics in the altar for gold."

Cadwr's expression cleared and he gave an uncomfortable chuckle. "Come now. Are not all, from pope to barefoot friar, working toward the church's best benefit?"

Michael lowered his voice. "It would do the church no harm to be parted from some of the legal protections they covet so. What of the murder of that bailiff of yours, two years agone? The knave who killed him had but to recite a verse in Latin to save his neck." This time he did spit into the fresh rushes on the floor. "And that wight no more cleric than Lady Bethany here."

She felt led to add her voice, though not as historical certainty. "I believe someday the church will be called to account. It is overfond of money."

"The root and cause of all evil," Michael responded. "By the rood, lady, you speak truth, and I agree. If we are to avoid more such cases as befell your bailiff, Cadwr, the king must rein in its worst abuses."

Cadwr looked both disgusted and frightened. "True, the king's justiciar could not touch him who slew my bailiff. But that was a small matter, and this a greater. It stands to hit us all deep in the coffers if allowed to go forward."

He drew breath, but before he could continue, he was interrupted. Trumpets rang out from a minstrels' gallery Beth had not noticed before, splitting through the clamor of talk in the hall.

Michael had clearly had enough. "Peace for now, brother. You will give us all belly cramp! Let us dine, and think no more on these matters till the time be meet."

Michael offered Beth his hand, and she rested two fingers on his wrist as she saw the other women doing. Cadwr, who apparently had a place at a different table, sketched a bow at them both—but Beth saw pure hatred in his eyes.

Watch that one. He'd do me a mischief if he could. I pray he doesn't get the chance.

A sumptuously dressed young woman drifted through the room at the head of an entourage of several ladies. She scanned

Beth as the others had done, crown to toe, and whispered in the ear of one of her groupies.

Michael chuckled. "It appears the Lady Royal would have you made known to her."

No attention, not now!

The Plantagenets who had so entranced Beth a half-hour ago now seemed sinister, their golden beauty threatening and foreign. *This is their time, their hour, not mine. I'm out of my depth. Lord God, let me not prejudice them against Michael, who will have to stay here while I return home . . .*

If I return home.

She waited until the covey got within a couple of yards, then as Michael bowed she attempted her best curtsey.

"Charming." Isabelle, the Lady Royal, had a soft seductive voice with a barely audible edge. "Quite charming, Lord Michael. I suppose a cousin? A ward?"

"God has placed Lady Bethany in my guardianship for the time being." He replaced Beth's hand on his wrist as if to assist her in rising from her curtsey. "My lady, allow me to make known to you Lady Bethany de Lindstrom, soon to be confirmed as holder of Trevellas manor."

Isabelle gave a gracious smile, but Beth noted it, too, looked sharp. The noble lady studied Beth's clothing in greater detail.

She herself wore two shades of mustard yellow. Her gown was finest samite, the surcote heavily embroidered in scarlet, its neckline and sleeves trimmed with ermine. Unlike her fair brothers, Princess Isabel had deep chestnut hair and brown eyes of a peculiar opacity.

"What a lovely design. Your maids must be very skilled, Lady Bethany."

"I marvel at their abilities, my lady."

Not bad, not quite a thumping lie. I never said my women made it.

Up in the gallery the minstrels launched into a tune one decibel short of raucous, with plenty of tambour pounding and a pulsing melody that set Beth's teeth on edge. Isabelle cast the gallery a single irritated glance.

"You hold Trevellas? Judging from its name, it must be in the west country."

One of the other ladies chirped a soft laugh.

"Indeed it is."

Isabelle gave a delicate shiver. "I cannot envy you, should my father's grace grant you the honor. Myself, I should not want to live sequestered in the country."

Beth's nerves felt raw. "*Au contraire,*" she said on a dismissive chuckle. "I find some of the Cornishmen quite sophisticated." She cast a glance at Michael that even the younger Isabelle could not mistake as casual.

The Lady Royal's eyes narrowed. "Alas, I know little of the—other classes. And less of foreigners. *Sans doute* your people come from the north, with so distinctive a name."

Beth gave a smile her questioner could interpret any way she chose.

"And I saw you speaking with Sir Cadwr. Such a *debonair.* So civilized though he comes from wild Wales where they all practice the strangest customs!"

"It must be the Mortimer connection, lady," put in one of her maids in a timid voice. "Certes that is where Sir Cadwr gets his gentle breeding."

"But that family is of good repute. I trust, my lady, that you do not blame the Mortimers for Cadwr ap Gwillem." Beth gave an involuntary shudder. "I regret to say he impresses me as one tankard short of a full banquet."

Michael coughed on a sip of wine. Isabelle gave a squeak of fury or laughter, Beth couldn't tell which. The princess's expression darkened, but only for an instant. With the air of a besieged castellan welcoming reinforcements to the garrison, she drew a passing woman into their conversational group.

"Lady de Lacey, tell the newcomers of our Mortimer cousins." Isabelle turned away as if unable to bear the conversation a moment longer.

"God's greeting, my lord de Veryan, my lady. What would you know of them?" After introductions, Lady Helewys de Lacey described the Mortimers she knew. "Of course Lord Roger is in high favor. My lady Isabelle is quite fond of him, and indeed, from what little I have seen, most of that kinship seems well-spoken and amiable."

Beth snorted. "Every family has its black sheep, *n'est ce pas*?"

"What have you heard?" Lady Helewys seemed much addicted to gossip, for her brown eyes lit and she leaned forward as if to solicit secrets.

"Heard—naught. Experienced myself, more than enough." Briefly, Beth related her opinion of Cadwr, and ended, "I insulted him, but not until after he affronted me beyond bearing. Sir Cadwr will get comeuppance either in this life or the next."

Lady Helewys's eyes rounded with shock. "You slapped hi—oh, your pardon, my lord. Lord Michael, Lady Bethany, allow me to make you known to Lord Edward."

With the silent stealth of a born soldier, Edward of Woodstock loomed beside Lady Helewys. He sketched a bow, to which Michael and Beth responded in kind.

Lady Helewys introduced them both, and Michael added his lands and titles. "Mostly in Cornwall, my lord," he concluded.

"Aye so," said the future Black Prince mildly.

Beth studied him. Of a height with Michael, he shared the Plantagenet features of intense blue eyes, high cheekbones and narrow, aristocratic nose. He wore parti-colored hose in blue and deep green, a surcote of the same blue color, with sleeves lined in deep green and heavily dagged in the latest fashion. Unlike his sister's, his attire made its statement through rich fabric and subtle good taste. Beside his golden good looks, Isabelle darkened and blurred, a photograph taken in insufficient light.

"I hear you are newly come to England, Lady Bethany. How do you find the Cornish?"

You just look around, and there they are. She bit the jest back, yearning to test the prince's sense of humor, but not daring. If he had none, nobody would be amused.

"They are the finest folk anyone could meet, my lord." She let this sink in before adding, "Those at Mossock in particular manifest truly Christian charity."

Apparently, the prince preferred blunt speech. "Where is your home?"

"At Truro, for the nonce." Beth felt a qualm over her false tale, but comforted herself that soon she must tell Michael the truth. "She who helped me first, Lady Alys de Tallac, believes I was set upon by brigands, and thereby lost both my traveling companions and my memory."

"Indeed." He frowned.

She blanched at the prince's scowl. She hadn't meant to suggest the idea of brigandage as an insult to the king's governance. Images of rat-infested *oubliettes* began to flicker in her mind.

"Since then," she hastened to add, "I must complain of the treatment I have received."

Michael's eyebrows went up, and the soft words on Lady Helewys's lips fell silent. Beth could see amused interest in the small group that had gathered around them. Would the newcomer dig her own grave by griping about the king's rule?

Instead, Beth smiled. "I have suffered overwhelming kindness, ever since I came. No unlucky wayfarer has ever been smothered with helpers so completely as I."

The prince's expression cleared, and he let out an immoderate chuckle, drawing more attention from courtiers nearby. Speculative glances aplenty, and a few frowns of jealousy that the baron's party occupied the young prince's time.

"Veryan, I like your lady. She lacks naught in wit and owns a ready tongue beside."

"Aye, my lord. Her tongue is none too slow out of its scabbard." With an exaggerated gesture, Michael placed Beth's hand back atop his wrist and patted it there as if to say, *Stay put, termagant, and sheathe that ready wit.*

The Lady Royal rejoined their group, her mouth pursed as if she'd eaten a raw frog.

Edward said, "Dinner will be served anon. Do you stay for the dancing?"

Beth looked up at Michael for his answer. "We should not stay," he replied, "for my lady is journey-tired. It is a long and weary ride from Truro, and I would not exert her unduly."

"But you must dine." Isabelle spoke, with a fresh glance up and down Beth's dress. She read mixed motives in that assessing expression. "Edward, we are all ladies at the second table. Come amuse us with tales of *chevauchée* in France, for we grow bored with our talk of gowns and embroidery. There is room for you also, of course, Lord Michael. Lady Bethany."

Michael bowed assent without speaking.

Helewys maneuvered next to Beth as they moved toward the table. "Pay Isabelle no heed," she cautioned in an undertone. "She has a sharp tongue and a sharper nature. Already she repeats whispers that you are Veryan's paramour, and his tastes have slipped since last he attended court." She gave a discreet chuckle. "But I do not believe it. He has the look of a man who wants, not one who has. My lady also says one so fair skinned can never aspire to true beauty. That only means she has weighed her own against yours, and found it lacking."

Beth bit back laughter. Imagine, in a royal court, simple jealousy over something as trivial as looks.

"I will take your good advice." With effort, she kept a straight face. "Please do me the honor of sitting beside me at dinner, Lady Helewys. That is, if you are not obligated elsewhere."

"With pleasure."

They followed Isabelle to the table since the Lady Royal's rank must precede theirs. Michael made sure to sit alongside Beth.

"If she says one word to discompose you," he said in a choked half whisper, "we plead fatigue and leave at that moment."

"So you saw it too? Set your mind at rest. It is nothing of any moment, Lady Helewys says, only woman-silliness. You have greater matters for your attention."

A page offered a spotless linen napkin. "Later, tell me the whole." He held back from further comment as wine was poured. "There are deep matters a-brew. I must put all my mind to keeping Cadwr's neck out of the noose he seems bent on wearing. I have spoken to Sir Walter, the king's receiver here. On the morrow, we will present our petition to the king's grace. I will receive his decision and pay my fine for your seisin. Once the council is finished, we return home." His grim expression lightened. "Perhaps by water. That should amuse you, sweeting."

"Home. That word is sweeter music than the minstrels', dear-my-lord."

"They do play rather badly. You must endure in as much silence as possible. It is but a few days, and then we can depart this court full of miasmas."

"It is almost overwhelming, is it not? You mislike it.?"

"I hate the strain I see here ever since I arrived. All talk of this new law. More than Cadwr fear it. High words over the barons' rights and the church's. Magna Carta has been mentioned. Gossip, half-truth, innuendo. Such tension is irksome and very hard to bear when it has no basis in truth."

"I understand how that is so."

"Each man eagle-eyed to make sure the king's will serves his own betterment. It is usually so, but more this time than I have ever seen. Pah! Everyone acts as if he might starve if another gets a furlong of land or a two-shilling benefice. As though there were hunger in this realm." He made a rude sound. "Since the sickness, I see little dearth. The villeins that remain are fat and their children survive, most of them. They demand, and we must pay, higher wages than ever before. Mayhap that breeds all the disquiet I see. The king and parliament pass laws to put their wages back to the old days."

He shook his head as if in disgust. "They would do better to try stopping the tide with a mattock. We cannot find harvest workers for less than sixpence, a gallon of good ale, and fine white bread. Before the sickness, they were wont to work for much less."

"In the face of such troubles, I should think the new law is but a trifle." Beth dipped her fingers in the *écuelle* and dried them on the napkin. "But if, as you say, every man fears to lose what remains, perhaps the church sees the new law writ larger than it is."

"By the rood, it is true. We have no choice—lords both sacred and secular must change with the new winds that blow, or be consumed by them. Better the harvest be taken up at great expense than rot in the fields." He lowered his voice. "As those facts, so this new law. It may be the right thing. You might lean closer to the truth that the church must play at justice on a level tiltyard with the rest of us."

Beth cast him a glance from under her lashes. "I cannot see how this new law will affect them much, truth to tell. And I should not speak of it. Did you not forbid it, my lord?"

He growled. "Women. Ever quick to obey, an it serve their own desire."

"As you wish, then, but not here. Some might misunderstand—willingly—that I talk of things outside a woman's estate."

His eyes lit. "We wait, then, until we are private." His voice softened on the word *private,* giving it tender connotations. His tone called up warm kisses and soft caresses, not dry discussions of church law and jurisprudence and serfdom.

He took her hand and lifted it formally in that kiss that made her breath come short. "Meet me on the battlements this night, and we will find our privy place, as we did in Truro. I await your views on the troubles of these modern times . . . and on many other things."

Twelve

The moon had risen over Windsor's Curfew Tower by the time Beth mounted the stairs. With a nod to the man at arms standing watch, she slipped into the shadow of a merlon to wait for Michael.

No doubt his vassals still engaged him in political conversation. All his talk with his retainers centered around their hopes and fears over the king's new statute.

She yawned. It was late and she longed for a half hour in restful conversation after the stress of a Plantagenet banquet. She longed also for warm arms and eager attention. On so pleasant a summer night she needed no cloak or mantle to keep her comfortable, but she did need his embrace.

A nightingale emitted its liquid, haunting notes, then flew away. She didn't have to wait long until soft footfalls approached in the star-blessed dark.

"By the rood, I'll be glad to get on the road," Michael growled.

"How soon, dear-my-lord?"

"My vassal at Kingsdown—he did not come, for his lady is just up from childbed—asks that I attend his manor court. Guillaume is persistent, but I may not leave until all business here be concluded, both that of the king's grace and our own." He snorted and slipped his arms around her waist, just as she had longed for him to. "He sent more ill news of Cadwr."

"Tell me."

"Apparently my brother has been in deep speech with Mortimer and a bishop or two. Not Lancaster yet, thanks be to all saints. While Cadwr spoke of it privately to me, it was safe enough. Now they whisper here in corners as though to create real hope of success. My brother is always grasping at this or that wild scheme that come to naught in the end. But an Mortimer be of one mind with them—he sits high in the king's favor. With him or Henry of Lancaster, or both, to speak gentle words of caution, the king may yet think twice. Failing sweet reason, they talk of appeal to the pope to void this new law."

He gave a disgusted sound and clasped his hands together as though to entrap her—though she felt in no wise constrained. Within his arms she felt secure.

"Full often the holy see wishes to grant ecclesiastical benefices, eke before they are vacant, to men of the pope's own choosing—foreigners who know naught of English speech or English ways. As useful they are for shepherds as a silk veil on a sow. They sit in their palaces, thinking grand thoughts and eating a great deal. Worse, they encourage resort to the pope and his Curia as a higher authority than the courts of the country."

"An ill thing, to be sure. But can anyone profit from the reversal of this practice?"

"We will all profit, save the church." He gave a chuckle. "Small grievances now heard in church courts can come to the lords' instead, and matters of the most weight to the king's. And the fines to their purses rather than the church's."

He shook his head with another soft and naughty chuckle. The breeze lifted a dark strand of his hair, making her want to smooth it back into place. But she dared not.

"Copies of the law have been broadcast. I have seen it. The language seems reasonable in my eyes. Any matter that belongs to lie in the king's justice, an it be transferred abroad, the culprit shall have two months in which to answer for contempt of the royal right. Fair enough—the litigants have enjoyed process, as any good Englishman should. Failing answer, they lose all rights, lands, goods, chattels." He laughed. "The king's grace means business this time, and none shall gainsay him. Cadwr and the others should not try to turn back this particular storm."

Beth nodded. The way her head lay against his chest made a verbal response unnecessary. His arms felt warm and sweet. Surely it was not a sin to indulge her need to be held, to listen and be heard, just this once . . .

"Not a bad thing," he went on, "to get back revenue the church squeezes from us and little to show in return. Moreover, opposing the king in this *praemunire* matter—or certes many another—is unwise. One does not challenge a prince unless sure of the outcome. Cadwr—and Mortimer if he be swayed by my oily-tongued brother—do ill to talk 'gainst it. The statute will do us great good and not ill."

"Either way, it will amount to little in the end."

He held her from him. "How say you this?"

She shuddered, wishing she had thought before speaking. "Forgive me. I spoke out of turn."

Michael glowered. "Nay. It will not answer. You have said other such things betimes, and then made excuse. I will not have it more. Tell me how you know this."

It felt as though a cannonball had hit her deep in the stomach. She drew a breath. "My lord—"

"The truth, this time."

Involuntarily she looked to the left and to the right. No escape unless she wanted to take a flying leap off the battlements. His arms, still loosely around her, felt more like a snare than a haven now. She swallowed through a dry throat. Perhaps God's law of truth had caught up with her at last, and the time had come to level with this man she had begun to love.

"Not here." She pushed at his arms, but she'd have had more success shoving the walls of the Curfew Tower. "Let us to a private place. I wish no eager ears to hear."

He said nothing but scowled and let her go as though he'd suddenly remembered he should not be holding something unclean.

Beth sought the door and the stairs that led down. In the tower's hall, she spotted a window embrasure and sought its shelter. Her heart hammered, the pulse sounding loud in her ears.

In the embrasure's privacy, she drew a deep breath to begin, but Michael forestalled her. "The truth, this time. Naught else."

She drew her paternoster from the pouch at her waist and kissed the cross. "I swear it. But, my lord, you must hear first, without interruption or question, while I tell my tale."

"I have listened to many of your tales. Is this yet another having no semblance to truth?"

"You must promise to listen without comment or I can tell you nothing. If you keep interrupting I cannot begin."

In the dim light, she couldn't see his expressions well enough. And it was important that she read how he received her story. He said only, "I will listen."

She inhaled to steady herself. Her next few words—and his reaction to them—might rend her world asunder, and yet she must come clean. God willed it, whether she stayed or left.

"When first I met Sir Geoffrey and Lady de Tallac, when first I came, I let her think I had lost my memory. I did ill to allow it, but I was much afraid."

She shifted her stance, unable to keep still. If only he'd take her in his arms once more and give her courage! A bad idea, for his embrace felt too comfortable. But she had the bit in her teeth now and would continue, come what may.

"I know where my family is, and my past. I came to Mossock from—" She drew another deep breath. "—another time."

"Another time?" His brow creased.

"Yes. I was born in the year of our Lord 1984."

His expression became, if anything, sterner still. "Continue."

"I came to England from—from another land, to finish my studies. I was a student at the university."

His face relaxed a trifle. "A woman, and no priest. Studying at a university."

"I will explain. I know it sounds impossible. I was to join a group at Oxford—"

"Ah, Oxenford." He nodded at her use of a name he knew.

Beth understood his desire to cling to what was familiar. When faced with the new and unnerving, the known gave comfort.

"My school gave opportunity to join English students for a summer. I had hopes—" She reached for memories of those hopes, but couldn't access what that eager, ambitious grad student had felt. "My travel arrangements got befouled, and a kind lady from Cornwall invited me to her home until I straightened them out."

"To Mossock?"

"Yes. I guested there my first night in England. In the morning I awakened quite early and wished to explore. It is such a fine old house. I entered a door into a passage behind the great hall, and . . . and something befell me."

"What?"

Slowly, as in a dream, she shook her head. "I . . . cannot say."

He glared in anger. "Pah. I should have listened to Cadwr when he warned me you were not to be trusted. You *will* not say."

"I would, my lord, if I could. I do not know the nature of what befell." No matter how many deep breaths she took, she couldn't seem to get enough air. "One moment I was exploring Mossock as it exists in my own time, 2010."

He scowled in a fresh spurt of bewilderment or disbelief.

"The next moment I was in Mossock of now—of 1353."

She changed her mind about plunging on. Let him process a moment.

"No brigands. No knock on the head. No loss of memory."

"No. I did bump my head, but the brigands were Alys's invention, none of mine."

"You say you came here from another time."

Though he looked as though he'd rather throttle her than learn more, his questions steadied her, gave her courage. How could that be when his eyes looked so fierce?

"Yes."

"How?" he demanded.

"I cannot tell. I tried once and again in that passage to journey back whence I came. It did not work."

"You came here against your will."

"Not in my will, no. But in God's. So I've come to believe. Before I arrived here, I thought such things impossible."

"You feel this was God's doing? He vouchsafed you this journey? To dwell here among us?"

His mouth remained grim. The disillusion in his eyes made her draw back. She moved as far as she could into the embrasure, her heart sinking at the enormity of the mistake she'd made in confiding in him. She searched for words that could convince him, but he spoke first.

"They say the Almighty loves a good jest. Now I believe it, to my sorrow, for the joke is on me."

"My lord—" What could she say that would take the disgust out of his eyes?

"Why came you here? If this faradiddle is true, tell me why here and not another place."

"I do not know," she returned with all the dignity she could muster. "I spend many waking hours by night, trying to guess at the answer. I have none, unless—" She stopped, the lump in her throat making it impossible to continue.

He doesn't believe me. How can he? If he'd come to my time and told me such a tale, I'd be rolling on the floor, laughing.

He regarded her, arms folded, body language closed and his eyes forbidding. "Tell me of your place. Your people."

"Where shall I begin?"

"Begin here. What would this keep look like, in your own day? What of Cornwall? Of England?" His tone challenged, dared her to tell him more and better lies.

Under her distress she almost laughed aloud at the idea of relating her impressions from riding in a powerful car speeding along the

M-4 or viewing the countryside from a 747 on final approach to Heathrow. "I know little of England, my lord. I come from another country. I had just arrived when I traveled to now—this year."

Words frustrated her. He wanted proof, but how to explain a land he'd never heard of, across an Atlantic no European had yet crossed?

"We dress differently than you. For example, women often wear—" She had to stop to think of the translation. "Breeches."

He looked as though he might keel over from shock, but didn't. "Go on."

"And no veils. Save for very special ceremonies."

Like weddings, which I may never experience in either era.

"Even girls cover their hair. You do not?"

She shook her head.

"Scandalous. Your women must be oft mistaken for harlots."

"Not unless they dress provocatively. And men seldom wear hats, except in winter."

He snorted. "Women. You travel hundreds of years in time—so you say—and can discuss naught but fashion."

"What would you hear?" *What does a soldier, a landowner, a leader of men want to know?* "Let me see . . . we have tools that might surprise you. Tools for mining in the earth and for farming. Ways to let one man do the work of twenty. Instruments—machines—that let people speak, be they separated by many miles. Flying machines that send folk long distances through the air. Carriages that need no horses to run fast along the roads."

"Pah." From an expression of mild interest, he closed off once more, refusing to believe. "Sorcery or lies."

Affronted, she said slowly, "I hoped you would believe me."

"That was ere you told tales wilder than piskies and the giant Cormoran."

She turned her back to him, for a long moment said nothing. At last, he yanked her to face him, and she peered hopefully into his face. She saw no laughter in his eyes.

She must challenge him to belief. "I believe you care for me. Can I trust the love you offer when you think I would tell you lies?"

He studied her, his dark eyes intent. By degrees they softened, but only slightly.

"I must think on't. Perhaps I judge overhasty. Until now, you have done me no ill, but only good. That is not reason to distrust." Frowning, he mused, "Cannot God do what He will? In truth, if He has sent you here from a distant time, then to disbelieve would be a grievous sin."

He hesitated before adding, "I am but a man. I make many errors, sin often. Perhaps this is no different, but my guts misgive me. I may be mistaken about the piskies and Cormoran after all."

Her heart lightened, but he was not finished.

"But I do not think it." He gazed out into the peaceful hall for some time, and she let him have a quiet space to think. In truth, she could not guess at what to say. It was imperative that he acknowledge her story, but she knew not how to achieve that blessed state.

"I do know none can travel through time, save through the black arts. Are you a witch?"

"I am not!" she cried. Tears welled in her eyes and spilled over, though she did succeed in holding back sobs.

He studied her face as if searching for truth in her damp eyes. "Very well. Let us say for the nonce that you speak true. Though it cannot be—" He took a half step back, which made him bump against the wall of the embrasure. "Neither of us can prevail, save if you have proof your words be true."

He held up his hand, forestalling her attempt to answer. "You say you are aware—I have been much taken with you in these days since you came under my care. But I have been wrong about women before. Love can come untimely, be misplaced, mistaken, deceived."

"You speak of Joan? Of your wife?"

"As you say, but leave her from this. An you be not lying or crazed or a witch, an your words are God's own truth, there's a reason why He brought you here. And that reason—heaven grant patience—must include me."

Her very soul quailed at the stark pain in his voice and the suspicion in his autumn eyes. "Dear-my-lord, I do intend you no ill, but only good. I told you my story and you said you would listen."

"But that is all I promised to do. Get you to your quarters, lady. I must put this from me and pray. I have a duty to my God and to my king. I must pray most ardently and most seriously consider whether that duty includes exposing you to the king's justice for sorcery."

Thirteen

A Traveler's Tale. Last night, all unprepared, I told him the truth. I don't know why it came out how or when or where it did—we were talking about this new praemunire *law, and the barons' reaction to it, and whether Cadwr the Surfer Boy might be planning some devilment. I never meant to tell him where I really came from.*

He doesn't buy a word of it. He says he's deceived himself about me. But he spoke of love.

Beth found nothing more to write. She lay her quill down, staring into the fire. Hours had passed since they'd parted in the embrasure, Michael's eyes cold and considering, unaffected by tears she couldn't hold back.

What was she supposed to do now? She wiped her eyes on the edge of her cloak. She'd spent the night trying to sleep, praying, finally giving up on the idea of bed, to wrap her cloak around her and try to dilute pain through the journal. On her floor pallet, Teagen snored, of quiet mind and noisy sleep.

Dawn's pearly light began to filter through the gaps in the wooden shutters. Beth gave up and sought clothing. Nothing too grand, for she of the swollen eyes and sorrow didn't feel up to splendor.

She tightened the gown's laces as best she could, sure that later Teagen would scold and do them up rightly. Donning her cloak, she crept out of the wall chamber and up to the battlements. Perhaps the rising sun held a remedy for grief.

Through a distant bank of clouds, in the direction great London lay, the sun began to make its impact on the land. She watched with a heavy heart as a new day arrived. She feared what today might hold for her, for yesterday that had begun in lighthearted banter, wonder, and warmth, had ended on suspicion and coldness.

She wiped her eyes on her sleeve. *Lord, I don't think I can take much more. I'm not at Mossock where I can seek the portal, but what matters that to the Almighty? Send me home from here, if You please. You see, I've begun to care what Michael thinks, far too much, and I had to see contempt in his eyes.*

A soft scuffing sound on the battlement to her right. She spun, hoping to see Michael, but did not.

"Good morrow, Sir Cadwr." Her heart fell into her shoes, so acute was her disappointment.

"What do you here?" His handsome mouth twisted.

"I seek peace. Since you must seek the same, I will leave you to it, my lord."

She attempted to slip past him toward the stair aperture, but he grabbed her elbow. "Stay. I would ask you certain questions."

"You may ask," she countered, lifting her chin, "and I may refuse to answer."

"An you care for my brother," he spat, "you will answer any and every question I put to you. Or I will toss you to the king's justice."

"On what charge?"

"Sorcery."

Though Michael's use of the word shook her to the core, Cadwr's moved her not a whit. "Pah. Bring forth your charge, for you have no proof and never shall. And you would toss anyone anywhere could it further your ambitions to more than you merit."

The best defense is a good offense. Right?

Cadwr laughed and released her arm. "I spoke with my brother—I do often, of late, knew you this? So far he refuses to support us who are longsighted in England's best interest." He must have seen scorn in her eyes, for he continued, "Oh, we are ample enough in number to get a fair hearing from the king's grace—an there be none of high enough influence to gainsay us."

"Do what you will," she said, "it will avail you naught."

"We *can* prevail, with Michael's voice added to ours. He is high in the king's favor, and Lancaster's—my worldly liege lord." Cadwr looked as though he wanted to spit, but refrained. "And in time, my brother must see reason—could do, if you were not present to exert your malign influence on him."

"Evil? I?" she laughed.

"Aye. Your bond on him is that of witchery. It is widely known the Templars secretly sell magic rings from Saracen lands that produce enslavement."

"Oh, this gets better and better."

"Leave here," he urged. "I will give you escort as far as Truro. Or wherever else—preferably abroad—you wish to go."

"I am not yours to command." She drew her cloak around her. "I come or go at Lord Michael's pleasure, and he has not expressed any wish to see me take ship or horse."

"Not yet." Cadwr's surf-blue eyes took on a narrowed, sly expression. "Not yet. But think again, lady—if lady you are, which I misdoubt. He will not keep you with him. If you hope for more, you are more fool than I think. He will not wed you, portionless and a witch into the bargain. You would do well to take my generous offer and get away. An you choose to stay, you may be of use to me . . . um . . . in other ways. But be warned, I *shall* protect my brother—"

"It is not your brother's well doing you plan for, but your own and that of your abbot," she responded.

He shrugged. "My motives are not your concern. Your own hide should be."

She let a little hissing sound escape her lips and drew her cloak close to prevent its hem from contacting him. "My lord." In her voice she let all her contempt show.

He bowed with a smirk. "My lady."

Beth sped down the tower stairs as fast as was prudent, out the hall door and across the grassy bailey of the upper ward. She passed through the Round Tower on the way to the chapel, for the bells of first mass pealed their call through the brightening morning. With a heavy heart she stood with other early risers and asked silently, in her own language, for forgiveness, peace . . . and an early passage back to her own time.

She did not expect Michael to join her in breaking the fast, but as she picked at a cold pasty, he pulled out the bench and took his place beside her. Nor did he speak, but motioned a page over for whatever refreshment the boy carried. Not until he had drunk it dry did he clear his throat and address her.

"I did not sleep."

"Nor I."

"Went you to mass?"

"Aye." She saw a question in his eyes, and her temper rose. "And it was not to confess lies, an you must know."

"A pox on all that." He waved a hand in the air and the watchful page, misunderstanding, hurried over to refill my lord's cup. "We will not speak of—your story here, but of other tidings."

She inclined her head. "You should know, my lord, that Cadwr came to me this morn."

"As your lover?"

Beth slammed her cup down on the table. "You already know that answer!"

"Speak, then." He ducked his head slightly. "Your pardon. I spent a pestilential night."

His contrition didn't touch her anger. "No doubt you spent it on your knees asking forgiveness. It is great sin to mention love and mistrust in the same breath."

"I did not," he responded. "Play not at words with me, my lady, but speak plain—if you can. What did my brother want of you?"

"My absence."

Michael swore a foul oath and a bite of pasty fell from his eating knife.

"He says, an you oppose his party on this new law, he will denounce me for sorcery and have me handed to the royal justiciar." Beth kept her tone level with an effort, though a qualm went through her on repeating Cadwr's threat. Would Michael believe this, since he had doubted her story last night?

"He has not the power to order you hence, and I give you no leave to depart."

"I am no man's to command," she spat back. "I stay or go on God's will and my own."

Behind the tablecloth he grasped her elbow, but his touch didn't revolt her like Cadwr's had done. "High words, my lady Tale-Teller."

She kept her voice low, that none of the other chattering diners might hear. "Last night I told you the plain truth. If I misunderstand the blessed Lord's intention in bringing me here—well, did you not say it best yourself? I am but a woman and cannot discern all the holy will."

His grip relaxed, though he still scowled fiercely. "Do not misunderstand. Where I love, I wish to believe. I would, but I cannot."

Beth swallowed. "I do understand that. There are moments when I cannot believe it myself."

"Then let us leave that for now and treat as best we might with the other obstacles before us."

He drained his cup and shouted at the page for more wine. Dropping her elbow, he attended to his pasty with renewed appetite.

"I have had another missive from Sir Guillaume, who nags me to attend court at Kingsdown as soon as may be, but I dare not leave with things still so unsettled here. Guillaume talks as if his villeins will be overawed by the sight of me, glowering in full armor and standing behind him while he gives justice. Pah! He has heard court for years. By now, he is well able to judge their small complaints. I think instead he wishes to meet you, the stranger-lady. In any case, we would fare better if the king's grace hasten on this *praemunire* matter, the better to get us on the road."

"You have many matters of more weight," she said, "to occupy your mind, than one unprotected woman with a strange story."

"In truth."

He finished off his pasty and reached to slice a generous portion off a great wheel of white cheese. Beth wondered irritably at his appetite. Shouldn't it be blighted like hers?

From the gallery above the dais, trumpets rang out. The entire company rose to its feet, for the king graced the hall with his presence. Beth's heart beat faster as the family filed in, the king first and on his arm a lady she hadn't seen before. Her figure under a red samite gown and surcote curved heavy with child and she looked tired, but her dark eyes scanned the assembly with kindly interest.

Philippa of Hainault. Has to be.

On their dais, the Plantagenet royalty still looked surreal, something out of a movie. But all too real—the man in the red and gold tabard had the power of life and death over every person here. Including her.

A boy approached Michael's table. Like his betters, the page also recalled Hollywood in red and blue parti-colored livery, the Plantagenet badge of a sprig of broom on his upper sleeve. "My lord, you have matters to present? The king will hold open court this morn."

"Aye, lad. This is Lady Bethany de Lindstrom, my ward. I would enfeoff her with my honor of Trevellas."

Michael's expression had cleared from the disquiet that had made it look forbidding. He rose, beckoning Beth to accompany him, and from his pouch drew a parchment.

Smiling, the page declined it, but beckoned them to a tall, heavyset older man in a short green surcote, and relayed their names. "Sir Walter will announce you, my lord baron."

The older man beckoned them toward the dais where the royal family was making a hearty breakfast of cold roast peacock, stewed pears and Gascon wine. While they waited, the king gestured Sir Walter to wait in order to bend his head toward a fidgety boy.

Kind affection glowed in King Edward's blue eyes, and all attention to the child. One of the sons. *John?* she wondered. *Lionel?* Either way, the leftover historian in her heart marveled at glimpsing the famous Plantagenets at close range.

She kept her gaze where Michael watched. Courtiers chatted; the women sized up her outfit. The tables began to empty as the noble diners, having satisfied the belly, moved on to more important matters, such as flirtation, gossip, and rumor.

Sir Walter ended his brief conversation with the king and beckoned them forward. Michael waited, for the king's grace must speak first.

When he acknowledged them, Michael bowed and replied, "God's greeting, your grace."

His tone sounded firm and clear. Beth thanked God for medieval mores that kept women silent. If she had to speak, her voice would quaver with nerves.

The royal voice rang with the tones of one accustomed to command. "Veryan, what business have you?"

"I have matters to lay before you, for I desire your counsel."

Slick. He knows his stuff, this proud lord of mine.

In few words Michael introduced Beth, described her situation, though he did not mention amnesia or time-travel—not that he bought her story. Explaining that since Joan's family had died in the pestilence and he had come into her dower lands, he made clear his desire to grant Trevellas and its income to Beth, subject to royal approval.

The king toyed with a great ruby hanging from the inch-wide gold chain around his neck and frowned. "Trevellas is one of your richer properties if memory serves. Have you no better use for it?"

Michael grinned. "None comes to mind. Many of the messuages lie abandoned, the lands unsown. I must make inducement for sufficient tenants to bring the manor into profit."

"Free tenants or customary?"

"Mostly free, sire."

I shall free the rest the day the king confirms my tenure, Beth decided. *Unless, of course, I burn for sorcery or find a way home first.*

Edward of Woodstock leaned forward. "One has heard something, Veryan, about freeing your serfs. Now you wish to give away your possessions?" His tone challenged.

"Just this one."

Chatter died. Beth felt her face flush scarlet at her effrontery in forgetting the studied, conformable silence of a medieval lady. Around her, courtiers made rude sounds or tittered behind their hands. She wanted to sink through the rushes on the oaken floor.

The king paused with a gold hanap of wine halfway to his mouth. Beside him, the queen gave a gentle smile as if to say she understood a lady's wish to speak for herself. Edward the younger gaped, then opened his mouth to respond.

The king lifted a quelling hand. "The lady has a voice, *n'est-ce pas?*" His gaze rested on her with appreciation. "Her wit, no doubt, is as great as her beauty. But leave this for now. An odd request, but we will take it under advisement."

"As you will, your grace. We wait upon your decision."

Murmurs of assent and approval. No matter the lady knew not when to speak and when to hold her tongue, Veryan respected court protocol and followed it.

"Attend me on the morrow," Edward said. He turned to Sir Walter, who bent close to hear the king's private word and nodded assent.

Beside her, Michael bowed. She felt a drop in the tension of his body language. So, that meant he trusted that the decision would be a favorable one. She dropped low in a deep curtsey of thanks, but didn't repeat her mistake of speaking.

The rest of the king's statement came through. *Wit and great beauty.* So Edward III thought her good to look upon. What a bone that'd make for Dave Graber or the Millards to chew! Not that she could share this, even if she did somehow find a way home . . .

Michael led her to a spot halfway down the hall, greeting some courtiers with a stiffish nod, others with a smile or a handclasp. Only when they'd accepted fresh wine from the same page—who this time barely concealed a smirk—did Beth feel as though she might risk a remark.

"My, that went well."

Michael sipped, eyeing the courtiers. At a signal from the high table, the minstrels launched into a tune she tried to recognize.

"Aye so. Except for your speaking out of turn, to which I myself have grown well accustomed."

"My lord, the splendor of the court has my wits full addled. Match yours not with mine, but have mercy on their weakened condition."

He gave a soft hoot of laughter, his first since hearing her story yestereven. "You will be weak-witted when I sprout wings and fly. Nay, to answer you true, it went not so ill. Now we wait upon the king's decision, and i' truth, I think it will be a favorable one."

"What of Cadwr and his plots? He mentioned the Mortimers, that they join the church to challenge the king's will. And why would the king listen to that family in any case? Did not the Mortimers cause his father's murder?"

She kept her voice low, guessing that Mortimers might easily be present in the king's retinue. A big, ambitious and acquisitive brood could take umbrage that Veryan called a relative foolish.

"Aye so. But Roger de Mortimer is in high favor. For that reason I have taken certain precautions." He sipped his wine, his stance relaxed from the tension he'd had when addressing Edward III. "I have spoken with Lancaster, among others. We have met and writ our thoughts down that we might more easily recall them at need."

"You can write?"

He looked miffed. "I can, though it is none so easy a skill."

"Have you books?"

He let out a soft guffaw. "Lies, truth, the king's favor, justice—all else pales when my lady wishes a book."

"I can read manuscript. At school I put in plenty of hours . . . "

"Tell me later." He drained his cup, keeping his keen eye on the room.

Beth subsided. He was right, of course. No reason he'd want to resume discussion of a topic that irked and upset him. Of course he didn't believe her. People did not travel in time.

The story was as true as the tale of a wild boar sprouting wings to fly. They did not. That made an end of it.

Fourteen

After their audience, Beth and Michael rejoined the courtiers, while others filed in and out of the royal earshot, ostensibly doing business both legal and personal. They soon found themselves attached to a group that included young Isabelle, the Lady Royal.

Due to her status as royal born and thus entitled to the floor, Isabelle talked volubly. Beth, in her present depression, felt relieved she didn't need to converse. She listened in silence, blessing the princess for leaving little time for anyone else's comments, save to agree.

Isabelle suggested a stroll outside in the gardens of the lower ward, an idea to which both ladies and gentlemen eagerly consented. She led the walk through blooming roses and speedwells, beds of sprouting herbs and elaborately trimmed trellises supporting flowering vines. The whole time, she extolled the superiority of French fashion, French cuisine, and French literature. Frequently she mentioned her betrothed and that gentleman's excellent taste. When she wasn't admiring French ways, she praised her elegant Mortimer cousins.

When she mentioned Cadwr, my lady spoke of his comely countenance and praised him for beautiful manners and admirable piety. Beth ground her teeth over a blistering retort, mindful of Michael's warning gaze upon her. With the lady's cataract of opinions and fawning agreement to steer the conversation, Beth found it easier to concentrate on the beauty of Windsor's elaborate, highly manicured gardens.

At one point, Lady Helewys made bold to comment on Isabelle's admiration of French poetry. "I have heard fine English love poetry—as well as French, to be sure. Does it not please you, lady?"

Isabelle sniffed. "Truly, I have found little to admire from English writers. But the French! Of course, since they invented it, they write best of courtly love."

Just wait till you get a taste of Geoffrey Chaucer.

Beth wasn't aware of making a tiny sound until Helewys nudged her elbow. The Lady Royal pounced. "Lady Bethany, you disagree? Is not Parisian love verse far superior to ours?"

Beth considered for a moment, smiling inwardly, since she'd read French—and English—medieval poetry unknown yet to these ladies. "I have heard little of it. And should the king's grace confirm Trevellas to my care, I will have little time for reading in any language."

Lady Helewys drew a long excited breath and spoke before Isabelle could. "You can read, Lady Bethany?"

Oops. Oh, baby. I mucked this one up. How do I squirm out of it?

"I did learn, Lady Helewys."

"Your father permitted this?"

"I was encouraged to it. I do not read well in English, of course."

Isabelle tittered. "Certes, you do not. Not even my father's grace reads it well. Not surprising, since there is no great quantity of English writing of any merit. Do you know *Le Voir Dit?*"

Having returned the company's attention where it belonged, Isabelle gave a long recap of the tale, adding the entire plot of a mystery she'd seen presented by street players in Caen. Beth picked a sprig of lavender, held it to her nose, and let her mind wander until a hand slid under her elbow.

"Allow me to escort you safely across the gardens, my lady." Michael's voice, edged with steel.

She bowed assent, noting that several gentlemen, having no pressing business, had joined them in the garden. Seeing that one bore a lute, Isabelle urged him to serenade them. Smiling, he invited them to sit on the grass and listen.

With a flourish worthy of an Elizabethan courtier, Michael spread his short cloak on the lawn for the Lady Royal. She giggled and took her seat on it with coy thanks. He returned her smile but bent near to murmur in Beth's ear in fine imitation of an accomplished flirt.

"Come with me as soon as you can break free," he murmured. "There is news. The king will hear petitions at law after dinner. I will present Cadwr's treachery in open court. You must give evidence, an you are called to do so." Glancing at her gown, he added, "You will wish to change your dress."

His eyes glinted warning into hers, and Beth's courage nearly deserted her. "My lord, I would gladly add my voice to yours," she returned in an undertone, "but how can I—a known liar and possible witch—be of any use to you now?"

"If I can use you without betraying your confidence, I shall. Depend upon it."

He bowed for leave to the young Isabelle, who let loose another giggle and waved them off. As they made their way back to the Round Tower, a page darted up.

"Your pardon, my lord—my lady. The king's grace requires your presence."

Beth startled. What could the king need Michael for now that he'd promised to rule on Trevellas in the morning? She cast him an anxious glance.

"Go, my lord. I will bide safe enough here in the garden with the Lady Royal."

Before Michael could answer, the page shook his russet head. "Not so, lady. The king summons you both."

Her blood went cold. For the last few hours, the Plantagenets had ceased to be an interesting species for a historian's detached observation and had become massed threat. Fervently she wished to be safe back at Truro, or Mossock, or even the unknown Trevellas, not here amongst people of power, whom she did not—could not—understand or trust.

From strength deep within, she mustered a smile. "So? Then I will come by all means."

She all but tripped over her own feet, fleeing up the narrow stairs of the Curfew Tower. Teagen helped her change, muttering as she did so about the laces Beth had tied all askew early that morning. And she cursed the gold net for the hair, yanking it off no less than thrice before it pleased her, and finally anchored the gossamer veil atop it with many pins.

"Lady, we maun go to London and seek different head coverings. By the rood, we must! Mayhap cauls can keep this muddle in better order, for sure I can make naught tidy of it . . ."

Beth gave her maid a distracted smile and let her wits wander, wishing only for a quiet corner in which to pray—and maybe weep off the tension.

A Traveler's Tale. If anybody around here feels six inches lower than a snake's navel, it's me.

How to figure men? A complete contradiction, Michael wanting her support when he didn't believe her story. Why would he want a woman to accompany him whom he feared was the worst sort of liar? How would he act when they stood together before the king? Would he repeat her story? Let her be accused of witchcraft? Find some way of linking Cadwr and his buddies to her downfall? It might seem a cheap price to pay to avoid a sovereign's wrath.

She met Michael at the foot of the stairs. The stern look in his eyes, the expression she expected to see since last night's confession, softened slightly as he looked her up and down. It eased her depression only slightly to know at least she had dressed becomingly, in the two-shades-of-green outfit Lady Amicia and her maids had created.

When they arrived in the hall, however, they found not the king but Sir Walter. "My lord baron," he said, "I regret the king is called to Staines on an urgent matter. Though he summoned you, he asks your indulgence. He will return by vespers and asks that you wait in patience until then."

Michael murmured something agreeable about the constant labors of a king. The harried Sir Walter smiled and hurried off to the next task.

So dinner. Fighting anxiety, Beth sat as usual at Michael's side. He did not bring up her story or his reaction to it, but talked of commonplace matters. This courtier, he told her, was in high favor, that one hoped to regain lands he'd lost. She knew not a single name he mentioned and in her current low mood cared less.

The ordeal dragged on through six courses, accompanied always by Princess Isabelle's strident chatter. She had an opinion on every conversational topic and peppered the dinner with all of them.

Cod, lamprey, sturgeon. Venison, goose, mutton and beef. Vegetables in every sort of piquant sauce. Fruit boiled or poached to mush, for the medievals thought fresh fruit unhealthy.

Between courses, entertainment took the center of the hall to divert the increasingly sated diners. A troop of gleemen tumbled and juggled small leather balls, sharp-looking knives, and flambeaux. A singer in a diaphanous gown shocked the Lady Royal with a plaintive ballad in the *langue d'oc,* which Isabelle claimed to understand.

Later a tame bear lumbered out, put through his paces by his trainers. When men baited the bear with a torch and sharpened sticks, Isabelle shrieked with laughter and clapped her be-ringed hands. Beth turned her face away.

"How soon may we decently leave?" she murmured under her breath.

Michael found her hand under the tablecloth, which shocked her. Should a man who disbelieved offer a squeeze of comfort?

"Anon. The entertainment is not to your liking?"

"Not in the slightest. Where I come from, we consider such cruelty an affront to God. Which it is."

"All men are capable of cruelty."

She thought of her own century. Lynchings, drug-related murders, pit bulls, terrorism, child abuse, prizefighting, two world wars. "You are right. Human nature apparently does not change."

"Sad, but so." He released her hand, looking thoughtful rather than sternly distrustful. His slight thaw heartened her. Was there hope?

At last the master of revels announced the subtleties. To a crash of cymbals, sweating servitors in Plantagenet blue-and-red trotted in, each pair bearing a huge silver tray with a fantastic pastry beast. A grinning cook followed each creation. The most elaborate beast went to the high table, but the servitors made sure the tables of Edward of Woodstock and the Lady Royal received the next best. Isabelle barely glanced at the subtlety, breaking off a piece of the gryphon's face and continuing her torrent of conversation. Beth marveled at the delicacy of the sculpture. The gryphon's candied-cherry eyes glowered a fierce challenge, its wire-framed wings of red-tinted spun sugar ready for flight.

"You do not try the subtlety, my lady?"

"It is too wonderful to destroy, dear-my-lord."

He smiled and broke off a piece of a rampant claw. "Destroy it we must or insult the cooks' mastery of their art." He chewed and made a mouth-full noise of appreciation. "Cherry, methinks. Go on."

Following his lead, she broke off a second claw. The beast had changed from menacing to funny, missing half his snout and an entire talon.

"Cherry, most definitely."

King Edward apparently returned from his urgent errand in time for the subtleties, for the page came to them while the high table demolished a lovely creation. Beth guessed that after twenty-some years as sovereign and a youth in the court of his homosexual father and adulterous mother, it took more than multicolored pastry engineering to thrill him. The boy led them down a short corridor and through the big paneled doors that led to the king's privy apartments.

"My lord, baron de Veryan and the *demoiselle* Bethany."

"Well done, Giles. Go and get your dinner."

The page bowed and left them. Michael approached the desk at which the king sat, looking weary and making marginal notes on a large script-covered parchment. At his side sat the queen and behind them hovered a magnificently dressed, heavyset man in his early forties, who favored one foot by standing heavily on the other. Nearby, two retainers in pale blue and gray livery stood at the ready. At a stand-up desk, a Cistercian monk in white worked on another parchment, moving his lips silently over words and phrases.

The king glanced up from his writing and laid his goose-feather quill aside with a sigh. "Ah, Veryan, so seldom seen at court. Earlier I neglected to mention the honor you do us by your attendance at this important time."

Beth glanced at Michael. A smile quirked his handsome mouth as he took a second to frame a reply. "My lord king, you honor me by noticing." He directed a respectful nod at the other gentleman and ignored those in blue and red.

"Yet you come now full of petitions and rumors. Very well. I suppose we must let this matter air, though I am not yet full ready. Let us return to the hall, and we will hear your public matter in open court. To complain behind the hand is not your way. What beside this *belle demoiselle* could make you do so?"

"Sire, ere we rejoin the court, I would explain."

Edward rested his elbows on the parchment. "I am all attention."

"I set out from home much troubled in spirit, for my bastard brother did visit Truro with so many complaints and ill tidings that I wrote to Lord Henry asking his counsel. While we were on the road here, I bethought me of Trevellas in regards to my lady. In that matter we await your answer in patience and confidence of your goodwill."

Edward grinned. "Go on."

"Since we arrived at Windsor, my brother confirmed—openly to my lady Bethany—that he is become ensnared in a foolish plot against your grace's stated will."

The king's gaze fell again on Beth, and she cast her gaze down toward the carpeted floor in due—but feigned—modesty. Under her surcote, her heart thudded in apprehension. "Lady Bethany, tell me what befell."

Beth swallowed. "My lord."

Although the queen looked sympathetic, the Cistercian studied her much as Father Stephen had done back at Mossock—as if she were a captured rabbit in a snare. His nose seemed to twitch as if he scented duplicity even before she opened her mouth.

Beth kept her account brief, relating only what Cadwr had said that affected the realm at large, omitting all personal threats and insults, and particularly eschewing any reference to sorcery or lies. Best, she figured, to stick to the facts as a man would.

"Aye—hmm. You say he wishes to draw Veryan into that party? To protect Lord Michael's interests should this law be put into effect?"

"So much he said, sire."

"Yet I read in your eyes that you do not believe it."

Beth admitted her skepticism.

"Very well. Why did he tell this to you—a woman?"

"I would answer," said Michael, and the king nodded. "Cadwr guested several days at Truro. Down to the spit boys, all there know the lady and I are much attached." He paused to let that sink in, ignoring her small sound of shock. "He had been blind and deaf not to notice. Your grace, my brother and I are in no wise close, but his claims he would protect my interests are blatant rubbish. He would drag me into this affray of the abbot's designing for his own ends. Cadwr cares not about my well doing. His true wishes are to advance *his* ambitions, and if possible, those of his liege lord."

Michael cast a glance toward the friar before adding, "Mayhap he feels some unholy envy. I made no secret that I would seek leave to marry."

Beth's heart skipped a beat. *He speaks to his liege lord of marriage?*

The Cistercian made a disparaging sound but was silenced by a glance from the king. "One has heard something of it. And, Brother William, Christians do well to join in marriage. The realm is sadly diminished in population, some shires by half. Since so many are dead of the pestilence, it is our will that good people live together in amity and breed up heirs." The king's astute blue eyes glinted with sudden mirth. "And of course, that those heirs pay just taxes to the crown and proper tithes to Holy Mother Church."

"Naturally, sire," murmured the Cistercian.

"Henry, what say you to this tale of priests and plots?" The king turned to the sumptuously dressed gentleman behind him, who had listened in silence. "I collect Cadwr ap Gwillem holds lands in the Marches of you. What do you make of this?"

Henry—of Grosmont? Beth swallowed hard as she recognized the gentleman as the noble and keen-minded duke of Lancaster. An unassuming-looking man with a tired posture and bags under his eyes, the duke nevertheless projected a quiet dignity.

"The lady's story cannot be false, sire," he said, his voice cultured, his demeanor indicating integrity and strength. "It fits well with Sir Cadwr's character. Would I could deny it."

He examined a thumbnail as if thinking. "These last years I ordered him to remain on his own lands, to give them due care. We lost many villeins in the Marches. Since the pestilence I see many who fear unduly, and trust not in our Lord and the efficacy of His saints. They count not on His provision but instead strive for their own welfare. Cadwr suffers much anxiety over money and the getting of it. Biding at home did not better his lands' condition, but worsened it. He plots out of fear, sire—fear he will be reduced to poverty."

Beth murmured, "I believe he means well but may be misled by others, and thus used by them."

Henry of Lancaster nodded slowly. "Not impossible. Does he bear you some grudge, Veryan?"

"His words betray him. He has come to see the whole world as enemy." Michael changed his stance to an aggressive one. "But I have remedy. Let me meet him in fair combat to decide between church and crown. My brother should not plot obstruction of your will, sire, but bring his concerns to you privily or through my lord of Lancaster. I shall prove his treachery on his person."

"That cannot be," said the king.

"My lord, by your leave, I insist."

"Nay, Michael, not at this time," said Lancaster. "Compose yourself in patience. Let his poisonous plant grow as it will for a little while, and we shall deal with it in fuller flower."

Michael released a feral growl. "By then he will flee incontinent in fear of my sword."

"In shame, rather," put in Henry gently, "at discovery."

"I doubt he feels much of shame, my lord," said Beth. "He sees me and Veryan not as children of God, but as means to an end."

The king stirred on his ornately carved and gilded chair. "Justice sees it differently, lady. My ruling, then. Since you are neither Veryan's wife nor chattel, you may not give evidence against Bridgnorth. And Lord Michael, I must offer you no justice, unfortunately. You shall not make the truth known on your bastard brother's body."

Michael bowed his head, accepting the king's decree, though with no show of happiness.

"However, lady, you have done us good service. What reward do you desire?"

"Sire, you are kind and gracious. I would have only Trevellas and peace. I know little of English justice, but your reputation is known by all. You will be fair. As my own lord, I would have the baron speak for me. His voice is mine."

Michael brightened visibly, casting her an appreciative look.

The king burst out laughing. "Take care, Veryan," he chortled, casting a meaningful glance at the queen. "Even an unwed lady knows ways in which sweet obedience may bend a man to her will."

At Beth's side Michael reached for her hand and raised it to his lips in the gesture she loved, the one she had longed for these past stressful hours. "Very true, sire. I shall tread carefully. Wise as a serpent, gentle as a dove is my lady."

"Veryan, ever you surprise us. First the wisdom of a graybeard, then the passion of an eager lover. You know, lady, that this madman frees his serfs? Look well to your lands, or he will practice his wild ways on those also. Is it your desire, Lady Bethany," asked the king, "that he free your villeins?"

Her mind sprang to attention. "With all my heart, sire."

"It takes a husband as well as a liege lord," put in Henry of Lancaster, "to do that."

His royal grace let out a booming laugh. Next to him, the queen leaned to whisper into his ear behind her hand.

"Aye so, my dear. It was ever thus. Let you to church," the king said on a last chuckle. He waved his hand and Lancaster poured him wine. "Veryan, get her soon wedded and well bedded. Oft with child and close to the hearth. Someday you may hope to tame that ready tongue."

Michael made a face. "Sire, I have reason to be full grateful to God for her, just as she is."

Marriage. The king speaks of marriage, and Michael isn't shuddering like a man under a dentist's drill. I can't say anything now, and maybe it's better to play the submissive maid a while longer. Later, though, dear-my-lord the skeptic, I may give you the short side of this ready tongue!

The king sobered. "Henry, Cadwr is your vassal, and you may do with the scut as you will. But we must hear the matter in open court. Later on, if all goes our way, I recommend disseisin. Bridgnorth offends honor by not voicing his concerns direct in your ears or mine. Instead he skulks and plots, unbecoming behavior for a knight. Enough. Lancaster, do you talk with Simon Islip. He can keep his unruly abbot in check. The godly faction is best dealt with in its own house, but see to those Marcher keeps yourself. They are too vital to entrust to such hands as Cadwr's. *Sans doute,* they need good oversight to make up for long mismanagement."

"Many lands in the Marches want for good stewardship, sire," Henry put in gravely. "A vassal comes to mind I have long wished to reward, one who fought with great bravery at Sluys."

The king's countenance brightened when reminded of his great naval victory.

Subtle, my lord duke, she thought admiringly. *Subtle and sly.*

"As you will. Now, what fine shall I take from Trevellas? Veryan, we will come to terms easily enough. *Zut,* why linger you here? Haste to your wedding, lest my good lady and I withdraw our royal blessing." The king winked at Beth, and she dropped him a deep and relieved curtsey.

Michael took her cue and bowed. The teenaged page showed them out of the presence chamber, and Beth could breathe again. Once the page left them in the corridor outside the great hall, she put a hand to her embroidered bodice and gave a deep sigh, the first it seemed she'd drawn in hours.

"As we say where I come from, whew!"

"We say that here, also." Without ceremony, not seeming to care if they were seen, Michael grabbed her hand and drew her out into the sunny bailey.

"Now, wench," he said into her ear. "We talk."

"My lord," she said, her heart dropping, "there is naught more to say."

"*Au contraire, ma belle.* There is a great deal more."

He kept tugging until they reached a corner of the lower ward, behind some stacks of shaved stone and large timbers intended for the construction projects. Here they were screened from all eyes.

Michael glared at her, but for some reason the ire in his eyes did not frighten her. "Well done. You have got what you wanted in all ways, I think."

"No, I—" Whatever she'd thought him ready to accuse her of, it wasn't this. "What do you mean?"

"That you, a dowerless, friendless stranger, with a wilder story than any wandering minstrel can fabricate, achieved the king's order to marry—" He compressed his lips for a moment. "—me."

Had he heard something different than she'd heard? "The king's grace gave no such order."

"Have you pottage in your ears? You heard him give permission!"

Though he raised his voice, strangely she still felt no sense of threat. His upset, whatever its source, did not reach her.

"Oh, that. Permission isn't an order," she said, relieved. "You know I must find a way to go back to my own time and my family. The king but meant it as a jest, I am sure."

"Not so. He did command us. But you know his grace so much better than I."

Beth smiled, certain now he was teasing. Through all this remonstration, he had not let go of her hand, nor had she released his.

"My lord, as you have already forgotten, I know naught."

"You have the right of it. You know nothing."

He seemed to realize he still held her hand, for he ran his thumb over her knuckles. Then he surprised her.

"If we are to wed, I should know more. You must tell me more of this strange land whence you came."

Fifteen

"Tell me," Michael said, "how you live. What you do."

"Did." Beth's stomach churned from more than the aftereffects of stress. To answer she must recall a life that now seemed a distant memory. "Remember, I do not know how to go back to my time. For all I know, I may never learn the way of it."

"You are frightened, and rightly so."

"Aye."

More than he knows. What am I supposed to do if he still disbelieves and feels forced to marry? If he loses this little affection he seems to have for me, I'll have nobody here. Nothing and no one.

"You claim you can prove this tale. I have never heard its equal. You must forgive if it is difficult of belief. I have many questions."

"Ask them. I will give you true answer."

He took a seat on a pile of lumber and stretched out his long booted legs. "Let us agree, for courtesy's sake, that this wild story is purest truth. I would know why. Why you and not another? This—this journey across the ages was something you desired? Did you pray God to permit it? Or have you machines in your time to make such journeys possible? Or do folk often tumble all unready into another time?"

Beth frowned. "No. I used no machine, no contrivance to travel. And I would not have dreamed to pray for something I thought impossible. But Michael, God is sovereign. When He moves, I must accept, though I don't understand."

He digested this for a moment. "What of your time do you miss?"

She sighed. "Plenty."

"Tell me."

"Oh, so many things. Washing. We bathe daily in a special small room with warm water pumped from a nozzle in the wall." She saw by his expression he didn't get *nozzle,* but she let it slide. "Ice cream. Pizza. Dark chocolate. Tomatoes. Shoes that keep out the wet. A hot drink called coffee, of which we are very fond."

"We will obtain it for you."

Beth laughed, her spirits rising by the minute. *He does care. He says I'm a liar or a witch but betrays how he really feels.*

"The coffee plant does not grow in England."

"What else?"

Looking down, she whispered, "My mother."

"Ah." There was sympathy in his tone. "And your father?"

"He died when I was but a child. I hardly remember him."

"He died of the pestilence?"

"We have no such. And for many of those illnesses, we have potions to heal them."

"You have no brothers, no sisters."

"No. There's no one except my mother."

He remained silent for a moment, and finally asked, "What miss you not?"

She considered. "Hurry. The idea that there is never enough time to do all one must. And certain stenches—I will not explain further, for those plants do not grow here either. And crowds. There are many more people in my time, and much congestion and noise. It seems peaceful here. At home, there is little quiet."

He gave her a tentative smile. "There is scant peace here either. What would you rather have—peace or your marvelous muzzle that spews forth wash water?"

"Nozzle," she corrected on a laugh. "I must go back to my own time . . . of course." *And yet . . . and yet . . .*

"Do you think you will go back?"

"Needs must."

"That would mean *le bon Dieu* makes mistakes."

"No," she said, startled. "Perhaps He sent me here to grow closer to Him. To regain the joy of first knowing Him."

His eyes gentled. "You have always known Him. The first day you came to Truro, I cared naught for caution, for I saw the love of God in your eyes."

She took her turn to offer a smile of gratitude. "You saw what wasn't there. At least, not yet. Before I came here, I did not even pray. But I offered Him my life once more, and I am determined to follow Him closer than I have yet done. I try to pray *in* His will now, and not ask that He do what I desire. At times lately, I wonder if He has work for me to do here. Some special task. Perhaps a thing people of this time cannot do."

He regarded her, his expression open and level, considering. "Cannot or will not."

She agreed. People here did have different attitudes, mores, mindsets than those she'd grown up with. Did those mindsets make this unknown task unthinkable for them, but not for a time traveler?

"Will not? Possibly. When I find the task, it might become clearer. You have much knowledge lost to us in my time. And, forgive me, but I know things that your people do not."

He shifted on the chair. "And this is your secret? While you prattled of losing your memory, this was the truth you did hide?"

"Aye, that's it."

"*Incroyable.*"

"You can easily understand why I hid it. If you, my lord who knows me best, cannot believe, what chance have I with others?"

"There must *be* no others. Tell no one this tale."

"Never."

"And you realize, of course, that you must say naught more of your own age." He considered her, frowning. "You know matters that have not yet fallen out?" She nodded. "Then you agree that you must not talk of them. Doing so might change what must be."

"I have thought so myself. My lord, if you knew what improvements I could suggest, how our ways could make your lives easier . . . "

"That is devilish temptation. You may not yield to it if you are to remain here."

She stamped her foot in frustration. "How can I know if I am to remain?"

He thought for a moment, his eyes lifted to the lowering sky above Windsor's secure walls. "A storm comes. Look you there. There is rain in those clouds."

Michael returned his gaze to her, and his eyes had softened to that tender autumn hue she loved. "God will vouchsafe a sign. If He permits us to come to the church door to wed, we will know His agreeable will. Bethany, sweeting, I saw from the first, though you withheld much, there was no guile in you. I would believe your story—I would, but I fear to do so. It runs against all I know to be true. And yet . . ." He sighed. "The priests say God's ways are unknowable by man. And how does your journey in time fit into so *inconnaissable* a plan? What base have we to understand? And yet, since He loves us true, why would He hide His plan for us?"

He shook his head slowly as if bemused. "My belief or unbelief I must put aside and trust Him who made us both. God has placed you in my path for His own purposes. If those purposes include taking me to husband—" He pulled her to him and pressed an unhurried kiss on her brow. "—who am I to say Him nay?"

Sweet that he let her know his heart. And yet though he said he wished to trust her, he freely admitted his fear. As he drew her close, Beth clenched her eyes tightly shut and gave herself up to the tender kisses he pressed on her face. For some moments she remained so, clinging to what could not be.

"Michael, let me go. We must consider, we must take care. What if we . . . marry?" Her heart constricted at the mere saying of the word. "What then if I'm called back to my own time? It could happen, you know. Mayhap a fortnight after. Or years. What if I must leave you? Our children? I could not bear it."

He gave her a firm kiss on the mouth. "That must not happen. I shall pray and offer rich gifts to holy church for your safety. If this story be true—and I do not say I believe, only that I am willing to agree that *you* think it true, in good faith—if true, our blessed Lord vouchsafed you to me. He will not be so cruel as to tear you away."

"But we cannot know that! We don't know His purposes."

He toyed with her light veil. "Do we not? For what other intent did He send you to my time, if not for this wild journey, to share my life and be my lady?"

She chose her words carefully. "I release you."

"Only the Lord God can do that." He chuckled and withdrew a pin. Beth clutched at the veil so it wouldn't slip off. "I thought not of asking God for anything, till you reminded me of it."

"You did not pray during the pestilence time?"

"Oh, aye. All did. We prayed and made vows . . . but you say we ought to pray *in* the will of God, not for our own desires. When I knew at last that I would have you stay, I asked if it be in His will, He would grant me this boon."

He removed another pin and the veil slid off. He snatched it up in his hand and stuffed it up his sleeve.

"In His great goodness, He has."

The veil no longer hid her ears so he kissed below one, making her shiver.

"Don't do that." She pressed her lips to his jaw, trying to distract him. "If we are to consider this at all, I must ask one duty of you."

"Name it."

She drew a deep breath. Once home had seemed a dream. Now it tasted more like a nightmare.

"To test my presence here. In the Bible, it says a believer must try every spirit to see if it comes of God. When we arrive again in Cornwall, I must to Mossock—and try the portal once more. I do not wish to return, but you see I can only try."

He opened his mouth for a roar of protest. She cupped her hand over his lips.

"This is no idle whim, but necessity. I would remain here, but that may not be my destiny. If I can go back, it must be soon, for I cannot live forever in between. Especially now. I need to know."

Into her kiss, she tried to put all the love in her heart. "If you love me, take me there. Once we are finished at court, let us visit Mossock."

"Nay. Mossock is where you emerged. It is too dangerous."

"An I visit there, and return not to my own time, then I will marry you."

"You speak lightly of risking all."

"I risk nothing lightly. Least of all the chance I might leave. And I risk nothing that was ever ours to begin with. You forget I was born in 1984."

He ran a fingertip over the front of her hair where the snood left it uncovered. "I forget naught."

Beth tugged her veil from his sleeve and gave a broken laugh. "Men—and women too—forget far too much when it comes to love."

The baron left her at the door of the Curfew Tower. His kiss to her hand made her knees weak.

"Until later, lady, at supper. Keep you far from my brother, and remember—tell none what you have told me. I must speak with Abbot Boniface, see if sweet reason can turn him from this ill-starred path."

"I promise it, my lord." She gave him a tender smile, for what could warm her heart more than his statement that he was willing to believe her? "After supper, I may find items that can prove my story to you, an you wish to see them."

His eyes widened. "I would see them now."

"Later. My lord." She bent her head and dropped him a curtsey. "I am sure there is sewing needing my urgent attention."

She climbed the stairs, wishing only for an empty chamber, that she might rest near the window and think over the tumult today had already brought. What more would the evening offer?

Stress. Regardless of century, there's always disquiet, always turmoil.

Blessed silence in her chamber. Beth stripped the snood from her hair, lay it and her crumpled veil on the bed for Teagen to see to later. She hung the green surcote on a wooden rod near the window shutters, opened them and gazed out at dark-gray clouds.

Storms. Ever these mists and storms.

Storms—the human kind—resulted from sin, and man's nature always to want advantage over others. Peace was found only in God. She realized that now. From the pouch at her waist she removed her paternoster and gazed in the failing light at the Man on the crucifix.

"Lord, You never promised there would not be storms. You only promised You would stay with me and never leave."

It felt right to get on her knees, so she did that. A flash of light from outside distracted her, so she closed her eyes. The thunderclap shook the shutter, and the first fat drops spattered against the thin strips of wood that formed its louvers.

Beth began to pray. As she whispered words of praise, tears came, and she bent double on the plank floor, her heart awash in contrition.

I walked far from You. You, who promised not to leave me—I left You, and now I have the temerity to ask for Your help.

Father God, I've sinned exceedingly in Your sight. My sins aren't the overt ones. I've done no murder, stolen nothing. My sins are the deeper kind: self-aggrandizement, ambition, and pride. I thought I could handle a short trip into the Middle Ages. A lark, something I could use to my own benefit. But I was wrong.

I can't handle it. I'm just about lost in my own age, and I can't cope with this one. I told Michael the truth without praying about whether the time was right, and of course he's skeptical. I don't blame him. In his shoes, I wouldn't believe me either.

"But he says he would believe what is unbelievable," she whispered aloud. "If that isn't love . . . I do love him and I'd stay with him, but only if it's *right*. Father, show me what I must do. Let me tread Your path and not mine. Lead me in truth, for in You alone I find the right way."

She sat back on her heels, wiping her face on both sleeves. While she'd wept, the rain had increased to a lash, as though the very heavens echoed her turmoil.

It's true what they say. Sin is the sharpest blade. It leads us into wrong attitudes and those separate us from Him. The problem is that after a while it feels so normal. One tiny step at a time away from His love.

She rose and went to throw back the shutters. Into the room the storm blew, but the rain hit as a cooling balm to her tear-scalded face. The thunder built to a crescendo, then slackened, dark clouds drifting away east, toward London town. She stood motionless, for as the storm ebbed it left behind quiet in her soul.

Pale, timid shafts of sunlight pierced the clouds from the west, contrasting starkly with the thunderheads and shedding gold mist over the upper ward. It glowed also in Beth's heart, telling her at long last she'd set foot onto a firm path.

No matter how comforting that thought, a first step was not the entire journey. She remembered Sheila's enigmatic words: "Passion isn't always easy . . . you'll need all of yours, and more of strength, to finish your journey well."

Passion she had, aplenty. It was God's guidance she'd lacked.

She turned from the window and went to the ewer on its stand in the corner. She splashed water on her face and donned a plain blue surcote over the green gown, twisting like a rag doll to do up the laces without Teagen's help. As though Beth's need had summoned her, the maid burst in through the door.

"I came to help you make ready, lady. The rain is gone, and for sure they are about to blow the supper horn."

"I managed." She gave Teagen a smile.

The maid clucked her tongue and re-did all the laces, patting the snood back into place and tucking stray curls back into their confines. Beth refused the veil, saying she'd had enough of feeling like a covered high table.

Supper at Windsor, she found, was conducted less formally than dinner. Though the diners were still seated according to strictest protocol, the master of ceremonies called them to prayer before the royals took their places at the high table. Servitors brought large tureens of soup and mixed greens in silver bowls big enough to bathe a baby. They served forth huge cheeses, roasted mushrooms, marchpane, berry comfits, meat-and-egg dishes encrusted in pastry, round, hot loaves of bread, and an entire roast goose swimming in a tinted pastry crust for each table.

Down the space between tables, jongleurs sang, pacing slowly with their lutes and gitterns. Beth recognized many French lyrics and occasionally a thread of English. Tumblers capered around the jongleurs and between them, mocking their elegant lyrics with raunchy paraphrases, and poking fun at diners and musicians alike.

Fortunately, no bear.

Michael entered late with Lancaster, Sir Andre, and other men Beth didn't know. He gave her a slight nod as he took his seat and accepted water from a skinny page bearing an ewer. Taking his nod to mean he had indeed been able to speak with the churchmen, she leaned forward, eager to hear good news.

"If only," he said crossly, "you spoke Cornish. I have much to tell you, and I dare not say aught here in common tongue. Too many eager ears."

"Teach me Cornish, my lord." She accepted his pewter cup of wine and drank from it, wiping its rim with the table napkin afterward so he could drink.

"It is none so easy a language to learn." His expression slowly relaxed as he chose a portion of goose and served it onto her trencher, then his. "Mayhap if I had many years for the teaching—"

He broke off, for all stood. The king's party entered, with Edward looking at ease. He gave an expansive gesture that the diners should continue, and they all re-seated themselves. Michael returned his attention to his trencher and to Beth, speaking low and inclining his body slightly toward her.

Beth understood his ploy and took no offense. As he whispered in her ear the gist of his earlier conversations, no casual eye would see more than a man in an amorous posture. When she responded in kind with little chuckles and lighthearted answers, his eyes warmed and his body language relaxed still more.

"You play the coquette well, lady," he murmured, pulling a curl from under the gold cords of her hair net. "Plenty of practice?"

"None whatever," she said, batting his hand down from her hair. She'd look like a Halloween fright wig if he didn't quit. "Leave my hair alone, *s'il vous plait,* and tell me more of what fell out."

"I was right about my brother." He released an almost inaudible sigh. "I had words with my lord Mortimer privily before I confronted Cadwr. The earl is sympathetic to the church's predicament, but will not flirt with opposing the king. One party wishes to travel behind the king's back. They would appeal to the pope to renew England's vassalage to the holy see."

She shook her head. "Like unto the matter of King John?"

He snorted. "I do believe you know England's past, sweeting. Aye, it would fall out like those evil days an we allow that to happen. It must not do! Mortimer, thank St. Petroc, says he has some sympathy for the scheme, but is not convinced. My brother, like a loose arrow, tells any listener that my lord Mortimer is totally sold on this *maudite* idea."

"He should not dare," she murmured. The idea that she, Bethany Lindstrom from Chicago, was embroiled, however nebulously, in an intrigue involving pope and crown, put her stomach on edge. She laid her eating knife down and beckoned a page for a refill on their shared wine cup.

"He dares much he should not," Michael went on, halting only for a moment while the page poured wine from a large silver pitcher, then withdrew. "Mortimer has the right of one worry, however. All know the king's privy purse carries a staggering amount of debt. Through that debt, the king might be influenced to make decisions that fall out ill for the realm—not just church or barony."

"Is this debt so vast, then?"

"None know for sure save the barons of the exchequer—and their lips are tight-sealed. But rumors say my lord owes obscene sums to Florentine and Lombard bankers."

Medieval loan sharking. Beth shook her head. "What can be done?"

"Lancaster and I have evolved a plan." He drank again and chose a slice of cheese, offering Beth the same. She shook her head. "I fear you must be silent party, if not actively involved, for Cadwr offered you grave insult. Because of that I must use your name to introduce my complaint."

"You broach the matter publicly as the king said?"

"Aye, here, tonight. In open court. Lancaster and I will play it out like mummers at Twelfth Night. You will see."

He munched cheese and looked mildly amused. Ire rose in her.

"You risk much through your playacting, my lord Veryan."

Michael turned to look her full in the face, mirth gone from his eyes. "Certes we play for high stakes. You must support me to your fullest, nor show fear, Bethany. Your safety may depend on our well doing."

Sixteen

At the end of the table, the jongleur ended his tune with a flourish and a huge grin. Michael dug in his belt pouch and pressed a small coin into Beth's hand. Copying the gestures of other guests, she flung it toward the minstrel. He caught it adeptly in midair, kissed it to her with a saucy wink, and bowed, grinning the while, before he moved on to another table.

Better than the mariachi band at the Guadalajara. With only a mild pang of nostalgia, Beth remembered her favorite south-of-the border restaurant. And then felt guilty over allowing herself the distraction.

For Henry of Lancaster took the jongleur's place, stepping forth into the lane between the guests' tables. He looked every bit the ranking duke, in tunic and surcote sparkling with cloth-of-gold sleeve linings and real gemstones. Around his shoulders he bore the great gold triple-S collar of Lancaster, and the Order of the Garter badge fastened his tunic collar.

He was worldly-wise, devout, and magnificent.

"Sire," Lancaster said in ringing tones, "there is a matter I would bring before your court."

Edward put down the drumstick of a roast goose, feigning mild surprise rather well, Beth thought. Michael had told her Lancaster's petition would be no shock. They'd already planned the scenario down to the last breath.

Now, Lord, be with them all, that it plays out aright.

"Since the pestilence—" Beth saw several diners make a doleful sign of the cross as Lancaster spoke. "—the realm has naturally been at some pains to come to terms with changes. Harvests are good, yet times are hard. The barons must pay ever more for labor on their lands, and villeins are not wont to follow the old customary duties with such good will as in our fathers' time."

"Aye so," and "Certes, it is true" were murmured from many throats.

Beth listened with rapt attention. What historian would not give his eyeteeth to watch Edward III's court hear a matter and render opinion?

"The church also suffers. On her lands labor is just as scarce as on ours."

More murmurs of assent, particularly from the table nearest the dais, a colorful assembly of red cassock, brown habit, white cope, and black monk's hood. "Those there are who fear the church in her necessity might require more out of England than is due."

As if on cue, Michael pressed her hand under the table, and rose. "My lord of Lancaster, I would speak."

"Come up, Veryan." Lancaster motioned Michael up and he strode to his place at the duke's side.

Beth's heart melted. Her lord stood equal to Henry of Grosmont, tall and square-shouldered, less richly dressed but every inch a baron amongst his peers. To her eyes, he had no equal, for there was not a man in King Edward's crowded hall she would look on twice with Michael de Veryan present.

"As you know, your grace, I have in my protection one lady, Bethany de Lindstrom by name," he began, but was interrupted.

Roger, Lord Mortimer leaped to his feet. "What has a woman to do with such dealings? My lord, Veryan's protection of this woman—who I am told practices the dark arts—can be of no moment here."

Beth felt her face drain white. But Michael seemed forewarned and forearmed. "My lord Mortimer, you listen overmuch to a bastard brother of mine, and one often in his cups."

Titters of laughter around the hall. From his clerical overlord's table, Cadwr glared.

Lancaster spoke as to the king alone, but made sure all heard him clearly. "Of Cadwr of Bridgnorth we will have more to say later, sire."

Michael inclined his head. "My lord Mortimer, I will speak no more of her than this—doubtless hoping to gain the lady's favor in merry dalliance, he did whisper in her ear of heavy matters. It is well to look to our own people and our own lands—church and baron alike. It is *not* well to take overmuch concern over the health of the realm. That is the duty of the king's grace. There are those who do plot to give England into the hands of the pope."

Gasps and cries of outrage came from around the hall. At their exalted table, the prelates glared as one man with one pair of eyes. The king sat up straighter in his elaborate chair as if he'd heard this only now for the first time.

Lancaster put out a hand as though to bid Michael hold his tongue, but he continued. "As it was in the days of John Lack-Land, so some would have it in ours. My lord, churchmen and a small party of barons speak against the *praemunire* matter. I contend they fear not for the realm's best good, but only for their own revenues. If complaints be brought to the royal court instead of church courts, will the crown not collect revenue from those fines, rather than the church?"

"That is so," said Lancaster. "Fines rightly belong to the court that decides a matter."

Michael went on, "Some see *praemunire* as a danger to the church's interests. This party fears that if abbot and bishop be squeezed for money—and with the villeins in such disarray, for sure they will be so squeezed—will they not turn again to ask still more from their vassal lords?"

"Well said," Beth heard whispered behind her. "When did the fat bishops ever suffer want without passing it on to us?"

Lancaster shook his head. "Veryan, you do overstate your fears—and the barons'."

"I believe not, my lord. Through Cadwr of Bridgnorth, via the delicate ear of Lady Bethany, I am convinced they plot in secret to send emissaries—and mayhap an attractive gift—to Avignon. They would ask the pope to void our oaths of fealty, making England a vassal state to the holy see."

The clerics' table reminded Beth of a bench-clearing brawl at a hockey game. All the younger ones jumped up and began shouting. The older church lords rose at a pained and slower pace. She noted how Cadwr edged, as if wanting to go unnoticed, to the side of one bishop and drew him into the shadows to speak urgently.

What fresh mischief is that?

A knight Beth did not know jumped to his feet in the aisle, face red, fist clenched. "It will mean anarchy. We will not suffer it!"

Lancaster strode down the hall to the knight. "Compose yourself, Alun. We but bring this out in the open in order to find a solution acceptable to all."

"What solution will the church accept—" Michael indicated the furious churchmen with a wide-swept gesture, "—save total capitulation to the will of any foreign legate the holy see wishes to send us."

The eldest bishop leaned heavily on his crozier as he made his way into the aisle where Michael, Lancaster, and the enraged Alun stood. He addressed his words to the king, but the vigor and volume in his voice belied any impression of fragile age.

"My lord, will you hear me?"

"Aye, my lord of Canterbury," said the king's grace.

Simon Islip, archbishop of Canterbury and primate of England, tugged on his little pointed beard. "Lords sacred and secular," he began, "part of what the baron de Veryan says is simple truth."

Murmurs of both shock and savage agreement rippled up and down the hall. But Canterbury was not yet finished.

"Like barons great and small, the church suffers much in these dark days since the sickness. In addition to serfs, we have lost many brothers, both lay and ordained. Priest, monks, friars, and a grievous number of the good sisters also have gone to God. And the law is meet that seeks to keep the villeins laboring at their old and just wage. Do not all agree this is only seemly? God has ordained they work for the best good of us all. But who among us complies with the wage laws?"

More murmurings. Beth saw nobody willing to jump up and claim he paid for farm labor only what the law allowed.

"The times change, and we must change too," declared the archbishop. "The king's grace justly fights for his rights in France, and money is short. My lord king, God cannot but be on your side against the perfidious French."

Lancaster saw the archbishop pause to draw breath, and leaped into the breach. "This is not the time to offend our Lord and His saints by grieving His church."

Beth thought she glimpsed a twinkle in Michael's eye. "Lords all, there must be a center path between offending heaven and becoming vassals to Pope Innocent the French. Nor do I suggest sending to Avignon for a mediator, but settling this matter as befits reasonable men. How can we keep English matters in English courts without flouting the will of Him who made us all?"

The archbishop cast him an astute glance. "We might, of course, consider such a middle path. My lord of Lancaster is a faithful son of the church, and his devotion is known to all. Might he be named to treat between us to find this middle way Lord Michael would tread?"

"A fair thought," said Henry gravely, "and with all my strength will I labor to find this good path."

The king rose from his chair. "Henry, draw forth your sword."

Beth stifled a gasp, but saw she was the only one in shock. What did the king wish Lancaster to do with his blade?

The duke complied with swift and accurate grace, reversing the sword in his hand.

"Come you all," called the king, "swear before the holy relic I am sure Henry keeps in the hilt, that you will take good counsel one of another. That you will hear fairly and resolve the matter of *praemunire.* It is our will that the question be heard and decided once for all by the lords and commons of England. Swear all to do justice fairly in all your courts—be they sacred or secular. My lord of Canterbury, answer for your church and all she names as hers. Lord Mortimer, Lord Michael, Sir Alun, Sir Cadwr, come you also and swear."

The king waited as those he named drew near to the sword Lancaster lofted high. "On pain of breaking faith with our heavenly King, and treachery to the earthly sovereign, I charge you all to swear."

Edward detailed what they must promise to do. He would suffer no papal legate to mediate this or any other English matter. They must consider dispassionately and each choose a speaker to address the legitimate concerns of his party. The king named a date in August on which parliament would meet. His challenge, Edward said in a ringing voice, was for them to accept the law he proposed, or put forth a better one.

Beth saw no overt reluctance to swear. Every representative lay his hand on Lancaster's upraised one, over the holy relics contained in the sword, and swore.

My word, she thought in awe. *He's quashed the plot.*

All was not sweet amity, though. She saw scowls on quite a few faces as the contenders withdrew to their various corners. The watchful minstrels struck up a cheery rondeau, and Michael returned to Beth's side humming a few bars.

"Well," he muttered as he lifted her hand to his lips, "I hope that turns a few points elsewhere."

"Will this swearing not put an end to the plot, dear-my-lord?"

"It should do. By the rood, it should do. But from the fire in some eyes, it shall but stay their hand for a time." He beckoned the page over with wine, and Beth saw that his tunic was damp with the sweat of stress. "My lord Mortimer worries over the sinful amount of royal debt, and i' faith he has the right of it. Lancaster says much of Mortimer's concern is fear the king might be tempted to rash decisions based on that debt. To owe a man money puts you in his power."

Michael drank deeply. "I have, of course, made several fresh enemies by standing in the way of this misbegotten scheme."

"And I with you, lord, for did not I stand at your side?"

"You do well, lady, to cast your lot with me, and not with my brother who insults you."

"As though I would! He knows I have never trusted him. It is as you say—he is a loose arrow." She accepted a refill, for her own cup was empty. "Yet I fear you have made a dangerous enemy on my account."

"Which?"

"Mortimer."

Michael made a soft huff and drank more wine. "Mortimer is a reasonable man. He will not account me an enemy for that I take a stance opposing his. Beside that, this is not the moment for him to irk the king. He stands high in Edward's favor and wishes to keep it, but one hears he's currying still more. He desires to be earl of all the Marches. He will do naught to imperil that. You need have no worries of his challenging me for my honors in the Marcher lands. An the king grants the earldom, Roger de Mortimer will have his hands full." He laughed outright. "Oh yes, he will have a loaded trencher. My bastard brother is due proof that the Welsh are mad to a man, and they will not lightly submit to any new earl no matter how strong he be."

"They will fight."

"Oh, aye, my love. As sure as your hair wishes to escape confinement, they will fight." He tugged on a willful curl, and Beth returned his smile.

So, we may have peace, at least for a while. And some uneasy truce between us, for the time being.

"There is yet more to tell," he continued, dropping the strand of her hair. "Lancaster tells me my lord of Canterbury is not at all pleased. Boniface of Valle Crucis is blamed for tugging Cadwr into treason. He promised succession to my lands if Cadwr succeeded."

"How can a baseborn brother aspire to your honors?"

"Simple. By either eliminating me or blackening my name here at court, hopefully dark enough the king would consider disseisin. But that is past. Cadwr's not only the loose arrow you name him, but a spent one. I misdoubt Mortimer will suffer him long."

"What will become of him?"

"For now, he would do well to go and sulk on his lands, and bother the powerful no further. Mayhap if war with France is renewed, Cadwr may acquit himself bravely—he is well enough in battle—and so regain favor."

A page clad in Lancastrian livery cleared his throat at Michael's elbow. "How now, child?"

"An it please you, my lord, your presence is required."

Michael wiped his mouth and flung the linen napkin back onto the table. "Ever something. Pardon me, *ma chère.*"

The page coughed apologetically. "Your pardon. Lady de Lindstrom is summoned also."

Beth gaped. "Me?"

"Aye. This way, please. The king and family have withdrawn to the solar."

Her stomach wished she hadn't drunk that last sip of wine. Beth rose as gracefully as she could and placed her hand on Michael's. The page led them to a staircase and up to the solar, drenched in the spring sunset's last light and well fitting its name. The lad bowed them in and vanished.

Near a merrily snapping hearth that allayed the evening's chill sat Queen Philippa and other women, including Isabelle. The king lounged on a cushioned settle, playing at tables with two of his sons. Beth found a moment to wonder if either was John of Gaunt, future "time-honored Lancaster", but the boys were close in age and similar in looks, so she couldn't guess. She and Michael made their courtesies to his grace.

"So, Veryan." The king moved his piece on the board and glanced up. "My good lady, and my good sense, demand I grant your request in the matter of Trevellas."

Michael grinned, gave a deep bow, and said nothing. His silence warned Beth that the king was not finished.

"One has, however, heard strange rumors circulating at court." He yielded to his son's clamor and moved again, which allowed the boy to capture the king's piece. "Well done, Edmund. A fair move." He shifted his castle and set Edmund deep into whispered strategy with his brother. "The *dits* say you lack any memory of family or your true home."

"That is true, sire." *Lord, forgive me yet again, for if Michael who loves me cannot believe, how could I expect the king to?*

"It is said also that you are portionless, that you bring Veryan no dowry."

"Also true."

"Yet you would have her anyway?" The king directed this next question to Michael, who hesitated not an instant before replying.

"She is a termagant, my lord, and difficult of management. Yet we treat rather well together, my lady and me. She is of that type of woman—she puts me in memory of Lady Nicolaa de la Hay—who does right well under strong protection."

Beth glared his way but Michael paid her no attention. The queen set down her sewing to listen with raised eyebrows.

"I trust she will become more complaisant with time."

"My lord, I am complaisant now." *And "she" has a voice of her own, thanks very much.*

The king guffawed. "Doubtless. Although I misdoubt Cadwr of Bridgnorth found you so. He repeats abroad that your hold on Veryan is due to witchcraft." The king's eyes, very bright and intelligent, fixed her motionless where she stood. "Do you practice the black arts?"

Her heart beat thickly, for life depended on her answer. "No, sire, never did nor ever shall. I serve only the Lord Christ."

"Well and roundly said." The queen spoke up from her corner. "*I* believe her."

"My good lady is a sharp judge of character," said the king. At his elbow, the boys clamored to resume their game. "Very well, *demoiselle* who be no witch. You shall have Trevellas to your dowry, and poor Veryan will pay a fine of—let us say—sixty marks."

Michael bowed assent. Beth sank into a deep curtsey.

"He shall have Trevellas back in any case." The king laughed. "See that it prosper, lady, that it provide rich dowries for your own daughters."

"With all my heart."

"What do you now?" The king directed his question to Michael.

"By your leave, sire, we head home by way of Kingsdown. I must treat with Guillaume and his manor court there. Then home to Truro. I replenish my purse and let my troop rest, and after go to Trevellas, that my lady may know what is hers."

The king's smile faded and his countenance darkened. "The road is none too safe a place for you at this time, Michael. Do you watch your back."

Seventeen

Lord Michael, baron de Veryan, departed the royal presence with suitable decorum. But the moment they'd crossed the upper ward bailey and gained the Curfew Tower, he tugged Beth toward the same embrasure they had used before.

He put his arms around her waist and drew her near. "I scarce know what to think," he growled. "You have told me a tale I should never credit but for the care I bear you."

He prevented Beth's answer by whirling her around in a mad *pavane*. She squealed and held on tight.

"I have you," he said on a laugh. "By heaven's bright gates, I have you!"

She squirmed out of his arms and patted her crooked snood back into place. "You have the king's consent to wed, and I have Trevellas through your kindness. Now you must consider well whether you truly want what you have won."

"Speak plain—an you can." His chest rose and fell, with mirth or exertion she could not determine.

"You, who claim me to wife, say you dare not believe me."

He ran a hand over his chin. "I would believe. I wish to. By the rood, I fear wishing it too much. It seems too fantastic a tale."

"Before we leave Windsor," she said, "I will show you things that will prove the truth of my story."

He brightened, then scowled again. "Those who love should need no proof."

Her heart softened and tilted toward him. "You do love me then. You do."

"Aye, sweeting," he whispered at last. "It came unbidden . . . but I do love you." He caught her back into his embrace. "Forgive me—can you ever?—for my failure to believe."

"Gladly. Of course," she teased, her heart feather light, "I will certes remind you of it every time you make a misstep."

"I expect you to. And you will wed me?"

"Aye. I cannot do other, for you see, despite your obdurate decision to distrust me, I do love you most sincerely." She smiled to tell him the truth of it.

"Bethany. You love me. I knew it!" He covered her face with kisses, a laugh half caught in his throat. When he'd done, he added, "After we are married, or before, it makes me no mind, I should like to see your future-clothing. You will wear it for me, in private of course?"

"I will," she said on a chuckle. "I warn you, you will be deeply shocked to see me in breeches."

"So you have said. And your mother permitted this? Amazing."

"My mother had little to say about it. Some women own nothing else, though I did not follow that style. When I came to England I brought what I liked best and what would wear well."

He shook his dark head. "A woman in breeches."

"There is worse, though I cannot show you."

"What would cause greater scandal than wearing men's attire?"

"Someday," she promised, "I will sew something we call a bikini." With few words, she described it.

Michael's grin widened and he pressed kisses to her face. "That will have to wait," he said repressively, though his eyes glowed approval, "until we are well and truly married. Otherwise you would shock me out of breath."

"My lord, you may depend upon it," she said with a wicked laugh. All conversation ceased, leaving her well pleased with her after-supper time that night at Windsor.

Morning mass in the chapel of St. George was not packed as full as the earlier days' worship had been. Beth saw many of the nobles had already left. She hoped Cadwr and others had taken an early departure, but unfortunately, she spotted him in a corner with his liege lord the abbot. Did the scut never cease lurking in dim corners?

She mentioned as much to Michael after mass. The day bid fair for travel, he told her, and save for the necessity of paying his fine to the king's receiver here, he too would have ordered the troop to horse.

"Depend upon it, if there is naught to keep my brother, he will scurry at an early opportunity."

"You promised the king's grace," she reminded him, "that you would not call him out."

"By the rood, so I did. Bad cess to it. Whatever possessed me?"

"If we do not set out this morn, I would join the women and do some sewing."

"You are not overfond of sewing."

"No more am I, but things can be heard in the women's quarters. I will make shift to hear what I can, before everyone leaves Windsor."

His brow creased in a scowl that was growing familiar. "It is too dangerous. You do not know these ladies and who is attached to whom. Moreover some of them are too clever and no faith with it. These spread untruths to their own ends. Their loyalties can shift like the wind of a Cornish winter. I forbid it."

"I will say naught save to you, but keep my ears open." She reached up to plant a kiss on his chin, and together they sought breakfast.

Afterward, working with redoubled enthusiasm on a surcote for Michael, Beth kept her ears well open, but heard nothing of interest. The ladies, lacking the queen, who was resting with a bellyache, talked freely, but only of who bedded whom and which cuckolded husband knew naught of it, while she took stitch after dutiful stitch, trying to imitate the skill of the ladies' long white fingers.

I'm not sure I'll ever get the hang of this. After we're married, I'll have to delegate as much embroidery as I can get away with.

Bored, she rose with a murmured excuse about the privy. Slipping down the stairs to the ground floor of the Round Tower, she heard raised male voices.

She ducked into a window embrasure. At last, a chance to serve Michael's interest and learn what she could!

Cadwr's voice, almost in a whine. So he hadn't taken the fair weather as his signal to skedaddle, had he? It could mean nothing good if he'd secretly lingered behind. Another man, whom he called "my lord" was apparently in the middle of delivering a stern lecture.

"I will have no further part in this. You promised success and you gained naught but failure. If you and your greedy abbot wish to play with loaded dice with the pope, you may, but I will not. By Christ's crown, you may have cost me the earldom."

"Surely not, my lord."

Cadwr had developed a nervous quaver in his voice. Beth took a moment to scold herself for being glad of his discomfiture.

"I know your type, man. You wished to attain Mortimer's patronage, but I will deal no more with you. Moreover, I have counseled many. They will offer you neither men, nor money, nor influence. You are not only on your own among the barony, but quite dangerously exposed." She heard spittle hit the floor. "You would do well to run home like a louse in sunlight and bide safe on your own lands."

"My lord—"

"Get you gone, I say. Mayhap this nonsense of the king's will fall under its own weight, but I will not add my bulk to its load. At parliament this summer we shall see what these holy schemers pull out of their sleeves. An this law fail or prosper, the king shall not hold me accountable."

Angry footsteps retreated. Beth put a hand up to wipe nervous perspiration from her brow and in the process, jostled the torch bracket. It rattled loosely and loudly in the quiet. She caught her breath and gathered her skirts to dash back upstairs.

Mortimer must have left Cadwr alone in the hall. Just as she rounded the turn of the stairs, she glimpsed large boots at the bottom of the staircase. Had he seen her? She prayed not, or, if he had, that he'd spotted only the hem of her skirts.

I just pray he didn't recognize me. She gained the women's quarters and stood for a moment outside the door, setting her hand on the stone wall while she caught her breath. It wouldn't do to rejoin the ladies looking rattled.

I heard way more than I should—more than I wanted to. He'll be livid that I witnessed his set-down at Mortimer's hands!

She reached for the door latch, intending to rejoin the embroidery team, but realized she must tell Michael what befell. With a sigh of resignation—for he would be ill-pleased when he discovered she'd eavesdropped—she descended the stairs once more.

Cadwr had left the hall. She found a moment to catch her breath and pray he'd taken Lord Mortimer's good advice and made tracks.

When at length she caught up with Michael, she found him near the lower ward buildings in which the men at arms and lower servants were housed. Two men, he told her, had fallen out over a wench, and he had just finished meting out discipline.

He gave the smarting culprits a last glare and gladly led her into the sunshine and wind of the bailey. In as few words as possible, making it clear she had but gone for the privy, she related what she had inadvertently heard of Cadwr's set-down by Mortimer, and how unhappy Michael's brother would be an he knew.

"Doubtless." He spat into the grass. "Petroc's bones, that is unhappy news. A vexed Cadwr is a dangerous Cadwr. You say he saw you not?"

"I do not think he did. When I bumped the bracket, I ran up the stairs. If he saw, he saw only a woman's skirt, and that cannot identify me."

"Still. We cannot take the chance." He tugged a curl out of the light veil she'd worn today, disarranging Teagen's careful work. "Go and speak to your maid, sweeting. I will ready the men. I intended not to leave till tomorrow dawn, but we must away." His expression grew grim. "Can you ride hard?"

"At need, I can do anything you ask me to do."

He put his arms around her waist and gave her a hurried squeeze. "Thank the Lord for you. Get you ready, for we must put as much distance between us and my brother as we may. Nor can we stop at Kingsdown, but come home by the shortest road." He released her. "I fear you heard too much. The king's grace can give justice if you are harmed, but I am not willing to take any such risk—justice can help only after the crime." He smiled a bit grimly. "No harm must come to my witch-woman."

They set off before Sext. Michael took counsel of Bifan to plan their route avoiding the high ways. They would not retrace their route here, for so Cadwr, if he intended treachery, would expect them to do. Instead, Michael proposed they head not to Truro, but to Trevellas.

"He may think of it if he wishes to do you mischief, but I doubt his brain pan holds wits that sharp. What say you, lady? Would you see your new lands?"

"With all my heart," she replied, guiding Caillin around a clump of prickly shrubbery that encroached on the road, "but only if it does not cause you any trouble."

"Lady, the day you cause me no trouble will be the day I summon learned physicians to see to your health."

They laughed and clucked their mounts to a smarter pace.

"Trevellas," said Michael, days later. "Welcome to your lands."

"How lovely in the sunshine. Tell me more." She sat up straighter, and though Caillin-the-Ever-Resentful danced aside in protest, she curbed the mare with the ease of practice. "You mentioned the lands produce well. What are their crops, dear-my-lord?"

"Corn, of course, and barley. Many messuages still lie deserted since the pestilence. Jacca has turned some of those to pasturage. Sheep do well in the rocky places, and the lands benefit from lying fallow." He winked and added, "Not to mention from all that the busy woollies do leave behind."

She wrinkled her nose and laughed.

In a stony pasture before them, work ceased. Men leaned on their scythes and gazed, for on so bright a day they were busy with haying. One man gave a tentative wave, to which Michael nodded, so she did the same. From the stares of the men, they didn't see the lord's entourage often.

The peasants looked similar to those she'd seen elsewhere, though fatter than the villeins along the road from Windsor. Either Michael's ways led to prosperity amongst the lesser folk, or crops grew better on this side of the Tamar.

"I trust they also grow vegetables. I grow hungry for a rich pottage like unto Alys's."

He smacked his lips. "Since you mention it, I could eat something."

"Then let us finish this weary journey," she suggested. "How far to the house?"

He pointed with the hand that didn't carry his peregrine. "Just over that rise, beyond the village. It is small and with some empty tofts still. You will see the manor house clearly once the village is in sight."

She gave a chortle of eagerness and put her heels to Caillin's sides. The mare obeyed with a little bounce to warn Beth she didn't approve of ideas she hadn't originated. Giffard snorted and kept up. Ever more capable in the saddle, Beth gained the top of the hill at a canter and reined Caillin in.

Below them lay a tiny village of the usual whitewashed wattle and daub. Several of its homes stood vacant. The shutterless windows stared out at the day, empty as the eyesockets of a skull. Beyond the last cottage lay a cluster of buildings. Built of Cornish gray granite, the structures on the right were surrounded with small sheds and hayricks, marking them as stables. On the far side of the stable range lay a good sized timbered barn, and beyond it several small holdings similar to those around Mossock.

Just visible was the roofline of a house of two stories, laid out in segments, as though conceived as a cottage, and then grown higgledy-piggledy over decades—or centuries. A wisp of slate-colored smoke drifted into the still air. The entire homestead was encircled by a mossy granite wall with a tiny gatehouse built into its thickness.

Mine. Through my lord's generosity, in my hand until we marry. This will be my learning ground before I'm a baroness with much more to manage.

Her heart swelled in approval. "Small, as you say, my lord, but tidy."

"Aye. Trevellas village can prosper, an the lands keep in good heart. At Michaelmas, they hold a fair, well attended though it lies so close to Truro. Trevellas fair is known all over Cornwall and eke as far as Devon for the quality of the stock traded here." He curbed Giffard, who sidestepped anxiously as though smelling a snug stable and a measure of oats. "Steady, lad. Anon you will be fed and happy, and myself also."

Caillin's ears pricked forward as they descended into the valley at a comfortable trot. As they neared, Beth scanned the outbuildings. In a fenced surround by the stables, several cows and an ill-tempered goat jostled one another for a first view of the newcomers. One of the cows lowed a welcome. To the right, a vegetable garden marched in tidy rows, peas staked carefully with sticks and hempen thread. A single guard near the gates called a challenge, and Bifan rode forward to announce them. The guard ran to swing the gates wide.

Michael greeted the guard in Cornish, to which Beth added her own *dydh da.* The guard grinned, showing browned and broken teeth, and let loose with a torrent of greeting in that tongue.

Beth gave Michael a helpless gesture, so he explained, "He would run to the house and tell Jacca we are come."

"Say I ask him to do so, if you please."

Michael nodded, a glint of pleasure in his eyes. "Aye so. You do well to take your place as lady of Trevellas from this first moment. All orders should come from your lips, not mine, the sooner to make you so." He grinned widely. "Unless it be in military matters. Then, for once, sweeting, I—and they—will expect you to defer to me."

She wrinkled her nose at him. "I shall at least try, dear-my-lord."

The party trotted past the stables, skirting the pigsties and a dilapidated dovecote. Past the farm, the manor house came into view. Michael curbed Giffard with a sound of consternation.

"Lady," he said in a choked voice, "the house is not in the condition I hoped."

Beth reined Caillin in and gaped. Her heart fell. Though the farm buildings looked sturdy enough, wanting a touch of repair here and there, the manor house itself . . . The only word that fit was *slum.*

She'd seen places slated for demolition in better shape. The window casements, once closed against all weathers in stout wooden slats, showed shutters broken to bits in some places, in others needing only a well-placed nail. The big oaken door hung ajar from one iron hinge.

From the roof of the separate kitchen building, thatch dripped in clumps onto the ground. More thatch moldered over the outbuildings and the privy. From between tatters, a cockerel screeched, regarding her with a dark and suspicious eye.

She rode Caillin up to the manor house door and curbed her, then waited for Michael to dismount and hand her down. He threw the reins of both horses to the gap-toothed guard who'd been first to welcome them.

"*Deus a ji.*" The guard beckoned toward the door and let loose something uncertain in Cornish. Michael shrugged and replied in that musical tongue.

"Jacca has been ailing," he said in a tight voice. "They feared pestilence, but none who took it had the signs of that, thank God. From the looks of things, certes he is at death's own door." Michael's broad shoulders drooped, a sure sign of dismay, and he spat into the dry ruts of the courtyard. "He would never let it fall to such a state otherwise. Despite the evidence of your eyes, he is a good and faithful steward, if overmuch concerned for sin. A poor welcome Trevellas gives its new lady."

"Let it not trouble you," Beth soothed. "If they can find us food, and a dry place to lay our heads tonight, we will do well enough. First, I would see to Jacca. I know little of leechcraft, but mayhap I can find some ease to offer him."

His troubled expression lightened. "Jesu bless you." He slid an arm around her waist. "Treasure of my house and light of my eyes. God knew His work when He sent you to me."

She laughed in sheer delight. "I do love you, my lord."

"Me, who doubted, you love? Thank God for it." He gave her a brief and fervent squeeze there in the courtyard before guard, cockerel, and decrepit thatch. "Let us hasten now."

They found the bailiff, but not in the big house as Beth had expected. The building's disrepair gave her the suspicion Jacca—or others—had appropriated its comforts for themselves. Her guess proved inaccurate, for he lay not in the hall, but in a hut attached to the house. A coarse hempen blanket clutched around his shoulders, the old man struggled to rise from a pallet near a sulky open fire and greeted them in the quavering, fretful voice of illness. The hut's smell alone betrayed that much.

Michael introduced Beth and lost no time in increasing Jacca's comfort. "Come you into the hall," he said, "and speak English, old trout, for my lady's sake. She has no Cornish."

With a strong arm, he helped the scrawny old man to his feet and supported his halting steps into the hall. Beth slipped outside to tell Teagen to find a sturdy boy to lay and light a fire.

The hearth lit after several tries. Her maid snapped at the frightened lad like any fishwife, then left to find others to tongue-lash into service.

Once the fire blazed up in a freshly tidied hearth, Michael sat Jacca down on a trestle bench. "Now. You are not the man to cheat your master or stand idle while others do so. Tell me."

"Sinful. Sinful." Jacca gave a cough that sounded like someone strangling a cat. "None here to greet you, lord, as is your due. All scurry about, intent on thieving, fornication . . . " His voice clotted in his throat, and he coughed some more.

The bluish tinge to Jacca's lips bothered Beth. She rose as the maid returned. "Teagen, please bring wine and a pan to heat it in. Then find whoever in this place knows healing. Bid them bring herbs efficacious for lung complaints."

Teagen eyed Jacca with suspicion and said under her breath, "This is the skulking *fainéant* who let the manor fall to ruin?"

"Hush! The bailiff is not to blame. As you see, he is ill. Anyone may fall sick and fail his duties, as well you know. Recriminations can wait. My lord and I will bring them to answer for neglect here, but not until Jacca is eased." Beth gave a dismissive gesture. "Go to."

"Aye, lady."

Due to Teagen's efficiency, in a short time Beth held a wooden mazer to Jacca's lips. He sipped gratefully of warmed wine. Silent women with reddened cheeks fled to the kitchens, murmuring to Teagen that they were concocting a pottage to feed the party and potions for Jacca's wheezy chest.

By the time the sun ambled toward dusk, Michael returned to the hall from setting the farm laborers back to their work. He'd had to use the sharp side of his tongue, he reported, and his riding whip on a few who preferred the easy days of Jacca's disability. Beth called it attitude adjustment.

Their mounts were being tended first, then the manor stock. Michael edged toward the hearth, for the fading day had cooled, with a brisk wind off the sea that smelled of rain. He'd sent villeins to cut fresh rushes for the new-cleaned floors, and after that, reeds for the thatching they must begin on the morrow—rain or no. Beth had already set two menservants to scraping up the malodorous rushes that had greeted her on entry. That, she figured, would help cure the obvious rat problem.

She shuddered, making a mental note to find fleabane. Above all, she would banish all fleas and rodents from the house. Once she'd succeeded here, she'd do the same at Truro. Already, though, after only a couple of hours of work, the sorry hall looked much improved.

"Now, Jacca." Michael stripped off his gloves before the snapping fire. "What befell here?"

"Lord, I wit not how it began. At first, when the fever came, we were much affrighted that the pest-maid had returned to sweep us away wi' her broom, us as survived her first embrace."

Trembling, he crossed himself. Teagen urged another draught of warmed wine. With a shaky hand, he clutched the blanket closer as if invoking its meager protection.

"But when the others recovered, we knew it for naught but common fever. Me it took worse than most, and I consigned me to God."

"The other servants?" Beth prodded. "Were they taken ill like you?"

Jacca nodded and gave another wheeze. "Some was. Several are gone to God. Mailie Brewster and old Tab the thatcher. Two of Simon at-Leat's childer." Teagen and the others signed the cross.

"Others, curse them, used the sickness as leave to do as they would. Andrew Porroc and his brother took to their heels." He coughed some more. "God alone knows where those knaves landed."

"So the manor lost still more," said Michael thoughtfully. "I would welcome farmers to take over their holdings, but those I cannot trust cannot return."

The maids beckoned them to table, and between spoonfuls of pottage and loaves of bread solicited from the village, Jacca continued.

"Every wight must have a lord. It is great error to leave. Others of them took women to whom they were not wed. Sinful, sinful. Petronilla the miller's wife now lives with Sim by-Brook, and Tom Miller himself has taken to woodcarving."

"Despicable," said Teagen. "And after you did free them, lord."

Michael shrugged and drained the best mazer of home-brewed ale. Teagen ordered it refilled with a curt gesture.

My lord offered the fresh draught first to Beth, then remarked, "In times of confusion, men make shift for themselves alone. Many have done since the sickness. Oft they find beggary and starvation instead of betterment."

"They had better to stay put and mindful of their place. The church suffers also, lord," said Jacca with aggravation. "So many forsake daily mass that the priest mumbles the liturgy in unseemly haste. He misses the old crowd who did listen."

"And misses his proper tithe as well," put in Teagen.

She rose with a comment about seeing to the maids. No poultice, by heaven, should take this long to concoct!

Beth patted the bailiff's shoulder, unwilling that he grow agitated. "That, too, then, we shall set to rights." She cast a glance toward Michael.

He gave her the barest hint of a nod. She could see shame in his eyes that he hadn't sent to Trevellas long ago to check on its well doing. He'd feel he had failed them, and to atone for his preoccupation he would help his overwhelmed steward.

Teagen returned to the hall with two others. One bore a pink mark on her cheek as though recently—very recently—slapped. The other bore an earthenware bowl containing a steaming, fragrant poultice.

Jacca eyed the bowl. "Nay, lady. The lord's hall is no place for physicking."

"Hush," said Beth. "The hall is warmest, and you need warmth." She stood back to oversee the maid with the stung cheek as she opened Jacca's shirt and applied the poultice.

Michael took up a knife and a stick of wood to whittle. His quick inquisitive glance told her now was the time to open the topic of Teagen and the reward they'd discussed on the road from Windsor.

"Tell me, Teagen." Beth couldn't restrain a smile. "Have you ever considered marriage?"

Teagen stopped so sharply her shoes skidded in the rushes. "Aye, lady."

"You would wed Ennis of Kenwyn?"

"Aye." Her flush brightened her alert dark eyes.

"It is a fair match. Do you wish to remain in my service should you marry?" Teagen nodded. "In that case, there is no objection. My lord and I approve the match. You may wed as soon as we return home to Truro."

The joy on Teagen's face served as the best reward. "Lady, lady, thank you! I'll serve you always. I thank you. I never thought—oh, my ivers, I must tell Ennis!"

Beth hid a laugh, unwilling to spoil her attempt at dignity. "Go, then. Do not make him wait longer. Men are poor at it."

Michael whittled, maintaining his dignity until Teagen bolted from the hall, letting the door bang the frame in joyful haste. Then he slapped his hands on his knees and hooted.

"Poor at waiting, are we? I do recall hearing someone asking forgiveness lately for impatience."

"Allow me to order you a bath. Your earholes need a good cleansing."

He laughed some more. "I hear well enough, saucy one, and you know it right well."

She approached the bench on which he sat, to squat down on the new-laid rushes. She took his hand and kissed his scarred knuckles.

"Dear-my-lord, I am often hasty of temper, especially when fatigued by a long ride. Your forbearance is great, beyond what a woman should expect of any man. I pray daily for patience. Thank you with all my heart for putting up with me so long."

Jacca, his breathing eased by the poultice, began to nod off in his chair. Michael cast him a single glance and extended a booted foot toward the warmth of the fire. Outside the broken casements, evening clouds lowered. It began to rain, but quietly, as if not to further try my lord's patience.

"Boy," he said, but softly so as not to wake Jacca. One of the serving lads scurried over, tugging his forelock. "Among my men you will find Ennis of Kenwyn. Send him here."

"A fine notion, dear-my-lord."

"You know not my mind. Compose your soul in patience, for I have yet more to do here."

She subsided, draining her mazer of the wine it held.

Ennis arrived on the run, damp-spattered with rain and flushed as though he'd been working hard. Michael didn't appear to notice the drops that fell from his leather jerkin.

"What say you, Ennis," he asked idly, as if the notion had just occurred to him, "to helping Jacca put affairs to rights here? The manor needs repairs he cannot undertake on his own. I daresay you will find methods of coaxing men out of their hidey-holes, for a wage."

The bailiff roused with a cough that sounded easier than it had before.

"That I can, my lord," said Ennis. "An it be acceptable to master Jacca, I will bide here a while."

"A good thought." Beth included Teagen in her glance as the maid slipped back into the hall. "And your wife-to-be also. Teagen is in no wise behindhand when it comes to the ordering of a house. She has my leave to stay if she like."

"Lord—lady," said Jacca, looking bewildered from one to another. "Right enough it would help, but you do me no justice. I thought you would turn me out, so laggard have I—"

Beth lifted a hand to stop him. "Enough. Speak not of turning any out. It is not my way to punish undeserved, but allow my people a chance to redeem themselves."

Michael gave a firm nod. "Peter, the steward at Truro keep, is no spring hatchling. If I'm to train a new one, that man will need experience in a smaller household. Jacca, will you train Ennis? On my lands—I mean, my lady's—is sufficient work for every able hand. Did you think because your body is weak for the moment, that we have no need of your mind?"

Jacca coughed again. "I mend apace, lord. Soon I will be able to ride out and turn those scapegrace serfs back to their duty."

"And until you are whole," Ennis added smoothly, "I'll learn from you. At your bidding I shall sieve out the willing workers from those who would do better elsewhere."

"We are agreed, then," Beth said. "Jacca, my lord has told me of your good and faithful stewardship of these lands. I would that it continue once you are well." From a large yellow round, she broke off a piece of cheese, looking from face to face.

Dear Lord, I love these people.

Michael's expression had set in the stern mask he wore in lord-of-the-manor mode. Teagen's hid eagerness, Ennis's seemed calm and determined, Jacca's bewildered, dawning toward pleasure.

She added one more comment. "Of course, I may suggest an improvement or two—here or there."

"Woman, are you never idle? What do you here?"

Beth tucked a damp strand of hair back under her head-rail as Teagen glanced up and bowed. "We do but devise a better floor for the kitchens, dear-my-lord."

Michael pointed to a hillock in the corner. "Sand? Do you mine for tin?"

"Sand will fill in the cracks between the flagstones. I plan to pave the entire floor. Do you look here, near the hearth where the men have already done. The stones will make all neat and tidy."

"And much easier to clean than any dirt floor, my lord," put in Teagen the Vocal.

"What says Jacca to this plan?"

"If it save work, he is all for it."

Michael snorted. "A new contrivance, therefore he is not at all for it."

Beth dusted her sandy hands on her coarse linen smock. "He will cheer it, once he sees how much labor it saves the kitchen-maids."

"See, lord? When they spill, they will not have to waste the rushes," Teagen explained. "And if the spill fall between the stones, the sand will take up all."

"There will be fewer vermin," Beth added.

Michael scanned the new-laid floor. "The kitchen wenches had best make sure it does well, then. Jacca will not approve anything new if it yield bad fruit."

He stretched his hand to Beth, and she sprang up from the flagstones by the hearth. Teagen sketched a curtsey and tactfully moved on to her next task. They'd found no lack of work for every willing or unwilling hand, due to the sorry state of the manor's upkeep.

"Is there nothing with which you plan not to meddle?" He dropped her fingers and slid his hands round her waist. "Phew. You smell of kitchen and moldy rushes."

"I smell of honest work." She put her arms around his neck. "Of which I am in no wise ashamed. Would that you had twenty more healthy tenants, my lord, and we would see swifter progress."

He sighed and settled her more closely against his chest. She rested there, secure as in a well-guarded keep, so deeply did she trust and love him.

"The youngsters make merry over your bounty on vermin. A rackety bunch. Ennis has no difficulty recruiting. Silver groats are the surest enticement. And certes, I am to blame. I should have been more diligent after the pestilence, but I was too taken up with problems on my larger honors. These lands produce as well as ever, so I did not inquire further as to the state of the house and its keepers." He scowled. "I was remiss."

"In the past, but no longer. We will put all to rights."

"God bless your sunny nature. And we shall. Do you order what seems right to you. You must oversee your own lands as you think best."

"Will you still say so," she teased, "when it forms my dowry?"

He laughed and dropped an unhurried kiss on her lips. "If I forget to give you praise, you may take yon broom to my head. I look forward to Trevellas becoming your dowry in truth, for that day will see us bound in wedlock." With one hand, he pushed the dusty head rail off her curls, and ran his hand down them. "I grow eager, sweeting." Another hearty kiss showed ample evidence of his eagerness.

"You may call me immodest," she said against his mouth, "for so do I."

How far their embrace might have gone, she couldn't say, for after a moment he cleared his throat and rattled a parchment she only now noticed. "You distract me. There is news from Lancaster."

"What news?" He took a stool by the hearth and drew her to sit on his knee. Beth looked around, and found them safely alone.

"He writes in haste. Cadwr has left court. He rode with Abbot Boniface for a pace, then struck out alone—with a strong troop, full-armed—before they'd reached Maidenhead."

She shook her head. "What matters that?"

"From there, the abbot's party would have turned north, toward Wales. Cadwr goes not there, sweeting, or so Lancaster guesses."

"Where would he go?"

Michael's face darkened. "I mislike the idea of his going anywhere, save home to Bridgnorth."

Fear struck her. So short a time, and already they'd moved from peace to turmoil. "What are you thinking? What will you do?"

"Get me to Truro. You must bide here. It is safer for you here than on the road."

She opened her mouth to object, for surely her place was at his side. He saw and quelled her with a lifted brow.

"I will write to my vassals and castellans from here—an you will help copy out the summonses." He thrust a hand through his tousled hair. "It is not so ill to have a wife who can write. Surely a strange creature . . . We will warn them from this ill-gotten plot. I must explain how it is foredoomed ere it hatches and will bring them no good an they think on casting their lot with the church's attempt to stop the new law."

He stopped to finger his chin and think. "I will also warn them of my private quarrel with my brother. They must offer him neither shelter nor men nor money. The sooner I get to Truro to give and take counsel of my vassals, the sooner I can return to you here." His hand clenched and unclenched around the parchment as though it were the hilt of his sword. "An Cadwr dare set his foot onto my lands, I will be ready." He gave a harsh laugh. "Aye, very ready."

Eighteen

A Traveler's Tale. Michael left this morn. It hurts like the time I put my hand through the storm door. I played the proper lady, though—smiled like a brave chatelaine, helped him arm, offered the stirrup cup. It ached, watching him and the men gallop up the valley. Since the hour we met, we've never been far apart.

Beth leaned back onto the coarse linen pillowslip in Trevellas manor's best curtained bed and brushed the quill along her chin, remembering Michael's leave-taking. He'd tightened his arm around her waist and kissed her with the pent-up heat she'd longed to taste but never had.

She had sighed in bittersweet joy, leaning into his strength. With God's blessings, if his efforts to keep his vassals on the right path prospered, she could count days, not weeks, until his return. Hard upon that, he swore, they would marry and enjoy each other in honor.

By the following morning, after breaking fast with Teagen, Jacca, Ennis, and very few others, Beth wondered how to pass the hours. The new lady of Trevellas felt grand . . . and lonely.

Teagen was supervising the maids in clearing away when Jacca entered, tugging his forelock, a courtesy she had told him to forget.

"Your pardon, my lady."

"Aye, Jacca?"

"Kei of Mossock, Sir Geoffrey's master at arms." Jacca's eyes looked worried. "He craves speech with you."

"Pray send him in."

Beth rose from the bench and took her seat in the single chair near the hearth. Simon the carpenter was already busy building another.

"Sir Geoffrey has trouble," she told Teagen, frowning. "He prefers not to let Kei go far unless needs must. My lord says they are related—wrong side of the blanket—and he and Sir Geoffrey are close tied in friendship as well as in blood."

Teagen nodded and directed the maids to scrub the table well. Kei entered, his expression bleak.

"*Dydh da,* Kei," Beth said. "Teagen, bring ale."

Kei fell to one knee on the rushes. "Lady, *myttin da.* Please excuse my hurry, but I have baleful tidings. My lady is taken bad with child. The midwife and herb wench have done all they know, even the leech can do naught but commend her soul to God. Sir Geoffrey is like to despair, but—lady, she asks for you. Will you come?"

Beth felt her jaw go slack. *This, this is what I was afraid of. They look to me in crisis, and I know nothing, can offer nothing. Yet how can I fail Alys, who cared for me when I couldn't look after myself?*

"As quick as I can don my habit."

Though her lord had bade her stay put, he could not mean for her to refuse so extreme a need—could he? It took Beth only a moment to decide he could not. "Teagen, Ennis must tell the lads to saddle my palfrey. He must put together as strong a troop as can be had."

"Aye, lady. My good Ennis will make you trusty escort."

Mossock's familiar gray bulk loomed into view sudden as a gray spirit, half hidden in a drift of rain and mist. Ennis blew his horn to signal their approach. Bruse, the stableman Beth had seen first when she'd arrived, darted out from behind the midden pile and gabbled something Cornish and incomprehensible. Ennis nodded and rode back to them.

"Lady, they are sore beset within and urge us to hasten. They have called the priest to shrive Lady Alys." He dismounted and tossed his reins to Bruse, then came to help Beth down.

"Pray for her, Ennis, and tell the others to do also. I am no midwife." She clasped his hands for a moment. "Pray that God give me the knowledge, for I have none."

"I shall, lady, and for sure He will."

Beth's stomach clenched, but she nodded and hurried to follow Bruse, who was still yammering in agitated Cornish. In the hall, Maude met her, wringing her hands. Her expression aged her ten years, and exhaustion trembled in her voice.

"Lady, my dear lady," Maude wailed. "Come quick, Lady Bethany. Taken bad she is, my poor young lady . . . "

Beth shook off Maude's laments. "Go and wash," she ordered. "Bring me water and lye soap to my hands. Let nobody enter the confinement chamber who has not washed to the elbows in strong soap."

Maude's expression went blank. Beth's voice snapped like a whip, fear giving it spikes.

"Go to! Or I'll post one of my lord's men here as guard, to make sure you return not above stairs."

She turned to go.

"Maude!" The maid spun back with frightened yet hopeful eyes. "See to it the kitchen puts the largest cauldron on to boil. I will need linen cloths boiled in that water, and a knife boiled also."

What else? Think. Think!

"And your stoutest linen thread, also well boiled. Touch nothing once you take it from the water, but wrap all in a clean linen rag and bring it thus to my lady's chamber. A *clean* rag, hear you? See to each matter yourself, or I will forget that I do not beat servants."

She wasted no time on Maude's response but waited until water came. After a thorough scrubbing, peppered with frantic prayer, she gathered her habit and hurried upstairs to the solar.

Maude had not exaggerated Alys's condition. The babe was not yet born, but Alys sagged against her pillows, too tired to cry out any longer. Beth's heart sank. What was she doing here? What could she hope to offer any woman in childbed, she who'd borne no baby herself?

Ela sponged Alys's forehead with a damp rag that didn't appear clean. Biting her lips, Beth bent near. Alys's brow was damp with sweat, her color poor, but she roused and tried to welcome her.

"Nay," Beth said. "Save your strength for the child."

She gave her friend her most encouraging smile, her heart sinking further. What was she, a historian turned vassal, to do with this muddle? She knew little about medicine and nothing about midwifery.

What little I do know, it's more than these.

That thought came from nowhere, and she thanked God for it. The notion brought comfort and firmed her resolve. She thrust terror aside and turned to Ela.

"How long?"

Ela's broad fair face creased in worry. "This is the second day. Mistress Ebrel—the herb wench fro' Perran, you do know—she stayed the night, gave her colewort and other simples, but did avail naught. This morn toward prime we thought my lady might be lightened, but the pains did slacken."

Beth nodded while quailing inwardly.

Forty-eight hours in labor? How is she going to survive?

"Bestir yourself. Replace that clout with a fresh one, wet with cool water. Throw that one on the fire. It stinks of sweat and your hands. Open the casements, let in clean air to refresh her."

"But lady—lady." Ela rose and twisted the used cloth in her fists.

"Go to! Then get to the kitchens and scrub your hands. Use soap. Maude will relay my other orders."

Ela obeyed with a bewildered curtsey. Left alone with Alys, Beth swallowed hard. It was time to kick her wits into gear and forget fear. She sank onto the edge of the big bed and took Alys's hand in hers.

"How is it with you, dear friend?"

Alys tried again to moisten her lips. Beth offered water from the pitcher on the bedside table. "None so well," she said in a hoarse whisper. "Not like when I bore my son."

"How close come the pains?"

She did not answer directly. "I thought he would be well born by now."

Beth clenched her teeth. "Will you permit me to find out?"

"Please." Alys swallowed, so Beth gave her another sip. "I feel like to tear apart. See if you can do aught for me. If you cannot, pray for my soul, for I haven't long."

No! Good Lord God, let me help her. Let me but keep her alive and I will ask You for nothing more. "Such foolishness. You will be here to counsel me yet for many a year."

Alys sighed and tensed as another long pain racked her. Beth waited until she sank back panting against her pillows, then turned the coverlet up and discovered what she could.

The child's crown should appear first, she knew that much. She saw a dark fuzzy oval. That was good—right? Right?

She sent up another frantic prayer for wisdom and strength, then peeked once more. Was the child's head too big? She had no way to tell, but something was amiss. Even a total ignoramus knew the birth should've been well over by now.

Despair shook her as she processed. "The child seems stuck."

Alys nodded weakly as if she'd sensed this, and Beth but confirmed her fears. "I've heard of such. Can you do aught?"

Beth's stomach and heart switched places. *Think!*

"I can but try." First things first—she'd pray, as she'd so grandly ordered the others to do. *Take your own advice, my lady Know-Nothing.*

Maude returned with the clean things Beth had requested. "Oh, lady, lady," she wailed. "My poor lady—by now t'other one were well born. Popped into the world like a greased piglet from a poke, he did, and a fair one from first brea—"

"What did you say?" Beth leaped up from her knees.

Maude's eyes filled. "That her son—God rest his little soul—was the fairest babe . . ."

"No, about the pig."

"A greased pig, lady?" Maude's damp and skeptical eyes grew rounder yet.

"Yes. Yes! Get you to the kitchen." Beth gave a furious, vague gesture. "Bring goose grease, butter, lamb fat, any grease they have. And not a little."

She bent over the pale, sweating Alys. "Have patience, my friend, and bear as best you can. We may get you a fair babe yet."

The maid's eyes all but popped from her head, and she let out a blast of hopeful Cornish. Beth saw she'd caught the idea. Maude set her burden down and bolted clumsily from the room.

Alys grabbed for her hands as another pain hit, and let out a deep groan. Beth let her squeeze so hard her bones popped, but held on, saying a fervent Ave aloud. Alys's dry lips formed the words, but she had little strength except to endure.

When the pain had ebbed, gently Beth wiped Alys's flushed face. "If this scheme of mine fail, forgive me." Her voice choked and she cleared her throat. "I can promise nothing."

Alys blinked. Her strength failed visibly. Beth trembled before the task, but she had no choice. It would work. It must.

"I—forgive." Alys gave a long, tremulous sigh. "*In manus tuas, Domine.*"

Maude returned with a stout earthen bowl. Beth echoed her words and set herself to her task. Truly, her work—and Alys's life—might lie in her uncertain hands, but in truth, more surely in God's. In the corner, Berta, Hawise, and several others whispered prayers.

Lord, stay with me, and strengthen her. Guide me and make all right that I do wrongly.

She had Maude hold Alys's legs as she applied the lubricant. The next pain—that would be the telling time. Beth watched and prayed harder that all the babe needed was to make like a greased little porker, to slide merrily into the world.

Alys gasped, then began to breathe harshly. A cry, in deeper pain. This was it—another contraction came to its peak. Hopefully the last. Maude held Alys's hands and Beth dabbed more oil where she guessed it was needed.

Take this chance, little one, or I lose you and your mother. Please, God. Please!

A shift. Under her fingers, slippery with oil, Beth felt the child reorient itself ever so slightly. Alys gave a huge cry and pulled on Maude's hands.

"Jesu! It comes!" She lifted her head and clenched her eyes shut.

From somewhere deep, Beth saw strength and determination rise, and Alys pushed. Beth positioned herself to be ready for whatever happened next.

The tiny dark head slid free of its prison. Beth sobbed aloud as she caught the child's blue-pink face in her hands. The baby rotated and a shoulder became visible. Then, quick as thought, the rest of the small, greasy body slipped from Alys's.

"Give me cloth," Beth snapped. "The thread and the knife. Quickly. And touch not the child until I say."

Alys sagged back, panting. "Does it live? Is it aright? What is it?"

With a fingertip, Beth wiped out the child's mouth and freed his face from its coating of oil. She scratched the bottom of one minuscule foot. The baby startled as if she'd awakened him from a pleasant dream, then screwed up tiny features and let out an experimental squall. His color changed from waxen lavender to angry pink as he filled his lungs, to release air again and again in lusty and outraged cries.

"He lives, lady. Your son is born."

Alys began to sob with tears of joy and exhaustion. Maude told Beth to wait until the bluish cord stopped pulsating, then she tied it with sterile thread in two places. Extra-tight knots, Maude said, and Beth obeyed because the maid seemed more knowledgeable than she about this step. Surely you couldn't kill a baby this way? Holding her breath, feeling nauseated, Beth cut the brand-new boy free of his mother. Gently she wrapped the wriggling baby in the fresh cloth and handed him over to Alys.

"Put him to the breast." Maude came to the bedside but obeyed Beth's instructions not to touch the baby. "Let him help bring the milk in."

Beth stood up to sag against the bedpost, exultant, shaky, exhausted. "Give me water to my hands," she said hoarsely to the gaping maids. "And wine."

Maude's gaze lingered on her face. She gave a sharp gesture to send Berta scurrying from the room.

"Anything you wish. You have but to ask."

When Beth turned away from Lady Alys, who lay pale-cheeked and feebly weeping, cradling her newborn son to her cheek, Maude swept her skirts in hand and curtseyed low to her, as one does to high nobility. "I'm yours to command, for this day have you saved our dear mistress."

Beth managed a smile. "Maude, give over. Pray rise, for your skills are greatly needed, and we have still much to do."

Her head dipped lower in penitence. "Forgive me, lady. I misliked you at first. You seemed so odd, so strange . . . "

"Yet you put aside your feelings and helped me, a stranger in need. It takes a large spirit to do so. Lady Alys sets great store by you. I understand why."

Maude wiped her eyes, still bent in shame. Beth took her shoulders and forcibly raised her. "Enough. It was little you did, and already forgiven. Let us go tend to your lady and the new de Tallac."

Alys gave both women a dreamy smile as her son rooted for nourishment. Before long he fell asleep, and she stroked his downy, dark head with a shaky finger.

"Look you." Her voice sounded spent but exultant. "Is he not lovely?"

"Beyond any babe I have ever seen." Beth couldn't stop smiling, giddy with relief and gratitude to God who had certainly guided her instincts. "None the worse for the greasing I gave him."

"A fair babe," Maude pronounced. "Although, lady, by rights he *should* have just a grain of salt on the tongue, for—"

"Nay!" said Alys and Beth together.

Both laughed at the dismayed expression on the maid's face. "Bring ale," Beth requested, "and perhaps a small loaf of bread and some cheese. I expect my lady has not eaten since the pains began."

"No, nor yet all today," said Alys. "I was afeared . . . sore afeared."

Maude hurried out to see to my lady's snack.

"That is past," Beth soothed. "Take nourishment and rest. Ela and Berta will see to making all clean and fresh. You need rest above all things. Later today you will rise from the bed and sit in your chair for a little, for this is the best way to prevent complications."

"I can do naught but obey." Alys nuzzled her baby, and in sleep he thrust a tiny hand against his wrappings. "Maude speaks true—your work this day saved my life and my son's." She caught at Beth's hand. "My husband will be beside himself. I could see from his face, he despaired of us both."

"That is well past," Beth reminded her with a catch in her voice. She tucked a sweat-damp strand of Alys's dark hair back beneath her bed coif. "When you are again yourself, up and able, what say we feast your new son into his family?"

Alys smiled once more, but Beth could see fatigue conquering. Probably once she'd taken sustenance, she would sleep like one drugged.

"There's Maude. You must eat, and by your leave, I will tell the menfolk you are safe delivered."

"Send Geoffrey to me. Pray, do not tell him it is a son. I owe you much, but I would tell him myself."

"Certes." Beth bent and kissed Alys's clammy forehead. "We are quits, lady. For your generous help when I came, I but repaid what you gave. You have earned the joy of telling your lord of his heir."

She felt like leaping up and down the length of the solar, but kept her dignity. Gathering her rumpled habit in her hands, she tripped, light with relief, down the steps to the hall.

First things first: Put Geoffrey out of the desperation that creased his face. "She is well." Beth raised her voice loud enough for the manor folk in the hall to hear. "The babe is born and cries strongly."

Geoffrey sank onto a trestle bench like a snapped bowstring.

"Go up to her, my lord. Lady Alys has someone to present to you."

Geoffrey sprang up and bolted toward the stairs. Hawise, her face alight with joy, came to offer Beth ale.

"I must get me back to Trevellas," Beth told Hawise.

"You are sore undone. You shall not travel until the morn." Hawise put the best silver hanap into her hand.

"Hawise, *you* give commands?"

The maid laughed. "When need be, lady. Any woman may make shift to look to the good of another."

"You speak true." Stress over, Beth felt she would melt into a puddle on the rushes.

Hawise indicated the second-best chair. "Sit," she said. "You are travel-tired, and not a little discomposed by your work above."

Beth could not do other than obey.

"How does my lady?" Hawise asked. "Truly, the babe is well?"

"Truly, she and the child are well."

Beth watched as the maid, flush with her importance as the chief of staff now with Maude absent, ordered the servants this way and that. They must bring cold meats and a pasty for Lady Bethany's refreshment.

When Hawise turned back to her, Beth explained, "It was stuck. I had to oil it before it could be born."

Hawise murmured something amazed and grateful in Cornish.

"Give all glory to God, girl, for sure I know naught of midwifery." Beth shook her head.

With a tired hand, she pulled her wimple off, dropping it onto the arm of the chair. For once, the maid didn't purse her lips at hoydenish behavior.

"I may have read of it at some point. I do not remember."

"I' truth God gave you the knowing."

"Bless His name." Beth traced a reverent cross over her heart. Though she wasn't in church, it felt right.

Not until she woke in her old chamber with a slender crescent moon shining in through the slats did she consider Michael's strict orders to stay put. It would be all right, she assured herself, for how could she ignore Alys at her time? Surely he'd understand. She was no complaisant and timid medieval lady. She had as good a head as he to see a friend's need and to meet it.

He'd be angry, though. She'd have to measure how he managed that anger, for though he'd been irritated with Cadwr's plotting, she'd never seen Michael in a temper before.

She turned over and punched the unyielding pillow into submission. Would he limit his wrath to bellows and curses, or was he that type of medieval lord who believed a sound beating made for a good woman?

Silly to worry about this. If he ticks me off, I can always try the portal. Right here at Mossock. This is where I should be if I'm supposed to try getting back to my own time.

Strange, how the idea didn't hold as strong a pull as it should.

She'd think about the portal tomorrow.

Nineteen

Beth and her troop took horse just after Prime. Sir Geoffrey waved Ennis away as the early rays of the sun pierced the sea-fog, saying he claimed the honor of lifting Lady Bethany to horse.

"My everlasting gratitude, lady. If ever you have a need—if ever I can do aught to your benefit . . . "

"Have done, my lord. Lady Alys would have done no less for me. We are quits."

He returned her joyful smile.

"We return for the christening. Do you send word to Trevellas, for that is where I must be by my lord's order."

"On my faith, we shall not christen the babe without you. *Dyw genes.* Fare you well."

Still grinning, Sir Geoff waved her down the courtyard to the gates and was still waving when she turned round to give Mossock a last glance. Guilt spurred her back to Trevellas to arrive in stealth, before Michael returned.

Though the portal had sung its temptation song, it played very faintly. She hadn't once ventured into that hallway.

Caillin clopped placidly through a misty morning as Beth took the chance of peace and quiet to think. Looking back over the past hours, she realized the portal was no longer a place of resort, but of fear.

I can always go back to Mossock. If I do, I might try it later. Maybe after the wedding, or when we come back for the christening.

The road, familiar from her earlier journey, lulled her into a half-dreaming state. She'd never thought to ride horseback with less than full attention, but such was the luxury of a lady, well mounted on a sturdy palfrey with a seasoned troop to watch out for her.

Ennis had gathered the stoutest—and most eager—Trevellas men to serve as my lady's escort. She knew none of them save Ennis, for none had dared speak to her. In Ennis's ability she had not the slightest doubt.

So, the road to Truro, then striking slightly north toward Trevellas and peace. Glad times awaited her, happy reunion with a successful Michael, who'd gathered his vassals and dependents, binding them more firmly to loyalty to himself and to the king. Soon after, God willing, her wedding . . .

She set Caillin to a gentle canter after they'd crested the hill outside Redruth. The mare responded with eagerness to her heel, shaking her head betimes to make her bridle jingle. Ennis and the troop easily kept pace.

Her heart beat faster with the sheer joy of the wind in her face.

They'd reached a small copse near a stream when a sudden shriek came from Ennis at her side. "Ware! Arms!"

The men, a horse-length behind them, rushed forward to surround her. Ennis had his sword free before his bellow of warning died on the breeze.

Beth saw the danger he'd seen, and her heart froze. A troop three times their strength had shot out of the copse, blocking their path.

"Leave us!" she screamed. "We are peaceful wayfarers only, and carry naught of value."

Sword rang on sword as her troop defended themselves and her. One by one, over a space that seemed to drag out forever but was mere seconds, the enemy troop cut her men down or disarmed them. Ennis at her side fought like a man possessed, but she saw a sword hit his mailed neck, the blade turned so as not to behead, and he fell from his horse to lie senseless in the road.

None were left between her and the assailants. “Let me be!” she screamed.

Caillin shied as one of the enemy grabbed her bridle. Another yanked Beth from the saddle. She kicked and fought, but her soft-toed boots made no impact worth noting. Hard hands grabbed her arms and a callused palm clapped over her mouth.

A malodorous cloth was thrust over her head, effectively blinding her. She struggled, mindless in panic.

From behind, she heard a foul oath in middle-English, and what sounded like, “Silence her! Master said bring her quiet to . . . ”

She didn’t understand the final word, and a second later something blunt struck her on the back of the head.

She woke with difficulty. *Man alive, this hurts.*

Her only reality was a skull-cracking headache. It took a long while to decide to open her eyes, the better to find an explanation. She spent a few moments longer actually forcing them open.

A dank, circular room, strange to her. Bare of amenities, its stone walls held no tapestries to keep out the draft or the musty, stale smell of disuse. In the walls she heard the scutter of mice—or worse. The room boasted no furnishings, not even rushes on a splintery plank floor. No equipment save for a decrepit chest near the ironbound door, and a few rusty pikes leaning against the stones.

Arms. Why do my arms hurt so much?

It must be her position, for her body felt off kilter. Lifting her head, she glanced around to see that she stood—sort of—against one of the walls. Her wrists had been tied together with coarse rope, its end looped through a rusty iron ring driven into the stone. The rope was fastened high enough that her toes reached the floor, but she couldn’t put her heels down. Short as she was, it was impossible to relieve the strain on her arms for more than seconds at a time before her feet cramped.

Strung up like a pheasant in a market stall. Terror froze her. And it hurt. How long had she been here? Who had done this? And why?

She tried to shift position on the wall and grunted with a fresh wave of discomfort. Twist as she might, motion didn't budge that great ring above her hands. If she persevered, eventually movement might loosen it. Right? From this angle, it looked as though one good heaving squirm might overtax it and set her free. Or maybe the rope . . . Like everything else in the room, it didn't look exactly new.

Beth set to work.

Every system has a weak spot. If not the ring, the rope. I can do this. I can.

Time passed. Her head throbbed. Her calf and foot muscles cramped as she threw her weight back and forth on the ring. Motion sawed the rope against her wrists, breaking the skin down. The strain on her arms migrated down into her chest and back. Pain made her clench her teeth, which in turn worsened the headache. Becoming dehydrated didn't help either.

She tried to take her mind out of her body, to focus attention on anything but discomfort. At times, working the bindings, she drifted in loose fancy, imagining herself cantering through spring-blessed farmlands with Michael humming at her side. Then she'd move wrong and jerk back into the painful present.

Why? Who? Michael will run mad when he finds me not at Trevellas. And what of Ennis? What have they done to him? Did any of the men win free to get word to Michael? If so, will he come . . . and walk straight into a trap?

No! He'll figure this out long before that happens. He'll find a way—

A noise. She froze in mid-twist, every sense alert. The door opened with the protesting whine of dry iron hinges.

She closed her eyes, feigning unconsciousness. Heard footfalls, felt unwashed breath in her face.

"Awake, are you?" A voice she'd heard before, speaking English. "*En fin*. You look better this way. Not so determined."

She blinked as though waking. "Cadwr." *Might've known*. She didn't bother keeping contempt out of her voice.

"Glad to see me, are you, *ma belle*? Mayhap you will treat me with better courtesy now than when last we met."

She lifted her brows. *What does he want? Why is he doing this?* It seemed best not to scream her questions, so she let him think her paralyzed with pain and fear, and didn't speak.

"You seem tongue-bit. So unlike you."

His fingers fussed with a strand of her hair that hung loose, no longer confined by the tidy wimple into which Maude had tamed it this morning. She wanted to turn her face away from his unwelcome scrutiny, but instinct told her to continue to appear stunned.

She let her eyes drop half shut and somehow avoided flinching when he withdrew his eating knife from its sheath and expertly sliced her surcote down the front.

"Better."

The gray habit that Alys's maids had so carefully altered gapped over her collarbones. She ground her teeth in helpless rage at the waste.

"Aye, much better. Current fashions do no justice to a lady's charms. But then, you are no lady, *ma belle*."

Whatever. Let him say what he pleases. As long as he thinks I'll cooperate, maybe he'll cut me down and I can figure out why he's doing this. What has he to gain?

Lord, please let him get me down from here. Everything hurts from my wrists to my toes.

He ran an idle finger over her collarbone, indecently exposed by her undertunic. "No," he said quietly, as though to himself. "No lady. But *sans doute* you knew I would guess that—did you not, witch?"

Beth managed not to react to the accusation. *Sort of. I feared it always. Just not that it'd be an ignorant git like you accusing me.*

She ran a dry tongue over her lips. "You are mistaken. I am no witch."

"No? I say you are. Certes you have ensorcelled Michael beyond reason."

"That is love, not magic."

He shrugged. "Call it what you will. It matters not a speck to me. You but want the Veryan lands, as do I, but I have so much more at stake."

Her lip curled. "I would not presume to his lands."

"You would presume to paradise itself," he sneered, "did it advance your purposes."

"I have no evil purpose toward any. I want nothing."

Not quite true. What I want, right now, is to get loose so I can claw his eyes out and run far from here. Can I persuade him into it? Trick him?

He tugged at the shoulder of her chemise. "Mayhap a few more hours will make you more pliable. Not that it matters what befall you in the end. I advise you consider the state of your soul. Your sins must be many and interesting. Mayhap I will even send a priest. If you speak me plain, I may give you the chance to confess and be shriven."

He wants to kill me? "Speak plain? I have spoken as plainly as I can." Her mouth hadn't enough moisture to spit in his face. Maybe that was a good thing. "What is it you want me to say?"

"Your true reason for coming to Truro." He twirled one of her curls, his hand too near her skin. "And to whom you really owe fealty. You were not set upon by brigands, and you suffer no convenient loss of memory."

Oh, to be able to spit! "You would not know the truth if you heard it. Plainly I'm but a convenient tool, since you have some old score to settle with your brother. Is that the reason you tried to kill him when you went hawking?"

Cadwr's mouth curled up on one side. "Surely if I intended murder, he would even now inhabit a grave. He came off his horse like an untaught boy. None of my fault an he be clumsy and have accidents."

"Accident my—" She bit back words. "Free me at once." She pretended to yank on her bonds, though without the energy she'd expended earlier. "Give over and Lord Michael may not cut you down like a runt puppy. You may have a chance to live, do you but let me go. Now." She waited a moment for the threat to penetrate his paranoia, and repeated, "If you tarry, I may not be so forgiving."

He gave a cold laugh. "Set you free? I think not."

He fingered his eating knife and for a panicked moment, she wondered if its next motion would be into her chest.

"Lord Michael will seek me. Do not deceive yourself. He will raze this—place down to its foundations stone by stone if he finds me harmed."

"He sets such great value on you, then?" Amazing, how thoroughly a sneer ruined Cadwr's surfer-boy looks. "Besotted, as I guessed. I will free him from your witcheries . . . and my true heritage also. In Wales it is no shame to be illegitimate. When I come into what is rightfully mine, I will foil the king's plan to beggar us all. Once I've sufficient men and money, Lord Mortimer will grant me his favor once more. If he add his strength to mine, we can see our way clear of this *praemunire* foolishness. We will have no more flouting of custom nor life turned upside down! We must not order life contrary to proper and God-ordained ways. No more king's justice overbearing the church's, of freeing serfs and paying the churls high wages. I can take my place at court, and—"

She forced a derisive laugh. "You are moonstruck."

Cadwr's smile made her blood run cold. "If I know my brother, he seeks you even now. What will you say, witch, when he kneels before me and pleads for your life—and his?"

"He will never plead before you," she spat. "You're no match for him. Here or elsewhere, he will have your guts for garters."

He didn't appear to hear. "Michael, the greatly favored. Our father first, then king and Lancaster after." His lip deformed in a sneer. "Do-No-Wrong Veryan. He charms them all, makes them blind to his folly. They hang on his every word as if he has some vision the rest of us lack."

He spat with force onto the bare floor. "Not everyone is as admiring as those highborn fools. My brother's pot-brained ideas are the laughingstock of his class. Freeing the serfs—imagine what mischief could ensue if this became common! They laugh at him at court, knew you this?"

"I heard none do. I doubt he'd care. And he does well to free his serfs. It is the right thing. No man should be owned by another, or bound to the land against his will."

History itself will prove he's right. Serfdom is doomed anyway . . . the smart money already senses Michael's on the right track.

He smirked. "More of your witchery ideas."

"You bore me, you hairy-nosed git, but I'll repeat it since you obviously lack wit to understand—I'm no witch. Michael will sniff you out. Depend upon it. When he does, you'll be the one pleading for him to spare your sorry hide."

Cadwr tested his blade's edge on his thumbnail. "A harlot should trust her master. Do not pretend you're not his leman, you use his name too easily to claim otherwise."

And I'll keep using it, for every time I do, fear rises in your eyes.

"Free me." Sparring, trying to gain insight into his delusions, exhausted her more than trying to twist the iron ring from the wall. "Let me go and my troop also. We will return to Trevellas. If you do so now, I will say naught of this—this misunderstanding to my lord."

Cadwr laughed and ran a finger along her throat as if slitting it. His touch froze her tongue with revulsion.

"It is you who misunderstand. Here you shall bide until my brother comes. And after I dispatch him, an it please me, I can always bring you up before the bishop on charges."

His handsome blue eyes turned off kilter, obsessed and ugly. "It might be pleasant to see you executed for sorcery."

Twenty

Shock. Beth opened her mouth to say he'd lost his mind. Her contempt must have shown in her eyes, for Cadwr slapped her with a savage backhand, slamming her head against the stones. She saw red and white stars. When she regained reality, he was gone like an evil shadow. She heard the key grate in the lock, footfalls retreating down the passage outside. Then silence.

"Steady," she murmured. "Steady. A bit more effort and the ring will give way."

She shook her head to clear it and gasped. The pain of the slap echoed dimly through greater pain. Since she'd conked out, the distress in her arms and chest had doubled.

She resumed her efforts to loosen either rope or ring, but it hurt more now. Her wrists, rubbed raw, had begun to bleed. The strain in her arms brought a strange constricted sensation, centered in midchest, making her breath come short.

Man alive. He's good at this. Must practice on his serfs.

Time passed. She judged its slow grind by the sun's fitful shadow, creeping toward noontime on the uneven floor planks. A lone high arrow slit served as the room's only aperture, and soon the sun's angle would no longer allow her to see its light. She heard her voice whispering a prayer.

Gradually, the seriousness of her predicament came through.

Gotta find some way. If he comes back—maybe I can convince him. Make him afraid somehow. If I can get free, in some way warn

Michael, that's even better. Lord, all strength comes from You. If You give me a way . . . Lord, if I'm to overcome here, I need power from You.

And a drink of water would be great.

Her chest vibrated with tight, constricted pain. Her arm muscles screamed with the nearly unbearable strain of supporting her weight for so long. The fullness felt as though it localized in her lungs, which she didn't want to think about.

Try. Keep twisting that rope . . . the ring's weakening, I'm sure it is.

It's only a matter of time. Right?

Doggedly she kept up her efforts, though by now she was beyond tired. The ring began a mournful whine of protest, scraping on the stone that held it.

Keep going. The pain doesn't exist. Meaningless. Keep trying.

How many hours had passed? Frequently now she must stop working on the ring, stop to catch her breath, to rest. Blood traveled in slow, tickly rivulets down her forearms.

Just a little longer, a little harder. Michael's looking for me, don't forget that. Oh yes, he'll search like anything, and he's too clever to blunder all unknowing into a trap. All I have to do is hang on till he gets here.

She developed a pattern. Twist as frequently as possible. Rest. Catch her breath. Push the headache, dehydration, and nausea to a manageable distance. Pray. Twist some more.

Master, Jesus, let Michael know what's happening. Michael, hear Him. My love, stay safe. But Lord, let someone come find me, 'cause I'm getting so tired.

She closed her eyes. Time to rest and conserve her strength for a fresh assault on the ring. Try not to lose hope. But . . .

"I'm afraid," she whimpered. "Come to me. I'll keep trying, but—*j'ai peur*."

At midday Cadwr returned to taunt her. She tried to show neither fear, pain, nor thirst, but speech came with difficulty.

"A trifle less contumacious now?"

"I can match words. If I wish." She had to stop to take in a long, shaky breath. "I save my con-conver-sation. For equals."

Don't let him see. Don't give him the satisfaction.

Cadwr chuckled. Dimly she felt his fingertip track where none but a husband's hands should go. "A few hours more, and we shall see what you will offer for your freedom."

"A few years. Make no difference." With all her heart, she wished she had enough spittle to fly in his face. "Do not forget. Lord Michael. Too canny not to spot. Trap. Seeks me as we speak."

She had to stop every few words. *Breathe. Keep your cool.* "If you are greatly. Favored by God. His mercy. Michael may let—keep your head."

"I would welcome him here," Cadwr sneered, "to see you suffer."

"Summon him. He will make you pay . . . "

Sneering, he left her.

She drowsed, woke, worked the ring some more, drifted off again. Outside the shabby window, noises as though Cadwr's troop practiced at arms in whatever court this place possessed. Steel rang upon steel, but she could not pay attention to its meaning. If indeed it meant anything . . .

By the time the gold glow of afternoon showed through her arrow slit, she lacked breath to work on the rope. Her body would no longer obey. Still she tried, though her motions had weakened and she couldn't do much more than rock against the wall. Though Cadwr returned once or twice to taunt her, he seemed distracted and did not stay long. She didn't waste breath or dimming energy to counter his needling or even to answer.

She heard him slam the door in rage. The sun fell on her tortured, cramped feet. She leaned her head back on the rough granite. Pain racked through her chest, arms, back, hands. She arched spasmodically against the wall. Despair coursed through her.

If I'm to die here . . .

A Traveler's Tale. In her imagination, she took up quill and inkhorn. Her mind felt foggy, tracing out the words.

I should've seen Cadwr was one tankard short of a feast. I thought he was a harmless idiot whose only fault was self-aggrandizement. Lord, I was daft. Why did I think I could sojourn here safely, untouched? Visit in a foreign land, make detached, scientific observations, and return home to write them up? Instead, I fell in love and ran afoul of my love's family.

What path do I walk now, Lord? And here I stand, unworthy to ask anything of You . . . I who left You long ago. In Your mercy, I ask You to forgive my many sins. Chief of those are arrogance and deceitfulness, walking in opposition to Your law of truth. Forgive me anyway, and protect Michael. Given this sixth day of June in the year of my Lord 1353. I think. God, have mercy and let Michael come soon. I cannot endure much longer . . .

Her heart beat thickly. Her breath came short. Her thoughts rambled, sometimes present in pain, sometimes sheltered. The noises in the courtyard intensified, then drifted into an unreachable distance. Shouting, the urgent ring of steel on steel, cries of distress, cries of warning.

They could not reach her.

Why had she put such stock in her career as historian? In ideas, writings, theories that after all could prove nothing? History consisted of so much more than dry facts. All she knew of medieval history could not assure her one more breath.

Michael, Alys, Teagen, Beth—they comprised history. History was personal. Why had she ignored faith, emotion, experience? Why, for that matter, did she consider it so important to find her way home, to do work that lacked all meaning? Wasn't *life*—the sheer thrum of her slowing heartbeat, the blood in her veins—wasn't living more important? What did it matter, truly, if this heart beat here in the fourteenth century, or at home in the twenty-first?

It doesn't. Lord, thank You for helping me see. Now forgive all my foolish mistakes, and let me follow You—here or home. I don't care anymore. It's life that matters. Your will, Lord, not mine . . .

She awakened, unaware of drifting off, to find her eyes stuck shut by dried tears. Then she stilled. The ring was coming loose, so in spite of the pain, she tugged a little harder.

A protesting squeal of metal against stone, and she tumbled free, falling face forward on the rough planks of the floor. A mouse squeaked alarm and scuttled into hiding.

Her face prickled with wood slivers. She moved a quarter inch, testing a run of dry tongue over paper-dry lips. She desisted and lay quiet, dimly glad of the change in position, too tired to figure anything out.

More change. At a far and incomprehensible distance, sounds. Pounding footfalls, cries whose words came without sense or clarity. The ring of metal on metal. Closer now. Who was making those irritating noises? She tried to move and couldn't.

Okay then. Someone's coming. Okay. I'm just so tired.

With any luck, swords made that clanging sound, growing ever nearer. In which case she would soon be free, one way or another.

So be it.

A thud. At the extreme edge of her dimming vision, the rough-hewn door crashed open. Beth blinked. Hands on her.

Okay then.

"Lady, lady, what has been done to you?" *Bifan?*

She blinked. A shadow blocked the light. Someone fell to his knees beside her, tore off a battered helmet and scooped her into his arms like a newborn babe. *Michael?*

"My love, can you hear me?"

She cried out at a sudden jerk on her bonds. More pain as gentle hands peeled the rope from the deep wounds on her wrists. She lost consciousness again.

She roused at motion, a strange motion as though she were carried. She knew that strength and the wood-and-leather scent of the man. She sighed and nestled into his embrace.

The light came clearer now, and she could see a little. Blood smeared her surcote. Not hers. His. She cried out again.

"You're hurt!"

"A nothing, sweeting," he assured her brokenly, "nothing if you but live."

His tears fell upon her face, but she lacked strength enough to lift her damaged hand to brush them from his cheek.

And suddenly, the healing, blessed dark.

Twenty-One

She came back with maddening slowness. Sun in her eyes. A spoon at her lips. Soft, coaxing words in a voice she knew. She drowsed, too tired to analyze. Warm liquid slid along her teeth, and involuntarily she swallowed.

"She mends, lord. See? She takes the cordial."

"Not enough. Keep trying."

The spoon. More liquid. She turned her head slightly so it wouldn't dribble out of the corner of her mouth, but made an inadvertent sound of pain. Everything *hurt*!

"Bless God. She wakes."

"Lady. Lady Bethany. Do you hear me?"

She blinked again. Slowly, excruciatingly slowly, an unfamiliar room cleared before her eyes.

"I hear."

"God in His mercy be praised." Michael's face, close to her own, his voice sounding strangely tight. "How much did I promise that simpering leech-monk?"

"A year's worth of fine beeswax candles."

"See for it."

"Aye, lord."

Beth blinked and tried to form words. Not much came out, and what she articulated was still a whisper: "How—how long?"

"This is the third day, lady." Teagen wiped a drop from her chin. "We were sore afeared, but Brother Simon's leechcraft served well.

He even said he should not bleed you, can you credit it? He said only foxglove tincture, yarrow salve, and rest would restore you, and praise all the saints, they have!"

"Dear Teagen." She had to stop to catch her breath.

When Michael bent over her, Beth tried to lift her hand to grasp his, and failed. Fatigue sent it flopping inert onto the coverlet. Michael, however, caught her fingers and held them to his lips. Her eyes filled.

"Dear-my-lord."

"Do not talk," he ordered. "Rest. Make certain sure, Teagen. Now she is awake, my lady will want to be up, but I forbid it."

He ran his lips over her fingertips, and his touch felt so good she couldn't repress a smile. When he replaced her hand on the coverlet he took care to lay it down gently, for neat linen cuffs bandaged her abraded wrists.

"I should be up." Gingerly Beth flexed her hands. They cramped and refused to obey. "It is always better . . . to rise early from illness."

"Nay!" both her caretakers said in unison.

Trying for a severe frown through the relief in his warm eyes, Michael added, "Brother Simon and I do agree. Do not even think to rise until he visits again at vespers. Mayhap you can cozen him around to your thinking, but do not try your woman's wiles on me."

Teagen tittered. "Can you take broth? I can hot it up here on the fire quicker'n you can say an Ave."

Beth felt too nauseated to eat, but the desert-dry state of her mouth won out. "Yes, please."

Michael had to lift her into a more upright position. Teagen insisted on wielding the spoon. Beth took a few blessedly warm, savory mouthfuls, and slept.

She drowsed away that afternoon and evening. Periodically Teagen urged more broth. As darkness fell, Beth found an appetite for larger amounts, plus a half goblet of well-watered wine. The sweet vernage gave her energy she'd lacked for . . . how long had Teagen claimed she was out? Two days? Four?

Evening brought a visitor: Brother Simon the leech-monk. Gravely he introduced himself.

"Though we have met before, I daresay you remember me not."

"Forgive me, good brother. I do not know you."

He undertook a gentle examination, then produced a small leather vial from the sleeve of his coarse woolen robe. "The wounds heal well. The swelling in the arms and ankles is much diminished. Hmm, we will offer no more than a small dose of foxglove tincture at this time and more good yarrow salve. I dare to hope that on the morrow we may forgo the tincture altogether."

Medieval medicine, but he obviously knows what he's about. Without modern drugs or anything, he saved my life.

"I was very ill. I am grateful for your care," Beth murmured.

He gave a "tchk" sound with his tongue, and though he didn't crack a smile, she saw gratification in his brown eyes. "God's mercy and fervent prayer. Though foxglove is efficacious for water on the chest, and the salve good for wounds, also your stars were auspicious."

Beth shivered in recollection of how awful she'd felt. "You excel at your craft. I would offer my thanks."

He perched on the side of the bed, taking his seat so carelessly she recognized it as long habit. From Teagen he took long strips of clean linen, and set about redressing her wrists.

"Express your thanks in good works. Alms for the poor give great comfort to the soul. God must have saved you for something very special."

She smiled, though the wrapping hurt. "I believe He has."

As if on cue, Michael rapped at the door and strode through it without waiting for Teagen to open it. It did her good just to look upon his face, and she felt her spirits rise at the sight of him. He wore clothing of the type for work in the castle, a plain blue gown, dun surcote, and hose and looked as though he'd partied too late or ridden too hard. Weary lines bracketed his mouth, and his eyes betrayed fatigue.

"God's greeting, brother," he said. "How does my lady?"

"Much improved. She needs no more foxglove after tonight. Her woman knows how to poultice the wrists and change the dressings, so I am finished here."

The monk rose and tucked his vial back into the depths of his sleeve. Did he have folds for every vial of medicine he used, or did he restock his sleeve afresh for each patient? Beth wondered.

"How soon can she travel?"

Brother Simon fingered his chin. "Not for a seven-night."

"We would go carefully." Michael scowled, taking the monk's seat at Beth's side and finding her hand. "I would have her home to Truro as soon as she can ride."

"Your pardon, my lord." Beth withdrew her fingers. "She mislikes being discussed as though she were deaf and dumb as a stock."

That brought Brother Simon's gap-toothed smile. "If you needs must travel in the next few days, lady, use a traveling-wain. I would not have you undo all my good work on horseback."

"Necessity wields a stout whip, but one that is obeyed." Firmly Michael reclaimed her hand. "I will watch close. She shall not ride until healed. May I taste ale nevermore, lady, if I let you out of my sight again."

Beth froze at the ferocity in his tone. Teagen's hands stopped folding linen for bandages. Brother Simon made his "tchk" noise and sketched a cross in blessing over Beth's head, and hastily she echoed the gesture. In silence Teagen showed the leech-monk out of the chamber, lit several fat candles to provide light, and shut the door behind her.

Beth waited until they were well and truly alone before speaking. "I think my lord has something to say."

"Indeed I do." His hazel gaze caressed her face. "First, however, I must answer the questions you have not asked."

"Forgive me. I suppose I should ask about Sir Cadwr and his plots, but in truth I didn't want to know."

Michael scowled, looking more fatigued than before. "He will not trouble you again."

Beth sighed. "I warned him your wrath would be terrible, but he didn't listen." She unearthed his thumb out of his clenched fist, and stroked it thoughtfully. "He said he meant to use me to set a trap for you. Where are we now? Where did he take me?"

"Gently, lady. All in good time." Michael reclaimed his thumb, rose and poured wine into two goblets on a small table nearby. He tasted before offering Beth hers.

"Mmm. A good flavor, this Gascon swill."

When she had sipped the wine, he resumed his seat. "My bastard brother learned our destination through court gossip. The king's friar let it slip I would show you your new lands at Trevellas. The git my brother can add two and two. He followed us from Windsor. He must have kept from the roads like any outlaw, to skulk thus unseen! By the rood, I came near to having Bifan's ears from his head for such carelessness."

She patted his hand and he calmed visibly. "When I left Trevellas for Truro, he lay in wait, then followed your party to Mossock. It was near there that he suborned a force of Mortimer's strong enough to take you when you left Mossock. Mortimer will have their ears for listening to his blandishments, but they thought they had their lord's order to go."

Beth shook her head as Michael emptied his mazer. "Cadwr made free with more than Mortimer's men," he continued. "He bore you away to a disused castle of Mortimer's in a wood near St. Austell."

"Where he bound me on the wall." Beth shivered and Michael put an arm around her shoulders. Grateful, she rested there. "I didn't think I'd ever get free."

"Yet you freed yourself. When we broke in, I found you on the floor, out of your senses, your arms still bound and the ring pulled from the wall."

"I did?" She sat up straighter in his embrace. "Well, well."

She savored the brief triumph. Not that her efforts had saved her. Michael, Brother Simon, and Teagen had together done that.

"I do not recall freeing myself. But while I hung, I felt like to die."

"When I saw you lying there, all white . . . I thought you dead." He glowered but she saw his barely suppressed shudder.

She had to change the subject. "Cadwr said he was as well-born as you and as deserving of your lands and honors. He spoke of the customs of Wales. He said once he had your lands and power, he would regain Mortimer's favor. Together they would put paid to the king's plan regarding the church. I do not understand."

He set his empty goblet on the table. "It has its roots in Welsh law. The Cymry are half mad with their inheritance customs, as well as many other things. Though Cadwr is in truth my brother, Welsh ways say that 'the son of the handmaid shall be heir with the son of the free.' He has always felt he was shortchanged in lands and honors and deserved more." Michael spat into the floor rushes. "He linked his well doing to Mortimer's favor and determined to have it all if he must kill both me and you to do it."

Beth took a shaky breath. "You stood in the way of his plans to regain his standing in Mortimer's eyes. And he believed me a witch for the spell I've woven over you."

"A spell you've woven indeed, though not by witchcraft," he said with a smile.

Sobering, he set his empty goblet on the table. "Through this villainous affair his full treachery has come to light. It is now clear he and others planned to send a huge gift to Avignon. Three thousand gold nobles were found on him. Money collected from the coffers of the church, which could've found better use for it. Cadwr worked hand in glove with Abbot Boniface and others to wrest true power from Edward and put England in the pope's hands. England might have become no more than an impotent vassal and with the holy see but a puppet of France . . . "

He shook his head. "But all his plots have come to naught. They rot in the grave with his bones."

"How learned you this?"

"From his men. They served Cadwr, but out of fear, not love. To save their skins after I bested him in battle, they told the same tale to a man."

She saw in his eyes that his brother's exposure as a coward gave him no joy. Impulsively she blurted, "Cadwr was older than you and still unwed. Was that the source of this enmity? Did he despise you because he wished to marry Joan himself?"

Michael thought for a moment, then raised his shoulders in an expressive shrug. "Mayhap. Our families were long connected, and Joan was comely enough to attract Cadwr's interest. She wished to wed no man, but become the bride of Christ as an abbess. Like you, she loved learning and books. She wanted not to 'waste her life' running a keep and bearing children." He shook his head. "Not Bridgnorth's and certainly not Veryan's."

"Yet you loved her," she whispered. "Everyone knew of it."

He shrugged. "Aye, I suppose I did, in a way. Perhaps I loved the idea of having someone of my own . . . "

When he cleared his throat, Beth realized she had never asked about the rest of his family. Her heart moved with repentance for her insensitivity and sympathy for the buried pain in his voice.

"In any event, I was unaware how reluctantly she wed me, till long after. Nor did I realize how she came to agree. Her father held old-styled ideas. He held not with the church's edicts requiring consent. To get Joan's compliance he beat her, starved her—saints know how he brought her to bend the knee. Forced consent is none at all, and his methods were worse than useless. Once I saw she had no heart for me, nor ever would, my affection did not last a twelvemonth. Oh, I did my duty, and Joan hers, but after a while we had naught else."

"Dear my lord, do not talk of these things if it irks you. Tell me instead how you found me and overcame Cadwr."

He scowled. "One of your troop played dead in the road. He found his way back to Truro to alert me. When he told me Cadwr's claim that Mortimer knew and approved the attack, all you learned at Windsor fell into place, and I knew at once he set a trap for me. I misdoubted even then that Mortimer was involved. Cadwr made free with Mortimer's property by taking you to a holding without his knowledge or sanction. He knew I should seek you at once if he took you to any place of his own. My vassals were already with me at Truro, so we made a strong force to set you free." He lifted her hand to his lips and did not hurry over the caress.

"And Ennis? He lives?"

Michael laughed and kissed her. "Certes, tender-heart. He was left for dead in the road, but his wounds were light. He heals apace. Naught more done to him than a sore brain pan."

She smiled in relief. "What then?"

"Why, we laid siege, of course. My only thought was the horrors you must be suffering, that the scut might well kill you just to spite me. The place was well fortified, though not well guarded. We had our work cut out to breach the walls and overcome the few he'd trained properly. Thanks be to God I met my brother in fair combat body-to-body, and I triumphed at last."

"He is dead. I am sorry for it."

"Aye." His mouth twisted. "I am in no way of gloating. However ill guided and pork brained, he was my brother in blood." He kissed her and cradled her close as if to give them both solace. "Sweeting, he will vex you no more."

"Unshriven." Beth signed the cross with regret. "Poor thing, for he had no chance to make peace with God."

"You are too tender of heart. He would have done you more damage if he could." Michael tucked her closer under his chin. "I failed in my duty to protect you. If I'd let him fly scot free, I would have failed twofold."

"We are safe now," she soothed. "His soul is in the hands of our dear Lord. We can only pray he found peace before you fell upon him."

"Aye so." He looked doubtful.

"And you were sore hurt in the fight."

"Pah." He waved her words away. "It was nothing. A scratch."

"Not so," she began, but he stilled her with his forefinger to her lips.

"You see I am fully recovered. I have much to do and may not stay. I would see you resting, as you promised me you would do."

"I recall no such promise."

"Then the promise I was about to extract from you." He released her to her pillows after giving her a sound kiss. "And I will take my ease as soon as I see you obey me."

She yawned. Hearing the story, filling in the blanks was tiring.

"I believe I will obey you now, dear-my-lord."

"You improve apace." He kissed her more tenderly and rose. "Sleep now, sweeting. If you have need, tell Teagen to summon me. I shall not be far away."

Fatigue stilled her reply. After he'd left, she lay staring at the ceiling timbers for some time. Though she felt tired enough, sleep eluded her. Her mind stayed wide awake, busy with too much to think over and way too much to figure out.

If Michael hadn't come in time, Cadwr would have killed me. I felt so lousy, I was almost ready anyway . . . They'd have put me in a grave here in Truro's churchyard. All Mom knew was that I'd gone to the U.K. on the dig. She'd never have learned what became of me.

God didn't let that happen. Why? To go back to my own time? To stay here? If I don't go back, I might as well have died as far as Mom's concerned. She'll still never know . . .

At last exhaustion silenced her questions, and she slept.

Twenty-Two

Never had her Chicago apartment looked so welcome as did Truro, twelve long and weary days later. Looming on a horizon drifted in fog, the towers shouted *home*. Michael's destrier pranced as if smelling his own stable and eager to get there. Ever true to form and impossible to predict, Caillin snorted and sidestepped, making Beth curb her sharply. *See?* the mare seemed to say. *Even after carrying you this long distance to Windsor and back again, I will obey when I choose, if I choose, or not at all, as I choose.*

"Calm yourself, my girl." She gave her palfrey a slap on the neck with her glove. "Steady, I say. Before vespers you will munch oats in your stall, and I will take my ease with my own dear lord."

"Vespers, sweeting? There's a happy thought. Father Gedren will say prayers for us in our own chapel."

His bright eyes lingered on hers, and it struck her how great a change he had undergone. From the taciturn man who said little, as Alys had described him, he'd apparently reverted to his old merry ways. Beth thanked God, for certainly no doctoral candidate time traveler could have achieved it.

"Peter atte-Well will be happy to see you returned at last."

"You speak true. Certes I have been too long away. Are you awearied?"

"No more than usual, and eager to be home. Look how the sun peeks out to shine on the water. There are the Kenwyn, the Allen, and the Fal."

She grinned at him. Michael had irritated her by insisting on taking the short journey home much more slowly than they'd ridden to Windsor. No more than a few miles did he permit, before he commanded the troop to stop and let her rest as much as possible.

The first hours, she'd tired much too quickly to suit her. Her stamina was much diminished since Cadwr's attack. But she held her so-called "ready" tongue lest Michael fret overmuch about her condition.

Though she no longer experienced shortness of breath and her hands barely ached, she'd be glad to dismount in Truro keep's bailey. The experience was sobering, for she only now realized how ill she had been. Michael, of course, expressed every intention of babying her, and this she could not allow.

In no long time they would receive word that Alys was ready to be churched, and then the christening of her baby. Per her invitation, they would visit and celebrate at Mossock. Beth would test her theory by seeking out the portal. Once she'd tried it, once she could trust she would not be snatched back to her own time, she and Michael would wed. And in no short order, with God's blessings she could announce to him that she was with child.

With these happy visions in mind, she rode alongside him into Truro town. On a warm June afternoon, the townsfolk bustled about, each on his own errand. The street crowds parted for the noble troupe, Bifan shouting coarse greetings and warnings to "make way, make way for my lord Veryan!"

Beth put aside the pain of lacking loved ones to stand with her at the church door. Lady Alys, Teagen, Michael—they made up her family now. Others would enter her life, she hoped, in time. Her current sorrow meant she'd welcome them the more warmly when they did arrive.

Truro's castle gates opened wide at their approach. Peter greeted them from within the bailey, glad eagerness in his voice and expression. "*Warlinenn, warlinenn!* God give you greeting, my lord!"

"*Fatla genes,* good Peter?"

"We do well, right well, lord. Greetings, my lady. God be praised, you look so well!"

She glanced at Michael who sketched the Cornish words with his lips. "*Meur ras,* master Peter."

The steward gave her a wide, surprised smile. "You learn *Kernewek!* This is pleasant hearing on my lady's lips. *Deus a ji.*"

"Come inside," Michael softly translated with a sly grin. Stable boys raced out to take their reins, and Beth accepted Michael's courtesy in a lift down from Caillin's back. Peter took charge, ushering them solicitously inside with many eager words and bows.

"I will use Cornish when I can," Beth warned the steward with a smile, "but you must be patient and speak me slow and easy. It is none so simple a tongue to learn, and I am poor at it."

"The castle folk will be delighted nonetheless."

"That is as may be, but Teagen still mocks my accent."

"She will not do for long, Lady Bethany."

Michael beamed at his steward and Beth could have kissed him. So gratifyingly different, this reception, from the cool and speculative glances at Windsor!

"The wains have arrived? My lord's baggage and furnishings?"

"All is arranged as you commanded, lady."

"What new whim is this?"

"I but sent a few simple instructions ahead with the carters, dear-my-lord. Do not worry. All shall be done as you desire."

Warmth flared in his eyes as he took a meaning she did not intend. She laughed, and borrowing his gesture, raised his fist to her lips. Michael's expression cleared, though his gaze lingered on her throat as he echoed her merriment. Handfast, they sought the comfort of wine and a warm fire in the great hall while Teagen and the others saw to their gear. Irksome and slow as she found mounted travel, Beth saw distinct advantages in having someone else to do the unpacking.

"Compose your soul in patience. We will be wed soon enough." With a grateful nod, she accepted cool wine from Peter and drank deeply.

He growled, "Not half soon enough for my liking."

"Nor mine. What think you, my lord, of a few days' rest here, then visit Trevellas and Mossock after? I would get this testing over and done, then hurry back home. The month end will see us wed, what say you to that?"

He affected a scowl and didn't answer. "Cicely! By heaven's bright gates, my belly thinks me beheaded. When's supper?"

The girl scurried to his side, wringing her hands though her eyes remained unafraid. "Anon, lord. The meats are but half cooked. There's pottage . . . "

"In that case, let them bring it," Beth said on a laugh, "and with all haste. My lord and I will be grateful for hearty food after our journey."

Cicely reappeared rapidly with bowls and spoons. On her heels, the serving men bore large fresh-baked wheaten loaves, cheese, and a pewter tureen of rich-smelling soup brimming with chunks of meat and leeks.

Beth could have kissed the servants' feet, so enticing were the aromas. Cicely drew up a small table, and the noble pair fell to. Michael applied his eating knife to the cheese and tore great steaming hunks off a loaf, serving Beth before himself. Then he dipped his bread into the soup and chewed happily.

"Hearty fare indeed. I grew aweary of the food at court—half of it overdone, the rest oversauced and overdecorated. Now, as to our wedding."

"The banns must be cried first, is that not so?"

He made an incredulous sound, then stopped his own voice with another spoonful of soup. "You, an historian, know this not?"

"As always, my lord, my inferior knowledge must bend to yours."

"Hah! That will be the day, my lady." He drained his mazer and gestured to Cicely for a refill. "However, since you wish me to take this in hand, Father Gedren will have the priest call the banns at St. Mary's starting this very Sunday. What say you to that?"

Beth nodded, putting her spoon down. Her tum grew soon full these days, since she'd lived on broth and watered wine. It wanted to rebel at the speed with which she filled it.

"A fair plan. We must see Ennis and Teagen wed and return them to Trevellas. To Mossock to celebrate Geoffrey's boy, then we marry."

His eyes took on a glint of mischief. "You did promise at Windsor to show me your . . . odd clothing. What time like the present?"

"My lord," she purred, "it would do better to wait till we are well and truly wed."

"You are overfond of bending me to your will, and I do badly to permit it. In this, I will have my way."

Beth smiled back. "Very well. Come above, but you may not enter my chamber till I bid you."

She insisted Michael finish dinner first, though she'd already done. After he declared himself satisfied, they set off handfast up the steps. "You will not be shocked?" she murmured.

"I shall try to contain it."

"Wait you here, then." She put out a hand to indicate the passageway that led past her small chamber and to the solar. "I hope Teagen is well occupied with work or with Ennis, for I have never shown any the contents of my traveling pouch."

"She is below." He gave her an impatient waggle of the hand. "*Vite,* or I will be tempted to enter where I ought not."

She smiled and shut the door. Her pouch was in its proper place in her larger coffer. She dug into the bottom to extract clothing she hadn't glimpsed in weeks.

The underwear constrained. The T-shirt didn't cover her bandaged wrists as was decent, and the jeans gapped at the waist, telling her she'd lost weight. Natural enough, considering her recent recovery from Cadwr's abuse. She donned the socks and shoes, then pushed her loose hair back—thank Heaven, it had grown somewhat less ragged—and called, "*Entrez.*"

Her heart beat thickly under a single layer of cloth. What would he think of her so immodestly dressed?

Michael left the door a few inches open behind him. His eyes widened as he took in her appearance. Beth moistened her lips. "You were forewarned of being shocked."

He pursed his lips and let out a long hissing sound. "*Belle sainte vierge!*"

She squirmed under his scrutiny. He found her ugly!

Michael paced around her three-sixty. Beth shut her eyes, but opened them again when she felt his hands at her waist.

He smiled and kissed her. "Have you other clothing of this kind?"

"No. This is what I wore when I came." She studied his eyes from close-up. "You think it not—lewd?"

"I dare not say for fear you will offer me the harsh side of your tongue." He kissed her again. "An this style become the fashion here, I tremble for what the lustier men might make of it."

"I knew you would not like it."

"*Au contraire,* sweeting, I like it right well. Too well."

She chuckled and relaxed, stepping back out of his embrace. "Then may I show you other proofs of my story? I have little, but they are things I promise you have not seen before."

He expressed interest, and she dug in her pouch for her wrist-watch and the few coins she'd had in her jeans pocket. He fingered the items almost reverently.

"United States," he read aloud. "This is your country, imprinted on this fine coinage? I have never seen its equal."

"Yes. It is a land across the ocean, past Ireland, and many days' sail from here."

"And this?"

She demonstrated her wristwatch, making it tick again after many weeks of neglect.

"*Incroyable,*" he said. "A timepiece so tiny. Is it accurate?"

"Quite, when I remember to wind it."

He set it down on the coffer and fell silent. Beth let him have the time to process, for she could imagine how he felt. What would she have made of artifacts from the twenty-sixth century?

At length Michael shifted his weight onto one foot and regarded her. "When first you told me your story, I could not believe. I dared not. And when I began to doubt my doubts—" He lifted one shoulder in a bemused shrug. "Misbelief and love cannot walk as yokefellows. I wanted to see these wondrous things, but you needed not to show them forth to prove your tale."

She stepped into his arms, and he willingly drew her near. "For that I did not trust at first, I ask your forgiveness."

"Willingly given. I love you." She lifted on tiptoe to kiss his chin.

"And I you, sweeting." He returned her kiss with interest, then set her back onto her feet and frowned. "And faced with our marriage, with all the joy we will share together, you would still go back to Mossock and try the portal?"

"I feel I must."

His frown grew very black. "I tell you, I mislike this testing you want. It is unwise to tempt fate."

"Fate has naught to do with it. It was God's sovereign will brought me here, and I must know if He will let me stay."

She picked up his hand and kissed the knuckles. His skin tasted faintly of yeasty bread and cheese.

"These things—this life I knew before—it is abhorrent to me if you be not in it. For long and long, I thought I *wished* to go back. That is dead in me. I had rather remain with you."

His eyes, holding hers, glowed with that familiar expression of *haste to the wedding.* "So, my love. Remain you shall. I am determined on it, be God sovereign or no."

All the following week it rained. A fickle wind blew smoke down the chimney where it lingered, a sullen cloud in the high rafters, before it dispersed. Beth wondered where their golden summer hid, but she'd learned that English—and Cornish—weather was as temperamental as any spoiled child.

Monday made a good day for indoor tasks, including the many duties of putting forward two weddings, one grand and the other modest. Michael had gone into town, freeing Beth to concern herself with women's affairs, but before leaving, he'd drawn her aside. On Wednesday next, the day after Teagen and Ennis enjoyed their nuptial festivities, their party would leave for Trevellas.

"Ennis professes himself eager to return to the place. Teagen seems equally keen. I shall tell Ennis today of the time for leaving. Do you inform Teagen."

"Aye, my lord."

"They'll pull hard on the bit once there. Young sprouts. They're alive to the honor done them and will see for your interests the more keenly. I see them growing into the post, helping old Jacca while they learn. He has given me good service since taking Joan's manors in hand, but anyone may fall ill at any time. Pride will not let him admit he's past the heaviest work now. I will not reward him with displacement."

"No, of course not. They are eager to learn all he has to teach."

"He will have his task cut out for him." Michael bent to fondle one of the grizzled hounds. Bran trotted up and nudged the other dog aside, to get his head in its rightful place. "Certes he will gain a new leasehold on living. If I know Jacca, he will spend at least six months telling Ennis who is virtuous and which are sinners, and the boy will learn little beyond Jacca's prejudices."

"We may safely trust Teagen to hold them both to their work."

"I daresay she will manage everything while the men think they accomplish all. Aye, me. It is the best solution I can conceive.

Between the three they will keep Trevellas in good order while its liege lady needs be elsewhere."

"It is a good plan, dear-my-lord. Teagen is well able to order a household."

After he had gone, Beth called Teagen to her from the chattering, busy covey in the women's hall. "I had the thought," she teased, "to make you a present for your wedding."

"I thought you might never mention it, lady." Teagen answered her in sassy kind, cheeks bright, eyes snapping. "The castle folk say you will be gracious and generous."

"Imp. You but cozen me to get your own way, as always." Beth gestured to a packet wrapped in plain linen, tied with a scrap of bright silk. "First, look whether my gift is to your liking."

Smiling as she watched, Beth took her seat near the fitful fire. For Teagen's wedding attire she had taken the liberal vocal advice of every maidservant in the keep. Everyone who'd made a suggestion she'd drafted to work on the secret project. Consequently, the women's quarters had been busy amidst much hiding and giggling, in purchasing cloth, cutting, sewing, and embroidering an outfit suitable to Teagen's wedding and subsequent promotion.

Her maid's advancement reflected well on her also, Beth reflected. It tickled her that Michael respected her opinion.

She hummed a lively rondeau to herself, feeling proud she'd helped in the creation of Teagen's gift. As the blue gown tumbled out, Beth observed closely for the maid's reaction.

"Oh, my!" Teagen held the simply cut surcote up against her bosom, swishing its skirt about her scuffed soft-leather shoes. "Lady, lady . . . " Tears filled her dark Cornish eyes.

"Do not take on so. The embroidery is but simple and done in haste."

"I care not. It is lovely. I shall wear it for the wedding."

"Of course," Beth said with a smile. "I hoped you would."

"This will be my best gown," she said dreamily, "forever and ever."

Beth laughed. "There will come a day you will call it old fashioned."

"Nay, never." Teagen wiped her eyes on her sleeve, draped the gown reverently over one arm and dropped to her knees in the rushes at Beth's feet. "I'll serve you always, lady."

Beth figured she'd better put a stop to all this praise, for she was getting teary-eyed again. Something about weddings must bring on this mushy streak. She put both hands on Teagen's shoulders and with a gentle shake, brought her back upright.

"Enough. Weeping ill becomes my sassy maid. Since you've promised to serve me, I shall hold you to it—at least for this day. Do you get a traveling basket together for me and for yourself also, for Wednesday next. You and Ennis must make all fit and ready. We travel to Trevellas soon, that you and your husband may begin your training for its stewardship."

Teagen gave her a wide, willing grin.

Beth laughed, enjoying her role as lady giver-of-bounty. "I see, for once, you are struck speechless. At last I have achieved it! Go to, and fret not. My lord has his way, and I agree, for he ever chooses well. All will fall out as I have said."

Twenty-Three

They saw Teagen and Ennis wedded with much merriment and an excess of music, dance, ale, and laughter. The next day they traveled to Trevellas.

At the end of their first week there, a most welcome summons came. Leaving the newlyweds to settle into their education, Michael and Beth took horse again for Mossock.

Beth found her medical recommendations had been followed, though Berta reported they'd scandalized every woman in four villages. Contrary to local custom that the new mother lie abed for several weeks, Maude had taken Beth's advice and gotten Alys up and walking the next day.

"It is due to that," said Alys after welcoming them with fond embraces, "that I am well so soon."

"Your natural strength, rather." Beth stripped off her gloves and accepted ale from Berta.

"Never heard of such in these parts afore," muttered Berta.

Alys, ensconced in a seat near the fire with her hard-won son in her arms, murmured softly to her maid.

Beth grinned. No matter how much under-the-breath muttering she heard, Maude would tolerate no complaint over my lady's instructions. Nor did she countermand any, due to her gratitude over Beth's intervention at the confinement.

Later, alone in her usual guesting chamber, Beth took out parchment, ink, and quill. Outside the casement, today's windless mist touched the land with the same tentative finger. Another indoor day, and she didn't feel like sewing. The men had ignored the damp and gone to Camborne to look at a possibility for mining tin. Alys had resumed a weaving project she'd abandoned as she'd grown near her time. Gerard slept in his cradle near the fire, under his doting mother's gaze.

She twirled the quill against her cheek, then dipped the quill into the inkpot. *A Traveler's Tale. Alys does well, and little Gerard grows daily. I vow he is heavier already, and such opinions! He will have this, will not have that. I tremble to imagine him as a teenager. I foresee great trial for Geoffrey and Alys with a son so headstrong.*

This will be my last entry for a while. We came here to Mossock in all haste so as not to miss the young de Tallac's christening day. I scarce had time to grab my pouch. In other circumstances I'd have planned where to hide this journal, but I've had no time until now. Yet I must figure out a place for it, and soon. Michael wants not to linger here once the feasting is done, but to go home to Truro and our wedding. He's invited the de Tallacs if they see fit to travel, and he's promised Geoffrey we won't leave till he can serve as Gerard's godfather, so I still have a little while.

Alys mends apace and will be churched this Thursday. At that time will they will christen young Gerard. So I have this tiny cushion of time. All here is joy and amity. She even liked the drawing I made for her of the blessed mother and Child. It hangs, fitly framed, near the dais and the high table.

I shall enjoy this little interval of peace with my beloved and with my good friends, to make my plans and test my theory.

She looked up to watch the sporadic drizzle and considered. Where would she find a fit hiding place? She clenched her eyes tightly shut and tried to recall the manor as it existed in the twenty-first century.

The memories had grown dim. This room, for example—had it endured, or been demolished? Had it fallen into ruin like so much else of the lovely ancient house? Try as she might, she couldn't recall much more than the great hall, its monolithic fireplace, and the passage behind.

The passage wherein lay the portal she must test.

She took up her quill once more. *I do not want to test time travel. The dear Lord knows I would rather leave this portal untried. I want to stay as I am, in joy to take vows with Michael. Yet I know I must try, and the idea shakes me to the bone and to the depths of my soul. How will I see when it is time to make the test? Father, I don't know Your ways, yet with my last breath will I trust You.*

Bethany de Lindstrom, Lady of Trevellas, betrothed to Lord Michael Veryan, baron of Truro, of Mossock, St. Anne, Kingsdown, Odiham, Ivel, and Trevorgas, holder of other honors in the wild Welsh marches. Given under my hand this twenty-fourth day of July, in the year of the Lord I serve 1353, in the reign of our sovereign King Edward III the twenty-sixth year.

She rose and tucked the parchment into the sleeve of her everyday gown. She'd racked her brain, but the only hiding place for her secret lay in the great hall and its portal-bearing passage.

"Lady Bethany." Berta beckoned. "Come see the weaving, almost done and a marvel it is!"

"Anon, good Berta. The privy." She made a vague gesture and escaped outdoors into the drifting, lukewarm mist.

The garden glowed with summer color even in the wet. From there she slipped into the back passage. A rat squeaked alarm and with his fellows scuttled behind two ale barrels, into the shelter of a gnawed-through sack of corn. Beth looked around, sure she was alone, and withdrew the parchment bundle that was her journal.

Only one place. Stone must shelter it, something secure she could find again if worse came to worst and she traveled forward to her own time. Beth closed her eyes and whispered an earnest, if hurried, petition to the Master. Cautiously she crept along the passage, going a little further back than ever she'd trod before.

There, in the rough-hewn granite stones of the hall's wall, two feet off the floor, she found what she needed: a chink with the mortar crumbled out. With her eating knife she pried a little more mortar loose, broadening the space. Folding her parchments into a tight bundle, she slipped them into the crack. Into the breach she jammed as many mortar fragments as she could find.

She straightened and inspected the chink. It resembled many another in this neglected passage. She remembered, dimly, how the hallway looked in the future, when Sheila had mentioned finding little here to interest old-house aficionado, remodeler, archeologist, or homeowner.

"It will bide," she whispered. "It must."

Returning to the hall, she found the maids cooing over Alys's project. The kelly-green cloth was a marvel of the weaver's art, fine as silk though made of wool, a jacquard design interwoven with fanciful leaves and blossoms.

As Beth added her approbation to those of the maids, Alys used broad iron shears to cut the warp free of the loom. It took her and Maude both to fold its length.

Alys stood with a smile in her dark eyes. "For you." She extended the kelly-green cloth to Beth.

"Lady Alys, no. This is too much!"

Alys folded Beth's fingers around the bolt. "If my eyes deceive me not, you will need a wedding gown ere long. Honor me by using it thus." When Beth opened her mouth to protest some more, Alys silenced her by saying firmly, "Do not say me nay. Did you not tell the maids just this morn, that contention and raised voices are bad for a new mother's health?"

Lady Alys was churched as scheduled. The maids had ceased to grumble about the household's newfangled ways that so new a mother be up and active.

Alys's newborn grew like he intended to set a new record, Beth thought. She handed him, once again changed and dressed in his best, to his mother. Sir Geoffrey's son thrived with such strength that the de Tallacs held the christening today, with the child only a month old. Beth and Michael stood as godparents to the boy, along with Sir Andre, who had traveled all the way from Odiham for the honor. Dressed in the best they'd brought along, the trio filed into church behind the proud parents.

Michael gave her waist a surreptitious squeeze. "You next, sweeting," he whispered.

The idea of carrying and bearing his child moved in her heart. "Oh yes, please. As God wills."

"As God wills," he repeated.

Father Stephen cleared his throat and threw them an aggrieved glance. He would never like her, Beth realized, but after Lady Alys's survival of a hopeless labor, he would make no further murmurings against her. Betrothal to Sir Geoffrey's liege lord must also help silence him. She might clash with the lazy priest in the future, but for now he posed no threat, and she was glad to let down her guard a trifle.

She stood proudly at Michael's side as he held the baby over the font for Father Stephen's attention. "I baptize thee, Gerard," said the priest. "In the name of the—"

"Father!" said Alys suddenly. "Add Michael to his name. I beg you."

The priest glanced for permission to the proud father.

"A fine notion." With a big nod and a bigger smile, Geoffrey squeezed Alys's hand. "*Très apropos.* Sorry I am that I did not think of it myself."

"Lord Michael, by your leave?"

Michael gave a huge, delighted grin. The baby wriggled in his grip. "You do me great honor. Of course."

"I baptize thee Gerard Michael," Father Stephen corrected. The baby thrashed and squalled satisfactorily at the chill of the holy water, for all knew that at this sacred touch the devil flew out of him. Young Gerard Michael did not like the cold and kicked so hard Michael almost dropped him.

Beth chuckled under her breath. Father Stephen, never her friend, scowled and lifted his voice to drown her out in a Latin prayer of blessing.

"Imp," murmured Michael beside her. "I hope you can restrain your mirth at our wedding."

"I promise naught, my lord."

"No. You would not, would you?"

Only that I will make you the best wife I know how to be. Lord, if it's in Your will, let me stay here. Let us have a while to love each other.

To Michael she let her eyes speak her promises, for it was time to leave church for hall and baptismal feast.

They walked back hand in hand through a fair summer morning. The fitful Cornish mist had fled to parts eastward, as if it blessed baby Gerard and all other new beginnings. Today's sun shone intensely from a crystal blue sky, as innocent as though it hadn't blown drifting rain for three days previously. Beth drew in a sigh of pleasure.

"Happy, sweeting?"

"Oh, yes. The very weather honors Geoffrey, Alys, and the babe. Look—not a cloud to be seen, and saw you ever such a rich blue?"

"Aye. Your pretty surcote." He winked and in a gesture she cherished and craved, he brought her fingers to his lips.

At that moment, something shifted. She froze and stared into Michael's October eyes. She felt almost dizzy with the shock of the change.

"Today," she breathed.

"Sweeting?"

"The passage. I must try. It must be today. Now."

His expression faded from contentment to anxiety. "Nay. I forbid it."

"You cannot forbid. You agreed to this when I accepted you to husband."

"I did not wish to agree." His step lagged, and as the party cleared the gates of Mossock, he drew her aside toward the garden wall. His gaze bored into hers, his brows drawn together in a fierce and worried scowl. "I hold it then as now—too great a risk. By heaven's bright gates, in a fortnight we marry. It is doubly dangerous now."

"It must be now. I sense it. I feel it."

He gave an impatient sound and led her back beyond the wall's corner. Once out of sight of the rest of the party, Michael yanked her close against him.

"You would leave me?" His voice sounded choked.

She began to sob, sagging against his chest. He pulled her so tight she could feel the fear-pounding of his pulse.

"Bethany, do not test God. He wills it not. Stay here, with me. You know it is His command that you remain amongst us. How else, why else came you here?" He covered her face with kisses, knocking her silk veil askew. "Did He not vouchsafe you to my keeping? If you believe this, and certes you do, do not tempt His pleasure. It is disobedience if you try to return to your own time." His voice cracked, and she felt him bury his face in her hair. "Bethany. Sweeting."

"Michael, I would not, but I must. This is no maidish whim, for I have no choice. How else can I know I am permitted to stay? Permitted to pass my lifetime as your wife?"

She took his face in her hands, shocked to find his eyes slitted and wet. He pressed his lips to her palm.

"Aye, I want with all my heart to have you to husband and to be your loving lady. But God may not wish it so. It is Him I serve. Do not forbid me, my lord."

Michael clenched his jaw together so hard she saw the muscles leap in his smooth-shaven jaw. "We are betrothed. You would break your promise?"

"By all I hold holy, never."

He breathed in and out. Beth's heart rocked at how her words had shaken him. Indeed, the trembling under her bodice made her feel ill.

"I will not have it."

"You see my path, and yet you would prevent me."

His voice cracked. "Would I could beat you to make you stop. Give over now and let us to the feast."

"Michael, God ordains this. I will not gainsay Him."

He ground his teeth, temper mixing with anguish in his autumn eyes. "If I say you nay, what will you do?"

"Obey my good Lord." She stood her ground. How could he fail to understand, who knew her true story and her call to obedience—he who loved her Master?

"I owe you all duty that does not belong to Him. You are my chosen husband, but He chose me before time began. As He chose you, my love. You cannot fight Him, try as you would to have it your own way. You are grown too used to command." She pressed his hands to her lips, covered his rough-skinned fingers with kisses. "In this age or another, I will love you until my last breath."

"No matter what befalls," he said in a hoarse whisper.

"No matter what befalls. But do not ask me to gainsay His will."

He remained silent a long time, his hands wrapped around hers. Tension thrummed in the air between them, almost strong enough to make her cry out. When finally he spoke, his voice came ragged and uncertain.

"Show me this place you would go."

"Here."

She took his hand and led him to the seaward side of the hall. A dirt path edged the back wall of the garden, the same dirt path on which a bewildered time-traveler had emerged months—no, a lifetime—ago. Strange, how difficult it was to remember. She thrust a shaking hand toward the small ironbound door.

"This is the place."

"Then I go with you." He drew another agitated breath. "Before God, Bethany, I have not waited so long in life to find my soul's true partner, only to lose you now. I cannot. I will not."

She put a hand to her throat. Would it happen? God knew she did not want to try. He understood, right?

Lord God, I don't know why, but this is the moment. What's Your best way? Give me strength to follow, for I'm Yours and Yours alone. And my beloved belongs to You as surely as I do.

She stared hard into his eyes. In their autumn depths she read determination and courage and a love so firm it warmed every cell in her body and every depth in her spirit.

She offered him a shaky smile. "I love you. Time cannot alter that."

"And I you."

"Hold hard, then."

Taking a shallow breath, clinging to his hand, Beth stepped into the passage and inched along the wall. One step, and then another. Surely all was safe . . .

Between one heartbeat and the next, the narrow passage went cold. Mind-numbingly cold. She gasped and tightened her hold on Michael's hand. But now his desperate grip seemed to dissolve, the fine bones and strong sinews losing their substance as her surroundings shifted and went dark, sucking her into a vortex.

Consciousness ebbed. Her knees buckled.

Cold. She cried out, dizzy and sick, collapsed against the rough stones of the wall, sunlight cascading over her upturned face, heating the tears streaming down her cheeks . . .

By degrees, the blackness ebbed. Her head quit whirling and the wall stopped quivering. Her world righted itself into a normal Cornish early morning.

She drew a shaky breath, weak with relief. Surely Michael had let go of her hand for only a moment and she'd find him glowering and muttering Aves just outside. The portal hadn't worked, for she could still hear unintelligible voices and the twittering of the birds. Surely those voices spoke Cornish, not modern English. Eagerly she stepped out into the warm, sunny morning she'd left.

But this was not the morning that should be.

Beth clutched at her throat, trying to steady her breathing and the trip-hammer pounding of her heart. To her right, the garden wall that had stood higher than her head a second ago had moldered into a ruin low enough to cross with a single step. High above, a jetliner left a silent white contrail. Instinctively her eyes sought the stables, where Broc and Caillin would surely poke their heads out, hoping she had a slice of stale bread to give them.

The stables weren't there. In their place stood a shiny black Land Rover. A bright and early sun glared like an obscenity off its waxed hood.

She staggered a step back. *Michael. Michael.* She sank to her knees on the path, rocking back and forth, sobbing. Like a mighty chord in her mind came the words of the mass: *Mea culpa, mea culpa, mea maxima culpa.*

"Lord," she cried in Middle English. "Lord, no!"

And yet, hadn't she told Him that His will held first place in her life? Hadn't she borne witness of that fact to Michael? How could she now tell Him no?

Beth hid her face in her hands and cried like a child. *Mea culpa.*

Rational thought trickled back.

It is but a moment. I can seek the portal yet again. Rejoin my Michael where I belong and rejoice with him that I left him not.

She struggled to her feet. Exhaustion similar to that she'd felt when first she'd traveled back in time made her wobbly. Clinging to the wall, she reentered the passageway.

How different it felt from the last time she'd seen it—in Alys's Mossock, warmed with the heat of the great hall's fireplace, aromatic with the cooks' labors for the christening feast, ringing with the calls and comfortable insults of the servants. Now, abandoned.

She closed her eyes, collapsing against the wall, feeling its sun-warmed roughness against her cheek.

"Please. Please."

She had no idea how long she leaned against the stones, begging. Her cries of supplication ebbed into soft, weary sobs of despair. Presently she wiped her sodden face on the sleeve of her second-best gown and stumbled out into the unwanted morning.

Twenty-Four

"Heavens! What are you about? And wherever did you find those clothes?" Sheila loomed into the sunshine, drawing a warm jacket tighter around her shoulders.

Beth jumped, pressing one hand over her heart.

No, oh, no. Sheila. Oh, Michael, forgive me.

She had to stop, take a deep breath, remember to answer in modern English. "I-I—"

Nothing more would emerge no matter how she tried. A lump rose in her throat and threatened to choke off her strongest attempts at speech.

"It's a lovely morning for a stroll, isn't it? A touch chillier than yesterday, but by noon the nip should be out of the air." Sheila studied Beth intently, top to toe, much as the Lady Royal had done, but with a much kinder expression. "I take it you're an early riser."

"I . . . " Beth gulped, " . . . think I need a cup of tea."

"Smashing idea." Sheila draped an arm around her shoulders, which steadied her slightly. "Why, you're cold as ice! A nice pot of tea will take the chill off. Run to your room and change out of your Faire costume while I get Gillian started."

Numb, bone-weary, Beth allowed herself to be guided into the house. But this was not the house that should be.

Within her built a great silent scream.

Father, I said I would follow Your will. Is this Your answer, to snatch me from my loved ones? Lord—why?

Once inside, Sheila allowed her to flee to her room without further questions. Beth stood before the mirror in her gown and surcote, shaking. Slowly, she put her hand to the embroidery at the neckline, feeling her pulse still bounding.

Michael. Michael. Her eyes looked huge with shock.

Somewhere in the house a radio played, its distant voice sounding tinny and artificial. Light flooded through windows that needed wooden casements or thick greenish glass, not clear panes encumbered by heavy damask curtains. "Her" room looked foreign and strange and far too large for one woman, unassisted, unaccompanied . . .

Teagen. How am I supposed to get this surcote unlaced without her?

Tears threatened. She'd tough it out, for there was no choice. She'd drink tea with Sheila in clothing that would feel strange, as strange as Alys's chemise had felt that first day at home.

Home.

Her throat tightened into a lump that already felt like part of her. She swallowed it. She must stay focused, try not to weep or scream. Instead she'd make plans to get back home as soon as possible.

Wriggling her body in order to reach the laces, Beth realized she'd come, unwillingly, full circle. Home was not twenty-first century Chicago. Home was wherever—*when*ever—Michael moved and lived and breathed.

I told him I must try, but I never believed, I couldn't believe . . . Why, Lord? Why did You bring me back here, now that at last I know where I belong?

Why had she not left well enough alone? Why had she insisted on taking the risk? She already knew the answer. Tears welled up, bitter with regret, and again she couldn't stop them.

She sank onto the edge of the bed. Disappointment and terror fell from her eyes. When she could restrain the sobs no longer, she sank onto her side, curled in on herself, and let the storm break afresh.

Fifteen minutes later, changed, shaky, and heavy of heart, she made her way down the great stairs of the "new" Mossock. True to Sheila's word, Gillian in a black sweatshirt and miniskirt was just setting out tea in the parlor.

Sheila patted the sofa at her side. "Do sit down, Bethany. Are you warm enough? If my eyes don't deceive me, you were shivering, out in the garden."

"Perhaps. I don't . . . " Beth shook her head, helpless to explain.

More lies. A lifetime here, a lifetime there . . . naught but lies.

Her inward speech patterns had altered. Her thoughts, on coming forth in spoken word, would sound foreign to Sheila, and no wonder.

"You were fine last evening." Sheila passed her a cup of tea, correctly doctored. "Do let me help."

Beth took a sip of the sweet brew. She'd missed tea, these past months. Coffee, too. But right now she'd trade a cartload of fresh-brewed frappuccino for one sweet mug of Mossock home-brewed ale.

"I'm not sure you can help." Sheila urged a slice of raisin-and-currant studded bread. Beth accepted it and set it on the painted china saucer untasted. "I think I met the Gray Lady."

Sheila's cup paused halfway to her lips, and she tilted her head to one side. "Gray Lady?"

"Yes. The one you told me about when I first arrived. You remember, all those months ago. The one who's like a cold, sad presence in the older parts of the—"

The mystified expression on Sheila's face made her break off with a catch of her breath. *She told me about the Gray Lady, but she's not grasping a word of this. What's to do?*

"Months ago?" Sheila carefully set her teacup back in its saucer. "You've lost me. You just arrived yesterday. Dear, are you quite well? We met on the flight from Chicago, remember?"

Beth took in Sheila's statement and steadied herself as its implications developed. Months had passed. But for Sheila, apparently only one night. How to discuss this? Her heart wrenched as she contemplated many difficulties. Her journey had started here, and to Mossock she had returned. That meant she owed Sheila the truth, just as she'd owed the man she loved. She sent up a swift silent prayer for guidance.

Michael. Michael.

"Maybe you'd better order more tea. It's a very long story."

"Of course, love. Of course."

Sheila, bless her, drank the entire pot herself in silence. Beth barely sipped it. Instead she described the cold, the dizzy sensation, the shock of emerging into Mossock's back garden, thrust six hundred years back in time. She told of Alys, Sir Geoffrey, Maude and Michael. She told of Teagen and Ennis, of Michael's kindness to old Jacca at Trevellas and the steward's constant vigilance over sin. She told of Truro keep and of Windsor, of Michael's actions, of the glittering, faction-filled court and her conversations with Edward III. She related baby Gerard's difficult birth, told of Cadwr of Bridgnorth and how Michael had rescued her. As her voice faltered again on that name, tears welled.

"My ivers," Sheila breathed. "You're in love with this man."

"With all my heart. We planned to marry."

But he's dead. Her stomach rebelled. *He's been dead for centuries. Michael, my love, why did I insist on my own way?*

"And you returned here," Sheila said in a wondering voice, "as a sort of test?"

"Not of our feelings for each other. We were full sure of those. But I wished to be certain I could stay—" Again her voice lost its tone, and she took a sip of tea. "I helped Lady Alys in labor. We came to Mossock to feast their son's christening and planned to return to Truro and be married once the feast was done."

"Yes. You say she almost died, but your idea saved her."

"I can't know for sure. But yes, I believe it helped."

The terror of trying to figure out what to do while Gerard Michael struggled for life; the maids' dumfounded stares when

Beth had insisted none must touch mother or babe without hand washing in strong lye soap . . . Those memories almost made her laugh. She choked back a chortle at Maude's dismay at being forbidden to sprinkle salt in the newborn's mouth to strengthen it. She remembered everything, for it had all happened less than a month ago . . .

"Earlier you mentioned a Gray Lady and that I told you a legend of an apparition. I've never heard of such a thing—not here at Mossock. Most ancient homes have their ghostie. But do you suppose this Lady Alys may have been that spirit?"

"I certainly don't see how. You said the apparition was always accompanied by a sense of extreme sorrow, as if—" Beth caught her breath.

Of course. The Gray Lady didn't mourn her lost loved ones, she mourned not being here for them. "Do you think Lady Alys once died in childbed, and my arrival there changed events?"

"It's possible. I do know there is no Gray Lady haunting Mossock as a sad ghost." Sheila chuckled, still looking ill at ease. "We can ask Bertie later . . . but I'm sure if Mossock had such a spirit all these years, he should have mentioned it."

"It did have a ghost. Once."

"And you changed that. Gave her a fresh chance." Sheila shook her head slowly as if in wonder. "There's no end to the mystery."

Beth's tea had gone gray with cold. She sipped it anyway, her grief a little eased at having told her tale.

"You believe me, don't you?"

"Of course. How can I not? You've changed. Nothing about you is the same. And don't forget, yesterday you wore a T-shirt and jeans. This morning I found you in a lovely Faire costume."

"It is no costume," Beth said softly. "It's my next-best surcote, the one Alys and her women made together, right here at Mossock. This surcote I wore to the christening. The rest of my clothes we sewed at Truro before Michael and I went to court at Windsor to seek my enfeoffment of the king."

The full force of her loss hit like a crossbow bolt, and she hid her face in both hands. Sheila rose from her sofa, came near, and hugged Beth's shoulders as again she wept.

Quiet fell over the parlor. Outside the big windows, birds—they could not be the same kind—twittered and scrapped, bringing an air of normalcy to a morning that could not claim it. Beth swallowed the last of her tears, though the incipient feel of them remained. Would the ache ever leave her?

Never. I will mourn him all my days.

"What will you do?" asked Sheila quietly.

Beth thought for a moment. If the portal would but open long enough for her to get back to Michael, run to his arms, and never let go, she would jump through without hesitation. She'd already traveled, not once, but twice. The only puzzle was why it had worked when she didn't intend to travel, and why not when she'd begged.

What methods should she use to accomplish what was undoable? With effort she cast her mind back to Sheila's practical question.

"Go to Oxford, I guess," she said dully. "Join the party at the dig. Write my papers. Make my name—for I surely have learned things others don't know about fourteenth century England. Live. If I can call this living."

"Oh, love."

"I know." Beth gave her a mirthless smile. "Hardly a triumphal chorus, is it?"

"I've a better idea." Sheila sat back in her chair and crossed her arms. "Stay here at Mossock a while longer. Get used to what happened. Do your crying and your praying here, where it's private and safe. You certainly don't wish to discuss this—happening—with others, do you?"

Beth shuddered. "No. Never. I'd be called every kind of a liar, maybe even unstable. Nobody would believe me." She clenched her stinging eyes shut. "For that matter, why do you?"

"Believe you?" Sheila rubbed an invisible smudge from the knee of her gray slacks. "I expect it's because you've changed. Yesterday you seemed little more than a child, with stronger dreams than any child has, and a cartload of fear. Afraid of your plans? Your future? I couldn't tell, but it struck me you used your learning to protect you from your dreams. Now your demeanor—even your voice—it's different. You've gained assurance and a tone of certainty. You've had authority and wielded it well, I'd say. You've conquered something, and grown in ways I can't even guess."

Sheila smiled. "Besides, any mother would notice—your hair's grown. And those dreadful scars on your wrists." She pointed, and self-consciously Beth drew the sleeves of her sweater down to hide them. "How long did you say you were there?"

"Four months."

"Yet a single night passed . . . enough. You say it's so. I choose to believe."

My journal. Beth sat bolt upright, forgetting the burn in her eyes and the ache in her soul. "I can prove it—I think. I hid something in the passageway behind the old hall. If it's still there."

Sheila's eyes lit with eagerness. "Show me?"

"Of course. It is your house, after all."

The women paced in silence toward the old hall and its capricious passage. Beth closed her eyes and tried to envision the dusty, abandoned hallway as it had looked yesterday—six centuries before. Here? No, a little further along, about two feet up. Perhaps less, since dirt floors tended to accumulate depth over time.

She slid a questing hand around over and between the stones. "Ah!" The chink wasn't as easy to find as once it had been. Grit, spider webs, rodent accumulations all made it narrower and less visible. She dug her short nails into the detritus and pulled out animal junk, dust, mortar, and a crumbled wall stone.

"Here it is. I hope." Cautiously, slowly, she drew out a fragile wad of parchment.

"My ivers," breathed Sheila as with slow care Beth unrolled it. "I can hardly credit it. We've had specialists in and out of here for generations, looking for historical artifacts."

"It wasn't here then," Beth said. "I wrote a journal, and none knew of it. It's been here over six hundred years, but in my time sense I hid it yesterday." Some of the parchment came away in her fingers, the edge crumbling as easily as shattered hopes. But enough remained. "Read it if you like. I don't mind."

Sheila perused the faded, cracked document. "Medieval parchment. Medieval ink. But American English." She raised bemused eyes to Beth's face. "My ivers. You are quite the traveler, aren't you!"

"You do believe me," Beth said without tone. "This must be proof enough for any."

Sheila straightened her spine and handed the journal back. "I believed you before you showed me this."

"It is hard to credit, though."

Yet Michael believed with less proof than I just gave Sheila.

"But since we met on the plane, there's been something—some *thing*—for you to accomplish here, and I'm a minor part of it. I spoke of passion when you came here. I felt it in you, some calling larger than yourself . . . " Sheila let her voice trail off, then gave a self-deprecating chuckle. "There now, you see? Off I go again, on one of my 'sensitive' tangents. Pure foolishness, Bertie would call it. But he's in Newquay." Sheila fingered the parchment very gently. "And then, there's the clothing."

"My gown? My surcote?"

Sheila nodded. "I'd like to take a closer look, if you don't mind."

Her journal in hand, together they went up to Beth's room. She'd carefully laid out her clothes—feeling more surely hers than chinos and sweater—on the bed, mindful not to let the fabric wrinkle unduly.

Sheila glanced at her for permission and picked up the surcote. Her second-best—not that even her court dress looked as fancy as the Lady Royal's—but her favorite gown of all Michael and Alys had provided for her. Teal blue, his favorite color. Her throat closed up in a spasm of pain.

"My word," Sheila breathed. "Pure wool, this. Summer weight, and so finely woven it feels like silk. The seams, all hand done. And embroidery, such fine stitches you can barely see them. I'd imagine one would go blind with such sewing. Who has the time or interest anymore for work like this?"

Beth remembered the cutting and sewing of the cloth. "We made it together," she said in a hollow voice. "Lady Alys had the cutting, because the lady always does. Maude and the others helped with the embroidery. I was poor at it, you see."

Sheila fingered the gown without further comment, then lay it back down. "Do say you'll stay. You have unfinished business. Do promise me you won't go to Oxford until you're sure in your mind that's your true course."

Beth gave another dry laugh. "My true course? There isn't a map complete enough to point that out."

"Stay anyway."

Beth shrugged. "You and Lady Alys de Tallac, two of a kind. I wonder if she isn't your distant ancestor, for you are both of a seemly charity. I'm not sure what good staying will do, but perhaps a day or two."

With a single finger Beth parted the curtain. A gibbous moon stitched silver embroidery across an unquiet sea. In the distance, an invisible animal scuffled through the underbrush, its hunting sounds audible through the midnight quiet.

Exhausted, she hadn't closed her eyes even once this night. This terrible night, separated from Michael and those she loved. When she thought of traveling to Oxford, away from Mossock and Truro and Trevellas, her throat developed a tight, painful lump. When she contemplated returning to Chicago, the lump grew hard and hurtful corners. She put a hand to the ache, willing it to ease. Would it ever? She couldn't see how.

Impulse gave birth to action. She rose and pulled her "old" cloak tightly around her nightgown, and tiptoed down the stairs. The soft grass bespangled her bare feet with dew as she crept down to the old doorway, eased it open, and slipped into the passage.

She put a shaky hand to the ancient stone and waited. The moon crept downwards, grew ruddy and misshapen as a squashed orange, sulking into a cloudbank offshore. She stood silent, counting the in and out of her breathing, watching, waiting, praying.

Nothing.

The eastern sky began to lighten with a hopeful spring dawn. Beth stumbled outside into the misty gray light and slumped against the exterior wall of the old hall. She let her face sink into her hands, and the tears trickled through her fingers.

"What am I to do?" she whispered in Middle English. The dewy grass soaked through her cloak to her bare skin underneath. "Tell me, Lord, what You want. What's to become of me? What am I to do, to be? And must I be it alone? With no one to talk to, nobody who can understand? And I'm not a historian anymore, I'm a noblewoman. I have lands and people to look after, a husband to cherish, a household to order. What of Trevellas, what will become of them?"

A wave of purest terror swamped her. C. S. Lewis had it right when he'd written that grief felt very much like fear.

"I don't see how I can go back to the life I knew before. When You sent me back in time You changed me, Lord. I don't care about history, unless it be the stories of those I love. *They* are important, *their* lives matter, not the writing of yet another book to add to the thousands . . . "

And yet it seemed only that remained for her to do. She lifted her tired head from her hands and gazed out at the first rays of sunshine peeping over the rooftops. In the distance the town's shingled roofs threw the light, reflecting it off television antennas, telephone lines, aluminum gutters, all the appurtenances of a modern life that she no longer wanted—or needed. All that awaited her in this life was cell phones, zippers, coffee, canned food, indoor plumbing. Not the dear ones for whom her heart ached with a pain already grown old.

I cannot. I must.

That day Sheila made several phone calls. On Wednesday morning, Beth would take a bus from nearby St. Agnes to Truro. In Truro, pick up the Inter-City for Exeter, then Oxford and archeology.

Beth couldn't see beyond that, but Sheila was right: one step at a time. A sensible plan. She kept repeating it to herself, trying to make it feel real. Sheila's advice had proved sound before and, after all, what else could Beth do in the circumstances?

How long would she have to hammer the necessity into her mind before this half-life became acceptable? With a groan, she kneaded her aching forehead with her fingertips.

Possibly a lifetime. Or more.

Oxford's "dreaming spires" loomed overhead, blurred by cool, smattering rain. Beth leaned on her trowel and tucked a strand of damp hair back under her slicker hat, trying to muster up some suitable degree of enthusiasm. She'd been here on the dig for three days, though it felt more like three months.

Her muscles ached almost as deeply as her heart. She leaned down and peered at a bone sticking out of the muck at the bottom of the carefully string-lined hole, her assigned grid-square. She took up a brush to free the bone of mud. Though the dig was sheltered by tarps from the worst of the rainfall, water puddled in the hole. She freed the head of a humerus, which further dispirited her. She'd been told to seek a jaw so that DNA could be extracted from the teeth.

Not that she cared anymore. She had reported to the chief investigator, provided him with her *curriculum vitae,* her letters of reference from Dr. Richards and the others. Any summation of her actual experience was little better than a lie. The paperwork must be enough. The eminent Dr. Thurston had looked them over with approval, and then voiced well-bred surprise at her obvious lack of passion. But his acceptance didn't matter.

What mattered were the evenings. She'd stopped at a stationer's and bought high quality parchment paper, the best they had, and pricey sketching pens that mimicked the blunt nib of her quill. In her room she cleared the small desk of all clutter and bent over the parchment. Faster than any drawing she'd ever done, Michael's face took shape on the page, correct down to the tilt of his eyebrows and the warmth in his eyes.

If ever I see you. She leaned back so tears would not blot the ink. *If ever we meet again, nothing and nobody will ever tear me from your side.*

She'd spent hours on her knees in the college chapel, explaining to the Lord and Master of time how she'd changed. Begging Him to call her back to the fourteenth century. Asking Him for another chance to live life the way it was supposed to go.

The chapel, accoutered in the spare trappings of the twenty-first century Church of England, felt bare and cold. She sought it anyway, imagining how it *should* look, with proper hand-embroidered altar vestments and bright, instructive wall paintings. Every time she mentally redecorated it, she longed for Alys whispering diligent Aves at her side or Michael muttering some new scheme when he should have been attending to the elevation of the Host . . .

Drawings of the Truro chapel, Mossock-of-old, Trevellas village, Windsor's Curfew Tower and other dear places filled the sketchbook.

If God did not call her back to the time in which she knew she belonged, she prayed she'd someday come to a way to deal with life here. She must, eventually, so she wouldn't miss Michael and the others she loved quite so much.

The ache was supposed to ebb, day by day. Right? It didn't seem to be working. Sheila had called last night, to check up on her, and Beth had sat in her chilly, bleak dorm room and tried to banish tears enough for conversation. That hadn't worked very well either.

Now she kept brushing, doggedly freeing the unwanted arm bone from the plague pit. Others enjoyed better success, and the skeletal remains were piling up nicely. Soon the team would have enough to bring samples to the university's medical lab, have the DNA extracted from any suitable bones, and draw their conclusions from the analysis.

Gradually, as she worked, under her sweatshirt, deep inside where she'd learned to listen for the Lord's voice, crept a certainty more dependable than her heartbeat or the raindrops in her hair. Her test was over, and she'd passed. The Master was calling, sending her back to those she loved to do the work He'd ordained for her from the beginning.

Why else, the certainty whispered, *why else would I have gotten the grant, been stranded at Heathrow, met Sheila, gone to Mossock? If my journey back in time was to end in futility, why vouchsafe it to me at all?*

Beth threw up her head so rapidly that her neck tendons snapped. A furtive afternoon sun tried to peek under the tarp, though it dripped with accumulated mist. Several of her colleagues raised their heads as well, glancing at the "odd American." She'd not indulged in much conversation with them after introductions, preferring to spend her evenings in her room rather than drinking in the local public houses. Their glances reminded her of prairie dogs popping up from their holes to gaze in fear at a predator flying overhead.

I'm done here. This is not where I am supposed to be. I can't take it one moment longer. Not one more second.

Gently she placed her trowel and her brush into their plastic tote. Climbing cautiously out of the muddy hole, she stamped as much mud as possible off her wellies, and then went to seek Dr. Thurston.

"Leaving? Miss Lindstrom, whatever for?"

"I have been called urgently to Cornwall." *None of your affair who's calling me.*

In words vague and few, she mentioned Sheila and Bertie, Mossock, a recently discovered batch of documents found in a chink between two stones in a medieval passageway.

"Fascinating. But—" He waved a scholarly pipe in the air. His office, unheated like the rest of the Oxford campus, smelled of cherry tobacco and old books. "We do need you here, actually. Take a few days then, settle your affairs, and then try to pick up where you left off. We need every hand we can muster on the project."

"You don't need mine," she said. "I've found none of the right kind of bones. I'm neither efficient nor lucky."

He stared at her. "But you will be back?"

"I cannot say at this time."

She stood her ground with dignity, staring him down. Visualizing herself in her surcote and gold-cord snood helped. Calm, unflinching, in possession of herself as befits a lady and a landowner.

"I may, but probably will not." She felt a laugh bubbling up, and suppressed it. "I suppose you could say I'm throwing in the trowel."

He blustered, making allusion to her fellowship-in-jeopardy, a negative recommendation to Dr. Richards, imperiling her degree. He mentioned the grant that must be withdrawn and given to a more malleable candidate. One who could take direction and work with others.

She barely listened, but waited, tapping a toe, until Dr. Thurston had talked himself dry. She couldn't make him understand, she'd been called home and it was *au revoir* Oxford. Rummaging in her messenger bag for the paperwork he'd need, she produced it and laid it on his desk. Without further conversation, she turned on the heel of her Wellington, and left.

One task remained before she could seek her fortune, as the fairytale demanded. She sat on the edge of the bed in her room and dialed.

"Mom? Have a little while to chat? I need to talk to you."

"Of course, dear." Her mother's voice caught. "What's the trouble, Bethany? Your voice sounds strange."

Beth took a deep breath and began. "I hope you don't have anything pressing. This may take some time."

She lifted her eyes to the leftover droplets making their slow way down her windowpane. The sun turned them to crystal, refracting a glory of light onto the sill. With God's blessings, she would soon be seeing that light in Cornwall.

"I have an opportunity to stay here."

"Stay?"

"Live here. Permanently."

"Bethany, what on earth—?"

"Hear me out." She rapidly explained she'd fallen in love, and would be living permanently in an ancient house in Truro.

That much is the simple truth.

"It's too fast," Mom objected. "Honey, you can't know this guy yet. Men say anything when they want a wom—"

Beth laughed and interrupted. "I have a commitment and a wedding date. You don't know him like I do, Mom. You must believe me." She let conviction ring in her voice. "This is the life I was born for. The life I *must* lead. I hate not hanging out with you, talking to you, but I've prayed heavy duty over this, and I know it's where I need to be." She could hear Mom's agitated breathing over the distance. "Trust me," she ended simply. "You always have before. I know I'm right about this."

"Stay where you are," Mom said after a short silence. "Don't move a muscle. I'm going to call the airline. What inn did you say you're at? We need to hash this out face to face."

I can't do that.

"Mom, I love you. I'm so sorry," she said. "Sorrier than you know. But you can't talk me out of this. I love you always, but I haven't got the time. A train leaves this afternoon for Truro, and I have to be on it."

"Exeter, please," she said two hours later at the train station.

The ticketmaster gave her an appreciative once-over. "Right, love. Single or return?"

She gave a rusty-feeling smile. "One way. I mean, single. From there I'll want a ticket to Truro."

"Right, let's see . . . seventy-four pounds."

She passed him two fifty-pound notes. Her heart lightened by the minute, telling her that now—finally—she saw the road clear before her. Mom had wept, remonstrated, warned, advised, and at length given her reluctant blessing and a promise not to hop on the next eastbound jet.

Though her mother thought she understood, she did not—could not. Beth walked in the exact center of God's will, and there was a lightness and freedom in it she'd not imagined possible.

"Keep the change. Buy a pint or two for your friends. I'm having a great day."

Twenty-Five

If only these clouds would break.

Beth stepped down from the train in Truro, longing for the sunshine that had blessed her earlier. It was nearly dark, for the connection in Exeter had taken longer than scheduled. Sheer impatience to be back in Cornwall had tired her beyond bearing. Now, though, she'd arrived, and fatigue didn't matter.

Graeme the Ever-Accommodating would pick her up soon. She paced up and down the pavement with her duffel slung over her shoulder, peering down the twilit street to spot a black Land Rover. Impatience had her dancing on the platform like a ten year old. Should she try the portal now, tonight? Or wait until dawn?

She'd done her praying while weeping for joy. Now, surely, was the time for action. Despite Dr. Thurston's bluster and Mom's tears, she'd felt no fear whatever while resigning her fellowship and giving her parent final farewells. Now all that remained was an electric sense of anticipation.

Bethany Lindstrom, PhD candidate, *adieu*. Lady Bethany de Veryan, noblewoman, holder of Trevellas, baron's wife, *bienvenue*.

Tires on pavement. Every cell in her body, every level of her mind, snapped instantly alert. She hoisted her duffel higher on her shoulder. The black Land Rover pulled up smoothly to the barrier, and she stepped up, head high, lips smiling, soul rejoicing.

"Hi, Bethany."

"Graeme, hello. How good of you to come for me."

Mossock glowed in the indigo twilight of a Cornish summer evening. Its big, deep-framed windows welcomed her with the shine of electric lamps, gently blessing her return. Sheila emerged through the front door, holding out her hands in welcome. Beth came to embrace and be embraced.

"So," said Sheila. "You're back."

"Thanks for having me at such short notice."

Graeme brought in Beth's duffel, and Wenna trotted up to sniff inquisitively at Beth's hand. She stooped on the hallway floor to scratch the dog around the ears, and Wenna whined in approval.

"You've eaten?"

Graeme laughed. "Good old Mum. Always trying to feed the masses."

"Go on with you." Sheila shooed him off. "Are you hungry, Bethany?"

Starving. For home-brewed ale and meat pies cooked over the hearth fire, and the man I love smiling at me.

"Thank you. I had a snack in Exeter." She gave a tired smile.

"Then what about a nice—"

"Cup of tea," Beth ended on a laugh. Sheila chuckled also, and led the way to the front parlor. The tall window on the ocean side stood open, and she could hear the murmuring of the surf some forty feet below.

A sputter and roar from Graeme's motorbike split the peace as Sheila poured out tea for them both, adding honey and a tiny bit of cream to Beth's cup. Beth accepted it and sipped in real pleasure.

"Sheila?"

"Yes, dear."

"How did you know? That first day I was here, you doctored my tea exactly right. How could you know how I like it? Do you offer honey to all Americans you've just met, or was that another of your 'seeings'?"

Sheila sipped. "To tell the truth, I don't know. I can't always tell, but at this age of me, I've learned to follow my instincts." She set her cup down on the Chippendale table and gave Beth a concerned frown. "Right now every maternal instinct I have is screaming. I assume the archeology project didn't go well."

"Not exactly, no." Beth sat back in her chair. She'd miss the flavor and comfort of good English tea once she went home to Michael. "I tried—truly I did. Then I . . . I suppose I just stopped. It came while I was yanking on a bone—someone's arm. I couldn't think of it as a *bone,* Sheila—it was part of a *person.* Someone with a name. Her own voice and hopes, her own special something that made her real. I was supposed to see her arm as a source of DNA for analysis. I couldn't do it, and besides . . . Well, I bailed."

She related her brief effort at resuming life as a twenty-first century historian. "In the end," Beth summed up, "I realized I didn't care about any of it. Not the PhD or the papers or the brilliant career. That is not how my life is supposed to go. I just want Michael."

"I think I understand. You came here because of the portal you think is behind the old hall."

"It *is* there." Beth dug in her tote bag for a large padded envelope. "This is for my mother, if you'll be so kind to put it in the mail. It contains the journal and some drawings, and as much of an explanation as I can give her. She and I talked, of course, but she doesn't understand and she's upset. I've taken the liberty of including your telephone number." Sheila nodded, agreeing to the necessity. "It's already addressed. I got stamps in Exeter while I waited for the Truro train and tried to talk myself out of doing this." Beth gave Sheila a helpless smile. "I couldn't. This is what I must do. I know it's right."

"Do you—" Sheila hesitated and then swallowed hard. "Do you want me to walk with you into the passageway?"

"No, you needn't. Just promise you'll keep me in your prayers. I don't think I'll try until morning, anyway. It was sunny when I came through the first time, and sunny when I came back." She smiled at Sheila. Between Lady Alys de Tallac and Mrs. Sheila Tyrrell, what time traveler could ask for better friends? "I have a good feeling about the sunshine."

"Then I'll rise early and go with you." Another brave swallow. "As far as I can."

"No. It might upset you. After all, remember, I've no idea what it looks like to an observer. It might be very scary. I was alone when I first went, and the second time only Michael saw. Don't come. I want you to remember me well, not with distress." Sheila's eyes filled. Without words, they embraced, and Beth felt her eyes sting. "Fare you well," she said. "I doubt you'll be seeing me again. At least, I trust you won't. And thank you," she added, "for everything."

She didn't sleep. Though she closed her eyes several times and tried to put herself to sleep by reciting the kings of England from Edward the Martyr through Elizabeth II, it availed nothing. Birds began to twitter an early greeting to the dawn. She rose and dressed in her second-best gown and the blue surcote Michael loved, and donned her cloak. Her belt-pouch, eating knife, silk hose and red leather shoes completed her outfit, hair left loose because she was poor at braiding it. Her veil sat properly anchored atop her curls with silver pins, his gift from St. Piran's fair.

Ready. She checked her traveling pouch for the umpteenth time. The items she needed were all inside. A lip gloss. A ceramic jar filled with antibiotic ointment, which she'd have to hoard carefully against times of direst need. A plain cloth folded and tied over several dozen aspirin. Her own toothbrush, which she would copy in native materials and hopefully end as an old woman with all her teeth.

And, for Michael's delight, a small bar of plain chocolate.

"Father," she prayed in Middle English, "*grand merci* for letting me come back here for a little while. Thanks for working things out as they must be. I just want You to know—if this doesn't work, if it's not Your will for Michael and me to be together—I'll be all right. Either way, You're first in my life and in my intentions. I sense Your way, Lord, and I'll follow. No matter what befalls."

She drew a deep breath and scanned the room to which she would not return. A short note for Sheila lay on the pillow of the tidily made bed. Her modern clothing, folded up on a chair. Nothing here she needed. Nothing she would grieve to leave behind.

Ahead of her, light and love and an adventure dear to her heart. She slipped out of the room, tripped lightly down the stairs and outside into the dawn.

A noise by the side of the old hall made her start. Wenna, the great hound so similar to Michael's hunting dogs, peered at her, big-eyed, from the edge of the ruined garden wall.

"Come here, love," Beth murmured. When the animal obeyed, she found the itchy places behind Wenna's ears, bringing soft ecstatic doggy-moans. "Stay with me?"

The dog cocked her head and trotted along behind as Beth made her way to the passage. At the door, Wenna plopped down on her haunches in the dew-damp grass and would budge no further.

"Farewell, then," Beth whispered. "*Adieu,* girl."

She slipped in through the heavy oaken door without glancing back. Wenna whined low in her throat. Beth waited in the passage, calm now, expectant and almost content.

No matter what befalls.

She waited. The sun climbed. Wenna, out of sight but not out of hearing, gave an almost inaudible sigh, then began a low, insistent whine. Beth heard the rustle of grass as the dog lay down outside, continuing to whimper.

A slight breeze entered through the door she'd left ajar, and teased the dust-motes into awakening. Beth waited. The zephyr held more than the chill of a Cornish summer morning . . .

She closed her eyes and set a hand flat against the rough stone wall. The chill grew deeper and her head began to spin. Around her smells changed, temperature shifted, Wenna's agitated whining morphed into human voices lifted in glad celebration . . .

A strong, sturdy hand clutching hers and the familiar aromas of meat roasting on an open spit, of bread baking, of the stable-midden and cool, damp earth. From the kitchen building came the crack of flesh upon flesh as Cook screeched imprecations at the spit-boy. Beth opened her eyes on the morning that should be.

I'm home. Home. Lord, thank You!

She blinked. Michael's hand, solid and very real, around hers. His face, scowling and relieved and oh so very smug. She barely heard her own voice lifted in thanksgiving, so acute was the joy.

This is Your doing. And marvelous in my eyes.

"Mutter Aves all you want. Let us away. Come away, sweeting—did I not tell you this *maudite* plan of yours would never work?"

She threw her arms around his neck and laughed into his eyes.

"*Deo gratias* that it did not. You see once again I am right. But sweeting, you must learn to restrain this constant and unseemly mirth."

"Never. I never shall, for God has put a laughing in my heart."

How can he understand? He might never fully grasp this, unless someday I find words to explain to him.

"Learn to listen to your husband. The next time I speak truth of a matter, I would have you own it." He tightened his arms around her waist. Was his inner self aware she'd been gone? Perhaps his heart knew, though his mind denied, for he clung to her as desperately as she to him. "And I was right about this folly."

He'd been right all along and could righteously prove it. Her heart swelled in a carol of joy. She could cope with a husband who was always right. What was that to a time traveler?

Beth answered his grin. "So you were, dear-my-lord. So you were."

Discussion Questions

1. Considering that God is omnipotent, could time travel be possible? Should a believer use common sense to decide something is not doable, or is this a violation of faith? Do we limit God when we say some things are impossible?

2. Beth's main challenge is regaining her close walk with God. She's sent to live in a time when everyone believes. How could a believer in such an environment lose his or her faith?

3. Michael privately questions why God allowed so many innocents to die of the pestilence. When disaster happens on so overwhelming a scale, where does the believer find understanding and a deeper faith?

4. Beth has to cope with living as a Christian while fostering a spirit of untruth. Can these two spiritual states ever walk together? Can you think of circumstances where it's acceptable to lie?

5. If time travel were possible, would it be wrong to save the life of someone in the past as Beth did? What implications might doing so have?

6. Have you ever faced a situation where all your possible choices seemed wrong? How did God help you sort out the right path from our human inclination to go our own way?

7. When Brother Simon treats Beth, he cites several superstitions the medieval people associated with healing. Do we of the present day still harbor superstition? What current ideas might a visitor from 600 years in the future find laughable?

8. What do you think your biggest challenge would be if you were to travel back to 1353?

9. Medieval Europe was almost exclusively Christian in culture and outlook. Would your walk with Christ be easier in an environment that is 99 percent Christian or more difficult? Why?

10. When Beth first landed in 1353 Mossock, she was frightened but not terrified. Why do you think she reacted this way? Would you react as she did?

11. What part did ambition play in Beth's life? In Michael's? Would you say either of them was ruled by ambition at the beginning of the story? At the end?

Glossary

Alestake: tavern
An: if
Assart: reclaimed land added to a farm or manor
Bedizen: dazzle, confuse
Bestiary: book describing real and unreal animals
Bliaut: woman's gown (prior to 1300)
Brilliant: diamond
Burh: Saxon town with earthen defenses
Cabochon: gemstone cut without facets
Candlemas: February 2, feast of Mary's purification after Jesus's birth
Canon: priest attached to a cathedral or large church
Canon law: church law; much more lenient than civil law
Caparison: horse draperies
Castellan: custodian of a castle for an overlord; not heritable
Chevage: fine for leaving the manor; paid to the lord by the villein
Childwyte: fine for giving birth outside marriage
Churl: peasant bound to the land (Saxon; also ceorl)
Compline: bedtime (Latin)
Consanguinity: relationship in the prohibited degrees, precluding marriage
Corpus Christi: holiday on second Thursday after Pentecost
Cottar: poor tenant living on less than a virgate (Saxon)
Crenel: square protrusion atop a wall to shelter defenders
Croft: homesite and the immediate yard around it
Cymri: the Welsh

Danegeld: tribute paid to prevent Viking attacks
Demesne: land retained by a lord for his own use
Destrier: war horse
Device: figure painted on the shield; a knight's heraldic symbol
Diddle: to fool someone
Disseisin: to remove a vassal from his lands, usually for cause
Ecuelle: water vessel for washing the hands (French)
Enfeoff: to grant a fief to a retainer or vassal
Eyass: young falcon newly caught, not yet trained
Eyren: eggs
Farm: the amount of taxes the king could expect from a manor
Fealty: loyalty; a man's pledge to serve his lord
Fewter: to settle one's lance before a joust
Fief: holding granted from a lord to a vassal
Frankpledge: system in which neighbors were held responsible for each other's lawful behavior
Fyrd: levy or militia (Saxon)
Hanap: fancy drinking vessel
Hauberk: chain mail tunic
Hayward: minor official entrusted with guarding the harvested hay
Headrail: veil
Hearthright: householder's right to his dwelling (Saxon)
Heriot: fine on inheritance of a property, paid to the lord
Hide: amount of farmland that would sustain a family
Hlaefdige: lady (Saxon)
Hlaford: lord (Saxon)
Holmgang: duel of honor (Scandinavian)
Honor: manor held in tenancy
Hosen: chain mail leggings
Housecarl: armed retainer (Saxon)
Infangthef: right to try and punish a thief caught on one's land
Jess: leash for a hunting hawk
Lammas: August 1, holiday to celebrate harvest's end (Saxon)
Leat: ditch or run-off stream (Cornish)

Leech: healer; one skilled in "leech-craft"

Leyrwite: fine for intimate relations outside marriage; paid to the lord by the villein

Liege: lord or sovereign to whom allegiance and service are due according to feudal law; a loyal subject to a monarch

Loge: bleacher from which to watch a tourney or joust

Lych-gate: gate between church and graveyard

Manchet: white bread

Martinmas: November 11, feast of St. Martin

Matins: dawn (Latin)

Mazer: drinking vessel, often of wood

Merchet: fine for privilege of marrying; paid to the lord by the villein

Merlin: hawk considered especially suitable for ladies

Merlon: square gap between adjacent crenels

Michaelmas: September 29, feast of St. Michael the Archangel

Mis-say: slander, diss

Morgengifu: "morning gift;" lands and/or money given by a bride-groom to the bride (Saxon)

Murrain: highly contagious livestock disease

None: about 3 PM (Latin)

Palmer: one who paid another person to go on pilgrimage for him

Pannage: turning domestic hogs out to graze in a woodland

Peregrine: falcon suited to royalty

Piskie: mischievous Cornish sprite or pixie, analogous to leprechaun

Posset: any soothing herbal drink

Pottage: thick soup

Pottle: four-pint measure for selling ale

Prie-dieu: prayer bench (French)

Prime: around dawn (Latin)

Pyx: communion bread (Latin)

Quadrivium: arithmetic, music, astronomy, and geometry

Reeve: overseer of the agricultural duties of a manor

Reresoper: after-supper snack

Revenant: zombie

Rood: the Cross (Saxon)
Rouncey: tall, sturdy mount bred down from war horse stock
Saker: hawk a minor nobleman flew
Sawsnach: stranger, outlander
Scutage: "shield-tax" paid to one's liege lord in lieu of knight service
Seisin: to confer a land honor upon a vassal
Serf: farmer tied to the land (see Churl, Villein)
Sext: noontime (Latin)
Sparrow hawk: hawk for common folk
Steward: overseer of an entire honor
Stews: red light district
Surcoat: var. "surcote": garment worn over the tunic as outerwear
Suzerain: an overlord of an entire land
Tables: board game similar to backgammon
Tallage: land tax
Thane: nobleman (Saxon); also thegn
Thrall: slave (Scandinavian)
Tierce: around 9 AM (Latin)
Toft: house or homesite
Treen: household items made of wood
Trencher: bread slice used as dinner plate
Trivium: grammar, rhetoric, and dialectic taught at college
Troth: faithfulness
Trow: affirm
Tun: liquid measure for ale or wine, something over 200 gallons
Vassal: one who held land of an overlord
Vespers: evening, sunset
Vielle: early violin
Villein: peasant, generally tied to the land
Virgate: amount of farmland that would sustain a family
Wain: wagon or cart
Warlinnen: welcome
Wergeld: man price, compensation paid to a murder victim's family
Whitsun: Pentecost